I0594942

N
W
E
S
KUNLUN
BAIYONELLE
NYSANOK
KITEZH
ANNWIN
SARGANAR
ORLON
THE MAGICAL REALM

LEMALOME
ALDWINELLE
TEARNANELLE
TEARNANOAK
LEMURIA
SILVERMAR
ZURZURA

CURSE OF THE GIFTED

THE TWIN KINGDOMS TRILOGY
BOOK ONE

A.M. AURELIA

PIDDLY PINCHERS PUBLISHING

Curse of the Gifted

Book 1 in the Twin Kingdoms Trilogy

A.M. Aurelia

ISBN (Paperback): 979-8-9928921-0-9
ISBN (eBook): 979-8-9928921-2-3
ISBN (audiobook): 979-8-9928921-1-6

Author's Note

This is a work of fiction. Any references to historical events, real people, or places are used fictitiously. All other names, characters, and places are products of the author's imagination. Any resemblance to actual persons, living or dead, or actual events is purely coincidental. Curse of the Gifted is a fictious portal fantasy romance with adult themes. It contains mature and graphic content that is not suitable for all audiences. Reader discretion is advised.

Content Warning: Sex, Language, Violence, Graphic Scenes, Death, Drug Use, Alcohol.

Edited by many people
Illustrations (interior and exterior) by Jai Design
Trailer by A.M. Aurelia

Piddly Pinchers Publishing
2025

To those who dare to believe in magic and the kind of love that burns hotter than any curse.

INTRODUCTION

Light Magic: All that is good. The entire universe and the balance of life depends on light magic that originates from the Gods in Empyrean. We all have a little bit of light magic in us that is the spark of life.

Innate Magic: Exists beyond our understanding or comprehension. It simply is. It cannot be manipulated, modified, or nullified by any person or substance.

Tangible magic: As its name implies, anything tangible that we can see, hear, feel, taste, or touch. There are many ways in which tangible magic exists. Those born in the magical realm are blessed with magic flowing through their blood and grants them extraordinary gifts.

Elemental magic: Magic that is harnessed in an object like the gems and stones harvested from the God Trees in the magical realm. Anyone can utilize elemental magic whether or not they, themselves, possess magic.

Intangible magic: Powers of the mind. Other than a few select creatures, who may possess telepathy or superficial empathy, intangible magic is rare and not much is known about it.

Rune magic: A type of blood magic that can be utilized by anyone who either has magic running through their blood or they've drank the water of Orlon thus infusing themselves with magic. Runes can affect tangible and intangible magic in various ways, but they cannot affect innate magic.

Dark magic is the corruption of any of the previous magics. Anyone who uses any form of magic to bring about harm, imbalance, or destruction will damage their souls permanently. When they are eventually caught or die, they will be banished to Mokor where they will forever never know happiness, satiety or pleasure. The soul eventually withers away into demon hood. If a demon escapes the realm of Mokor...well The Gods help us all.

What if magic is whispering to you but you're not listening so it starts to scream? Quiet your mind and open your heart. When you hear it, don't be afraid of it, don't hide from it, just direct it. Play the magic like you would play an instrument. From the heart.

~ Ambrose Reston

PROLOGUE: AVA

"Ava!"

Ignoring the woman's shouts, Ava picked up the pace. This foster mother was nicer than the one before, but the concern in her voice was still fake. She didn't care about Ava. She just wanted the money that came along with fostering a kid. No one actually wanted a fourteen-year-old, green eyed, red-headed girl with an attitude.

"Ava, come back! Please." The woman sounded desperate, almost worried.

Shouldering her backpack, Ava turned a corner, leaving the yelling woman and the apartment building behind.

Hands in pockets of blue jeans that were too big for her, she fisted the wad of money. Five-hundred and sixty dollars of freedom earned from helping people take out trash, unload groceries, clean their house, walk their dog, anything someone would pay her to do, she'd done it.

Ava had gone door to door in the apartment building and surrounding condos asking for odd jobs for cash. It wasn't long before word got out, especially among the elderly residents, and eventually people started seeking her out for help.

No job was too big or too small, and she was always very enthusiastic to take any monetary offer made without hesitation or negotiation. Other than earning money, it also provided a distraction from life. An escape from reality while simultaneously funding her actual escape.

Gracious patrons laid on praises.

"Oh, you're such a sweet young lady."

"Your parents have done a great job raising you darling. They must be so proud of you."

The compliments made her uncomfortable. She wished people would keep their thoughts to themselves. All she wanted was the money, not the commentary, but she maintained the façade of innocent bashfulness, responding with the expected 'thank you' in a sweet voice, before hungrily snatching up the money.

She wasn't the sweet young lady they thought she was, and she didn't want to be. She was a vengeful animal, biding her time until she could be free, and the work had finally paid off. She had enough money to fund her extrication from the foster care hell she was trapped in.

The young Ava walked casually down the street. The summer sun warmed her olive skin and made the rusty tones of her red hair shine bright. No one took much notice of her. That's how it was in the city. Everyone minded their own business. Aside from the path of icy silver flowing through the right side of her bright red head, she was just another nondescript person walking down the street.

Each sequential step lifted Ava's spirits higher as she put more distance between herself and the foster system. Year after year she'd bounced around to countless foster homes. Most people were nice enough but none of them ever truly cared.

One couple couldn't have kids of their own, so they attempted to fill that void by providing a home to an unwanted child. It only took three months for them to realize Ava wasn't the answer they were searching for.

Another couple thought they could be the saviors of the broken, forcing her to attend church and give thanks to the Lord God Almighty who would save her lost soul. When she couldn't be saved, they too gave up and exchanged her for a more pious individual.

She was a burden, tossed around to the next willing, albeit unenthusiastic, volunteer. No one really tried to get to know her. It was always about them and how she could fit into their life and their world. When she inevitably didn't fit, they traded her in for the next kid in line. Like trying on shoes at a department store, if it wasn't the right color, size, style, and comfort then it was tossed aside to try on another contender.

But her life wasn't someone else's puzzle piece to force into a picture they deemed acceptable. This was her life. It was time for her to take control and be her own caretaker. She didn't need anybody, and she didn't want anybody to need her either.

Painful memories of the Hansons popped into her mind, the only love she'd ever known. They offered her a home after finding out about her secret instead of kicking her to the curb.

"Hey, you ready to go?" A young female voice interrupted her reminiscence, pulling Ava back to the streets of Charlotte North Carolina, and her runaway plan in progress.

A slender brown-haired woman stood against a light pole smoking a cigarette. The woman wasn't much larger than the light pole itself. Sarah was the closest thing to a friend that Ava had. She lived a few blocks away from Ava's current residence, and was older than her by a few years.

Sarah always challenged the rules, sneaking out to go roller skating, see an R rated movie, or hang out with other older kids, smoking pot. Ava wanted to go with her, and tried to on several occasions, but her foster parents seemed to always be one step ahead, catching her, and locking her in her room.

They liked to assign tasks to keep her busy. Study, clean, tutor the other kids. They thought they could fix her by giving her endless activities to do.

"Busy hands, idle mind," Mrs. Johnson would say.

The Johnson's fostered eight other kids, varying from four to seventeen years old. All the other kids were complaisant and followed the rules like good little boys and girls. Not Ava though. She vexed her foster parents routinely and caused disruption amongst the other kids at home and school. No malice or ill intent, just disregard of the rules. Rules were too confining. Ava did whatever she wanted, whenever she wanted, and didn't feel the need to justify herself to anyone.

They all lived in a small three-bedroom apartment on the fifth floor of a building that didn't have an elevator. Ava shared a room with three other kids, and a bottom bunk with a little girl who pissed herself every night. Ava always smelled like urine these days. She could smell it on herself now. She didn't want to spend the next four years of her life stuck in that tiny apartment sharing a bed with the pisser. Besides, it was only a matter of time until they discovered her curse and sent her packing anyway.

Ava decided to beat them to the punch. She'd leave before they discovered what she was. So, when Sarah asked to run away together, it didn't take much convincing for Ava to agree.

Sarah lifted an eyebrow.

"I'm ready," Ava said flatly.

"Did you bring the money?" The woman's eyes narrowed. The piercing in her nose, that was too big for the pale face it sat upon, twinkled in the sunlight.

"Yes." Pulling out the wad of money from her pocket, Ava held it out.

Sarah grabbed it greedily and shoved it into her own pocket. Ava looked questioningly at the taller woman.

"I'll hold onto it for us, so you don't accidentally lose it." The older girl smiled wickedly.

Sarah had a driver's license, and according to her, her parents were low life drunkards that didn't care what she did as long as she stayed out of their hair. So, she was always out at night partying, and getting into other mischief.

Today, Sarah had stolen her parents' car, and with it the two girls would run away to Hollywood. Ava didn't care much for movies, but

Sarah loved them. She wanted to be an actress. Ava just wanted to be as far away from North Carolina as she could get. California met that criterion.

Sarah sauntered over to an old silver four-door sedan, and seated herself into the driver's spot, adjusting the mirror to put on some lip gloss.

Unease twisted Ava's gut. Ignoring the feeling, she hopped into the passenger side front seat next to Sarah. The engine started after a few turns, and the two girls drove away from the city, and the problems it held for them. Ava would finally be free to live her life the way she wanted. Well, and the way Sarah wanted too, of course.

Ava stared out the window, watching all the familiar buildings pass by until they reached the edge of the city, and left it behind. A sense of relief and anxiety stirred inside her, oil and water, together but not mixing well.

They continued for several hours, and through a few more towns, before Sarah turned onto a dark gravel road. Ava looked out the back windshield at the disappearing lights of the last town. The sun dipped below the horizon, leaving the road nearly imperceptible as darkness consumed it. Only dust, reflected off the red gleam of the rear lights, was visible.

Sarah assured her this was the shortest route to Hollywood. At fourteen years old, Ava had little concept of distance, so she believed her friend, even though her heart started to beat a little faster with every mile they headed deeper into the woods.

As they traveled further into the country, the trees leaned in closer, and the gravel road became bumpier and narrower. Ava swallowed down her nerves. Sarah slowed and turned onto an even smaller dirt path. This road was nothing more than two brown lines with bunches of grass growing in the center that tickled the underside of the car like thousands of spiders wearing tiny tap shoes danced on the undercarriage. The sound sent an unsettling chill down Ava's spine.

The road was riddled with potholes and the two girls bounced around like shoes in a dryer. It was dark, so completely dark, the only light was from the headlights of the car.

Ava's palms sweat, and the hairs on her arms thickened and turned black. It'd been four years since the wolf had taken over her body, and Ava was so shocked by its presence that she momentarily forgot where she was.

A large pothole bounced her sideways. She hit her head on the window. "Ouch." Rubbing her head, Ava glanced at the dashboard. The gas tank was almost empty.

They wouldn't make it much further, and there was no gas station in sight. Anxiety twisted her stomach. Her shoes fell off, and her socks dangled loosely around wolfish paws. She had to get out of this car.

"I need to pee," Ava blurted.

Sarah narrowed her eyes. "We're almost there. Hold it for another five minutes."

Ava took deep relaxing breaths, begging the wolf to stay hidden. It was difficult to admit, but she was glad the wolf was back. It also made her nervous, because she couldn't control the shifts. She didn't want to scare away her only friend in the world, who also had all of her money, and the car that she needed.

Finally, Sarah stopped the car at the edge of the dirt path, in the middle of nowhere. They were surrounded by trees, darkness, and a lake spread out before them.

"Get out," Sarah commanded, not a hint of friendliness in her tone.

Ava reluctantly exited the vehicle. After closing the door, the headlights went out, and they stood in near darkness, except for the almost full moon and its reflection in the water.

"Not the best night for this." Sarah glanced up at the moon.

What's that supposed to mean?

The lanky woman walked to the edge of the water and stared out. The water was a mirror, reflecting the perfect silhouette of the almost full moon. Frogs and crickets croaked, and leaves rustled in a slight breeze.

Apprehension flooded Ava. Her hands were gone now, replaced with paws. She quickly hid them behind her back.

"I know what you are Ava," Sarah said into the empty night.

Ava stiffened; eyes wide.

"I'm like you." The tall girl turned to face Ava, a serpentine smile on her slender face. Not exactly an unfriendly smile, but it wasn't innocent either. "I can help you. I can take you to where you're from." Sarah extended a hand toward Ava who backed away a few steps. Annoyance flashed on Sarah's face.

"Do you think you were born in this pathetic world? We are so much more powerful than these humans." She curled her lip up at the word *human*. "You could be one of us, help us." She paused, picking at one of her fingernails. "Or you could be our enemy. Your choice."

The casualness of her tone frightened Ava, but Sarah said, *us*. There must be more people like her. If that was the case Ava wanted to know.

"What are we?" Ava was scared to know the answer, but she needed to know just as badly.

"Well, we aren't exactly alike. I'm more powerful than you, and I'm immortal. You can't kill me, so don't try. That would only make things worse for you. You're a shapeshifter, and more importantly, you're mortal, so I can kill you, easily if I wanted to. But I don't want to do that." Her voice was patronizing, and her smile was replaced with an overexaggerated pouty lip.

"I want us to be friends. What's your animal? Show me." The hunger for answers danced in her brown eyes like hyenas circling a kill.

Ava backed up a step. "I don't know." Red fur began to take over her body. Sarah noticed the change and smiled wryly.

"Let's find out shall we. I'll show you mine if you show me yours. Deal?" She paused for a moment. "Well, go on then. You first."

"I....I...I can't, I don't, I don't know how."

Sarah barked out a laugh. "You take control of that fear and anger, and you channel it into what you want. Stop letting it control you. You control it. You will it so, and your body obeys. Would you like me to go first?”

Fangs grew in Sarah's mouth, lengthening to lethal points. Fur sprouted on her body like fresh new spring grass pushing through the dirt. Sarah removed her clothes and tossed them to the ground a few feet away.

Ava eyeballed the pants that held her money. Everything inside Ava screamed to run away, but she wanted answers so desperately that she ignored her senses and stayed glued to her spot. She needed to know what she was, not only for herself, but for the Hansons.

In two heartbeats, a monster stood before her. The beast was covered in brown dingy coarse fur, and reeked of rancid meat. Six-inch tall ears jutted straight off the top of her head, coming to a point, but the real points that terrified Ava were the ones protruding from her half human/half monster fingers.

The monster lunged. Ava fell backwards, and her pants became warm and damp. The beast chuckled.

Ava's clothes became suffocatingly tight as the body beneath them changed into a small red wolf with a black mane, four dainty black legs on tiny paws, and a white poofy tail. Round ears sat atop her red and black face, which had a long slender muzzle with razor sharp small teeth.

The monster cocked its head then shifted back to the woman that she was before. Curiosity distorted her naked features.

Ava was a tiny pup, barely fifteen pounds. That monster was easily four times the size of a human. Ava backed away hackles rising.

“Hey, little pup. It's ok. It's me, Sarah. Remember me?” Sarah extended a hand palm side up. Ava snarled at her.

The bone-thin woman sauntered to her pile of clothes and dressed again. Sarah pulled a little box from her pocket. The box had weird glowing shapes etched onto the sides. Sarah opened it and retrieved two identical objects; rings. She put one on her right pointer finger then knelt in front Ava, and held up the other one.

“I have a present for you, but you need to shift back to have it.

Look, I have one too." Holding up the hand where she'd placed a dull silver ring, she wiggled her fingers playfully. "Like friendship bracelets, only they're rings, because we'll be best friends." A wry smile tugged at the corners of her mouth.

Ava didn't believe for one minute that Sarah was her friend, but what choice did she have? She was in the middle of nowhere and had no control of her own body.

"Breathe out slowly and clear your mind. Tell your body you want it to be human again. That's it. Relax into it and let it happen. Your mind commands and your body obeys."

Concentrating, Ava closed her eyes, commanding her body to shift. Nothing happened.

Pain erupted over her cheek. Ava yelped and fell backwards. Sarah slapped her.

"Feel that pain. Use it to fuel your determination. You command and your body obeys. Your body is your slave. It does what you want. Don't let it defy you. Get mad and force it to do what you want."

Determination throbbed in unison with Ava's cheek. She had no control of anything in her life. No one respected her. Everyone treated her like shit, and abused her. There was one thing she could control though, herself.

With a confident internal voice, she yelled at herself, demanding her body to shift. A ripple swam over her skin as red fur retreated into the pores. Her legs lengthened and her toes and fingers grew back out. Her nose shortened and her black mane turned red again, except for the silver streak. She smiled widely at the achievement.

"See, I knew you could do it. Here." Sarah held out the ring. "Besties?"

Maybe Ava was wrong about her. Sarah had a tough life too, and it made her tough. Ava needed to be more like her. Learn to be cold and calculating, and leave no room for inadequacy. She took the ring and put it on. It slipped over her knuckles loosely.

"It's too big."

"You'll grow into it. Now, put some clothes on for fuck's sake, and meet me at the water."

Ava dressed quickly. Her face heated at the wet spot between her legs. "Can we buy me some more clothes on our way to California?"

Sarah didn't respond. She just stared out at the water again. Ava followed her gaze, and once again, saw nothing but the moon's reflection. Water rippled with disturbance as the brown-haired woman walked a few steps into it.

"What are you doing?"

"I'm not traveling with you soaked in piss. It stinks. Come in and wash off, then we'll leave."

Kicking off her socks and shoes, Ava stepped into the water. It was cool, but not cold, kind of refreshing. The slimy silt squished between her toes as if she walked through jelly. Sarah grabbed her arm and tugged her deeper until they were both waist deep.

"This is far enough. I can't swim."

Sarah continued to pull her further.

"Stop! What are you doing?"

Sarah's grip tightened around Ava's arm, and the water grew colder as they got deeper.

Ava tried to wrench her hand free, but Sarah was impossibly strong. If she gripped much tighter, Ava's arm would snap in half.

"What are you doing?" Desperation made her voice crack.

Sarah snarled, jerking Ava so hard that she fell face first into frigid water. Sarah pushed Ava down and fear consumed Ava.

The silty ground vanished, leaving nothing but endless freezing water. If she didn't drown then she would die of hypothermia. Sarah kept pushing her down. Her ears popped under the pressure. They were at least eight to ten feet under, and still, Sarah continued to push.

Shift, she told her body, but it did not obey. She couldn't breathe, her lungs burned from the lack of air. A current pulled her down, and the pressure lessened as a faint glow appeared beneath them. Sarah's grip slackened for a moment and Ava took advantage.

Kicking out violently, she hit Sarah in the abdomen. Bubbles trickled out of Sarah's mouth, and her hand let go of Ava.

Kicking frantically toward the surface, the bright moon her only beacon of hope, Ava swam. Her lungs fought against the effort to not gulp down the water. She reminded her body not to breathe yet, just wait a bit more. Ava breached the surface, gasping for air. A brown head surfaced a few feet away, taking in a deep breath of her own, then locking eyes on Ava. Sarah glared daggers.

Ava kicked furiously toward the water's edge. Instinct and fear teaching her to swim, but not well. Water splashed in all directions as Ava wildly kicked her arms and legs in an inefficient pattern, but it was working. She was getting closer to the shore.

Before she reached it, one of her ankles got stuck. Claws dug into her flesh. Ava kicked, making contact with Sarah's nose, feeling the crunch on her heel. Blood gushed from Sarah's face, and Ava's ankle was free again.

SHIFT! SHIFT! Ava screamed internally, but nothing happened. As soon as she hit the bank, she clambered up the side, digging into the mud for purchase. The ring fell from her finger and her body immediately shifted into wolf form.

Even though the pup was not graceful, she was stealthy, fast, and could see in the dark. At the same moment that Ava reached the edge of the tree line, Sarah crested the embankment of the lake and shifted to the hideous beast-wolf.

Birds flapped, owls screeched, and other creatures scurried away from a blood curdling howl that ripped through the night.

Ava ran as fast as her legs would go, tracing her steps back to the car. Shifting back to human form, she opened the driver's door, and hopped into the seat. The keys were still in the ignition. She'd never driven a car before, but it couldn't be that hard. She'd seen plenty of her foster parents do it.

Turning the key, the engine revved then gave out after a few sputters. She turned the key again with the same result.

Branches and twigs snapped a few yards away. The beast was getting closer.

Ava smashed the gas pedal down and turned the key again. This time the engine turned over fully. She slammed the gear stick into reverse. The car lurched backwards and rotated sideways as she sharply turned the wheel. The bumper smashed into a tree behind her, popping the trunk open.

She shifted into drive, and the car jolted forward, executing her commands without faltering. Turning the steering wheel furiously to either direction until she got it straightened out, Ava punched the pedal down, and drove as fast as the car would go. Her head hit the roof a few times when the car slammed into potholes, and the trunk bobbed up and down until it finally clicked into place, firmly closed.

Glancing in the rearview mirror, she saw the large hideously angry wolf-creature chasing her at an impossible speed. The car revved loudly when she smashed the pedal down to the floor as far as it would go. She could barely see over the dash, and another pothole sent her face smashing into the steering wheel. Blood poured from her nose and lip. Ava tasted metallic, but her adrenaline masked the pain.

The creature finally started to lose distance, fading out of sight the further away Ava drove, but she didn't slow down. A red gas light popped on. She hoped there was enough gas to get back to civilization.

A gut-wrenching roar ripped through the atmosphere, but Ava didn't look back. She kept driving until she hit paved road, then she headed back the way they'd come.

Maybe she wasn't quite ready to be on her own just yet.

CHAPTER 1
SIBYL
MARCH 13TH/ARINN FIROQ-2

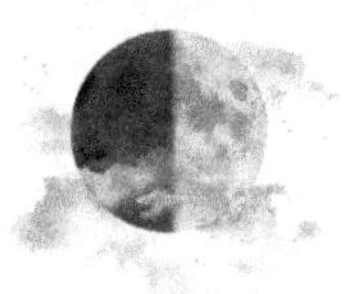

Staring out the window of her second-story bedroom, Sibyl listened to the ticking sounds of rain on the metal roof. The computer went to screen saver mode several minutes ago, but she was too distracted to notice.

A buzzing noise startled her. Yawning, she picked up her phone and checked the text. Melissa was checking up on her. All her friends were having a great time in Cancun on spring break while she stayed home studying like a good college student. Boards were in eight months. That one test determined her entire future. Would she be a doctor, or would she be a failure?

Sure, she could retake the test in six months if she failed, but you only got three shots before you're banned forever, then her veterinary career would be over before it even got started. She couldn't even think about that possibility. It was too stressful. This was no time to party, besides her heart wasn't in it anyway.

Closing the computer, she massaged her temples, attempting to relieve the headache that squeezed her skull. When she looked out the window again, a large horse stood at the edge of the woods. Her heart skipped a beat.

Deep mahogany fur covered his entire body, not a spec of white anywhere. Jet-black mane and tail and matching black irises that currently stared at her, made him mystically beautiful. Swallowing down a ball of anxiety, Sibyl stared back, afraid to move, lest he spook and run away like he usually did.

This mysterious horse had popped in and out of her dreams for most of her life, and she had no idea why. In the last several months, he showed up not only in her dreams, but in reality as well. Her therapist said it was *just* stress hallucinations like it was no big deal. But it was a big deal. She was hallucinating, but it seemed so real.

Hands tingling, she grabbed a pill bottle from the desk and dumped one into the palm of her shaking hand. The horse still watched her. Sometimes she thought he was trying to tell her something, but she never could figure out what.

He wasn't like the other monsters she sometimes saw in her dreams, the ones that scared her to the point she'd wake up screaming in a sweaty panic. Heinous beasts that brutally maimed and killed people right in front of her. It felt so real. She could smell the rancid decay of their breath, feel the pain and terror of their victims as they futilely fought for their lives.

After the monsters dispatched whoever the poor soul was, they'd turn their attention to her, but before they could get to her, she'd wake up. So far, none had ever entered reality, so that was a relief, but this horse was in the real world. Or was he?

Putting a hand on the desk, Sibyl rubbed along the maple wood grains. *Real.*

She walked to her bed and rubbed one of the pillows, feeling the cotton fabric beneath her fingertips. *Real.*

Her therapist called it grounding. It helped orient her into the here and now so she could easily identify things that weren't real, like a giant horse popping up at random times.

If it's always out of reach or doesn't feel as expected, then it's not real.

After she was confident of her lucidity, she looked out the window again. The horse was still there, watching attentively. One of his ears twitched.

She could practically read his thoughts. *What are you doing? Come out here.*

Unlike the beasts from her nightmares, this horse made her feel calm and peaceful. A beacon of serenity within the center of her mental turmoil. The horse invited her to embrace the adventure of madness.

She studied the pill and pondered her options. She could chase down a figment of her imagination possibly confirming her lifelong fears; she was insane. Or, she could take the pill and it would all go away. She would return to her life, pretending like all was well and normal. If she did that then she'd always have that question on the back of her mind. Was she crazy?

Shoving the pill into her pocket, she grabbed a coat, dashed down the stairs and out the front door. It was always better to know.

When she approached the edge of the woods the horse turned and trotted off. Sibyl cautiously followed. The rain was ending, leaving behind a blanket of mist so thick that she could almost reach out and grab ahold of it. The waterlogged atmosphere enhanced the pine and oak scents of the forest.

Sibyl's family moved between their two homes in North Carolina. One was on the coastline, and this remote cabin nestled in the Appalachian Mountains of the tiny city of Boone. There was an overabundance of love and support in the Murphy family, but Sibyl struggled with crippling anxiety that would frequently cause her to pull back from social situations like a turtle hiding her head in her shell.

Her parents said the forest was just another hiding place, but they didn't realize that it was actually freedom from the anxieties that constantly plagued her. The forest was a reprieve and the trees were her friends, always present, never judgmental.

As the horse traveled deeper into the woods, Sibyl found herself in new territory, surrounded by unfamiliar trees. Trees had to wait for newcomers to find and approach them, and this far into the forest meant these trees rarely met anyone new, especially a human. Sibyl was one of the few who would ever interact with them. She was honored by the sentiment.

The horse snorted excitedly, kicked up his heels, and bolted off as if he was playing a game of tag. Picking up a jog, she trailed after him.

Thunder rumbled softly. The horse nickered, matching the storm's baritone. The gray sky was full of dark puffy clouds, and a half-moon silhouette, barely visible from the light of day, peeked between the clouds. Bright green leaves sprouted from the tree branches, waking up from their wintry nap.

Stepping from around a tree, Sibyl came face to face with the horse. His sleek red fur shimmered under the mist that clung to him. Tossing a jet-black mane over his muscular neck, he stomped one of his giant black hooves and snorted.

She didn't move a muscle. This was the closest she'd ever been to him.

"Hey there fella." Holding her breath, she extended a hand toward him and took a step.

As if a whip cracked, the horse bolted sideways and galloped off.

Not wanting to lose him, Sibyl ran. Excited energy radiated from the forest that encouraged her to keep going, rooting for her to catch the animal. After a ways, Sibyl had to stop to catch her breath. Another thunder rumbled in the sky, ceasing the woodpecker's cadence and twitterpated blue jays' songs. Frogs awakened and the rain started falling in heavy thick sheets. She was thoroughly soaked within minutes, and a chill coaxed out goosebumps.

A whinny sounded nearby. The horse peered at her from a meadow of colors before turning and disappearing behind a group of trees.

Picking her way through the underbrush, she stumbled clumsily onto the edge of the large meadow. Knee-high flowers gently rocked in the breeze. An ocean of yellow daffodils, white daisies, purple echinacea, and every other color of the rainbow, coalesced in a tapestry of natural floral art.

Butterflies, bumblebees, and birds dodged raindrops in unorganized flight patterns. Some of the flying creatures looked odd, like tiny lizards with wings. It was difficult to get a good look because they flitted around so quickly. Sibyl dismissed it as an optical illusion.

The horse stood in the center of the meadow surrounded by the chest high wildflowers. His nostrils flared. He was larger than the average horse by at least two hands.

"Hi," she called.

He walked to her. Heart hammering, she waited for him to approach. She would finally discover if he was real. Once he was within arm's reach, Sibyl dipped her chin submissively and stood perfectly still. He sniffed her, then nibbled her hair.

She giggled.

He backed up a step.

Slowly she raised her head. When their eyes met, her breath hitched. A large obsidian horn protruded from his forehead about two feet long and ending in a sharp point. Golden veins that reflected the sunlight spiraled through it.

Her heart could have fallen out the bottom of her stomach. This couldn't be real, could it?

Tingling took over her hands, pulling her toward the horse as if an invisible bungee tethered them together. These sensations usually prefaced a panic attack, but this time it felt more like an invitation.

Reaching her hand out, her fingertips barely grazed his forehead. "Rea-"

Whispers scratched the back of her mind, cutting off her train of thought. Fear slithered up her spine.

The unicorn reared, pawing the air, and Sibyl fell on her ass. The horse turned, and with his tail in the air, he ran into the forest, disappearing behind the trees.

One of the beasts from her nightmares stepped into the meadow. Thick saliva dripped from its large maw. It had a wolf-like shape and appearance, but was at least four times the size of any wolf Sibyl had ever seen. Its hair was brown with a coarse texture, sparse on its body, but thick on its legs. It was positively horrifying.

The beast sprinted toward her.

Panic overtook all her senses. Frantically pulling herself to her feet, she ran toward home, weaving the trees haphazardly.

She tripped over a root and nearly face planted. Catching herself before she fell all the way down, she sprinted off again. Her heart pounded so hard she thought it may explode.

When she was a safe enough distance away from the meadow, she stopped to catch her breath. Hiding behind a tree, she grabbed her chest, trying to massage the pain away. Spots danced in her vision as her body struggled to pump enough oxygen into her head. That was the closest she'd ever come to one of the monsters.

Timidly, she peered around the tree and saw nothing but an empty forest. Laying her head against the rough bark, she inhaled a deep breath and waited for her heart rate to slow to a normal pace. Nausea swept through her as the adrenaline surge wore off.

Summoning a bit of bravery, she glanced back one more time and confirmed the beast was gone. Nothing and no one was there.

"Hello?"

Frogs answered in a harmonious chorus of croaking. Concern for her sanity at the forefront of her mind, Sibyl made her way back home on shaking legs. It was completely plausible that she was, in fact, crazy.

——— **May 20th/Teargem Lasq-1** ———

The sidewalk was an energetic river of people gearing up for a Friday night of fun. Sibyl regretted walking to school now that the temperature was dropping. It was atypically chilly for this late in the year. The day started sunny and beautiful with a spring-summer cusp breeze, but now the T-shirt and jean shorts were not enough to keep out the bite of the chilly night air. Not entirely uncommon behavior for Georgia weather.

Jogging to help keep herself warm, Sibyl dodged around people that siphoned in and out of restaurants and shops. The crowd consisted of families or college students enjoying their weekend evening in town. Their eyes scanned over her, judging her.

Was it the freckles that made people stare? She looked like someone threw brown splatter paint all over her face and body, and with her pale complexion, the freckles stood out like spots of mud on white carpet. Maybe it was her striking hazel eyes with a weird yellow halo around the center pupil that drew their attention. Maybe it was the blonde unruly hair that never stayed smooth, no matter how much she brushed it into place.

She wouldn't say she was an unattractive woman, but she was a different sort of pretty that some found odd. Regardless, she hated when people took a second look at her, or looked for longer than the accepted norm.

Anxiety bubbled to the surface as more and more eyes darted in her direction, even if only for a brief glance. Their curiosity and judgment poked at her mind, making her feel insecure.

Buzzing from her pocket interrupted her self-conscious machinations. Momentarily forgetting the illusory stares, she retrieved her phone: Melissa.

Slowing to a walk, she answered. "Hey, what's up?"

"How was your shift on the ER phone?"

"I got one call the entire night. Other than that, I got a lot of studying done, and it nearly bored me to sleep."

"Lucky. I got maybe a dozen calls on my shift. You study too much. You need a break. Are you coming to Daytona Beach with us?"

While two weeks on the beach sounded fantastic, she really didn't want to watch Melissa and her boyfriend be sickeningly happy the entire time.

Melissa and Trent started dating in the first semester of veterinary school. The connection they sparked grew quickly into a loving relationship that Sibyl envied.

Sibyl's most recent break up was the longest relationship she'd ever managed to keep, and it still paled in comparison to Melissa and Trent. Despite Melissa going out of her way to make sure Sibyl wasn't treated like a third wheel, it still ended up feeling that way most of the time.

Trent was from Florida originally, and his family had a beach cottage down there so the trip would be basically free. There was no excuse not to go.

"It'll be the last time we'll get to hang out together before we start our real lives, and you didn't go to Cancun, so you *have* to come to Daytona with us."

"I don't know, I probably should just go home and study."

"No, I don't want to hear it. That's all you've done since the break-up. It's not healthy. He's not going to be there. You can take a two-week break and then spend the rest of the year after graduation studying for boards. You're coming. I won't take no for an answer."

Sibyl relented. "OK, fine."

She had to remove the phone from her ear momentarily at Melissa's squeal of joy.

"I have the ER phone again tomorrow then I'm done. I was planning on going home for a few days before graduation."

"Don't you go home with your tail tucked between your legs like a whipped dog. You waltz in there like the fucking badass you are, drop your shit off, and we'll leave from the graduation ceremony. We're going to celebrate the fact that we just completed the toughest four years of our lives. Get your head up, pull yourself out of this slump, and forget him. We're going to party like it's 1999. Do you understand me Dr. Murphy?"

"Yes Dr. Rathern." She paused for a second before saying, "thanks Melissa."

"You can thank me when we're roasting on the beach, drinking strawberry daiquiris, and staring at hot guys surfing."

Sibyl chuckled, said goodbye, and resumed her walk home. She really shouldn't be partying. There was too much to do now that school was ending. All her classmates applied for jobs or residencies; some had already signed contracts. But she and Melissa hadn't started the job search yet.

Melissa was waiting for Trent to propose before making any decisions, but Sibyl had no excuse. Her life and career were stagnating when she should be taking off like a new bird spreading her wings and learning to fly. She just couldn't help feeling like there was something else she should be doing. So, she procrastinated making any life altering decisions, and just studied for boards.

This trip would consist of watching Melissa and Trent ogle over each other, and their other friend, Ashly, trying to get Sibyl laid every night, with a little bit of beach and studying in between. Sibyl was on the fence about her enthusiasm level.

An alluring smell of grilled burgers enticed her to change from her original plans of going home, to seek out food and warmth. A big juicy burger was the perfect solution to her grumbly belly.

Five minutes later, she pushed through a large wooden door into the restaurant. The heat of a kitchen in full swing of dinner rush, and the tantalizing aroma of cooking food enveloped her.

A skinny high school aged girl scanned a paper after Sibyl requested a booth for one. Fake nails tapped on the laminated paper with an obnoxious *tick, tick, tick.* Sibyl fidgeted slightly. Surely it couldn't be that difficult to find a booth for one.

While the girl continued the apparently impossible task of seating a single person, the door behind Sibyl opened, and the evening air bit at her back, causing another chill to consume the little bit of warmth she'd just procured.

She turned to glance at the offender who dared to open the door and found herself face to face with Chris, the ex-boyfriend, and Megan, the beautiful, un-freckled, perfectly manicured, blonde-haired, Sibyl replacement girlfriend.

All three of them froze. Panic paralyzed Sibyl as if she'd stuck her finger in a light socket, otherwise she may have run screaming out the door immediately. Heat flushed through her face and chest, chasing away all remnants of the cold. Neither thoughts nor words formed. \

The hostess started speaking, but Sibyl couldn't comprehend what the girl said. Her mouth moved, but the words didn't match up, like a bad Chinese movie dubbed into another unintelligible language.

"What?" Sibyl finally snapped out of her stupor.

"Your table is ready. Would you like to follow me?" The hostess said, perfectly coherent, fingernails clicking on the plastic menu in her hand.

The hunger pangs that were present only moments ago were now replaced by nausea. Any second she would hurl all over the hostess, or Chris, or his new girlfriend, maybe all of them. It may even be a little satisfying, but also very embarrassing and reprehensible. The last thing she wanted to do was sit alone while her ex was in the same room, with front row seats to how pathetic she was without him. She had to get out of there.

"I think I left my wallet at home. I'm sorry. I'm just going to leave." Turning quickly, she headed to the door, avoiding making direct eye contact with either of them.

"Sibyl, you don't have to leave," Chris said.

Even though her legs were jelly, thankfully they agreed with her desire to leave and sped up in response. Reaching for the door, she tried to push it open, but it wouldn't budge. The giant wooden door stood firm, barely budging at her feeble attempts to push it open. She may as well attempt to push over the building because of its lack of compliance.

What is wrong with this stupid door? Fucking open, you fucking piece of shit door! she screamed at the door in her mind, and pushed harder, becoming more frantic.

A hand reached in front of her, grasped the handle, and pulled it open.

She recognized that hand. It had wrapped itself around her waist more times than she could count. That hand was strong, warm, steady, and it dried countless tears, and rubbed her back and neck when she was sore after hours of studying. It had caressed her body and breasts with love and passion on many steamy occasions. She knew every callous and wrinkle. She'd tasted the saltiness when her lips nibbled on the fingertips.

Habit and desire made her own hand reach out to his. She met his blue eyes and the smile that was creeping over her face dissipated instantly as his expression clearly conveyed pity and guilt, but no affection.

A waterfall of memories cascaded into the rocky cliff face of her mind. Just four months ago, he sat in her living room, telling her he didn't love her anymore, and how sorry he was about that. He never meant to meet someone else, it just happened. He wished her the best, and asked her to not hate him.

She didn't hate him. She loved him. Even after he'd broken her heart, she still loved him. She hated herself for loving him.

Devastation settled into her heart like a boulder of pain rolling down a mountain to find its final resting place at the base of a large ravine, never to move again. She suspected that this was how her heart would always feel. Suffocating under a great weight, never to get out from under it.

As if she'd laid her hand on a hot skillet, she jerked away, and stared at her feet. The floor was suddenly very interesting. She backed up a step, and he opened the door for her.

"Thank you," a trembling voice spouted from her mouth as she passed the threshold and escaped. The chilly night air was refreshing.

Chris followed her out the door, but she increased her pace and was out of earshot within seconds. Even though she heard him speaking, she couldn't make out the words. She didn't want to hear what he had to say. She'd already heard everything he had to say. He didn't want her. He didn't love her, and he was sorry about that. Like one would say sorry for spilling a drink on someone's shirt. He was just sorry he didn't love her. What else was there she needed to hear? Nothing.

Her feet kept moving, getting faster and faster until it was difficult to breathe. Panting heavily and choking on sobs, she finally slowed down. Her muscles ached, but that pain was refreshing. It diverted the burden from her heart, at least temporarily.

A tight knot formed in her throat, and the scenery became hazy through a film of tears. She sat down on the sidewalk before she fainted, thankful that she'd run to a part of town with no pedestrians.

A million different scenes had played out in her head about what she would say or do whenever she inevitably bumped into him again. In a small town it was bound to happen sooner or later. But seeing him in person, standing there, looking amazing with his beautiful new girl-friend who was everything she wasn't, she'd forgotten all her rehearsed conversations. Her mind went completely blank. She was so embarrassed.

Tears trickled down her face. Four months wasn't enough time to heal, but the pain had finally decreased to a dull ache. Now it was back in full force and compounded on itself. A dam broke inside her and sobs escaped. Little by little, the weight lifted from her heart, the agony pouring out with every tear that fell, and after a few minutes she could breathe again.

The pain of a broken heart seemed impossible to survive, but for some hellish reason she did. Every single night she went to bed thinking her heart would burst in her sleep, but every morning she awoke, heart still beating. It was miraculous how resilient a heart could be. Despite constantly fighting an emotional battle, every day it continued its job physically unfazed.

Her family said she needed time, and her friends said she needed distraction. Time was helping, but not fast enough, so she decided that distraction was the next thing to try. If nothing else, maybe it would at least provide a reprieve.

Pulling out her phone and quickly typing with shaking hands, she sent a text to Melissa. "Can't wait to be sitting on the beach." Followed by a gif of frozen drinks with little umbrellas.

Wiping her face, Sibyl stood, took a deep breath, swallowed the knot in her throat, and walked home. Her body was numb to everything. Hunger, cold, grief; she felt none of it. At least it was better than pain.

The phone buzzed. A gif of two girls dancing on a bar.

Sibyl smiled.

CHAPTER 2

AVA

JUNE 18TH/CANKIT LASQ-3

Sweat clung to Ava's temple and hairline, dripping down between her breasts and lower back. Georgia heat was unforgiving in the summer, especially this far south in Savannah.

Her ankle twisted when she stepped off the sidewalk. Unintelligible curses spewed from her mouth as she sat down on the side of the road. Cars zoomed by pommeling her with a jolt of hot air that smelled like asphalt. Her body swayed from the force of it. Getting run over would make a shitty end to a shitty day, so she shuffled further away from the traffic and rubbed her ankle vigorously.

"HEY, get your ass up and get to work!" An overweight lady wearing an unflattering navy-blue uniform glared at Ava.

Using the trash poker for support, Ava hoisted herself up, glaring back at the public works employee who'd already moved her attention back to her cell phone. That woman had too high a regard of herself. Ava could outrun her easily even with a bad ankle. She could probably take her in a fight too, but that would defeat the purpose of being here, so she abstained from kicking the shit out of the insufferable woman. At least for today, she'd be a good little convict.

A skinny woman wearing baggy clothes wandered over. "You ok?"

The woman's pathetic brown eyes matched her pathetic smile that was missing several teeth. Side effects of methamphetamines. They'd only known each other for a few weeks since they did their community service together picking up trash on the side of the road.

Cassie was the nicest woman to rotate through the program since Ava was assigned to it. Even still, Ava had little interest in socializing with anyone. No matter how unfriendly she was though, Cassie never seemed to get the message, and tried to befriend her every time they worked together.

Other than Ava and Cassie, there were half a dozen women of varying states of deplorability. All around the same age, mid to late twenties. Other than their age, they had little to nothing in common, except being low level offenders of the law and sentenced to community service.

They barely spoke to one another, and Ava preferred it that way. She just wanted to keep her head down, do her time, and leave. She was only ten hours from being done. Five hours after today.

"Yeah, I'm fine, just twisted my ankle, but it'll feel better in a few minutes. I just need to walk it off."

Cassie nodded her head and stabbed a piece of plastic with her trash poker. Cassie was dangerously thin, resembling a skeleton with thin dull skin wrapped around it. Greasy brunette hair fell to her shoulders. Ava thought the weight of her hair alone may topple the malnourished figure.

They resumed picking up trash in silence. Six disheveled women, seven if you count the public works employee, wandered around the side of the highway poking at debris, dragging around large orange trash bags.

All of them had committed some misdemeanor offense that landed them here. Unlike the others though, Ava was innocent. She took the fall for her dumbass boyfriend, ex-boyfriend. The crime was truly ridiculous and embarrassing. When people asked what she did, she lied and said that she throat punched a parking attendant who scratched her car.

She didn't even own a car, but they didn't need to know that. When Cassie asked one day why she took the bus, she said her car was in the shop getting the paint job repaired. Cassie bought the lie, hook, line and sinker.

"Hey, this ain't stand around and enjoy the weather time! Get to work. If I have to ask you one more time, I won't sign off on your hours," the overweight woman yelled from the comfort of the air-conditioned van.

Ava stabbed a Styrofoam cup with so much force that it broke into four tiny pieces. Now she had to bend over and pick up all the pieces with her hands which pissed her off even more. Tossing the pieces into her orange trash bag, she continued to hunt for more trash with as much enthusiasm as one feels about a gynecological appointment.

It was so damned hot. Pulling the hair off her neck, she fanned herself and glared daggers at the woman in the van. Ava hated her. She was so angry. Angry at the fat woman in the van, angry at the world for the shit hand she'd been dealt, and angry at the stupid *ability* that only seemed to make her life worse and bring her nothing but pain. Mostly, though, she was angry at herself, for all of it.

For taking the fall for him, for falling for him in the first place, for letting her life get to this place. She was twenty-six years old, picking up trash on the side of the road in ninety-degree weather, wearing a hideous orange vest that clashed with her bright red hair and olive skin, sweat dripping down every crevice of her body, making things very uncomfortable. Looking around at the other women, she thought they may actually have more in common than she wanted to admit.

The sun relentlessly bore down, burning her skin. By this evening, it would be a not-so-flattering shade of red that would rival her hair color. This was torture. She only had two days left, including today, but she couldn't take much more of it.

Pulling out her phone, she checked the time. Glancing back at the fat lady sitting in the van watching them blister and melt in the sun while she sipped on a pink, icy lemonade, Ava pursed her lips.

"I thought the U.S. didn't allow cruel and unusual punishment."

Utilizing her best whiney voice, she followed with, "It's so hot out here, I feel like I'm going to faint."

The other women groaned their agreement, wiping sweat away from their brows and buffeting their shirts to help get wind under their sweat soaked clothing.

A chubby hand reached up and removed sunglasses from its accompanying face, revealing bored green eyes. She checked her phone while a few of the other girls did the same.

Hopeful faces with pleading eyes watched the woman. They'd been out there for four and a half hours. Hopefully she'd take pity on them and call it a day.

"Fine. Come on." She rolled up the window and unlocked the doors. Apparently, she did have a heart, or at least a small bit of sympathy for the overheated convicts.

After dropping off the orange trash bags at the designated pick-up area, they all piled into the van. The stink of sweat overwhelmed the vehicle, but no one cared. The only single focus was the air conditioning vents, of which there were only four, and too many bodies to fit in their wake radius.

Ava took the third seat so she wouldn't be part of the pushing match. Cassie plopped down beside her. Even though they didn't get to directly feel the blast of fresh air, it was still much cooler in the van than it was outside. Leaning her head against the window, Ava closed her eyes.

"I'm moving to Florida."

Ava opened her eyes, sighing in annoyance. For a split second, she thought about telling Cassie to fuck off, but she thought better of it since she had no friends, and Cassie was literally the only person who ever went out of her way to talk to her.

"Really? Why are you moving to Florida?" Ava asked, feigning interest.

"My sister has a restaurant in Daytona Beach, and she said I could be a dishwasher while I get my life together. I'm supposed to start a rehab program." Cassie smiled with closed lips. "The program my sister picked out has a great success rate so hopefully I'll be able to stay clean this time."

"That's great. Good luck." Ava stared out the window again, hoping Cassie would get the hint.

"You want to come with me?"

The question surprised Ava. "Why would you ask me to come with you? You barely know me."

"You're nice, and you seem lonely, like me."

The van jolted forward. Ava thought back to about a month ago when one of the other women tripped Cassie and she fell face first into a mud puddle. Ava helped clean her up. That didn't seem like an overly nice thing to do, just the right thing. Ava hated bullies. That's when Cassie started trying to befriend her.

"I don't want to go alone. My sister can be kind of a bitch. She has the perfect life; rich, handsome husband, kids in private school, big house." Cassie put her hands out to the side and bobbed her head back and forth mockingly.

"She likes to shove it down my throat, and remind me how much of a loser I am. It'd be nice to have someone around...." Cassie trailed off.

"Who's more like you, or who will stick up for you?"

"Someone who'll be my friend. I don't have many friends. No good ones at least." Cassie stared at her tattered shoes, scraping them nervously on the van floor.

Ava wasn't sure if Cassie was playing her or being sincere, but her gut said it was the latter. Ava wasn't sure who was more pathetic, drug addict Cassie or herself. They were both alone, friendless, with no prospects in any facet of life. What did she have to lose? But moving away with someone she barely knew, and only knew through criminal activities seemed like a terrible idea. Not to mention the fact that everyone she got close to either got hurt or killed.

How much worse could it get for Cassie though? She was already throwing her life away by being a druggie. Of course there was death. Death was worse. But a drug addict toyed with death all the time, so how much more risk would Ava be to her really? And Cassie thought she was nice. That was a first. No one, other than the Hansons, had ever thought she was nice.

"I'll think about it."

Cassie's head shot up like a bullet from a gun. The missing side teeth made her smile more pathetically endearing.

"Really?" She sounded as excited as a dog watching his master tease him with a large stick to throw.

"When does your community service end?" Ava asked.

"I have fifteen more hours after today, so another week. I was going to leave next Friday."

"I have one day left."

The van pulled up to the public works building. All the women filed out one by one. The officer signed their papers upon disembarkment. Ava was happily surprised to see that she approved five hours of time.

"Thanks," Ava said with a small smile.

The woman nodded once and shooed her away with a wave of her hand.

Ava made her way to the bus stop where she sat on a bench under the shade of a tree. Cassie sat down beside her.

"What are you doing? You don't usually ride the bus," Ava said.

"I know, but since we finished early, I have some time before I have to be at my job, so I thought I'd sit with you until the bus comes." Cassie smiled pleasantly.

Ava nodded.

"What's your favorite movie?"

Before she could respond, Cassie started talking. "My favorite movie is *Happy Gilmore.*" She droned on for ten minutes about how funny it was, and that her favorite actor was Adam Sandler, so she could watch anything with him in it.

Ava filled in small breaks with brief smiles and 'uh huh.' Somehow by the end of the conversation, she promised Cassie that they'd watch *50 First Dates* together after she admitted to never having seen it.

A large city bus turned the corner and Ava stood up. The pain in her ankle was completely gone now.

"See you Thursday," Cassie said excitedly.

"See you."

Cassie left once Ava boarded the bus. She watched the skinny woman walk away until she turned a corner and was gone from sight. Ava wondered where Cassie lived. It was obvious she could barely afford to feed or clothe herself. How did she survive? Maybe her sister was sending money.

Thirty minutes later, Ava stepped off the bus in front of a large corporate building. Most of the lights were off, sans a few illuminated windows randomly throughout the five stories. Pulling out a bulky set of keys, she pushed open one of the large glass doors, walked through, then closed and locked it behind her. Retrieving a rolling trash cart laden with miscellaneous cleaning supplies from the closet, she donned a small vest and ball cap.

Ava spent the next eight hours going from room to room and floor to floor, emptying trash cans, sweeping, mopping, wiping down surfaces, and cleaning toilets in the bathrooms. As she exited each room, she sprayed a fragrant spray, then closed the doors behind her.

A few times she entered a room with people having late night meetings. It was lawyer talk so she didn't understand any of it.

Quietly, she retrieved the trash, and replaced the liners. Some of the people threw their drink cups and random detritus in the bag as she walked by, but most ignored her as they argued or took notes.

The last task was the hallways. She swept and mopped her way back down to the first floor. By the time she took all the trash to the dumpsters out back it was almost midnight. Returning all the supplies to the closet, she punched her timecard, and exited the way she entered.

The night air was humid and hot, but not nearly as bad as the day had been. Her burned skin appreciated the fresh air more than the cold AC in the building.

The granola bar she'd eaten on the bus ride left her unsated, so she ducked into a fast food restaurant a few blocks down the road and got some food before heading to the shelter.

Ava signed in at the front desk of the homeless shelter and smiled at the lady behind the counter. The woman rifled through a cabinet for a moment before pulling out a backpack and handed it over to Ava. It contained all of her belongings that she'd left there for safe keeping, Two sets of clothes, toothbrush, toothpaste, an assortment of toiletries, one very worn-out red fox stuffed animal, and a small, tattered blanket.

Stopping at the bathroom, she took a quick cool shower to clean up and soothe her burning skin, then changed into some clean clothes, stuffing the dirty ones into her bag to take the laundry mat tomorrow.

All but three of the twenty-five beds in the shelter were occupied. A few people read books, some did crosswords or played cards, but the majority of the people slept.

Finding a vacant bottom bunk, Ava plopped down. Removing the stuffed fox from her backpack, she laid on top of the covers and clutched the stuffed animal in her arms.

Sleep didn't come. She thought about Cassie's invitation. Why shouldn't she go? Even if it was a bad idea, what did she have to lose? She had nothing and no one. Cassie was the closest thing to a friend that she'd had in a while. At least she was nice. That was more than she could say for herself. According to almost everyone she'd ever befriended or bedded, Ava was a bitch. Maybe Cassie could teach her how to be nicer to people.

Her phone buzzed. The text was from Justin, a friend of her ex-boyfriend. It said that Willy was in jail for attempted robbery, and he needed bail money, $800 to be exact. Of course, they would turn to her for help. A quick check of her bank account confirmed she had $204.98.

"I don't have that much money," she replied.

"Yes, you do. Don't hold out on us. He's in real trouble. He needs you."

"Fuck off. We broke up. He's not my problem anymore, so stop texting me." Ava blocked the number and set her phone back on the table, closing her eyes.

Sleep found her this time because she'd decided what she wanted to do and was satisfied with her plan. She'd go with Cassie to Florida. A change of scenery could be good, especially a beach.

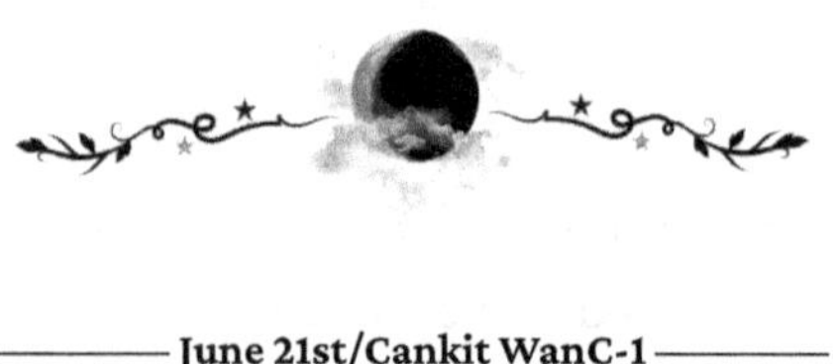

————— **June 21st/Cankit WanC-1** —————

Ava took a job as a server in the restaurant that Cassie's sister, Melody, owned. Melody was a hard boss, but a fair one, and Ava took every spare shift she could get. She planned to sign up for a few online classes through the community college, so she needed the money to pay for tuition and books. She finally had a real chance to start over, again, but this time she'd do it right. No getting into trouble or getting mixed up with the wrong people.

Melody let them stay in a small apartment above the restaurant. There was only one room so Ava slept on the couch, but it was free so she wouldn't complain.

On her days off she went to the beach with Cassie. She bought a bathing suit, and some other clothes. For the first time in many years, she had more than two sets of clothes.

Cassie was actually a good roommate. She cleaned up after herself, was quiet after hours, and respectful of privacy. Overall, Ava was happy with her current living situation.

When they weren't working Cassie went out most evenings. She spent a lot of time at her sobriety classes, and she checked in with her sponsor, via the phone, several times a day.

As a friend, Cassie was great, and Ava had grown quite fond of her. They watched every Adam Sandler movie ever made, went to the beach, and ate most of their meals together when Cassie was home.

Melody popped in a few times a week just to check up on her

sister's sobriety progress. During her visits, she would casually stroll around the apartment, and help clean for twenty to thirty minutes. It was obvious to Ava that she was searching for drugs, but Cassie thought her sister was spending quality time with her. In a way it was quality time, so Ava made herself scarce. Today was different though. Melody seemed agitated.

"Cassie, can you please go help Hank bring in the food from the truck?" She spoke to her sister in a tone one would use with a toddler.

Cassie jumped up, eager to comply. The two sisters were strikingly similar in appearance, except Melody was a lot healthier. The pallor of her skin, her weight, and strength, all conveyed she was at the prime of her life, fitness, and health, whereas Cassie was a thin little scrub that looked like she'd fallen into a gray paint bucket. Even chunks of her hair were missing.

Cassie left and Melody turned to Ava. "I think Cassie's using again," she said, getting straight to the point, Melody never wasted time with small talk.

"Really? Why do you think that?"

"She's out all hours of the night, she's skinny, and has terrible bags under bloodshot eyes, and she stutters a lot."

Now that Ava thought about it, Cassie was gone the last three nights until the early hours of the morning, and sometimes she slurred her speech so bad it was hard to follow what she was saying.

Ava never thought anything of it. She just assumed Cassie was out with friends, and that's the way she talked sometimes. Cassie never woke up before 10:30am, and she was always tired and run down. Ava just assumed Cassie wasn't a morning person, plus Ava had never lived with anyone long enough to learn normal human habits and behaviors.

In the shelters, they all left at the same time, when the shelter workers woke them up. Her foster families weren't much different either. They all woke up for school and work, got dressed, and left. She never paid enough attention to other people's comings and goings to remark on any patterns.

"Yeah, I guess I can see that."

"So, what should we do?"

"I have no idea. What do people normally do when someone's using drugs?"

"Intervene." Melody said, matter of factly.

"What does that entail?"

"We need to sit her down, tell her how bad it is for her, and explain what she needs to do to stay sober."

"I think she already knows those things. She's not stupid. It's a disease, right? She can't help it."

"Well, what would you do then?"

"I don't know."

"You're not helpful." Melody turned on her heel and left, slamming the door behind her.

Ava wasn't sure what she should do. Cassie was a grown woman. She made her own choices. It wasn't Ava's responsibility to do anything but be a good roommate. She shrugged and went back to perusing what classes were available next semester on the laptop that Melody lent her.

Despite trying to convince herself that it was none of her business, and she had no reason to get involved in their family drama, she succumbed to worry over Cassie. It was difficult for her to admit that she did actually like Cassie. A good friend would try to help somehow. So, she researched drug addiction signs, symptoms, and how to help someone. It didn't sound very optimistic from everything she read, but she figured she'd try.

Ava waited up for Cassie to return. Around two in the morning, she finally heard steps coming up the stairwell. She paused the movie and waited for Cassie.

A gaunt figure stumbled through the door. Despite Ava's unconventional upbringing, she'd never known a meth addict before, so this was all new to her.

"Whoa, what the fuck dude?" Cassie swayed unsteadily, then walked toward her bedroom.

"Wait, Cassie." Ava jumped over the back of the couch. "You're using again, aren't you?" Ava tried to sound as cool as possible.

Cassie turned around and pushed Ava so forcefully that both girls stumbled backwards. A lamp fell to the floor when Ava bumped into the side table. Luckily the bulb didn't break.

"You don't know shit. Stay the fuck away from me."

Stunned, Ava said nothing as Cassie meandered into her room and slammed the door closed. After returning the lamp to its rightful place, Ava slumped back down on the couch.

Cassie, normally so meek and kind, shoved her with the force of a two-hundred-pound man. It was impressive, but also concerning.

Ava clicked off the tv and laid down. They would figure this out tomorrow. Tonight, they both needed sleep. She wouldn't be able to talk to this version of Cassie right now anyway.

When Ava awoke, the apartment was quiet, as usual. Everything seemed completely ordinary.

Grabbing the box of Cocoa Puffs, she went into Cassie's room. Purposefully making a lot of noise, she fell onto the bed beside her sleeping friend and opened the box of cereal, crinkling the plastic bag obnoxiously.

They were out of milk that didn't have chunks in it, so Ava removed a handful of dry cereal and shoved some pieces in her mouth.

"What time is it?" Cassie asked in a scratchy voice.

"10:00am."

"Oh, really, man I was dead to the world." Cassie sat up, and rested against the headboard next to Ava. Deep blue circles surrounded her eyes, making it look like she'd been punched.

Ava offered her the box Cocoa Puffs.

"Thanks dude, this is awesome. Breakfast in bed. You're so romantic." Cassie smiled.

They both ate a few handfuls of cereal.

"So, are we going to talk about it?" Ava asked.

Cassie started to fidget with a string hanging from one of the bed pillows.

"No, it's all good. I'm going to quit. I promise. Last night was a one-time deal. I just wanted to get it out of my system one last time before I get serious." Cassie laughed in a non-convincing huff of determination.

"OK." Ava decided not to push too much. "But your sister's probably going to want to talk about it."

"Shit, she knows?" Cassie's head slumped backwards against the headboard with a loud thud. "Ouch."

They both laughed. Cassie threw a handful of Cocoa Puffs at Ava. They laughed even harder, and Ava returned a doubly large handful, after which Cassie dumped the entire contents of the box over Ava's head.

"Oh my god, we're going to get mice in here and your sister's going to be pissed," Ava said while laughing and pulling Cocoa Puffs out of her hair and eating them.

"Yeah, somehow I think the Cocoa Puffs and mice will be the least of her concerns." Cassie avoided Ava's gaze.

"We'll figure this out." Ava shoulder bumped Cassie.

Tears welled in the bottom of Cassie's sunken eyes. Ava wrapped an arm around Cassie. She had no idea how to help or what to say, but she could provide a shoulder to cry on. The rest, they'd figure out later.

CHAPTER 3
SIBYL
JUNE 23RD/CANKIT WANC-3

Cold saltwater splashed up Sibyl's legs, sending a deep chill into her bones. The water paused briefly, reversed direction, then raced back to the sea as quickly as it washed in. Another wave rushed in, enthusiastic to take its place. The sound was so tranquil that Sibyl could almost fall asleep while standing.

Melissa was correct, the beach was exactly what Sibyl needed. There was no threat of running into Chris in Daytona Beach, and there was no responsibilities or schoolwork. At least not that anyone knew about. Sibyl studied at night, in her room, when everyone else was either in bed or playing video games. Other than that, she could rest, heal, and find herself again.

Seaweed wrapped around her ankles like eels trying to pull her out to sea, or perhaps trying to prevent themselves from being pulled back out to sea. Her feet sank into the water-logged sand and little mole crab's butts poked up.

The weight of life became lighter as her worries washed away with the tide. Hot sun beat down on her pale freckled skin providing a stark contrast to the cold water. Her skin prickled pleasantly at the temperature war. Closing her eyes, she listened to the static noise of the ocean, seagulls, shouts of laughter, and conversations around her.

Tingling blossomed in her hands. Crisscrossing her fingers, she scanned the beach for anything that might have initiated the sensation. Nothing was amiss on the beautiful sunny day. Why was this happening now? It didn't make sense. This ailment had plagued her at random times throughout her life, and it rarely made sense why it would occur.

Following the years-long habit that helped calm her when she felt out of control, she breathed in through her nose, held in the smell of ocean, salt, and sunscreen for a moment, then exhaled slowly through her mouth. After repeating the process a few times, the tingling dissipated, and her heart calmed down again. Thank god. She really didn't want to have a panic attack in front of her friends and tons of strangers on a public beach.

While the medications and meditation exercises helped, she still felt like there was more to it than simply a panic attack. Firstly, why would she have a panic attack when she was completely relaxed and happy, like she was right now? There was no stressful stimulus. It happened sometimes regardless of how she felt or what was going on.

Secondly, it usually began as a physical manifestation, not emotional. The anxiety followed the tingling, not the other way around. If it was a panic attack, shouldn't she feel anxious first, then have physical symptoms follow?

Doctors ran every test imaginable, but everything checked out normal. Sibyl was a perfectly healthy twenty-six-year-old girl. Her official diagnosis was anxiety and panic disorder.

Water washed over her feet again, and with it, the last bit of tingling sensation evaporated. Inhaling a final meditative breath, she scanned the horizon. A patchwork of white puffy clouds within a pale blue sky met the perfectly straight line of the horizon. Dark water gradually faded into the deep blue sea as it traveled thousands of miles to the sandy shore beneath her feet.

It was curious that the horizon appeared straight despite the fact the world was round. The optical illusion made it understandable that humans used to think the world was flat, and ended at the edge of the sea. The justification of that point of view was obvious when standing here, looking at the horizon. Without the technology to discover the world was round, it made perfect sense to assume it was flat when your own eyes told you so. Another perception not to be trusted.

Screams grabbed her attention. Trent carried a flailing Melissa into the water. Once he was about waist deep a wave took them both under the water. A head popped up a few feet away from Trent who laughed hysterically. Melissa threw seaweed at his face. Sibyl laughed at their spectacle then headed to her chair that was wedged into the hot sand.

Courtney and Ashley lay next to her on their stomachs. Behind her, several people dodged around playing volleyball, sending up large puffs of sand. Luckily, the wind blew in the opposite direction, so none of the sand came toward her.

Sibyl picked up a book and flipped to the page she'd left off last. Staring at the page, her mind wandered off. She studied her hands and pondered the tingling sensations for about the millionth time in her life. It couldn't just be anxiety, could it? If not, then what was it? She'd waited her entire life for some big revelation, but nothing ever happened. She heard her psychiatrist clearly in her mind.

"The brain can convince the body that an unsubstantiated insecurity is a real threat, and the body will respond accordingly. Our job is to alter the chemical pathways in the brain with medication, meditation, and reasoning so that it can function normally. Then we can control our emotions and reactions," Dr Cudgel explained. It was all very logical. She suffered from a chemical imbalance in the brain. That's what was wrong with her.

"You ok?" Ashley asked.

"Yeah, just thinking about some things." Sibyl pretended to read again.

Ashley nodded and lay her head back down.

Forcing herself to focus on the words, Sibyl soon forgot all her worries and lost herself in the story.

"You ready?" Melissa looped her arm through Sibyl's elbow.

"Yes. I'm starving. Let's go before I eat the pool noodles."

Melissa giggled, but Sibyl wasn't kidding. She was borderline hangry at this point, and her burned skin wasn't helping her mood. She was practically on fire. She should've used more sunscreen. The thin green T-shirt and jean shorts scratched at it painfully. She would definitely peel in a day or two.

The restaurant was a mile or so up the beach, so they walked, which meant that Sibyl was positively famished by the time they got to the restaurant. Thankfully there were rolls on the table for an appetizer. She grabbed one and shoved it in her mouth like a starved animal.

"Damn. Were you raised in a barn? Slow down before you choke," Courtney said.

"Yeah, ok," Sibyl said between mouthfuls. It tasted so good. Her belly grumbled in appreciation followed by a weird humming of her skin. Odd. Maybe it was the sunburn.

"What would you like to drink?" the waitress's jade-green eyes looked at Sibyl impatiently. Her bright red hair with a silver streak down the front right side was mystical and alluring.

"Water please," Sibyl said around her half masticated ball of bread.

The woman nodded and moved down the table, getting everyone else's drink orders. The weird hum faded. Shaking it off, Sibyl turned back to her friends and fell into a mind-numbing conversation with Ashley, who regaled them with the unwanted details about her most recent hook up. Sibyl was almost relieved when her skin started humming again, giving her an excuse to ignore Ashley.

When the waitress set a glass of water down, Sibyl's fingers exploded into intense tingling. She flexed and extended her fingers, but the sensation didn't ease up until the waitress walked away.

What the hell? Her anxiety never behaved in this manner.

Sibyl gawked at the tall red head whose name tag read, 'Ava.' She had naturally tanned skin, and she was beautiful. All the men at the table gave her second and third glances. If the woman noticed at all, she didn't let on.

When Ava returned a few minutes later, the mysterious humming came back as well. She took their order and when she left again, the humming did as well. Interesting. Sibyl was enamored with Ava for entirely different reasons than the men at the table.

The next couple of hours were a roller coaster of intermittent weird sensations, followed by physical and emotional silence, all while trying to carry on normal conversations with her friends. It was dizzying. As closing time neared, most patrons filtered out, and eventually only their group remained.

They'd finished eating a while ago, but were socializing and killing time before the beach party. Sibyl wished her friends would hurry up. She wanted to get as far away from this Ava person as possible.

Amid a conversation with Courtney, Sibyl reached for her glass at the same time that Ava picked it up to refill it. Their hands brushed against each other and a sharp zing shot through Sibyl's hand. The glass dropped, spilling the contents on her lap.

"Oh shit, I'm sorry. Here, let me get that." Ava grabbed a napkin and leaned over Sibyl, cleaning up the mess.

A swarm of pins and needles erupted all over Sibyl's body. *Shit.* A full-on panic attack was about to happen.

Sibyl got up, nearly knocking Ava down. She bolted to the bathroom before the panic attack could fully set in. She ran to the sink and splashed cold water over her face.

"Please stop. Please stop. Breathe."

Attempting to assuage the building anxiety, she took long slow breaths, in through her nose and out through her mouth. She pictured waves crashing on the beach, imagining the feel of sand between her fingers instead of the burning numbness. Rubbing her fingers along the granite countertop sink, she noted that it was smooth and cold. *Real.*

Despite the meditation, tingling continued to build.

The door opened and Melissa came in. "Are you ok?"

Sibyl nodded. "Sorry. Just a panic attack."

"Do you want me to do something?"

"Can you get my purse, please? It has my anxiety pills in it. I need one."

"Sure." Melissa rushed out the door and returned a moment later with the purse.

Sibyl dug through it and found the pill bottle. Immediate relief washed through her just at the sight of it. Taking a pill out, she tossed it in her mouth, and swallowed. She'd be ok in just a few minutes.

Melissa rubbed her back.

"I'm good now. Sorry. I don't know what happened. You can go back to the table. I'll be out in a minute."

"Are you sure?"

Melissa had seen many panic attacks over the years. Sibyl appreciated the support, but sometimes she just wanted to be alone. It was embarrassing enough to be afflicted with this disorder, having a witness was salt on the wound.

"I'm good. I promise. I'll be back out in a minute."

"If you're not back out in five, I'll come check on you."

Sibyl smiled through the mirror.

Melissa left.

The tingling gradually subsided as the relaxing effects of Ativan set in. Sibyl took in her pale complexion. The freckles never paled, of course. They stood out more in times like this, making her look even more ridiculous.

She splashed some water over her face, then dried off. Running fingers through a few unruly blonde hairs, she took a deep breath, and headed back out.

The mess was cleaned up and a new glass of water waited for her. Taking her seat, she downed the entire glass. The cold water helped settle her queasy stomach.

"You good?" Courtney asked.

Sibyl smiled and nodded. Everyone resumed normal conversations as if nothing was amiss. Good. She didn't want to draw any more attention to herself.

Trent paid the entire bill for everyone, and they all toasted their thanks to him. Melissa beamed at his side and looped her arm through his elbow. They were so sickeningly happy. Sibyl swallowed down another gulp of water to help wash down her jealousy.

Courtney and Ashley got up and headed for the door. Sibyl weaseled her way between the two women and threw her arms around them. Ashley, who was already drunk, threw an arm around Sibyl's neck and started singing "Girls Just Want to Have Fun" at the top of her lungs. Courtney joined in loudly and out of tune.

The happiness was infectious. Sibyl got as close to her friends as possible, hoping to absorb some of it. Nestled between the two obnoxiously loud, overly happy women, she sang and danced her way down the beach, to the party.

About a mile or so later they arrived at a house that was at least twice the size of the one they were staying at, and it was currently overflowing with people and music. A large bonfire sent blades of wispy orange flames into the night sky. Nestled safely in a ring of miniature sandcastles, the fire was far enough from the ocean so that the waves didn't pose a threat to it, and far enough down the beach that the flames weren't a threat to the houses. People sat around the fire, some close enough to make out their profiles, and others outside of the light's reach, granting them a modicum of privacy.

Their group passed by the fire and went straight to the house and up a large set of stairs. Dozens of people hung out on the deck that led into a large common room that was also filled with people.

Trent gave them a brief run-down of where bathrooms, alcohol, and drugs were located, then everyone dispersed. One by one, Sibyl's friends broke off in different directions until Sibyl found herself alone in a room full of strangers. She was completely uninterested in any person or activity, so she fished for her phone.

Her pockets were empty. "Where's my purse?" The realization hit her. "Shit." The last place she remembered having them was at the restaurant, in the bathroom.

Sybil made her way over to Ashley who was in the corner flirting with some guys.

"Hey, can I use your phone to call my phone? I think I left it at the restaurant."

Ashley pulled out her phone, pressed a few buttons, and handed it to Sibyl before resuming her conversation. It rang twice before a woman answered. She recognized Ava's voice.

"Hey, that's my phone," Sibyl blurted.

"Hello, Sibyl," Ava said.

It was difficult to hear Ava over the background noise. "You have my phone. Wait, how do you know my name?"

"I looked through your purse to try and figure out who it belonged to. I found your I.D." She was basically yelling, but wind noise made it difficult for Sibyl to understand her.

"Where are you? I'll come get it."

"I'm at the beach, behind the restaurant. There's a path cut through the sand dunes. I'll be here for a while, so come on over."

"Ok, thanks. I'll be there soon."

Handing the phone back to Ashley, Sibyl headed out.

Once she was back on the beach, she removed her flip-flops, and picked up a light jog.

The prospect of being around this Ava chick again wasn't appealing. Hopefully the Ativan was still in Sibyl's system, otherwise she'd have to endure the weird effect this girl had on her. All she had to do was get her stuff, say thank you, and leave. She wouldn't be around Ava for very long. She could do that.

The wind was blowing away from the party, so the music faded out not long after Sibyl left. The lights from the street were blocked out by large sand dunes, and the waning crescent moon provided very little illumination, so it was very dark. She could barely see the bonfire from the party at this distance either.

Once she arrived at the restaurant, she scanned the beach, and saw someone sitting in the sand just out of reach of the waves. Puffs of smoke rose above the person and were quickly swept away by the wind.

Red hair, pulled back in a messy ponytail, whipped around furiously, like a bold red snake writhing in frustration at its inability to escape the binds of the hair tie.

Tingling tickled Sibyl's fingers. Damn, the Ativan already wore off. Oh well, she had to get her purse and phone. There was no choice.

When she got close to Ava, Sibyl noticed another really skinny woman lying in the sand next to the red head, nearly invisible in the darkness. Both women looked up when Sibyl approached.

"Hey, are you Ava from the restaurant?"

"Yeah, you must be Sibyl."

"Yes."

Ava handed over the missing purse. Ignoring the tingling in her hands, Sibyl grabbed the purse and examined the contents: wallet, money, phone, and everything else she carried were safely tucked inside. Relief flooded over her.

"Thank you."

Ava nodded then took a hit off a joint before offering it to Sibyl.

"No thanks."

"It'll work better than Ativan."

Sibyl's jaw unhinged. "That's a total invasion of privacy."

Ava shrugged before returning her gaze to the sea. A wave rushed inland, almost making it to their feet, then headed back out. Try as it might, but the sea couldn't reach them; yet. It would keep trying, over and over, until they left, or it succeeded.

The tingling intensified. Sibyl glanced back at the spec of a bonfire in the distance. She could leave now and these weird feelings would all go away, but, what if there was a reason this was happening? She could stay for a bit and try to find out.

"You going to stand there all night?" Ava blew out another puff of smoke.

Sibyl sat down and attempted to act cool. "Ok, I'll take a hit."

Ava handed over the joint.

Sucking in a deep breath, Sibyl's lungs spasmed at the smokey insult, and she coughed violently.

The girl laying in the sand next to Ava laughed. "I remember my first time."

Embarrassment bled through Sibyl. She passed the joint back to Ava.

"Are you ok? Have you ever smoked before?" Ava asked.

"Yes, it's just been a long time." Defensiveness gave Sibyl's words a bite.

"Just asking." Ava threw up her hands.

The three women watched silently as the water tried desperately to connect with them. The drug worked quickly. The tingling lessened and Sibyl relaxed into the gentle calm of THC induced tranquility. Ava was right. It was better than Ativan.

"I'll take another hit," Sibyl said.

"You sure?" Ava asked.

"Yes. If you have enough."

"Yeah. It's the last of it though. You can finish it off." Ava handed it over.

"Thanks." Sibyl sucked it down. Although no one could ever describe coughing as dignified, she made her best attempt at it. Neither girl laughed at her that time.

Ava laid back in the sand next to the other woman. Sibyl followed their example. The stars winked in and out of view as clouds rode by on the wind. The sky rippled in its own mesmerizing atmospheric sea and time slipped away.

How long they laid there, Sibyl had no idea. She didn't care. She enjoyed being still and relaxed, listening to the ocean sounds, feeling the sand, watching the clouds.

"I have anxiety, and I get this feeling sometimes, like pins and needles poking me everywhere." She wasn't sure why she said it, perhaps the weed lowered her inhibitions or sense of judgment.

"Maybe it's not anxiety," the skinny woman said.

"What do you mean?" Sibyl asked.

"Maybe it's your sixth sense." The woman's voice took on a mocking mystical tone.

Sibyl couldn't tell if she was making fun of her or being serious. As if on cue, the tingling returned stronger than before. Usually, it affected her hands first then crept up her arms and into her chest, but this time it traveled up her spine, through the back of her neck, and into her eyes. She was immediately sober as the sensation slowly took over her entire body.

"Hey, are you ok? Your eyes are weird." Ava asked.

Sibyl did a double take. Ava was covered by the faint silver haze. Flowing like a river from the silver streak of hair, Ava glowed mystically. Her hands and fingers were longer than the average human's and red fur covered her arms and legs.

Sibyl couldn't tell if it was the drugs or her anxiety that was creating the unusual hallucination. Her sanity was definitely questionable.

"What's wrong?" Ava's eyebrows furrowed.

Sibyl reached out to touch the stream of silver, but Ava jerked away.

"Dude, I think she's trippin'," said the other girl.

Sibyl's confusion doubled as Ava grew fluffy red ears and her nose elongated into something resembling a snout. The translucent form of a dainty red wolf took shape, overlaying itself onto Ava's body.

Ava tilted her head back and forth in an animalistic manner. Suspicion pushed into Sibyl's mind, an extrinsic force taking up space somewhere it didn't belong. Ava rocked onto all fours, glowering at Sibyl.

"What are you doing? You're both trippin'," the other woman said.

They ignored her, too focused on each other to pay her any mind.

Normally, Sibyl was unable to control her mind or body when a panic attack came on. The anxiety took over all facets of her being. Just the possibility of having a panic attack could precipitate anxiety. Over the years, she'd built a mental and emotional wall of meditation and Ativan against it, but this time, she didn't feel out of control, so she allowed the feeling to spread through her without hindrance.

When she hit a mental wall, she simply removed it. As if she'd blown pappus seeds from a dandelion, the barrier disintegrated and blew away with the wind.

Closing her eyes, Sibyl reached toward the epicenter of emotion instead of cowering away from it like she usually did. Once inside, she discovered the sensation was more of an awareness. She felt Ava's thoughts and emotions. Not caring if it was the drugs or something else entirely, she let her instincts run free, exploring this newfound atmosphere of awareness.

Ava wasn't entirely human. There was something magical about her, wild, wolf-like. Ava, herself, didn't fully understand what she was either. Born in a different world and orphaned in North Carolina as an infant, Ava was scared and cold. A tiny baby left on the street all alone. No, not alone. A stranger picked her up, ripping her hand from someone she'd been holding onto. The baby Ava started crying.

Violently shoved from her apperception, Sibyl opened her eyes and stared directly into Ava's angry face. She was on top of Sibyl, pinning her down in a choke hold.

"Who are you?" Ava snarled. Small fangs poked from her mouth.

Sibyl squirmed beneath the redhead who smelled like a musty wet dog. Ava's expression was feral, and her grip around Sibyl's neck was a vice.

Fear gripped Sibyl.

"Are you one of them?" Ava demanded.

Sharp claws dug painfully into the side of Sibyl's neck, right over her carotid artery. One wrong move and she wouldn't walk away from this night.

Ava's grip tightened, and lightning ripped through Sibyl's entire body. An urgency was hidden within the pain. Her heart thundered wildly. This wasn't a panic attack. It was a plea from herself. Her mind begged her to run, but she couldn't. She could barely breathe. Ava cut off her air.

Sibyl flailed her arms, punching Ava's shoulders, and frantically clawing at her face, but it was no use. Ava was impossibly strong, and Sibyl was weakening by the second.

"Hey, Ava. What are you doing, dude? She's turning blue. Let her up," the other woman pulled at Ava's shoulder, but the redhead didn't budge. She didn't even blink. Ava stared into Sibyl's face as if she was trying to decide whether or not to kill her.

Sibyl's vision closed in at the sides, her head throbbed, and her lungs spasmed. Just a few more seconds of consciousness left in her life.

Please, Sibyl begged.

Ava's eyes widened, and her grip loosened a fraction, just enough for Sibyl to take a breath. The smell of rotting flesh and decay enveloped her. She recognized that smell.

No. Impossible.

Ava's head snapped to the side a split second before she was dislodged from on top of Sibyl, as if she'd blown away on the wind.

Coughing violently, Sibyl sat up and sucked in deep painful breaths. The feel of air in her lungs was a relief, but the feeling of relief fell away as quickly as it came on. One of the beasts from her hallucinations was a few yards away, fighting savagely with a lanky red wolf.

Legs, hair, fangs, and bodies tangled with each other. The skinny woman stumbled over to Sibyl, and they both stared at the fight, completely dumbfounded and helpless.

The monster was easily five or six times the size of the gangly little creature and quickly subdued the little red wolf. Humanoid hands with deadly claws swiped furiously, but the small wolf blocked it with impressive skill and strength despite its size, but it was still no match.

The beast had the upper hand in strength, size, and brutality. The little red wolf sank into the sand beneath the giant monster. Claws raked at each other, but the beasts were longer and sharper, and cut into the little wolf as if its skin was tissue paper.

The little wolf howled, and pain ripped through Sibyl as if it were her own. She grabbed her shoulder. It was fine, no wound, and still in the socket, but that wasn't so for the little wolf. Its left front leg lay limply at its side, blood gushing from a deep laceration. Sibyl felt the little wolf's terror just like she felt for the victims from one of her nightmares.

"What the hell is that thing?" the other woman yelled.

"You can see it too?" Sibyl asked.

"Ava!" the woman shouted.

Sibyl followed the woman's path of vision to the wrestling wolves. The small red wolf resembled the shadowy silhouette that was imposed over Ava's body earlier. It couldn't be, could it?

"Get Off Her You Ugly Fuck!" The woman threw a small seashell at it. The shell bopped it on the side of the head. It snarled at the skinny woman. She backed up, tripping over Sibyl, who still sat on the ground, frozen in panic.

Sibyl jumped up. A voice inside her mind screamed to run. Her legs were poised and ready, but she couldn't leave that little wolf, who may actually be Ava. Although Ava did almost kill her a few minutes ago. Still, she couldn't leave someone to die, especially not at the hands of a beast that she may have somehow brought to life.

She found her purse in the sand a few feet away, and pulled out the canister of pepper spray that she kept in case of emergency. This seemed like it met the criteria. Stepping in front of the unknown woman, Sibyl aimed the pepper spray directly at the beast's face. Its black eyes held her stare with vicious intensity. The monster was so large and its arms so long that it could easily swipe the pepper spray out of Sibyl's hands without even leaving its spot.

"Let her go." Sibyl's voice sounded more courageous than she felt.

It snarled in reply.

Heart pounding wildly, eyes wide with terror, and hands shaking, Sibyl depressed the button.

CHAPTER 4
AVA
JUNE 23RD/CANKIT WANC-3

Thick slimy drool, that smelled of rancid meat, fell onto Ava's furry muzzle. It oozed like a slug onto her lips, the horrible taste triggering an immediate gag reflex. She spat in disgust. The beast wasn't focused on her. It watched Sibyl who stood several yards away, stupidly holding up a canister of pepper spray.

Stupid girl. RUN!! Ava's temper and desperation flared. Craning her neck, she tried to locate Cassie, but searing pain from her injured arm paralyzed her. The wound was deep, and her shoulder was dislocated. Thrusting her slender rear legs upwards, she raked her claws over the beast's torso. Tiny drops of blood dripped onto her. The monster didn't even flinch. She was but a mosquito on an elephant.

Her legs quivered with exhaustion. They wouldn't hold against the monster much longer. She tried to wiggle free while it was distracted. Its head slammed into hers, and the world tipped sideways. The beach fell away as a mental fog drifted over her. She tried to stay focused, but her head throbbed, and pain ripped through her chest when one of her ribs cracked.

Sinking deeper into the sand beneath its weight, she whimpered helplessly. Defeat was imminent. All the weight of her life came down on her at that moment. She'd been running for so long, and she was so tired. She could accept her fate and let the monster end her right here, right now, and she would finally be at peace.

But, what about the Hanson's? What about Cassie and even stupid Sibyl? She couldn't abandon them, and she couldn't let go of her vengeance. Ava didn't want to run anymore. She may be outmatched in size and strength, but she possessed the fortitude of a category five hurricane. It was time to fight.

"Let her go." Sibyl's voice was lethally calm even though her hand trembled.

The beast stared at the blonde. Ava's heart pounded in rhythm with the pain that throbbed in her wounded shoulder. A roar tore through the night and the weight lifted from Ava. Sibyl doused its face in pepper spray. Seizing the opportunity, Ava bit down on its wrist.

Yanking its paw away, the monster roared again.

Every breath stung as Ava scrambled away. A large paw swiped at her. She dodged it, just barely. The monster wiped at its face like a mad man, then swiped a paw in her direction again. He missed by centimeters. She felt the wind from his punch as it passed by her face. Finding purchase on the spongy sand, she scurried away on three shaky legs as quickly as possible, but she wasn't fast enough.

Incisive pain racked her hind quarters. Sky and sand blended into a jumble of confusion, followed by pain hammering into her uninjured shoulder. Rolling to a stop at the edge of the water, she pushed herself sternal. The beast was between her, Cassie, and Sibyl, their positions triangulated around it.

Finding untapped courage and strength, Ava stood again. The monster advanced in a disoriented pattern, swiping at its face. Since it lacked dexterity, it ended up scratching itself with its claws, which angered the beast even further. Another furious roar pierced the atmosphere. Sibyl and Cassie covered their ears.

Blinking repeatedly, the beast looked frantically side to side. Saliva and tears ran down its face. Choking on a cough, it looked right at Sibyl then turned away again, searching the beach, and sniffing the air. Its senses were temporarily blinded from the pepper spray. It couldn't see or smell anything.

All three women realized it at the same time and sprinted for the path between the sand dunes. Maybe running away one last time wasn't such a bad idea after all. Tripping over her injured leg, Ava fell. Sibyl and Cassie were almost to the pathway already, so close to escape, but Ava had fallen dangerously close to the beast. Its head snapped in her direction.

Ava froze. Holding her breath, she watched the beast's unseeing eyes scan the scene. Her heart beat so loudly, she feared the monster may hear it. Some slight thudding sound stole the beast's attention in the opposite direction, and it sprinted away toward the invisible target.

Sibyl was throwing seashells. Cassie ran to Ava. Sliding to a halt, she sprayed Ava in a blanket of sand.

"Get your ass up!" Pulling on Ava's scruff, Cassie helped the waist high wolf to her feet.

Ava's heart swelled with guilt and gratitude.

The monster circled in disoriented rage about twenty feet away. They didn't have much time before its senses would recover. The two of them limped slowly toward the dunes. Sibyl abandoned shell tossing and came to Ava's other side. Grabbing the lanky wolf around the waist, she pushed their advance.

Another wave of shame washed through Ava. The only reason they were in danger was because of her. They may die tonight, trying to save her. More victims to add to her conscience.

Sibyl's arms dug into Ava's abdomen, painfully. A trail of red sprinkled behind them like rose petals tossed out to woo a lover. If the monster got close enough, it would find that trail, and even with muted senses, it would be able to track them.

The creature howled in disapproval, sensing their escape. With one last furious shake of its head, the beast centered its gaze directly on them, swollen eyes narrowing, and pupils constricting in perfect unison. It sprinted, claws digging deep into the sand, propelling its massive body faster. It would be on the cumbersome trio in three strides, three heartbeats left to live.

They weren't going to make it. With determined resolve, the red wolf pinned her round ears flat against her head, and whirled around accidentally knocking Cassie down. Hackles raised, she growled with as much ferocity as she could muster, positioning herself between the beast and the other two women.

Two-inch-long pearly white fangs shone grandly. Compared to the six-inch daggers adorning the beast's maw, hers were laughable, but she'd break them off in its flesh if she had to. Fear pulsed through every fiber of her being, but she refused to let anyone else die because of her.

Out of the darkness, down the beach, two shadowy figures approached at an impossibly fast speed, as if they flew just above the sand.

The beast leapt into the air with outstretched front legs.

The newcomers also leapt. Large timber wolves, one as black as the night, with matching ebony eyes, and the other, a shimmering silver color, like ice under the light of a full moon, with molten metallic colored eyes. The new wolves were twice the size of an average wolf, but only half the size of the beast before them.

They intercepted the snarling monster in midair. The beast rolled to the ground in a flailing heap. Once it came to a stop, it got to its feet and looked toward its prey. Anger and confusion danced within its menacing eyes.

The two wolves didn't grant it the opportunity to orient itself. They attacked in unison.

The fight was brutal and bloody. Wounds appeared, seemingly out of nowhere, all over the creature's body. The mythical pair went unscathed. The lithe wolves moved with preternatural skill, working together with such precision that it was difficult to tell where one wolf stopped and the other started.

When the beast swiped its paw at the silver wolf to its right, the black wolf embedded a bite into its left leg. When it tried to kick the black wolf off, it was gone, and the silver wolf snapped at the back of its neck, leaving behind a deep laceration.

The beast howled in pain, swiping frantically at the silver wolf, but once again, the wolf was gone. Holding its neck, the beast whirled around, trying to get its bearings. Whenever it deflected an attack from one side, it was bitten or scratched on the opposite. So, the dance went.

The girls watched, dumbstruck. With every passing moment, the beast's rage increased exponentially, rivaling the number of wounds it collected.

Finally, the black wolf bit down on an extended arm, with such force that even from several yards away, Ava heard the bones snap. A deafening howl rang out, and the monster punched at the black wolf with a blow that could have crushed its skull. Alas, the only thing it managed to strike was its own broken arm, because, yet again, his assailant was not there. Another deafening howl erupted.

The pair of wolves drove the beast back. Distance between the girls and the beast, slowly increased.

Defeat and fury broiled behind its still swollen eyes. Holding the broken arm at its side, blood dripping from countless wounds, the monster glared at the pair. Blood dripped from the maws of the two wolves, but it wasn't their own.

For a moment everything was calm. The wind died down, the water went glassy, and the sound muted. The entire world paused, waiting to see who would make the next move. Ava held her breath.

Time slowed to a crawl as the monster's powerful hind legs coiled like a spring. Rocking back on strong haunches, legs poised with so much inertia that the sand beneath its feet almost vibrated, the beast leapt into the air, soaring over the two wolves. An impossible jump, spanning an even more impossible distance.

Landing with such force that the ground tremored, it stood up to its entire nine feet height right in front of Ava. Before she had a chance to react, it struck. The world went black.

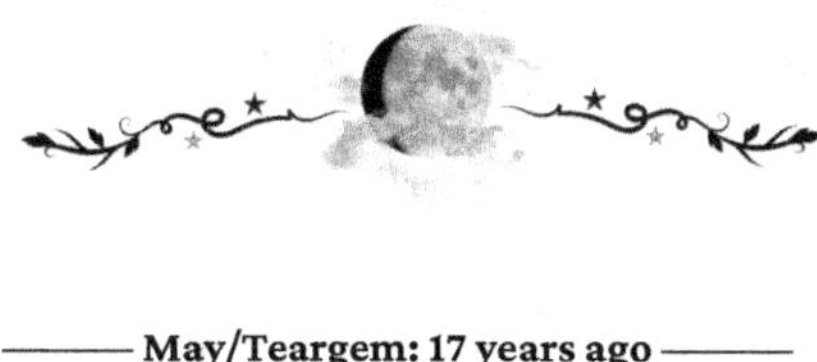

———— May/Teargem: 17 years ago ————

Standing on the sidewalk in front of a quaint little townhome in Raleigh NC, Ava stared at the two-story brick building as if it were a funeral home. Another foster family. The thirty-sixth one in her nine years of life. The Hansons seemed sincere, but they all did at first.

"Come on in dear." Mrs. Hanson led the way inside. Ava's room was to be on the second floor. It was simple and small, but she wouldn't have to share. That was a step up from the last, and most of the other places, at least. Usually, she shared a room and sometimes even a bed. Placing her suitcase on the floor, she sat on the bed.

Mrs. Hanson took her suitcase and set it on the dresser. She removed the contents, then neatly folded, and hung all of Ava's five sets of clothes. "We'll have to get you some new clothes. These are pretty worn out."

Ava stared blankly out the window.

"Would you like that? To go shopping? We can go tomorrow."

Ava nodded but said nothing.

"How about we let you settle in. We'll have dinner in a couple of hours. Come down anytime you're ready." The woman smiled.

Ava laid on the bed, turning her back to Mrs. Hanson. There was no sense in getting to know them. It was only a matter of time before they'd make her leave. Sighing, she gripped the small, tattered blanket tightly. The one possession she had that meant anything. Closing her eyes, she pressed the blanket to her cheek, finding comfort in its softness and familiarity.

The world shifted. Pieces of her soul shattered into nothingness. The floor came up and slammed her into a chair. Ava looked around, confused and disoriented.

A man with a gray mustache that matched his frizzy beard sat across from the Hansons at their dining room table. Wearing a perfectly tailored suit and a fancy blue tie, he rummaged through a leather briefcase and removed a stack of papers. "They want to adopt you, Ms. Smith," he said with a sincere smile.

Ava's mouth dropped open, and her mind went blank. If someone could melt, she would've collapsed into a puddle on the floor. Too stunned to talk, she just stared at Mr. Avraham, the Hanson's lawyer, in dumbfounded silence.

"What do you say about that young lady?" he asked.

Ava moved her mouth, but no words came out. She'd dreamt of this day her entire life, and especially the last year with the Hansons, but she never imagined it would actually happen. She'd learnt long ago that dreams never came true, yet here she was, sitting at a table listening to the words she'd wanted to hear from the earliest moments she could remember.

The hairs on her arms stood up and darkened. The sensation shocked her. Usually when she changed, it was from fear or anger, but she felt neither of those emotions right now. In fact, she couldn't even remember the last time she'd been angry or scared. She hadn't changed shape in a long time.

Tears welled in her eyes, blurring her vision. Squashing down the ripple flowing through her body, she jumped from her seat, which fell backwards in a loud crash. Tackling Mr. Hanson, who was the closest to her, she hugged him fiercely, happy-sobbing into his shoulder.

Mrs. Hanson's hand touched her shoulder, and Ava threw an arm out, wrapping it around the woman's neck, pulling all three of them into a hug that rivaled all hugs.

"Thank you," Ava whispered. "I love you." The first time she'd ever said those words to anyone.

"We love you too."

The words echoed into her subconsciousness. Ava saw their faces.

"I love you," Mrs. Hanson said after opening the Christmas gift Ava got her.

"I love you kiddo," Mr. Hanson thumped her teasingly on the nose.

"I....lo...." The words drifted away as did their faces. The beautiful sound of their voices warped into unintelligible muffled mechanical roaring.

The bus's engine revved and sputtered out. Ava glanced around in a daze of confusion. Sitting in the front seat, she watched as a man under the hood of the large yellow bus tinkered with some tools and other gadgets.

"Try it again!" the man yelled.

The bus driver turned the key, and the engine roared to life. The kids cheered joyfully. Finally, they were on their way again, after forty-five minutes of engine trouble.

The bus stopped exactly five blocks from the Hanson's townhouse. Descending the steps in one large jump, Ava hit the pavement and ran down the street as fast as her legs would take her. Everyone would be waiting on her, and this was the most important day of her life. It took all of her control to not shift on the bus ride home.

Home. Such a great word that she could finally use.

Rounding the last corner, she practically rocket-launched up the steps to the door of the townhouse she now called her own. She paused to catch her breath.

The front door was ajar. That was odd. The Hanson's never left it open. Deep claw marks were gouged into the wood, and a metallic smell wafted through the doorway. Blood.

Slowly pushing the door open, Ava stepped through the threshold. Bile rose in her throat. The once organized living room, of the elegant but modest city comforts, lay in tatters. Shelves were toppled over, all of Mrs. Hanson's figurines were shattered into thousands of pieces. The coffee table was smashed, and a cake was wedged in a messy blob between the broken boards. Blood splattered the curtains, and a balloon that said, *Congratulations!* bobbed against the curtain rod, stuck in a current of air from a vent in the corner. It was as if a cyclone tore through the room and destroyed everything in its wake.

Amongst the destruction were the mangled bodies of her would-be parents, ravaged to such a horrific degree that they were barely recognizable. Mr. Hanson lay atop his wife, belly up, as if he'd tried to shield her from their attacker. Entrails hung from his midsection.

Among them were her almost-grandparents, the C.P.S. case worker, Mr. Avraham, and another lady Ava didn't recognize. All seven bodies were speckled with various wounds and their eyes stared vacantly. The wound that ultimately ended their lives was obvious. Their throats were ripped out. Pools of blood congealed under each body on the beautiful Persian rug that Mrs. Hanson took so much pride in.

On the floor, amongst the shattered debris of their once happy home, was a blood-stained stack of papers. Ava picked up the messy jumble of papers. The adoption packet, signed by Mr. and Mrs. Hanson, Mrs. Hanson's parents, and Mrs. Lenell, on behalf of the State of North Carolina.

Below all their signatures was a little yellow sticky that pointed to a blank line where Ava would have signed to make it official. She stared at the blank line. Her heart was just as empty as that line was. Tears streamed down her face.

Choking on a sob, the ten-year old Ava backed away, despair and terror overcoming her senses as the grim reality of her circumstances permeated into the depths of her soul. A lump in her throat physically obstructed airflow. Desolation filled her. A water balloon of agony that was overfilled and about to burst at any moment, the thin layer of rubber latex, her skin, was the only thing holding her together. She was about to explode into oblivion. No, that was bile, she was going to explode literally.

She doubled over on her hands and knees as vomitus violently ejected from her. Sucking in a deep painful breath after the contents of her lunch spilled onto the floor, she knelt for a moment, waiting for the world to stabilize.

Refusing to look into the living room, Ava stood back up onto shaking legs. The adoption papers fell from her hand absent-mindedly, and she walked out the front door, leaving her destroyed family behind.

Bright sunlight slapped her in the face. Visions of her almost mother and fathers' mangled bodies filled in the amaurosis. Shielding her face, she fell down the stairs. Each of the five steps bit into five points of her body: hips, buttocks, knee, elbow, palm, finally hitting the sidewalk in a wrecked heap of a girl. The lights mingled with the pain, confusing her senses.

Clenching her eyes tightly closed, she reached out for someone, anyone, something to grab hold of and help orientate herself. Her hand brushed on a hard surface.

Opening her eyes to bright swirling blue and red lights, Ava took in her surroundings. She was in an alley next to a dumpster. How had she gotten here? A white streak lined her vision every time she blinked. A uniformed man knelt before her and spoke into a device attached to his shoulder. The officer's lips moved, but Ava didn't hear what he said. There was no sound in her reality.

She was naked and despite the cool evening temperature, she wasn't shaking. She'd been there for days, as evidenced by the flies dancing on her swollen eyes and desiccated lips. Ava resigned herself to die in that alley, next to a dumpster full of trash with all the discarded rubbish of the city.

Fitting, that's exactly what she was; a dreg of society, unwanted and unloved by anyone still living. So, she let the wolf slumber and waited to be reunited with the only family she ever had.

Another uniformed man arrived with a brown blanket. He tossed it over her then scooped her into his arms. She fought weakly, her movements sluggish and non-threatening. A tiny kitten swatting at a gorilla. His embrace was strong and secure. He deflected all her pathetic blows in a gentle manner that infuriated her.

Barely cognizant of who he was or what he was trying to do, she even tried to bite him, but he was ready for that too, and her teeth found a fist full of blanket.

Gently, he placed her in the back of a police car. Despite her best efforts to assault him, he remained calm and unharmed. His expression was one of devastation and sympathy. It reminded her of what she lost. The Hansons. Her family. They were gone. The pain burned hot again.

Ava screamed in a scratchy pathetic decibel after the door closed. Losing herself in pain and rage, she assaulted the backseat of the car in a temper tantrum that could rival a toddler. Other than a few fingernail scratches in the interior, nothing she did harmed the vehicle in any way. Ava panted in frustration.

Anger slowly consumed her; anger at whoever murdered the Hansons, anger at herself for not being able to help them, and anger at the world for, once again, robbing her of happiness. After a lifetime of rejection, mistreatment, and devastating loss, the only parts of her that remained were anger, pain, and defeat. Life had thoroughly and irrevocably defeated her.

The overwhelming despair was so heavy that she briefly thought about ending things. But vengeance fueled her will to live now. She would find the person or persons responsible for the murder of her family and she would kill them.

Rage took over. She saw red everywhere. Blood trickled down the windows in the cop car, obstructing her view of the outside world. The blood flowed toward her, as if it possessed a consciousness of its own. Sitting back against the seat, she pulled her legs up and closed her eyes. Heart pounding wildly, she rocked back and forth, waiting for the blood to absorb her.

Opening her eyes again, she stared at an ugly red wall. The psychiatrist's voice echoed in the small room, but Ava wasn't listening. She was too focused on that stupid red wall. Why did the psychiatrist choose that horrible color? It looked like blood. It made the room seem small and suffocating. Fitting for the insufferable personality of the woman who insisted they talk about all the painful things Ava had been through.

The psychiatrist used words Ava didn't understand like purgative and cathartic. She also liked to bring up the incident when Ava was six years old. That's when she first started to change forms, and it was the worst memory of all, other than the Hansons.

At first, she didn't know what to make of it. Like all the shifts, the first time was completely out of her control, and only happened because she was afraid.

One of her foster fathers tried to force himself on her. She'd never seen a naked man before, and what he presented to her, between his legs, frightened and repulsed her more than anything she'd ever encountered in her life, until that point.

The change happened in a matter of seconds after he moved his hand between her legs, under her nightgown. The feeling of his hand on her thigh made her want to vomit. She could still feel the slimy sensation of his touch as if it were yesterday. She wanted to peel his fingers off her, but she was too disgusted and scared to touch him even to fend him off.

Her wolf form wasn't afraid of him though. The wolf was brave and vicious and would not allow Ava to be assaulted.

He never got a chance to go further than her thighs because the wolf bit his arm so badly that the nerves in his hand were permanently damaged. It scared her, almost as much as he scared her. One minute, she was a little girl sleeping in her bed, the next, she was fending off a predator by transforming into an actual predator.

She could still taste his blood in her mouth. The power, instincts, and anger of the wolf overpowered her weak, scared human self. It was as if the wolf was a separate being altogether. She wondered if her curse was some form of schizophrenia. Maybe she had multiple personalities, and one is so strong it could physically transform her.

She shifted back to her human self just as quickly as she'd shifted into the wolf. Her foster father gaped, cradling his wounded arm. Ava stared at her arms and hands with confused curiosity.

He and his wife told the social worker that Ava attacked him, unprovoked, with a piece of broken glass that she'd hidden in her room. They made her out to be a monster and, if she was being completely honest, she felt like one.

Ava told the social worker what the man had done, leaving out the part of her becoming a wolf. They wouldn't believe her, and it would only make her sound crazy. She barely believed it herself.

They launched a full investigation and discovered several girls that he'd assaulted over the years. He went to jail. That brought some satisfaction to Ava. Justice was served for her and the other girls who were victimized by him.

Still though, she didn't want to revisit these memories, but that's what the counselor was determined to get Ava to talk about. Talking about them didn't make her feel better. It reminded her of all the pain and suffering she'd caused and endured, and she just wanted to forget it all.

The doctor put her on antidepressants which made her feel disoriented and tired. After the first dose, she flushed the pills down the toilet every day.

She learned how to pretend to be what the system wanted her to be, and she played the role every day, most of the time at least. Ava carried herself behind a shield of placid anger and disconnected calmness, biding her time until she could escape and exact revenge. None of her plans required therapy, medication, or talking to accomplish.

"Ava, you need to talk about these memories, so they don't continue to haunt you."

She ignored the counselor.

"Ava?"

She stared out of the window. A dark storm cloud rolled in.

"Ava."

"Ava." A female voice called her, but it was far away.

Ava watched the darkness slowly take over the sky.

"Ava. Can you hear me?"

She knew that voice. The black clouds surrounded her.

"Ava, wake up."

Cassie! Recognition dawned in her mind. Opening her eyes, she met the worried brown eyes of her friend.

"Thank God. Welcome back." Cassie smiled widely.

The room was familiar. Their apartment. The small hum of the window AC unit droned in the background. Ava laid on the couch she normally used as a bed. Two other people she'd never met sat at the kitchen table, along with the girl from the beach, Sibyl.

Ava bolted up. "What happened, and who are they?"

CHAPTER 5
SIBYL
JUNE 23RD/CANKIT WANC-3

Still shaking, coming down from the rush of adrenaline, Sibyl sat at the table, listening to everyone argue. Preoccupied with her own thoughts, she wasn't comprehending much of what was being said.

She'd stood her ground against one of the monsters from her dreams. No, it was real. They'd all seen it. That proved it was real. All these years, they were real. She wasn't sure what was worse; being crazy and not in danger or being sane and in danger the entire time.

Her head and neck throbbed from being nearly choked out which, ironically, was the worst of her injuries, and it didn't come from the monster. The table vibrated in rhythm with her jigging leg, and she chewed on her fingers to the point that one of them started bleeding. The tang of metallic taste didn't stop her from gnawing even more flesh off though.

It's a good thing the two people, wolves, what the hell ever they were, showed up when they did, otherwise, they'd all probably be dead. When Sibyl thought about it, she was really stupid actually. She should have run, but she couldn't live with herself leaving others to die.

She wasn't a hero. She saved lives in a hospital, not in a fight. She'd done very little, except delay the beast and anger it more. Still, she fought back instead of cowering, hiding, running away, or worse, fainting. That was something.

After the beast knocked Ava unconscious, the two wolves drove it into the ocean where it finally gave up and swam out to sea, which Sibyl thought was odd. Why did it swim out to sea? That was one of the many questions racing through her mind. She didn't know where to start sorting it all out.

A large caramel toned man pulled up a seat in front of her. His beautiful silver eyes blinked slowly, and he said something that she didn't understand. This man was supposedly the silver wolf from the beach. Ava was the little red wolf, and the other woman was the black wolf. It all made perfect sense.

The man snapped his fingers right in front of her eyes.

She jumped back into reality. "What?"

"Are you ok? Your neck is bruised. Want me to take a look at it?" He pointed to her neck.

"No. I'm fine. That's from Ava." She rubbed her neck protectively and glanced at Ava, who didn't look remorseful in the slightest, in fact she narrowed her eyes at Sibyl. What the hell was she mad about? She'd nearly choked Sibyl out. Sibyl should be the mad one. In fact, she kind of was, now that she thought about it.

Who are you? Sibyl heard the question in her mind. It was Ava's voice, clear as day, but her lips didn't move.

What the hell? Sibyl tore her gaze away. No. She didn't hear that. Her mind was confused from all that had happened tonight.

"Ava did that?" Yilfin, that was the man's name, looked surprised. Both the women looked at him, confirming the answer with just their expressions. He walked over and whispered something to Fulcinia, the woman who he came with, then sat down next to her.

To say Yilfin was good-looking would be a drastic understatement. He was devastatingly gorgeous. Muscles stretched the fabric of his shirt and well-filled out pants drew the eye of anyone in his presence.

A black beard and mustache merged with hair via sideburns that were uniformly trimmed to about half an inch in length, wrapping his head and face in a blanket of black velvet that handsomely accented his beautiful skin and eyes. Every woman, and likely many men, would appreciate a perfect living work of art such as him. You'd have to be blind not to.

Then there was Fulcinia, his wife, or mate, as they preferred. The slender dark-skinned woman rivaled his beauty but with a more feminine refinement. Her muscles may not challenge the fabrics of her clothing, but they were very well honed, granting her a lethal beauty. Her ebony eyes were just as dark as her skin and long microbraids weaved down the back of her head falling elegantly to her waistline where they were tied into one large plait.

On their left arms were nearly identical tattoos. A small band that spiraled around their arms a few times before wrapping around their shoulders and disappearing under their shirts. The pair was as intimidating to look upon as they were in a fight.

It was difficult for Sibyl to process all the information. They were shapeshifters, all three of them, Ava included. Magic existed, and the most important discovery; she wasn't crazy. It was all real, the monsters, the visions, all these feelings she'd struggled with for her entire life. Even after seeing it with her own eyes, she was still in disbelief. She supposed she'd get used to being sane eventually, if this was considered sanity.

"MOTHER Ffffff.....!" Ava swallowed the rest of the curse within deep breaths. Fulcinia had pushed her shoulder back into the socket. Ava got up and rolled her arm around a few times, pacing back and forth.

Fulcinia took her seat at the table next to Yilfin once again. Even though he towered over his mate, they matched in posture. Confident, intimidating, unafraid, and uninjured, not even a scratch. Their outfits also matched, black tight leather pants and red shirts with vines and leaves sewn into the fabric. Fulcinia's was a sleeveless, corset style shirt, whereas Yilfin's was loose, like a T-shirt. They had no weapons that Sibyl could see, but they didn't need any. They were living weapons.

Fulcinia wore a cuff around her arm adorned with dozens of gems of varying sizes, shapes, and colors. There had to be thousands of dollars' worth of gems on that cuff. A tempting lure for any thief, although you'd have to be really really stupid to try and steal from either of them.

"Ok, who wants to explain what happened out there?" Cassie asked. Sibyl finally learned her name too. Sibyl studied the two shape shifters who seemed like ordinary people right now, except for their outfits, jewelry, and intimidating aura. Ok, they were different. Sibyl's skin kind of hummed the closer she got to them too, like they put off some sort of frequency only she could feel, like those stupid dog whistles or something.

"What are you?" Sibyl asked.

Yilfin cleared his throat. "We're Mages."

Sibyl's eyebrows shot up. "You're what?"

"Mages. I think your world would call us magicians or wizards," Fulcinia clarified.

Cassie laughed. "Wow. I think you may have bumped your head."

Sibyl's mind raced through everything she'd seen and felt tonight, and all her memories of the monsters. "What was that monster?"

"I'm sorry you went through that tonight, but the best thing for you two-" Fulcinia looked at Sibyl then to Cassie, "-is to go home and forget this ever happened. You're not in any danger if you get away from us."

"Us?" Ava asked.

"Yes. You're one of us," Fulcinia said.

Ava's eyebrows dropped. She was obviously lost in her own world of confusion, just like Sibyl was. A wave of disbelief poured from Ava. Sibyl could tell she had as many questions as she, herself, did and Ava was having just as difficult a time sorting it all out.

But Ava knew she was a shapeshifter. Sibyl had no idea magic existed until thirty minutes ago. She'd always known there was something different about her, but she never imagined it was this extraordinary. She wouldn't simply be dismissed when she was so close to unraveling a lifetime of confusion and anxiety.

"I deserve some answers. I've been seeing those things my entire life. I thought I was the only one until now," Sibyl said.

"And I live here, so I'm not going anywhere without some answers." Cassie crossed her arms and leaned against one of the large support pillars in the room.

"What do you mean you've seen those things your entire life?" Yilfin asked.

Sibyl explained her dreams, the monsters, and the realistic hallucinations. She left out the unicorn. One type of hallucination was enough for now.

"Can you shape shift?" Yilfin asked.

Sibyl shook her head.

The two Mages exchanged speculative expressions.

"I told you, you have a sixth sense," Cassie said.

"Sixth sense?" Fulcinia questioned.

"On the beach, before that monster attacked us, she said that she gets pins and needles sometimes, and that she has anxiety disorder and panic attacks, and-"

"Ok, we don't need a run-down of my mental disorders," Sibyl interjected. "I don't have a sixth sense. I just have anxiety and panic attacks and sometimes stress hallucinations. Or I thought I did. Since you guys could see them though, now I'm questioning everything.

"Sometimes I get feelings or hear things...voices." She sounded crazy saying it out loud. They're going to think she's schizophrenic. She probably was. This whole night could be one big psychotic break. "God, I sound crazy. I'm going crazy." Sibyl laughed hollowly, and put her head back, rolling her neck trying to work out the pain.

Can you hear this? Fulcinia asked.

"Yes," Sibyl answered without looking at the woman.

"You're a telepath," Fulcinia said.

"What?" Sibyl jerked her head toward them.

"You can hear thoughts, and you may be an empath as well, I'm not sure." *You can hear my thoughts, right?* Fulcinia asked, but her lips didn't move.

"What the hell?" Sibyl mumbled.

"It's a rare gift for a human to have. Usually, it's something more animalistic magical creatures possess, since they don't have vocal cords like we do," Yilfin said.

"Magical creatures? Like the one on the beach?" Cassie asked.

"No. That was a cursed creature," he said.

"Cursed?" Sibyl shook her head. This was all too much. Getting up, she walked around the room. She put her palms against the wall. *Real.* She went to the kitchen, turned on the faucet, and splashed a handful of water on her face. *Real.* After taking a sip of water, she put her hands on the counter and rubbed her palms along the surface. *Real.*

"What are you doing?" Ava asked.

"Grounding myself, making sure this is real." Moving to the window, she put her palm on the glass. *Real.* Gripping the curtains, she felt the texture of the fabric between her fingers. *Real.* If this was a hallucination, it was an extraordinarily convincing one.

"Ok, weirdo. Back to the original question. What was that thing on the beach?" Cassie asked.

Ignoring the question, Fulcinia addressed Ava. "You're a Mage, and you're in danger in this world. We've been looking for you for your entire life, and we'd like you to come home with us. You'll be safer there."

It was Ava's turn to look shocked. Good. At least Sibyl wouldn't feel completely alone in the disbelief department.

"Right, just because you know I can shapeshift doesn't mean I'm trusting you. I've made that mistake before."

"We can do more than shapeshift and so can you. You haven't even scratched the surface of what you can do, and we can show you." Fulcinia crossed her arms.

"Well, I still don't trust you, don't know you, and have no interest in getting to know you. I appreciate the help, but you can leave now. So can you." Ava nodded her head at Sibyl.

"You're in danger here," Fulcinia reiterated.

"Yeah, I know. I can handle myself." Ava walked to a dresser in the corner, opened the top drawer and dug through it. "The most important lesson I've learned, in my life, is to trust no one, that includes you, so please leave." Pulling out a large knife, she closed the drawer then went back to the sofa and sat down, casually spinning it in her hands as if it was a toy.

"Whoa. Where'd you get that?" Cassie asked.

"Thank you, by the way, for saving our lives," Sibyl said.

"I already said thank you. Now, I'm inviting you to please leave," Ava said, watching the knife spin in the palm of her hand. She moved fluidly, not like someone who'd just been gravely injured.

"How are you doing that?" Sibyl asked.

"Practice." Ava didn't take her eyes off the spinning knife.

"Not that. You're moving like you're not hurt at all. Your arm was nearly ripped off, you had a concussion, and you were bleeding from a large laceration on your side. Now, it's as if nothing ever happened. I can barely move my head, and I wasn't hurt nearly as bad as you."

Ava froze; jade-green eyes wide.

"She has enhanced healing." Fulcinia sat back in her chair, smiling smugly.

"Wow. Really? You heal super-fast Ava?" Cassie asked awestruck.

Ava looked like a deer in headlights.

"So, you guys have healing powers too?" Sibyl rubbed her neck. A twinge of jealousy pulsed through her. That would be useful right now.

"She can." Yilfin nodded his head toward Ava.

"But you can't?" Sibyl asked.

"No. Only those with gold blood can heal. We have silver blood which grants us Mage magic and shapeshifting. Gold blood provides shape shifting and healing magic. Ava has silver and gold in her blood, so she can do all of it. However, we gave her additional gold to heal the wound faster since werewolves have anti-gold in their claws. It wouldn't have healed without our intervention," Yilfin answered.

The three women gawked at him like he had three heads.

"That's one reason the werewolves want you so badly, but we can explain all of this in Orlon so pack your things and get ready to leave," Fulcinia demanded.

"I'm not going anywhere with you," Ava snorted.

"If you want to live, you'll come with us, and it would be a lot easier if you dropped the attitude." Fulcinia's nostrils flared. Her temper boiled under the surface. A tiger on the end of a chain with a link about to snap.

"OK. Why don't we calm down and have a conversation about our options?" Sibyl said.

"Why don't you leave? I don't know you, and I don't want to. You have no business here either, so you can leave with your new-found friends," Ava spat the last word like it was poison in her mouth.

It pissed Sibyl off. She'd risked her life to help Ava. She could have just run away, but she chose to stay and help. Ava did have a point though. They didn't know each other, but she felt a weird connection, like they were supposed to stick together.

Despite the harsh words, sadness and fear radiated from the red head. Ava felt alone, truly alone, despite everyone sitting in the room. Sibyl could relate to that. She'd felt alone most of her life, the constant anxiety her only company. While Sibyl kept herself locked behind a façade of calm, Ava secured herself behind a shield of rage.

"We've been searching for you for twenty-six years, Ava. You're in a lot of danger here, and so is anyone associated with you." Yilfin's words were much softer than his mate's.

Images flashed through Sibyl's mind. Two mangled bodies, unrecognizable from their wounds. Blood and gore splattered everywhere, inside the living room of a quaint little home. Their deaths were slow. Sibyl felt the torment they'd endured before finally succumbing to their wounds. Terror and devastation rippled through Ava which spilled into Sibyl's mind.

Spiraling further into her shield of anger, Ava stayed silent, but Sibyl sensed everything.

Empath. She could feel other people's emotions. Relief settled into her. With every passing moment, as things became weirder, she felt better about herself. Despite nearly dying, being totally confused, and not understanding anything or how to control any of it, she was relieved that her problems weren't just anxiety. Empath seemed much less ominous.

"Why are you here now? How did you find me?" Ava asked, barely audibly.

"You've been difficult to track, moving around so much. Every time we got close, you vanished again. Sometimes we found the werewolves who found you first. We dispatched most of them, but a couple of times, they got to you first." Sadness flickered in Yilfin's eyes for a moment, but guttered out in one heartbeat, immediately replaced with steel countenance again.

"Werewolves?" Cassie asked.

Yilfin took in a deep calming breath, and the whole room seemed to let out a breath in unison, dispelling the tension with it. These were the answers they wanted.

"Yes. That was a werewolf, a cursed Therian. They're very dangerous, hard to kill, and one scratch or bite from them can kill you. Even someone with enhanced healing can be killed by them." Yilfin nodded to Ava.

"Wouldn't we turn into a werewolf if we were bitten by one?" Cassie asked.

"No. That's a myth. They breed just like everyone else. If you're bitten, you die," Fulcinia said. "It's only a matter of time before they realize we haven't left the spot where they saw us last. They'll send an army after us. We need to leave."

Cassie laughed so hard she snorted.

"Is something funny?" Fulcinia's exasperated tone shut down Cassie's laughter.

"No, yes, I don't know. I just thought you two were werewolves. I mean you do turn into wolves. That thing on the beach didn't look like a wolf. How do we know you aren't one of them, just pretending to be on our side?"

"That's an excellent question," Ava said.

"Some of the stories of werewolves, on this planet, are extrapolated from shapeshifters, like us, who've been seen over the centuries. Not all shapeshifters turn into wolves."

"Twenty-six years ago, the people born in the kingdom of Tear-nanoak were cursed. Instead of being Therian shapeshifters, they started to become those beasts instead. Sometimes they can't control their shifts, or their actions, like at the new moon. Other times, they shift at will and are well aware of their actions."

"I thought they were immortal, but you said they're hard to kill, not that they can't be killed," Ava said.

"They're not immortal, although they like to believe they could be. They live regular human life spans and can be killed. It's just really difficult because they have gold blood granting them enhanced healing since they were born in Tearnanoak."

"I think I'm more confused now than I was a minute ago," Cassie said.

"You don't need to understand." Fulcinia shifted her gaze to Ava. "Only *you* do, and we promise to explain everything when we get to the safety of Orlon and Tearnanelle." Her tone was urgent.

A nervous energy pulsed from Fulcinia. She wanted to leave. It made Sibyl nervous that a hardened fighter was this anxious about their situation.

"What about me? I can't do any of those things, and how come I can't hear anyone's thoughts, but hers?" Sibyl pointed to Ava. "And I can feel everyone's emotions, except Cassie?"

"You can hear my thoughts?" Ava shot her an incredulous scowl.

Sibyl slumped down sheepishly.

"The short answer is, we don't know. There aren't many humans with telepathic and empathic abilities. Mage Guards, like us, are trained to shield our minds from mental intrusion, which is probably why you can't access my thoughts, but I guess our emotions are free game. If you want to come with us, we can try to help you," Fulcinia said.

Sibyl thought about the offer. If she could learn to control this *ability,* as they put it, then maybe she could finally get control of her life. Maybe she wouldn't need medication. She could regulate the feelings, or magic. She could live a normal life.

But, she couldn't just leave, disappear in the night. Her friends and family would be worried. Curiosity and the hope of a cure from this affliction she'd been plagued with her whole life had her debating it though.

"How does one travel to your....planet?" She felt stupid even asking, but if she was seriously considering going with them, she wanted to know all the details.

Yilfin rifled with something in his lap for a moment, then produced what looked like a marble with swirling ripples of green and blue water inside it. It was mesmerizing, seemingly holding the entire world within its sphere, but so small that it would be impossible to hold more than just a few drops of water.

"This is a bubble," Yilfin explained. "It's our way home."

Ava, Cassie, and Sibyl moved in closer for better inspection.

"It can take you anywhere, in either the magical realm or living realm, you want to go, but only once. Once you use it, it'll be gone."

"So that tiny thing transports people?" Cassie asked.

"Yes," Yilfin answered.

"How?" Sibyl asked.

"It contains the magical waters of Lemuria. Water is the only medium that's present in equal density and molecular structure in every world in the universe, and all water is magically connected, thus you can travel from world to world through it, like a conduit," Yilfin said.

"Mermaids and Nokks are the guardians of the water portals, and the only creatures in the universe who can travel anywhere at any time through those portals. They live deep in the oceans of Lemuria where the boundaries of the worlds are blurred. That's where bubbles are harvested, which is how the rest of us travel between worlds."

"Ok, so that made perfect sense," Cassie said. "Let's travel through space by traveling through water, that's in a bubble marble, harvested by Mermaids."

"Basically, yes." A hint of a smile tugged at Fulcinia's lips. "And we really need to leave ASAP before the werewolves come back."

"OK, I'm game. Let's go," Cassie said, shrugging her shoulders.

Fulcinia cleared her throat. "You have a life here. You have family and friends, and you're human. You stay." She looked at Sibyl, her ebony eyes soft. "You have a choice. You obviously have some magic unknown to us. I'm sure our library can offer you some answers and assistance, but you also have family, friends, and a life to consider. The choice is yours."

Sibyl sighed. Library, books on magic and telepathy, possibly a method to control this affliction. "We can come back at any time we want?" Sibyl asked.

"Yes," Yilfin said.

"I'm going," Cassie blurted. "Ava's my best friend. I don't have anyone else, either, except my sister, who basically hates me anyway. I'm going." She huffed and crossed her arms. An immovable stone at the base of a mountain.

"How long does the journey take?" Sibyl asked.

"Usually about thirty seconds," Yilfin answered.

That was unexpected. She thought it would take days or hours, at least.

"Does it hurt?" she asked.

"No. It kind of feels like your lungs are being sucked from your chest, and you can't breathe for a few moments. There's some pressure, and it gets ice cold, briefly, before normalizing again. Kind of like being held under the water twenty feet deep, then suddenly being on land again, standing up perfectly straight, like nothing ever happened," Yilfin said.

"That sounds terrible," Cassie exclaimed.

"I think I know the feeling you're talking about, actually." Ava told them about a time when she was fourteen and unwittingly went with a werewolf who was pretending to be her friend. The woman lured her out into the middle of nowhere then dragged her under the water in a lake.

"I thought she was trying to drown me, but maybe she was trying to travel through the water, because she didn't have one of these bubbles?" Ava asked.

"Yes. There are some water gates on every planet. Usually in the ocean, but every now and again, a rift will open up a lesser gate. They can be turbulent, and not always a straight shot." Fulcinia glanced at Yilfin. "We need to tell the Mermaids about that one to make sure they patch it up, if they haven't already."

Yilfin nodded his agreement.

"You're lucky you got away," Fulcinia followed.

Ava pursed her lips and slouched back onto the couch in a huff.

Sibyl thought about her options. She could go with them, get information that could help her, then come back. She'd be gone a day, two tops. Assuming she could trust them. Her gut told her she could. Everyone always said she was a good judge of character. Was that part of her empathic senses? So many questions that she wanted answers to, and she was so close to getting them.

She couldn't keep living like she was, especially now that she knew these monsters weren't just in her nightmares, but real beasts who could hurt or kill her. What about her family, her friends? She needed to find out if she could somehow block the visions and monsters, to protect them.

"What guarantee do we have that we can come back?" Sibyl asked.

"I give you my word." Yilfin put his hand over his heart. "That's all I can give you. You'll just have to trust us if you're coming." He went to the faucet and got a glass of water.

"What's that?" Ava pointed at him.

He turned around and raised his eyebrows. "What?"

"The tattoo on the back of your neck. What is that?"

He rubbed the back of his neck.

Fulcinia turned around and pulled her hair up to reveal a Gemini symbol tattoo on the back of her neck. It had a faint iridescent silver shimmer to it, and it was nearly identical to Yilfin's. Sibyl hadn't noticed it before, but she wasn't really looking at the back of their necks either.

"Yes, that. What is that?" Ava asked again.

"It's the mark of the Mage Guard." Fulcinia dropped her hair and turned around again.

"It's the symbol of the Gemini," Cassie said.

"That's Tearnanelle and Tearnanoak, The twin Goddesses. Your planet calls the twins the Gemini. We call them by their names, which are also the names of our kingdoms," Fulcinia said.

"That's the second time you've said that; Mage Guard. What is that?" Ava asked.

"The Mage Guard are Mages who are hired to protect the kingdom. It's our version of the military. We protect the people and serve the Aruka. That's similar to what this world calls a queen. Everyone who serves on her guard gets this mark," Fulcinia said.

"My birthday is August thirtieth. When I was found on the street, I was wrapped in a blanket." Ava went to the dresser, again, and pulled out a small blanket that looked like it was white at one time, but was now a dull yellow. She unfolded it and held it up. In the center was the same Gemini mark sewn into the fabric.

"I've always wondered why I was wrapped in this blanket since I'm not a Gemini."

Fulcinia took the blanket and rubbed the symbol between her fingers. A faint smile played across her face. "Your mother made this for you."

"Was she on the Mage Guard for the Twin Kingdoms, like you? Is that how you knew her?" Ava asked.

"No." Fulcinia handed the blanket back to Ava. "Your mother was Aruka of Tearnanoak."

Ava's eyes widened, the green so vibrant they were nearly blinding.

CHAPTER 6
AVA
JUNE 23RD/CANKIT WANC-3

"Did you say Ava's mom was a queen?" Cassie asked. "Holy shit, dude. You're a princess." Cassie elbowed Ava playfully.

"Sort of." Yilfin scratched his beard. "A king, queen, prince, or princess, as your world defines them, is a person born from a royal bloodline, who is granted rulership. The position was established by the people and offers no actual power other than political or religious."

"An Aruko, Aruka, Arukan, or Arukas are chosen by the Gods to share a portion of the God's magic and act as a representative and monarch in the God's nation in Orlon. A chosen heir will be marked, on their body, with an unalome."

Yilfin pointed to Ava. "That's the streak in your hair. It's the mark of the Goddess who chose you to inherit the magic and the throne. Once marked, you're considered royalty."

Yilfin paused, then added, "Since your mother was an Aruka, that technically makes you a princess, even if you weren't chosen as an heir, but Orlon doesn't recognize those titles. Even if we did, Arukas supersedes princess, so you are Arukas."

The room fell silent as everyone stared at Ava. She wasn't usually one to be bashful or shy, but for once she felt slightly insecure under their stares. She ran a hand through the silver strands of her hair, a mark of the Gods. She was chosen to inherit their magic and the throne. No way. This was crazy talk.

"That's absurd. I was abandoned on the street, the day I was born. I'm not a princess, or Arukas, or whatever you said. You two are obviously just as deranged as her." Ava nodded toward Sibyl.

"Hey," Sibyl exclaimed, her eyebrows knitting together.

"You weren't abandoned." Fulcinia made to say more, but Ava spoke over her.

"I was left on the sidewalk, outside of a thrift store, in the middle of the night." Ava's voice cracked with the struggle to hold in her emotions.

"Your mother did what she had to do to ensure you survived." Fulcinia's voice grew louder.

Ava made to counter, but Sibyl stood up and spoke first. "This is a lot to process. It sounds like you guys have information that would help us both." Sibyl looked at Ava encouragingly. "We could go for a day or two, find the answers we want and then come back when we're ready. What do you think?"

"We?" Ava spat. "There is no 'we.' I don't know you. No one asked for your opinion."

"I'm just saying that it sounds like they have answers to questions that we've both had for a long time. It wouldn't hurt to see where you're from, and what I am, and how to control it." Sibyl spoke to Ava in a patronizing tone.

"Don't talk to me about what you think I need or want, or what I should or shouldn't do. You don't know anything about me."

"I know enough." Sibyl crossed her arms and glowered at Ava.

"Really? Because you've read my mind a few times. Please tell me. What is it you think you know about me, Sibyl?"

"I don't have to read your mind in order to figure you out. You're as transparent as glass. You pretend you don't care about anyone, so you don't have to admit that it hurts that no one cares about you."

"Hey, I care about her," Cassie said.

"You act all big and tough, but underneath, you're just as scared as I am that whatever we are will put the ones we love in danger." Sibyl looked at Ava as if she could see into her soul.

Ava hesitated. The words hit home, but she wasn't ready to admit it. She laughed hollowly. "You're so far off, it's laughable. See? I'm actually laughing at how stupid that is."

"Whatever." Sibyl rolled her eyes and sat back down.

"Ok, enough," Fulcinia said. "Sibyl, you're welcome to come with us, if you want. Ava, please come with us. Please come *home*." She enunciated the last word with a pleading tone. "Your mother would want you to come home. We all do."

Ava saw the sincerity in her face and heard it in her voice. Ava's fortitude wavered, but she didn't want to give Sibyl the satisfaction of thinking she'd won some asinine argument. Ava shot a glare at Sibyl, but a tinge of guilt resonated through her.

Sibyl's wind-blown hair, ridiculous number of freckles, and giant necklace of bruises around her neck gifted by Ava herself, completed the picture-perfect portrait of pathetic. It was hard to take her seriously, but, as much as Ava hated to admit it, there was truth in what Sibyl said. Ava did kind of want to go.

She'd been angry her entire life and purposefully kept everyone at arm's length. Cassie was the first person in a long time to weasel her way into Ava's heart, and if she was being honest with herself, she wanted more. Maybe there were people in Orlon who would actually want her. She felt stupid even entertaining the idea, but hope had a funny way of making people think and do stupid things.

As if Fulcinia could read her thoughts, she said, "your mother loved you, Ava. She would want you to come home and be with what remains of your family."

Ava jerked her head up. A ripple of shock tore through her like a lightning strike. "Family?"

"Yes. Your aunt is Aruka of Tearnanelle. That's who we work for.

We're on your aunt's Mage Guard. She sent us to find you and bring you home," Fulcinia said.

Just when Ava thought she couldn't handle any more life altering revelations, they dropped an atomic bomb on her. She had living family. Only one person, but at least it was somebody. A fissure in her heart opened. She would never meet her mother, but she could meet her aunt. She really wanted to go now, more than she cared to admit.

Ava ran her fingers over the symbol on the blanket, tracing the pattern. She knew every thread by heart. She'd cried into it, yelled into it, cuddled with it on millions of occasions. She met Fulcinia's raven eyes then she looked at Yilfin. The mark on the back of their necks matched the one on her blanket. That couldn't be a coincidence.

They saved her tonight when they could have killed her or just let that beast kill her. Ava didn't exactly distrust them, but she had no real reason to trust them either.

She was so tired of running and not knowing anything about herself or her family, though. If they intended to make her a prisoner, at least she'd know who her family was, even if they were horrible. It's better than staying here, waiting for those beasts to come back, and potentially hurting or killing anyone else Ava loved.

Cassie who was serious for once. Ava found the answer to what she wanted to do in her friend's face.

"I've been running my whole life. There have only been two people who I ever loved, and they were murdered because of me." Ava pushed down the guilt that threatened to undo her. The chest in the back of her mind where she'd locked all the painful memories grew legs and came to the front of her mind. She slammed a door in front of it.

"I'm done running. I'll come with you." Steeling herself, the anger shield snapped firmly back into place, she nodded at Cassie. "If Cassie wants to come, then she can too." She held her chin high, challenging the pair to argue.

They nodded.

"Yes!" Cassie hissed, wriggling excitedly.

Ava figured Cassie was in danger already just by knowing her. She didn't want to leave Cassie here alone and defenseless. She also presumed that their world, her world, probably didn't have meth. What better rehab for her friend than taking her to a place where she couldn't get the drug? Ava would ensure her safety and get her clean at the same time. Melody would appreciate the last fact, at least.

"I want to come too." Sibyl looked at Ava as if she was waiting for permission. Ava met the weird hazel eyes then her gaze dropped to the bruises around her neck. They were getting darker by the moment. The guilt grew darker with them. Maybe Sibyl was just trying to find her own answers. She didn't seem to pose any real threat, and Ava should probably keep her close until she figured out what Sibyl was up to.

Ava nodded to Sibyl who smiled faintly and dipped her head in return. A mutual agreement. They'd both get what they needed and stay out of each other's way.

"Great, we leave in ten minutes. Get your things together," Yilfin said.

"Wait. I need more time to gather what I need and let people know I'm leaving. Like you said, I have family and friends. I can't just disappear. They'll be worried about me," Sibyl said.

Fulcinia clicked her tongue. "Every minute we stay, we risk them finding us."

Sibyl negotiated for them to give her an hour. Ava rolled her eyes. Must be nice having people to consider. Family and friends, plural. A surge of jealousy rippled through Ava. Pushing down the emotion, she worked on gathering her few belongings in preparation to leave.

An hour later, Sibyl returned with an overstuffed backpack and an anxious aura. She twisted her fingers on top of each other in a manner that looked painful. Ava remembered seeing her do that when they were on the beach too. Odd.

"OK, everyone, grab on to each other," Yilfin commanded. "If you aren't touching me, or connected to someone who's touching me, then you'll be left behind. Do you understand?"

Each person collectively grabbed onto Yilfin, himself. He pulled the glowing bubble from his pocket. The tiny gem brightened with every passing second as if it knew it was about to be activated. Spots followed Ava's vision after she averted her gaze.

Aqua light mixed with silver and green streaks exploded from Yilfin's hand once his fist wrapped around it. A surge of excitement and anxiety coursed through Ava. There was no turning back now.

Wispy beams swam around the room like hundreds of shimmering eels. Amorphous light spread out through all the available space in the room, slowly engulfing everything and everyone, until they stood in a room resembling bioluminescent water. Ava reached out. It felt like air, but the drag was that of liquid. Her fingers were completely dry.

Five thick intense beams snaked out from Yilfin's hand and approached each of them, individually. The beams of light stopped about six inches from their faces. Similar to a curious dog cocking its head sideways, the beam tilted in front of Ava.

Even though it should have been blinding, the light was pleasant to look upon. Ava's eyes didn't hurt. In fact, she was transfixed, cocking her head sideways, mirroring its actions.

Without any warning, the beam dove straight into her chest. She fell backwards in an explosion of blinding particulates. Everything around her disappeared instantly, and she couldn't breathe, as if she was submerged deep under water, but she wasn't wet.

She couldn't feel or see anyone. Reaching out for Yilfin, her hand found nothing. Suspended in an aqua-colored atmosphere, Ava flailed her arms and legs in a panic, trying to reach someone or something, but she found nothing and no one.

She opened her mouth in an attempt to yell, but no sound came out. There was no way to gauge inertia, distance, or existence in this place. Pressure built around her, squeezing her body. Her ribs pressed into her chest, laden with an invisible heaviness, but she could freely move her limbs without resistance.

This place defied all laws of physics. It was impossible to expand her lungs and take in a breath, but at the same time it was unnecessary to breathe. It didn't hurt, but it didn't feel good either.

Goosebumps consumed the surface of her skin as she instantly went numb with cold, skipping the shivering stage and going directly into paralytic hypothermia. The cold penetrated so deep that her bones ached. Frost covered her eyelashes, and her eyelids closed of their own volition, obscuring the blue-green nothingness into absolute darkness. Her eyelids froze to her eyeballs.

Would she be able to open them again? This must be what hypothermia feels like. You fall asleep then you die.

Shit. I need to wake up. Open your eyes! Ava forced her eyes open.

CHAPTER 7
AVA
CANKIT FIROQ-2/JUNE 23RD

A warm breeze kissed Ava's cheeks. Her rib cage expanded and fresh crisp air dove into her lungs. Spears of sun rays poked through the tree canopy from above. The temperature was perfect, a beautiful summer day right after an afternoon storm, much milder than what the end of June normally was.

Once her eyes fully adjusted, she scoped out the unfamiliar forest. Tall trees that looked and smelled similar to regular pine and oak varieties surrounded her, only they were much more vibrant and magnificent. There was an aura in this forest unlike anything she'd ever experienced.

Energy pulsed through her. She felt strong, alive, powerful, like she was in wolf form. Double-checking her body, Ava verified she was, in fact, human at the moment. But everything was so much more invigorating than normal human senses usually perceived.

"What is this place?" she murmured to herself. Ava spun around, taking it all in. Cassie stood nearby with the same gawking expression that Ava had. Fulcinia and Yilfin huddled over Sibyl who was lying on the ground unconscious.

Ava rushed to Sibyl's side. Cassie followed.

"What happened?" Cassie asked, her voice laced with concern.

"I don't know. All her vitals are normal." Fulcinia checked the freckled wrist for a pulse.

"Do you think she had a panic attack and passed out?" Ava asked.

Fulcinia shrugged. "I guess it's possible. I don't know what else would be wrong with her." She nudged Sibyl's shoulder. No response.

"I don't think she's waking up any time soon. I guess we'll have to carry her." Yilfin glanced at Cassie. "You get the first mile. I'll trade up with you for the second mile."

Cassie's mouth dropped open. "Dude, I can't carry her. Look at my arms." Holding one

skeletal arm out to the side, she pointed at it. "I don't offer brute strength to this outfit."

"What do you offer?" Fulcinia teased.

"Genius ideas." Cassie tapped her temple with a finger and smiled wryly.

Yilfin chuckled, bent down and effortlessly hoisted the unconscious Sibyl over his shoulder. After balancing the cumbersome load, he turned and walked off. Everyone followed him through the unknown forest.

"Where are we going?" Ava asked.

"To the castle. To Tearnanelle," Fulcinia said.

"How far is it?"

"About two miles."

"Two miles? Damn. Why didn't we just bubble straight into the castle? That would've been a lot quicker and easier." Cassie was already out of breath, and they'd barely walked a hundred yards.

"Bubble transport is forbidden within about five miles of the God Trees. The God's have blocked them for the protection of the civilians. Otherwise, an enemy could just bubble right into the middle of the castle and attack us," Fulcinia said.

That made sense, Ava supposed.

The trek was slow because Ava and Cassie kept getting distracted by all the remarkable vegetation, wildlife, and insects. Exotic birds that sang foreign songs, flowers that glowed in the shade then changed color in the sun, bees that looked more like spiny dinosaurs with wings, birds that resembled peacocks with flowing plumes of feathers streaming behind. It was so much to take in.

Ava could have sworn she saw a winged horse flying above the treetops. The forest was so dense, though, she only caught glimpses of the flying creature before it flitted away into the evening sky.

"It was night when we left, but now it's daytime here. What's the time difference?" Ava asked.

"Tearnanelle is only a few hours behind American east coast time. It's on a different lunar orbit, but equal to that of Earth so you shouldn't experience any significant lag effects," Fulcinia answered.

After a while, they came to a wall made up of tree roots and branches that were interlaced so thickly that even air would have a difficult time permeating through it.

The base of the structure was made up of dense roots growing up from the ground, securing it firmly in place and ensuring no one could dig under. The roots and branches were about the circumference of an elephant's leg, looping and twisting around one another, creating infinite knots that had no beginning or end.

Every two to three inches a razor-sharp thorn tipped in silver sprouted from the branches within the wall. Silver sap dripped from the thorns, creating shimmering streams cascading down the wall. Bending her neck backwards as far as it would tip, Ava discovered the wall extended far beyond the treetops.

A path ran adjacent to the wall in each direction. They turned left and followed it.

"Where are we going now?" Ava asked.

"Toward the Southern Gate into Tearnanelle," Fulcinia answered over her shoulder.

After about another hour of walking, the wall changed its outward appearance and texture. The silver thorns took on a pattern that was difficult to discern this close up. Yilfin and Fulcinia stopped and looked up expectantly. Ava backed up to better appreciate the mosaic.

Cassie did the same. Thorns formed a pattern of a large intricate tree shape.

The ground rumbled as the tree mosaic split down the middle and doors opened. The doors had to be at least forty feet tall and ten feet wide each, easily enough span to fit a blue whale, maybe even two on top of one another.

The wall bridged over the top of the doorway so that when they were closed there was no discernable gap. The only clues there was an entrance here were the two watchtowers on either side and the design of thorns.

Ava followed Yilfin and Fulcinia through the archway. A cool mist drifted up from a cliff face on the other side of the wall. A wooden fence ran along the cliff's edge.

The left side of the fence dead ended into the massive fortress wall, and to the right the fence went on for miles. On the opposite side of the fence was a giant gorge.

Ava and Cassie leaned over the fence and peered down to a river falling over a deeper cliff into an expansive cave opening. The river and the cave disappeared under the wall and flowed out of Tearnanelle. Now she understood the fence. It was to prevent people from accidentally falling over which would no doubt lead to their death either from impact or drowning.

Backing up, Ava craned her neck upwards. This side of the wall was riddled with staircases, doorways, and platforms, all made up of pure silver. People stood watch every few stories until, at the top, she could see people marching up and down the wall on either side of the gate. The same creature Ava thought she saw before soared overhead.

"Holy shit. It's a Pegasus." Cassie pointed and squealed. Normally Ava would have made fun of her girlish screech, but right now, she was in a similar state of amazement and would probably sound the exact same if she tried to speak.

"Come on, Sibyl's not getting any lighter here," Yilfin yelled. He and Fulcinia headed over a bridge that was almost completely surrounded by trees and moss creating a mystical tunnel. Cassie and Ava followed, with their mouths hanging open. The doors closed behind them as soon as they were clear. The swiftness of the action defied their large mass.

The two girls froze in paralyzed awe for a moment, watching the doors close securely back in place. Yilfin and Fulcinia's footsteps echoed on the bridge, beckoning Ava to follow.

The floor of the bridge was a glossy silver wood grain that reflected the light from lamps hanging from the tree tunnel canopy which grew from the bridge's railing. Tree roots dangled over the side, all the way to the misty river below. The roots were twice as long as the trees were tall, and the trees cascaded over the bridge, creating an archway tunnel that extended along the entire length of the bridge. No one from above would be able to see this bridge because it was so densely covered by the trees.

Peering over the railing into the river below, Ava inhaled a deep refreshing breath. Mist floated up, mixing with the evening air, creating wispy clouds beneath them. Trailing a hand along the railing, Ava noticed that silver strands ran through it. Like veins in a body, the silver flowed within.

"Look at this." Cassie stared at one of the lamps hanging from the middle of the tree canopy. It was a diamond the size of a basketball encased in a tangle of green vines and gray moss. The stone emitted light that was gentle enough to look directly at, but strong enough that it permeated the dim environment of the tunnel for a long way.

"What do you think that thing's worth?" Cassie asked.

"More than we could ever spend in a lifetime, I imagine."

By the time they reached the end of the tree-tunnel bridge the sun was nearly set. The evening sky magnificently illuminated a monstrous tree atop a small mountain that stood just beyond a garden meadow. It was the largest and most beautiful tree Ava had ever seen or could imagine. It was so tall, the tree canopy disappeared into the clouds.

Cascading from its branches that extended outwards for hundreds of feet, were waterfalls of silvery moss that shimmered in the late evening sunbeams. Built within the tree was a castle.

They followed a pathway that snaked through the meadow like a river with many branching streams. Well-manicured gardens, straight out of a medieval story book, sprawled out over dozens of acres. Sweeping branches from the majestic tree-castle hugged the gardens on either side, boxing them in.

Winged women with bodies that resembled large cats picked flowers along the side the pathway. Centaurs casually walked arm in arm. People that looked almost exactly like humans with long spindly fingers tapering to sharp points cleaned up what appeared to be remnants from a gathering or party. Their ears stood so tall and thin that they blended with their hair, which also stood straight up like it had been put in an electric socket.

"Was there an event here?" Ava asked.

"Summer Solstice party. We hold it annually. It's the largest celebration of the year. Too bad we didn't find you a few days sooner. It's a lot of fun. You probably would have enjoyed it," Fulcinia said.

"Too bad." Ava said dismissively.

Little creatures that resembled tiny humans with translucent wings darted back and forth, dodging the pedestrians on the pathways. Statues and benches littered the shoulder of the walkways. It was so fantastically amazing, and Fulcinia and Yilfin marched past it all as if it was just an ordinary park.

Most people and creatures gave a slight nod or bow to Yilfin and Fulcinia. For Ava and Cassie, they had questioning glances and apprehensive smiles. Glancing back a few times, Ava met staring wide eyes or gaping mouths.

When they reached the other side of the meadow, the tree-castle was in full, unobstructed view. To describe it as magnificent would be an injustice to its magnificence.

"Whoa," Cassie said.

"My thoughts exactly," Ava mumbled.

Long braided roots draped over the mountain sides like hair coursing over someone's shoulders. The roots continued downward until they burrowed into the ground. The mountain was manicured into concentric rings that tapered upwards. Each ring was a floor level decorated with balconies and terraces. There were at least thirty levels, but she didn't have time to count as Yilfin and Fulcinia briskly walked on.

The tree was an oak variety, if compared to trees on Earth. Long sweeping branches dipped down to the ground, kissed the terrain then launched back toward the sky again. The branches were as big around as an SUV and the tree's trunk was the diameter of the stone mountain it sat upon. An assortment of exotic bird noises radiated from the tree.

Their group entered the front of the castle via a large opening at the structure's base. Ava felt like she was an ant entering an anthill. Uniformed guards dressed similar to Yilfin and Fulcinia stood at the entrance. They looked at Yilfin questioningly, nodded to Fulcinia, glanced over Cassie and their faces turned to surprise when they saw Ava, which was getting old real fast.

The same diamond type of lights lined the perimeter of the foyer, which was easily the size of a football field. Entrances into hallways lined the entire right side of the room. A guard stood at every door. Just like everyone else they'd passed, the guards surveyed her with a mixture of shocked and curious expressions. Ava sighed deeply, swallowing her discomfort.

To the left was another grandiose and elaborately decorated room, a ballroom perhaps? Everything was decorated in an ancient medieval style with elaborate statues, tapestries, and paintings.

Adjacent to what Ava presumed was the ballroom, was a five-story tall wall of glass windows. Rows and rows of books and tables were behind the glass windows and doors. People lounged behind the glass and on the balconies within the room she was in. They were reading, writing, drinking, and quietly conversing as if it was just a normal day.

The ceiling was barely visible high above them. Balcony after balcony rose up as far as Ava could see. The walls tapered inward as the outside of the castle tapered until, finally, the balconies met and formed the top of the giant room. A large vine chandelier with dozens of gemstone lights randomly placed within its framework hung from the ceiling.

At the far end of the room was a throne on a large dais. In keeping with the décor with the rest of the castle, the throne was made of tree roots, branches, and vines that all converged back into the main trunk of the tree behind it. Silver veins laced throughout the framework of the chair, making it shimmer. Little green leaves sprouted out of its sides, and a plush scarlet red cushion sat on the empty throne.

Giant ornate double doors at the back of the room behind the throne were currently closed and guarded.

This was, quite possibly, the most beautiful place she'd ever seen. Excitement overwhelmed her. She'd traveled to another planet and ended up in a paradise that was beyond her wildest imaginings.

"We'll take you to the guest rooms. You can get washed up and some food will be brought to you. As soon as Sibyl's awake, we'll take you to the Aruka," Fulcinia said.

Ava and Cassie nodded, stunned into silent compliance.

They were led through a door on the far side of the library and up a stairwell. Cassie was panting heavily by the time they finally arrived at the sixth floor. Fulcinia and Yilfin then led them through a maze of hallways, taking several turns that thoroughly confused Ava. She wasn't sure she'd be able to find her way back out, if she needed to, which made her a tad nervous.

Voices sounded behind some of the doors and occasionally a head popped out, glanced at them, then retreated back into the room's depths, timidly shutting the door again.

"How many people live here?" Cassie asked.

"In the castle? Several thousand. In the lands outside of the castle, our last census estimated our population around one-hundred and twenty-five thousand," Yilfin replied, without looking back.

"You guys have a census? Do your citizens have social security numbers? Do you have I.D.s and licenses? Do you require passports to travel?" Ava asked.

Fulcinia smiled. "We do not require any of that and our citizens are not numbered, but we do know them all. The innate magic of Orlon has everyone recorded in the census that's kept in the cave vaults below the castle."

They finally came to a door that looked just like the dozens of doors they'd already passed. Fulcinia held it open for Yilfin, who laid the still sleeping Sibyl on an elaborately carved four post bed.

The room was decorated in a similar fashion to the rest of the castle they'd seen so far. The same gemstone lights encased in vines and moss were evenly spaced in sconces along the walls. Lush aqua green carpet covered the floor in the room instead of the silvery wood grain marble of the throne room and hallways. The walls were light gray roughly textured oak boards. Two matching king-sized beds, a dresser, and desk furnished the room, and there was a bathroom off to one side.

Through another door, on the opposite side of the bathroom, was an identical room with another two beds. It was similar to the set-up of a hotel room, only much more fantastical. All the beds had matching scarlet red velvety-soft blankets that were as soft as a cloud.

"We'll have someone bring you some food and send in a healer to examine Sibyl. Don't go wandering around until you're properly introduced and acclimated, please." Fulcinia smiled then headed to the door.

Yilfin walked out, but Fulcinia paused and turned back to Ava and Cassie. "Welcome to Tearnanelle." Then she closed the door, leaving the two girls in stunned silence.

CHAPTER 8

SIBYL

CANKIT FIROQ-3/JUNE 24TH

Hazel eyes fluttered open and stared into four jet-black non-blinking eyes. The ping-pong ball sized bug slowly came into focus. A blue and red striped body with gray hairs all over, including its six legs, perched happily on the tip of Sibyl's nose.

Screeching loudly, Sibyl swatted the bug off and quickly stood up, putting as much distance as possible between herself and the bug. The insect scurried off at an impossibly fast speed that was disproportionate to its size.

Brushing herself off, she surveyed her surroundings. There was nothing and no one familiar. A warm summer breeze blew in the scent of pine and oak, but with a more exotic feel, similar to what she felt sometimes in her hallucinations.

"Where am I?" she whispered.

Hello, Sibyl.

She jumped around and came face to face with the bay horse. It was the same horse she always saw. Same large stature, deep red fur the color of lava, mane and tail as dark as vantablack, and black coral irises that currently looked directly at her. Mouth agape, she stood transfixed.

Did he just say hello?

Yes. The horse's lips didn't move. A breeze tousled his mane like a ripple of black water, but he made no intrinsic movement.

"What the heck? A talking horse." Sibyl sighed. "Oh man, I am going crazy."

I've always been able to talk. You were just unable to hear because of all the medications you took. It's because you are Druid that I'm able to speak telepathically with you.

Sibyl just stared, frozen and silent.

The horse chuckled. Apparently, horses can chuckle.

My name is Solstice.

"Um, nice to meet you, and how do you know my name, and what is a Druid?"

I've known you since you were born. The Gods requested I try to help guide the next Druid, but it's been challenging since the downfall of Tearnanoak, and you being on a different planet, and the mind-altering substances you consumed on the regular. I thought you would have stopped taking them sooner.

Ignoring the remark about her anxiety medications, she asked, "Wait. Another planet. You mean Earth?" She remembered the events from a few minutes ago, hours, days? Where was she? When was she? Where were the others, and more importantly, how long had they been separated?

"I traveled here through a bubble portal with some people. Have you seen them?" She spun around, but saw no one other than the horse and an empty meadow.

Calm down. You're in Orlon, and the others are in Tearnanelle with you. You're all safe within the castle.

"I don't understand. I'm here, but I'm there too?"

Yes.

"OK. I'm kind of freaking out here. Can you please explain what's going on, where am I, and didn't you have a horn last time I saw you?"

My horn is here. As if it had been there all along, the ebony horn appeared on the horse's forehead. Sparkling streams of gold spiraled through it.

"Ok. A pseudo-unicorn isn't making me feel better."

Let's answer your questions one at a time. You are a Druid, which put simply, means you perceive magic. When you passed through the portal into Orlon, you were overburdened with magic, and your body shut down to preserve function.

"That sounds bad. Am I ok?" She checked her body. She appeared normal.

Yes. You're fine. Your friends have taken you to a safe place. The unicorn's expression softened. Sibyl could tell he was smiling even though his face didn't change. She felt the emotional change within him and knew he was smiling.

In the world where you were born, there is very little magic as we define it here. When you're in a world that doesn't have much magic, you feel very little. When you go to a world that's immersed in magic, it can be over-whelming if you're not accustomed to it. Your mind is overstimulated. That's all. You'll acclimate soon enough. Solstice walked toward a brook across the meadow. Sibyl followed.

To answer your next question. I called your spirit to me, like I've done many times in the past. This time we are finally able to communicate freely now that you're unhindered by medications.

This ability is called Druid Dreaming or Druid Walking. You can project your spirit anywhere you want while your physical body stays behind. Some-times, you can even pull others along with you, which is how the werewolves showed up a few times. You accidentally left a pathway for others to enter the reality you created.

"So, none of it was a hallucination?"

No. They were Druid dreams.

"But I was awake for some of them."

You don't have to be asleep to Druid walk. You can pull a spirit to you while you're awake. But for your spirit to separate from your physical being you need to be in a deeply relaxed or meditative state similar to sleeping.

"Oh boy, I think I'm more confused?" Pressing her thumb and forefinger into her eye sockets, she gently massaged in tiny circular motions.

Things will make more sense as you learn about the magics.

She followed the horse to the water's edge. A gentle breeze rustled the tall grass and whispering sounds brushed her subconscious. She knelt and listened carefully. The grass whispered as if it was having a secret conversation. She wrapped her fingers around a few seed pods and curiosity flowed through her.

The unicorn took a drink.

She scooped up a handful of the clear water and took a sip. It was as cold and fresh as melted snow after a thaw in early spring. The water's adventurous spirit tingled throughout her body. Brushing her palm over the surface of the water, Sibyl felt a rush of excitement swimming within the currents.

She had a sudden urge to run down a mountain, jump over the edge of a waterfall, and dance in the shallow mud of a river. She saw the water's journey in the Silvermar mountains, through meadows, valleys, and forests to end up here.

"I can feel the water's spirit. I can feel everything." The energy of this place was unlike anything she'd ever felt.

In your world, there is a legend called the Fountain of Youth. Have you heard of it?

"Yes, of course."

It references the waters of Orlon. While drinking it will not keep you alive forever, it will renew your energy, increase your stamina, and make you feel dauntless, at least for a time. Over the eons, the legend morphed, and now people think that if you drink the water, you'll be young forever. While that's entertaining, it is not true. You, however, can commune with the water's spirit, as well as feel its effects.

The horse splashed into the brook and crossed to the other side.

Following his lead, Sibyl splashed through the brook. Water crested the top of her shoes, numbing her feet in the wet cold. Another jolt of youthful energy rippled through her. Once on the other side, she rested a hand on the unicorn's shoulder and gazed at the meadow, reveling in the feel of Orlon's magical atmosphere.

Her life on Earth was empty in comparison to this. She felt all the spirits around her. The flowers dancing in the wind, birds flying in the sky, frogs croaking, and insects scampering about. She could feel it all as a whole and individually.

There had always been a void inside her. On Earth, it was filled with anxiety and sadness. Now, it was filled with positive energy. If only there was a way to harness this feeling and take it back home with her, so she'd never feel empty or anxious again.

"This is awesome. I feel amazing."

There is something you must understand about this gift, Sibyl.

Her heart sank. "That doesn't sound good."

Intangible magic is reflective. If you are scared and insecure, the magic will be unpredictable and dangerous. If you are confident and strong then so will the magic be. If you lose control of your emotions, you could be a danger to yourself and everyone around you.

Using medications will not fix this. You must learn to control your emotions, thoughts, and mind. Only then will you master the Druid magic.

"What do you mean by intangible magic?"

Intangible magic is anything that is not of a physical nature. Mages can create objects, change their shape, and manipulate the environment around them. That is tangible magic.

You can feel, as well as push any feeling into another. You can hear thoughts, as well as push thoughts into another. You can sense someone's magic, and even transfer magic between beings, like a current of energy.

Most of the rest of us who have intangible magic, only have a limited scope of a single capability, unless we have an enhancement helping us. He glanced at the sky.

You possess the entire spectrum of intangible magic, but currently, your emotions are...unstable, which makes the magic unstable, which makes you vulnerable and potentially dangerous.

While that made sense, it wasn't that easy. She couldn't just snap her fingers and not be sad, or angry, or anxious. What did he want from her? To magically become brilliant, competent, and have no anxiety. It wasn't like she didn't try to be normal. It's a disorder, a chemical imbalance of the brain. She could tell herself all day long to calm down, but the mind was powerful and didn't always listen to logic when it's in freak out mode.

What a cosmic joke that someone with anxiety and panic disorder was given mental magic, and the only way to fully control it, was to control her emotions and mind. Like she hadn't been trying to do that her entire life.

I'm not judging you. These are simply the facts.

"Are you listening to my thoughts?"

It's hard not to hear when the door to your mind is wide open.

Sibyl didn't know a horse could have a reproachful expression until now.

Anyone with telepathic magic will be able to hear you, if you don't learn to shield your mind. And there are some who could extract memories, manipulate your perceptions, and even control you and use you for their own nefarious ambitions. It's vital that you learn to shield your mind.

"Ok, how do I do that?"

Picture a barrier of some kind, and put it around you.

Sibyl frowned. "That's it?"

Simply enough, yes.

She thought of the shields around spaceships in movies and tried to create that. After a minute of deep concentration, the only thing she had was a dull ache behind her eyes. Sibyl huffed in frustration. How was she supposed to make something real that was based on something intangible by nature? This was absurd. There was no way she'd ever be able to do it.

Solstice walked into the woods on a tiny hoof-print laden trail.

"Who would try to get into my mind and use me to do bad things?"

The demon who defeated Tearnanoak has seduction and mind control abilities. She's unable to feel or hear you, but she can get into your mind, if you are susceptible to outside influence. She works best in dreams. I believe your world would call her a succubus.

Sibyl scrunched up her nose. "Don't they seduce you while you sleep, like sexually."

Yes, and once they have a claw securely locked into the mind of their victim, they warp the desires of their subject, like a drug binding a receptor.

A succubus makes the victim feel empty without them. Their victim will crave their seductress more than life itself. Cravings so strong, it overpowers even their base needs. A fully bonded victim of a succubus will do anything asked of them, even starve or thirst to death just to be in the presence of their master.

They'll tell all of their secrets, share all of their memories, and they will also allow her to use their body as a conduit. The demon will see through their eyes, feel what they feel, experience everything through their body. A succubus is not fully alive.

Without a subject to control and use, it is ethereal at best. Unable to walk in the waking world, feeling nothing, unseen, trapped in Mokor, only experiencing life as if through an impenetrable looking glass. They can only interact with the living in dreams.

Those who fall victim become its body so that it can see, feel, taste, and be somewhat alive. When a succubus's victim is aroused, it feels the pleasure of both. That also pertains to pain and all sensory stimuli. That's why they like sex so much. Could you imagine experiencing your own climax simultaneously as your partners?

Sibyl fully understood the gravity of his words and was disgusted by them.

Since you have the entire scope of all intangible magic, you would be a gold mine for Alyssium. She could feel and see everything through you, and I'm afraid she could use you to do terrible things amplified to their most extreme potential.

"Alyssium? That's the demon who usurped Tearnanoak?"

The unicorn nodded.

"But I'm not sexually attracted to women so she wouldn't be able to seduce me, right?"

Succubi seek out those who would be most vulnerable to their seduction tactics. Since Alyssium is female, the easiest targets would be those attracted to females. She can sense that in a person. However, any succubus is perfectly capable of seducing any sexual orientation. It just wouldn't be as easy for them to convince their victim to go against their natural inclinations. So, they mostly stick to what they're good at.

If a person loves music, they don't have to play every instrument to be in the band. They play the instrument that suits them best, but that doesn't mean a musician couldn't learn to play any instrument with enough time and effort. The same applies here.

"Look, I have no intention of learning to use this Druid magic or cause any trouble. I just want a way to control it so I can go home and live my life. I won't be a threat to anyone once I learn that, and then I'll leave."

Not knowing how to control and use your magic doesn't protect you from being vulnerable to another's intangible snares. Just as you will learn to use the magic with time and practice, so could your captor. You can't run away from this responsibility. Your world has a saying: With great power comes great responsibility.

Sibyl's hackles raised. "I'm not running away. I'm just saying that once I learn how to block it, I won't be a threat anymore, and then I'll leave, so the demon succubus won't be able to get to me. That's why I came here, to learn how to make it go away. I don't have any desire to do all the other things a Druid can do, so I won't waste my time trying to figure that stuff out."

Disappointment seeped into her. It was coming from Solstice. Her heart sank. She didn't want to disappoint him, but she also didn't feel obligated or motivated to be a master at Druid magic, she just wanted it gone. She didn't owe him anything. This was her life, and she could live it how she wanted.

The trail widened and the trees thinned out. "Where are we going?" Sibyl asked.

I have something that will neutralize your magic until you acclimate to Orlon.

Sibyl's heart jumped. That's what she needed, something to make it all go away.

It's meant to be a temporary tool until you learn to control it on your own, which hinges on gaining control of yourself first.

"Yeah, I understand." She rolled her eyes. He was starting to sound like a broken record, just like everyone else in her life.

She was so sick of everyone telling her how she should think and feel and live. If it were that easy, then no one would have anxiety, or experience heartbreak, or panic attacks. Emotions aren't something you can just boss around like an obedient puppy. Sometimes the heart and mind think and feel what they want, regardless of what you actually want, and sometimes in defiance of each other.

If she knew how to be different, she would be. But people constantly fussing at her to *be better, do better,* or *just calm down and relax,* was not helping. She was trying to do all those things.

They came to a thicket of no more than two acres. The grass was short, as if it was recently mowed, and a small cave mouth opened at the base of a hill. Grass covered the mound on all sides, camouflaging it amongst the ground.

A dozen horses of varying colors and sizes grazed. They raised their heads at the approaching pair. Ears erect, they stared for a moment then went back to the grass, obviously unfazed by her presence. Likely because she was accompanied by Solstice.

He walked up to a dapple-gray horse with a black mane and tail. Describing this horse as large was relative. Next to Solstice he was dwarfed, but it was still a large horse by any standard measurements.

The meadow became very quiet, and an emptiness filled Sibyl, as if they entered a void. The grey horse stood silently, head swiveling from Sibyl to Solstice, then back again. She fidgeted under their stares. The grey horse walked away and the void lifted. The energy of Orlon fully embraced her again. A welcome feeling, like submerging oneself into a nice hot bubble bath. She had to admit, she'd miss this feeling when she left. She'd only been here for an hour and Orlon already felt like home.

Every unicorn has a special ability that is related to the make of their horn. My horn is ebony which imbues stability, power, protection, and balance. For that reason, I'm the leader of the unicorns. I protect my herd, keep the balance, and make sure the power of the realms remains stable. My mate, Emmaline, has an ammolite horn, which holds the power of love and rejuvenation.

A flirtatious love emanated from Solstice just at the mention of his mate. It made Sibyl smile.

Oberon's horn is made of osmium which is a funny element that is a bit of a conundrum of sorts. It is one of the most powerful objects in existence, but it holds no power at all.

"What does that mean?"

It neutralizes all light magic around it. No tangible or intangible magic can be used on it, against it, for it, or around it. Anyone who is within the radius of its effects will be rendered powerless, just a biological creature subjected to natural laws. Effectively, it equalizes the playing field of anyone within its reach. For that reason, it is sought after, very valuable, and highly dangerous to those who need their magic to defend themselves.

Currently, Oberon is the only creature in the universe who possesses it. That's why he remains here, deep in the forest, where no one can find him. Previous Osmium unicorns have been hunted, almost to extinction. In fact, most of my kind has. That's why I've hidden my herd here.

Other than the God trees, we are one of the only other carriers of magical objects. I will not let my herd become extinct from Orlon. This is the last planet that we exist. We've been driven to extinction on all other worlds in the living realm. I will defend them at all costs.

A horse so white it was almost purple came running across the field from the cave where Oberon just went. Sliding to a stop, it halted, throwing chunks of dirt at Sibyl and Solstice. Its horn was a beautiful pastel blue with opaque swirls. The unicorn watched Sibyl while the two horses nickered at each other as if they were having a conversation.

Sibyl noted how beautifully manicured their manes and tails were.

No knots, twigs, or anything in them, as if they'd just been groomed. Someone obviously brushed them, she wondered who.

Oberon has completed the separation. He's too weak to walk right now. You must come to him to retrieve the stone.

Sibyl and Solstice followed the purple mare into the cave. Oberon lay on the floor, laterally recumbent and breathing heavy. Rushing to the horse's side, Sibyl laid a shaking hand on his sweaty neck.

"What's wrong with him?"

No one answered.

White foam lathered his neck, his heart raced, and his breathing was labored. Sibyl stroked the horse reassuringly. He nickered weakly at her. Without medicines or tools, she could offer the horse nothing except comfort. Solstice pawed the ground. Sibyl looked at him and noticed a dull gray nondescript rock Solstice's hooves.

Sibyl crawled over and picked it up. "This is it, isn't it?"

Silence met her. Sibyl looked up at Solstice, but he was gone. Everything was gone. Not gone, changed. She lay underneath the softest red silk sheets she'd ever felt in a dimly lit room. Cassie lay sleeping on an identical bed nearby. The room was beautiful and smelled of essential oils.

She flipped the covers off and a rock fell to the floor. The osmium stone.

Picking it up, she cradled it close to her chest. This was her ticket to success. This stone neutralized the magic she didn't want. No one's thoughts or emotions would plague her anymore. The incessant tingling sensations would cease, the hallucinations, and the Druid Dreams would stop. It would all go away, and she could live a normal life.

Clutching the rock as if her life depended on it, she laid back on the bed and sighed, letting the relief wash over her. For the first time in her life, she felt free.

She was also wide awake. There were no windows in the room. The only light was from weird looking diamond gems along the wall. Her backpack laid near the nightstand. She retrieved her phone from it and read the time; three in the morning. That explained why everyone else was asleep, and it was so quiet.

Opening the drawer of a small nightstand next to the bed, she found a book titled *Legends and Myths of Silvermar*. She remembered something about that from the river in her Druid Dream. On the cover of the book was a blue Dragon flying over snowcapped mountains. Exchanging the book for the stone, she closed the drawer, safely securing the rock for now.

Nature called so she set the book on the nightstand and crossed the carpeted room to a door she was certain was the bathroom. The wooden door opened soundlessly when she turned the ornate silver doorknob.

Sibyl's mouth dropped open. This was the most extravagantly beautiful bathroom she'd ever been in. The tile was a white marble with glittery silver grout lines and warm on her bare feet. Upon entry, diamond lights around the perimeter of a large vanity mirror above twin sinks lit up to a dusky tone, allowing her to see easily, but not overpowering her tired eyes.

After relieving herself, she washed her hands and surveyed herself in the mirror. Semitransparent flakes of skin peeled from her shoulders. The fresh skin underneath was pink and tender, but also smooth and clean. Her complexion was quite a bit darker too. She was no longer pale and fragile looking. The days on the beach highlighted her cheekbones, and the freckles weren't as stark a contrast against her skin.

Gently tugging the dead skin, she rid herself of the last few layers, leaving her body clear of all enfeebled skin. She was a snake shedding an old layer of herself. The scared, fragile, nervous Sibyl of the past was slowly being replaced with a confident, strong, and curious woman, no longer hindered by the shackles of anxiety.

The idea of being a Druid felt like pulling on an old pair of jeans, long forgotten at the bottom of a drawer, now discovered but fitting perfectly. Something so familiar that she'd known her whole life but was hidden from memory for a long time. Most importantly, Sibyl was finally satisfied that she wasn't crazy.

She'd been a hollow shell of herself for most of her adult life because of this *gift* that felt more like a curse, and now, she had a cure.

Hopping back into bed, Sibyl removed the rock from the drawer. It looked like any ordinary gray rock you'd find on the ground. Nothing special about it, but apparently it nullified her Druid abilities. Rubbing fingers along its surface, she concentrated on the texture.

Real.

Her thoughts drifted to Oberon. She hoped he was alright. Solstice said he wouldn't let any harm come to his herd, so surely the unicorn wasn't seriously hurt by giving her this. Pushing the worry from her mind, she set the stone back on the nightstand. Obvious they weren't in any danger otherwise Cassie wouldn't be sleeping so soundly so the best thing to do, at the moment, was to stay put and wait for everyone to wake up. Tomorrow, she would find Yilfin and Fulcinia, get another one of those bubble things, and go home, just like she planned.

She grabbed the Dragon book off the nightstand, and by the faint glow of the diamond-looking wall lights, she lost herself in stories about the kingdom of Silvermar and the Dragons that lived there.

CHAPTER 9

AVA

CANKIT FIROQ-3/JUNE 24TH

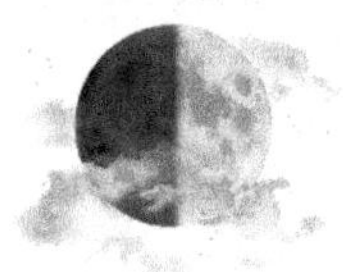

Fulcinia and Yilfin lead Ava, Sibyl, and Cassie through the maze-like halls of the castle. Wainscoting vines and flowers twined their way down the walls alongside them. Ava wore a similar outfit to Fulcinia, black leather shorts and a dark red, sleeveless, corset-style shirt with silver vine and leaf embellishments. They were the nicest clothes she'd ever worn, and the fit was perfect. Comfortable, easy to move around, and flattering. Ava liked it very much.

Three outfits were given to them, but Cassie and Sibyl refused to wear theirs, preferring their regular clothes instead. Sibyl was stylish for Earth's standards, but Cassie wore the same baggy, ill-fitting, thrift store ensemble that she always did, making her look like a bum. Ava wished Cassie would wear something different, but she was determined to embrace the dirty hippie look and no amount of arguing could convince her otherwise.

"Good morning," someone said to Yilfin as they passed by. Most nodded cordially to Yilfin and Fulcinia, they sort of gawked at Ava, and had curious expressions for the other two.

Ensuring her hair was pulled into a tight plait like Fulcinia instructed, Ava stuck her chin out, refusing to let the staring people get under her skin. Cassie didn't seem to notice or care that people stared, and Sibyl was too distracted by the surroundings to notice. She hadn't seen any of the castle yet, since she was unconscious on her way in yesterday. She'd slept through most of the night too. When dinner arrived, they tried to wake her, but she was out cold.

The food was so amazing that they ate not only their own portions, but Sibyl's as well. Ava felt a little bad about it, but not bad enough to stop herself. She recognized some of the foods like chicken and asparagus, but it was seasoned with exotic spices and herbs that brought out entirely new flavors. The rest was unfamiliar, and wonderful, so she ate every bite of the strange new foods. By the time they got to dessert, Ava was so full she thought she may explode, so she got a shower instead.

The shower stall was made of natural stone tile and the ceiling glittered with hundreds of tiny diamonds, creating the illusion of bathing under a starry sky. There were no adjustment knobs, yet the temperature and pressure were perfect.

The water from the double vanity sinks was also the perfect temperature as well. As if the water could read her mind, it was warm when she washed her hands and cold when she wanted a drink.

Diamonds lined the rim of the mirror over the sinks. As with all the lights in the rooms, they lit up and winked out as if they were on mental motion sensors. They also brightened or dimmed depending on your needs as well. Cassie and Ava debated the merit of water and lights having a consciousness, and being able to read minds, concluding it must work on some sort of magical telepathy.

After her shower, Ava finally had room for the dessert, which was just as wonderful as the entree. Not long after that, she fell into a sleepy food coma for the night. It was still early when she woke this morning to Sibyl sitting in bed, reading a book.

Already showered and wide awake, jittering as if she drank a pot of coffee, Sibyl jabbered on about meeting a unicorn in her dreams who gave her some weird stone that neutralized her magic. Something about her Druid abilities made it possible to bring back an object from a dream. Ava thought that was weird but, like everything else here, she just accepted that it worked somehow.

An older woman named Melinda brought in a cart with breakfast, and the clothes that Ava now wore. Melinda was the kingdom's medical director. She, Sibyl, and Cassie had an in-depth conversation about medicine, healing herbs, and magic. Orlon hadn't advanced its healing arts to what modern day earth described as doctors because 'we don't need that type of medicine when we have healing magic,' the woman explained.

Sibyl's quick grasp of the subject wasn't surprising since she was basically a doctor. Cassie seemed to enjoy the herbal medicine educational overview as well, but Ava found it boring. After Melinda left, it wasn't long before Fulcinia and Yilfin showed up to take them to meet Ava's aunt, the Aruka of Tearnanelle.

Rounding the last corner, the group entered the throne.

"Oh my god." Sibyl's jaw dropped. The yellow halo in her eyes was strikingly bright.

The throne room buzzed with activity. A desiccated, dinosaur-looking, biped with a caved in skull, and large black, insect eyes gave them a wide berth as they walked by. A group of angelic looking, feathery men and women conversed in front of a painting. A few people dusted statues or cleaned the floor and dozens of others meandered about leisurely. They zigzagged around everyone, making their way to the dais.

A guard stood at every door, and a queue of people lined up on the opposite wall from which they entered, leading to the front of the room where a beautiful middle-aged woman sat atop the tree throne. Ava's heart skipped a beat. Her aunt.

The woman slouched to one side of her chair, an elbow propped on the armrest, supporting her head. She wore the same shorts as Ava and

Fulcinia. One of her long, elegant legs crossed on top of the other, her bare foot bobbing up and down, jingling a gemstone anklet.

Like Fulcinia, she wore a cuff on her right arm decorated with dozens of gemstones. Unlike Fulcinia, though, she wore silver armor around her torso, throat, and wrists, laden with gemstones of various colors and sizes. It seemed a little over the top. Maybe that's how this world displayed status, because she wore no crown like one would expect a queen to wear.

The Aruka's entire left arm was covered in a tight sleeve that looped around one of her fingers. Her demeanor was one of power, dominance, and boredom. Her eyelids fought against their own weight, trying not to close as she listened to a man who knelt at the bottom of the dais before her.

When the group neared, the Aruka's eyes shifted, locking onto Ava. Her green eyes lit up, and her face changed from boredom to eagerness. In one fluid motion, the woman stood and sucked in a breath. The room fell silent, including the kneeling man, who stopped talking mid-sentence. All heads turned to them. Ava wasn't normally self-conscious, but when hundreds of people stared, it was hard not to be.

"Mr. Shaefer, I am so sorry that your daughter has gone missing. Of course, we will do everything in our power to find her." The Aruka talked quickly and snapped her fingers behind her. A guard came forward.

"Please take your photo to our Captain, and he will organize a search party for her."

The man thanked her several times, tears streaming down his face, while the guard escorted him from the room.

"Attention everyone. I must pause the appeals."

Grumbles broke out from the line of people. The Aruka narrowed her green eyes to lethal slits and the room fell silent again.

"Please return after lunch, reform the line in the same order it is now, and I will resume all appeals. I apologize for any inconvenience. Please visit the castle kitchens and food will be provided to you."

Disappointed faces transformed into smiling ones as they siphoned into a hallway, happily chatting their way to the dining hall.

Fulcinia signaled for Ava and the others to wait at the base of the dais. Yilfin signaled to some of the guards lining the walls and four of them came to stand behind Ava, Sibyl, and Cassie. Ava stiffened.

The large opening to the meadow out front was a straight shot, but now there were four uniformed men standing between her and the exit, not including all the ones who lined the dozens of hallways down the side of the room. Pushing down her anxiety, she squared her shoulders, and took a calming breath.

Sibyl glanced behind her and started crisscrossing her fingers. She sure was a nervous creature. She needed to learn to hide her insecurities better. Ava wondered what Sibyl would do if things went south. Pepper spray them? Ava suppressed a laugh.

Fulcinia and Yilfin ascended the dais steps. Yilfin grasped the Aruka's arm and gave a slight bow of his head. He dwarfed the Aruka, but she didn't seem intimidated at all. In fact, she held onto his arm and pulled him in to kiss him on the cheek. Once released, he went to the throne and casually leaned against it, folding his arms across his chest.

Fulcinia embraced the regal woman. Warm smiles transformed them from warrior and Aruka into two friends. They spoke in hushed tones for a minute before finally turning to face Ava and her two companions.

"My Aruka, may I introduce Sibyl Murphy, Cassie Newbanks, and Ava Smith." Fulcinia waved her arm like she was introducing the next contestants on a game show. "Ladies, this is Serellina Filmar, Aruka of Tearnanelle."

Cassie and Sibyl bent their knees and bowed their heads. Ava shot them incredulous looks. Were they serious? Bowing?

Fulcinia coughed and narrowed her raven eyes. Ava sighed, put her hands by her sides, and gave a quick nod. A few people gasped and whispered, tossing scornful glances at her. Ava was thankful to have naturally darker olive colored skin, otherwise people may have noticed her blush. Should she have done a bigger bow? Kicking herself, she stood tall and feigned confidence. Too late now, so best to pretend like it was purposeful.

The Aruka clapped her hands loudly. Everyone's head snapped forward, including Ava's. Serellina's hair draped down to her breasts and was more strawberry blonde than Ava's true deep red color and lacked the silver streak. Their eyes were a similar green, but the Aruka's were a bit lighter than Ava's. Her skin was also not as dark. If she were on Earth, she'd look more Irish than Ava, but otherwise, there was a strong resemblance that the two women shared, making it obvious they were related.

"Can I have the room please?" Her voice boomed with authority.

As one, all the remaining people headed to the nearest exit. After every last person was gone, the guards along the walls filed out and closed the doors behind them. The only guards who remained were the four flanking her group. Those four stood with their hands behind their backs and chests puffed out arrogantly. They wore belts with gems, just like Yilfin, and they were unarmed. Ava guessed that they didn't need weapons to be a threat.

The bubble thing transported people, and the diamonds provided light. Ava was piecing together that the gems weren't just accessories. They held magic. She noted the various stones on each of the men's belts, and the women's cuffs, and wondered what each of them did.

Other than Fulcinia and Yilfin, there were now only the two women in the corner who silently watched them. And, of course, the Aruka, who was obviously powerful in pretty much all aspects one could have power.

Ava sighed. She was outmatched and outnumbered, but she'd been in worse situations before. If this went badly, she could get herself out by transforming and making a mad dash to the opening behind them, but Cassie was completely defenseless, and would slow her down. Now she regretted bringing her friend. How was she supposed to protect Cassie if she could barely protect herself?

The Aruka descended the three long flat steps of the dais with the regal grace one would expect from a royal. Her bare feet were silent on the marble floor, but the anklet chimed with every left-footed step. Stopping in front of Ava, she stood just inside of Ava's comfort zone, but Ava wouldn't back up, no matter how uncomfortably close the woman stood.

They were about the same height, but where the Aruka stood older, elegant, and regal, Ava stood young, defiant, and brazen. They were so similar it was like looking through a time portal, seeing herself twenty years in the future, but family didn't mean Ava would automatically trust her. Taking a deep breath, Ava willed her heart to maintain a calm rhythmic pace.

Serellina smiled. "You look just like your mother."

Ava rocked back in surprise. Damn. She broke first. She wasn't expecting a comment about her mother.

"But you act like me." The Aruka's smile got bigger, and her green eyes gleamed with playfulness. Ava's heart and mouth dropped. She didn't know what to say to that.

"I miss my sister every day. We were very close. We were twins after all."

Unable to find any words, Ava just stood with a dumbfounded look plastered to her face.

"You didn't know that? Fulcinia didn't tell you?"

Ava shook her head. Her breathing came quicker now, and her heart rate increased, disobeying her command to remain steady.

"Yes. She was my twin sister, Serenilla. I am Serellina. We are.....were identical. We used to play tricks on our parents and friends by switching places." Serellina's eyes drifted sideways, as if she was remembering something. After a moment, she snapped back to Ava.

"I can tell you have her spirit. Our spirit. Defiant and stubborn. We should get along well, Niece." A mischievous smile played across her face.

Ava relaxed a little, but still couldn't find her voice. Her brain was completely deactivated. She couldn't think of anything else except that word. *Niece.* It sounded wonderful. She wanted to hear it from her aunt's lips again. She wanted this woman's approval. She wanted her aunt to like her. What was happening? She wasn't normally so sentimental. She needed to get a grip.

Serellina reached a hand toward Ava. A silver lock of hair had come loose from the braid. Her aunt brushed it back behind Ava's ear, and Ava's heart fluttered. Her aunt's face fell into an expression of disappointment, and she jerked her hand away.

Ava felt as if she'd been slapped. Had she done something to piss her aunt off already? Shifting uncomfortably, Ava looked away. Damn. Another submission.

The Aruka walked away. Just like that, Ava was dismissed. Anger and hurt bubbled under her skin. Was her aunt disappointed because she hadn't bowed? Damn it, she should have bowed. Too late now. Sighing, she put her hands behind her back and stood tall, mimicking the guards behind her.

Unlike Ava, Cassie was star struck and everything Ava wasn't. She groveled, bowed, and thanked Serellina for the food, told her how beautiful the castle was, and even how beautiful the Aruka, herself was. Serellina smiled sincerely and accepted the compliments, shaking Cassie's hand.

Ava was annoyed at how subordinate Cassie was being and how benevolent Serellina was in return. Her aunt seemed to really like Cassie. She wasn't fake like Ava would expect from someone in such a position. Overall, this woman was destroying all of Ava's preconceived opinions of her.

Once Serellina stood before Sibyl, who gave a quick uncoordinated bow, her aunt's features hardened into the arrogant formal Aruka that Ava had expected to meet.

"So, you're the one who has mysterious intangible magic," the Aruka said. Not quite a question, but not a statement either.

Sibyl shifted her weight back and forth, twisted her fingers all around, and stuttered over her words like a child being scorned. It was hard to believe that she'd actually pepper sprayed a giant werewolf just twenty-four hours ago.

Perhaps Ava's snap judgement and actions were misplaced. Sibyl did stay and help her on the beach when she could have run away, after all. That proved she was a good person, and there was some bravery buried underneath all that pathetic anxiety, right?

Sibyl twisted her fingers to an unnaturally painful angle. Ava winced. The bravery must be buried really, really deep.

CHAPTER 10

SIBYL

CANKIT FIROQ-3/JUNE 24TH

Sibyl crisscrossed her fingers on top of one another, trying desperately to calm her nerves. Serellina's eyes dropped to Sibyl's hands. Quickly putting her hands by her sides, Sibyl wiped her sweaty palms on her shorts. She felt like she was in front of a jury awaiting the judgment of a life sentence or execution.

"Hi. Yes. I suppose I have intangible magic. I just learned that I'm a Druid."

The auburn-haired woman in the corner gasped. Yilfin and Fulcinia exchanged a look. Sibyl glanced between them all, nervously. Was being a Druid a bad thing? Solstice didn't tell her it was a secret. Shit. She hoped that wasn't a mistake.

The Aruka's eyes widened. "A Druid? How did you manage to figure that out?"

"I met a unicorn in a Druid Dream last night, and he told me."

The Aruka furrowed her eyebrows. "You spoke to a unicorn?"

"Yeah."

Sniggering broke out behind her. Two of the four guards tried, and failed, to hide their laughter. The smallest of the four guards held a baffled expression. The largest of the men wore an unreadable expression, but his eyes told a different story. Deep brown with a hint of yellow and a mahogany red ring around the pupil gazed at her as if he searched her soul.

Sibyl's heart flipped over itself.

He wore the same outfit as Yilfin, which complimented his physique very well. He crossed his arms over his chest and narrowed his eyes at her.

She quickly turned away. She'd been staring like some love-struck teenager. How embarrassing. Raking her fingers through her hair, she attempted to smooth down any unruly strands.

"Interesting." The Aruka crossed her arms in a strikingly similar manner to the man behind Sibyl.

"A Druid." She tapped her fingers on the side of her folded arms and studied Sibyl for an uncomfortable amount of time. "Orlon hasn't seen a Druid in hundreds of years. If you are, in fact, a Druid, then we are truly blessed to have you." Serellina walked back up the dais to the auburn haired woman in the corner.

"How did you come to meet my niece at the exact same time that she was attacked by a werewolf?"

Like magnets, Sibyl's hands found themselves and her fingers entwined into a tangle of nervous fidgeting. Holding the Aruka's gaze, she forced herself to stand tall. She was intimidated, but she wasn't weak. She willed herself not to pass out, no matter how erratically her heart beat.

"I've wondered that myself, your majesty." Sibyl dipped into a quick curtsy which she immediately regretted when she heard more laughing from behind her. The hairs on her neck stood up. She turned and glared at the two men who laughed at her. They immediately went silent, stood up tall, and pretended not to notice her. Sibyl's eyes trailed to the other guard, meeting his cognac eyes.

His jaw ticked.

"And what conclusion did you come to?" the Aruka asked.

Sibyl turned around. "What?"

"How do you explain the coincidence of meeting my niece at nearly the same time as my advisors and a werewolf?" Impatience bloomed in her voice.

"I don't have an answer that makes sense. It does seem like a huge coincidence, but also, I felt-" Sibyl paused and thought carefully about her words. "I felt like I was pulled there. I guess by magic, now that I know it exists." Great. She sounded just as crazy here as she did on Earth.

The auburn-haired woman walked down the steps. Her hair fell down to her waist. Ivory skin, long legs, and a tiny frame made her homely, yet pretty.

"Clark will orient you to Orlon and help with anything you might need, in reference to learning your magic. She's the librarian's apprentice. You will also be escorted by two guards at all times to ensure your safety and ours."

"I'm not staying," Sibyl interrupted.

The Aruka's features morphed into surprise.

"Sorry. I don't mean to be rude. I appreciate the invite, but I don't need a guard or an orientation leader. I don't want to inconvenience anyone. I'll just be going home."

"Go home?" Serellina's eyebrows shot up.

"Yes. I came here because I've had problems my whole life with hearing voices and seeing things. They told me if I came here, you could help me figure out what it is and how to control it. I already did all that.

"I'm a Druid, which means I have some sort of telepathic magic and that explains everything. I also have a way to control it now, so I'll just be going home."

The Aruka looked to Fulcinia, who nodded. Sighing, Serellina turned back to Sibyl. "You already figured out a way to control it. How's that?"

"As I said, last night I had a Druid Dream and met a unicorn. He gave me this." Pulling the gray stone out of her pocket, she held it out for everyone to see. As if all the air was sucked out of the room like the barometric pressure dropping before a pop-up storm, everyone gasped.

"This is osmium. It'll neutralize....."

Before she could finish her sentence, the man from behind her, along with the smallest of the four guards, grabbed her arms, and dragged her backwards so fast that her feet failed to keep up. The stone dropped from her hand, bouncing loudly on the marble floor. The men forced her to her knees between them, and they gripped her shoulders so tightly that she thought her bones may snap in half.

"Ouch." She tried to wiggle free. That only caused the men to grip her tighter.

The rock lay on the floor at Cassie's feet, who stood in stunned silence, just like Ava. Fulcinia and Yilfin stood in front of the Aruka, acting like a protective shield.

Sibyl's heart pounded as hard as a war drum. She tried to think of some way out of this situation, but her mind wasn't working. There was nothing she could do. She was no match for any of them.

"Get that thing out of here," Serellina ordered. Fury consumed her features.

One of the guards who had laughed at her, picked up the stone and headed toward the closest exit in a rushed walk. He held the rock by his thumb and forefinger, arm stretched out as far in front of him as possible, his nose scrunched in disgust, as if it was some foul object that might infect him.

"Wait. Please don't take it from me!" Sibyl struggled against the men restraining her. "Let me go!" she demanded. She glared at the large man. Her eyes connected with his beautiful red-brown ones that held no sympathy for her. A chill snaked down her spine, and she withered under his stare that was equally as strong as his hold. The last thing he intended to do was let her go.

She tried to control her breathing and keep calm, but it was a nearly impossible task as the gravity of her situation crashed down on her. They could imprison her, execute her, do whatever they wanted, and she wouldn't be able to stop them. She had no way of getting help or notifying her friends or family. She should never have come here. How stupid could she have been?

Tearing her eyes from his, she mustered up what little bravery she could find within herself. "The rock neutralizes my magic. Without it, the magic will overwhelm my mind, and I'll pass out, like I did yesterday." Her voice cracked as the last bit of courage left her. She fought the tears that threatened to spill. She didn't want to show that amount of weakness. She was already vulnerable enough. Breaking down completely would make her look pathetic.

"So, you're using the rock to neutralize your own magic?" the Aruka questioned.

"Yes. What else would I use it for?"

"To neutralize an Aruka, half a dozen of the most powerful Mage Guards, and the heir to a kingdom all at once." Serellina fanned her arms out, accounting for all the people present in the room.

Understanding dawned in Sibyl's mind. She unwittingly brought a weapon with her. A powerful one. How stupid could she be? She should have thought of that.

"Take the rock back to Sibyl and release her." the Aruka commanded.

The two men didn't just release her, they shoved her away as if she were contagious. After dropping the rock in her lap, the other guard joined his comrades. All four men stood in formation again, but this time they flanked her more closely. Sibyl's resentment toward them and this place grew exponentially. A tear trickled down her cheek. She quickly wiped it away before anyone saw it.

"I'm sorry. I didn't know. He didn't tell me. I didn't think." Sighing heavily, Sibyl's shoulders slumped. Her best bet now was to grovel, and hope they would understand that she'd been ignorant, not malicious.

The Aruka's face was calculating, calm, and full of suspicion. Sibyl's blood chilled. The next words out of the woman's mouth could determine Sibyl's fate.

The Aruka waved a hand around in a weird pattern then she backed up a few steps and repeated the behavior. Backing up a few more steps, she waved her hand again. Now Sibyl was concerned for the woman's sanity instead of her own. What on Earth was she doing?

The Aruka repeated the odd behavior a few more times until a silver shimmering knife appeared in her hand. Sibyl's mouth fell open. How did she do that?

With another flick of her wrist, the knife vanished. Magic. Real tangible magic. That was the coolest and scariest trick Sibyl had ever seen.

"Sibyl, I do not believe you intended any harm, but your actions put this entire kingdom at risk. I don't know where you got that stone, but it cannot be in my presence or in my court. Until you learn to control your magic without the osmium, you are not to be any closer to me, members of my council, or my niece than the current distance between us now, which from my guess is about forty feet. You WILL be escorted by two guards at all times while you're in Tearnanelle. This is for everyone's safety, including your own. Do you understand?"

"I just want to go home." Her voice quivered. She wasn't beyond begging. "Please, just give me a bubble and I'll leave, then I won't be a problem for anyone."

The Aruka's voice softened. "That stone cannot leave Tearnanelle. You can go without it, or you can stay with it, under guard."

"That wasn't the deal!" Finding untapped courage, Sibyl stood up. Despite her shaking legs and hands, she practically yelled at the Aruka.

Serellina's eyes widened. "So, what's your plan? To take that stone with you everywhere you go for the rest of your life?"

Sibyl's anger rivaled her level of anxiety. Who was this woman to judge her? Serellina had no idea what her life was like, and Sibyl wasn't under her subjugation. She was an American. She had rights. She was free to come and go as she pleased. Her hands gripped the stone so hard her knuckles turned white.

The Aruka sighed. "When you shower, sleep, participate in hobbies, sports, take someone to your bed. Will that stone accompany you?"

Sibyl didn't say anything. She just glared at the Aruka.

"What if you lose it? What if it's stolen? What will you do then?"

Sibyl's grip on the stone loosened. Color bled back into her fingers. The Aruka did have a point, but those were problems for another day. She'd figure it out when it became necessary.

"We will all work toward the same goal of understanding how your magic works so that you can learn to control it on your own. Then you'll be safe to return home. Did the unicorn also tell you that, as a Druid, you pose a danger to all those around you if you don't learn to control the magic?"

Yes. Damn it. She was right. Sibyl couldn't use the rock as a permanent shield against her magic. She must learn to control it herself. Her shoulders slumped. A hand gently touched her arm, startling her. Sibyl met Ava's jade-green eyes.

"It'll just be a few days, like you said." Ava smiled sympathetically.

"Niece, Arukas, you put yourself and Tearnanelle at great risk keeping her in your direct company. I must insist that you back away from her."

Ava looped her arm through Sibyl's and faced her aunt defiantly. "I'm good."

Sibyl's mouth could have hit the floor. Yesterday Ava nearly choked her to death. She still had the bruises to prove it. Now Ava was coming to her defense?

"As I stated before, these measures are necessary for all our safety, including her own."

When Ava didn't budge, the Aruka sighed heavily. "If you wish to help restore the fallen Twin Kingdom, and take your place as Aruka one day, then we need to keep you safe until you're ready."

Ava tensed. Her face froze like a deer in headlights.

"I'll be Aruka one day," Ava mumbled to no one in particular. She swayed a little.

Sibyl gripped her arm tighter. She knew that look. She'd experienced it more times than she could count. Ava was having a panic attack.

Cassie came to the other side of Ava and helped steady her friend.

"Just breathe," Sibyl whispered.

Ava took a few deep breaths, and the tension slowly left her body. "Aunt, Aruka, I don't know my place in this world yet. This is all new to me. I've known for most of my life that I was different, but I never imagined to such a degree.

"I've been powerless my entire life and have only been able to rely on my non-magical strengths. So, being in the presence of some rock that takes away something I never knew I had, isn't threatening to me. I've lived my entire life just as I am now." Ava glanced between Cassie and Sibyl and smiled softly.

"Only, I was alone. Sibyl and Cassie are my only friends, I trust them, and I want them by my side."

Sibyl wasn't sure what changed Ava's mind, but right now she needed someone in her corner, so she went with it. Gripping Ava's arm tighter, she squared her shoulders. All three of them stood taller, daring the Aruka to challenge them.

Serellina pursed her lips. "Whether or not you're accustomed to having magic doesn't matter in the grand scheme of things. The facts are, you are heir to the throne, and you do have great power. You must accept this fact and learn how to be Arukas." Serellina sat down on her throne, running a hand down the arm rest of the tree-like chair.

"But I do understand the overwhelming responsibility that has been thrust upon you. Friends are important." Serellina looked to Fulcinia, who smiled warmly.

"Keeping a trustworthy council is one of the most important decisions an Aruka can make. Those people are your eyes and ears, as well as your protectors, and most importantly, your friends. While I would choose my council members a bit differently, I understand that sometimes they come into our lives organically. I will not mandate who you associate with, but I will advise you to make smart decisions. Consider what is best for everyone, and not just what you want."

The Aruka's voice and face hardened. Liquid lava transforming to cold dark stone. "I would also encourage anyone who truly cares about my niece to consider what is best for her. If being in your presence is the very thing that could destroy her, are you truly a friend?"

Sibyl's grasp on Ava's arm loosened. Before she could pull away, though, Ava put a hand over Sibyl's hand, securing her firmly in place.

"The only mandates I will insist on, is that you do not sleep in the same room. There's no need to render you powerless and unconscious. And, you will not be permitted to leave the safety of Tearnanelle's walls. So long as you stay within the walls of the kingdom and sleep apart, I will not interfere with who you choose to keep company with. These terms are non-negotiable." Serellina leveled a stern look at Ava.

"Keep in mind, Sibyl, when you want to practice using your magic, you'll have to leave the osmium behind." She meant for Sibyl to practice also, which meant Sibyl would have to muster up the courage to face the world without the pacifying object at some point.

"I think that's a fair compromise." Ava turned to Sibyl. "What do you think?"

"I..." Sibyl hesitated. She didn't like any of it. She wanted to go home. She met the Aruka's uncompromising eyes. There was no point in arguing.

"Yes. I agree."

"Excellent." The Aruka smiled.

"And," Sibyl followed up.

The Aruka sighed dramatically.

"As soon as I prove I can control the magic without the stone, you'll give me a bubble so I can go home." This point, Sibyl would not compromise on.

The Aruka stood, a large cunning smile on her face. "Deal."

Relief flooded through Sibyl. All she had to do was learn to control the magic. Now that she knew it wasn't anxiety, she was confident she could learn how. She could learn anything with enough practice and study. That, she was good at.

"Now that that's settled. Niece, I'd love for you to join me for lunch. I want to hear about your life and what it's like on Earth."

"Oh my god. I'm starving." Cassie dropped Ava's arm, and practically galloped to the Aruka. Grabbing Serellina's arm, Cassie pulled the woman toward the door that led to the dining hall. Serellina's eyebrows shot up, but she allowed herself to be escorted out. Cassie either didn't care or didn't realize the invitation wasn't for her.

"Come on. I'll sit at the end of the table with you, forty feet away from the Aruka," Ava said, with mock formality. "I'm sure Cassie can keep my aunt occupied for now."

"Thanks," Sibyl mumbled.

They walked arm in arm, sufficiently behind the others. The four guards followed them closely. Sibyl glanced back and her eyes immediately found him. His face betrayed nothing of his thoughts.

"If you have to be followed around by an entourage of guards, at least yours are hot," Ava whispered.

Sibyl's cheeks heated, and she turned away. This was going to be an interesting couple of days.

CHAPTER 11
AVA
LEOMAR FULM-1/JULY 1ST

Ava surveyed the Mage training yard. Dozens of men and women sparred, several practiced with conjured weapons, while others stretched, jogged around a track, or participated in random exercises. They all had one thing in common. They were extremely fit.

She was a decently fit person, but compared to the people here, she was out of shape. She had a lot of catching up to do. Ava hadn't been the weak one in a long time. Ever since the Hansons' deaths, she trained in martial arts so that she'd never be vulnerable again. This was the first time in her adult life that she was at a disadvantage. Something she planned to remedy as quickly as possible.

Many of the men were topless and half the women wore sports bra style corsets. She pulled her shirt off, since it was blazing hot outside, and planned to go in her sports bra too. More than half of the people had silvery tattoos on the back of their necks, the same as Fulcinia and Yilfin, and several people had similar spiraling tattoos on their left arms.

She learned that they were mating bonds. During a bonding ceremony their arms were wrapped in a magical rope and the pattern was burned onto their skin to signal they were taken. Orlon's version of wedding rings. Ava preferred the tattoos over rings. She hated wearing jewelry. The magical gems for their currency were enough accessories for her.

All of the women had their hair up, probably to help keep them cool and to keep it out of the way of fighting. She plaited her hair in a tight wrap around style braid, at her aunt's instruction. It wasn't just to keep it out of the way when sparring. Serellina wanted to keep the silver hidden as much as possible to avoid any unnecessary attention. Ava was one hundred percent ok with that.

Being the Arukas automatically made her the highest rank here, other than Yilfin and Fulcinia, who were nowhere to be seen. Everyone stared at her as if they were sizing her up. They were curious to see if she deserved the rank, because she certainly hadn't earned it, yet. Taking a deep breath, pretending not to notice, she stretched.

The stretch poses offered her the opportunity to steal glances at everyone. The men's bodies were nothing short of exquisite. After nearly losing her balance on a stretch, she tore her eyes away.

Shaking off the distraction, she studied the women instead. If she were attracted to women, she'd find it difficult to concentrate as they, too, were nothing short of beautiful.

Across the yard, one lady was kicking her partner's ass in jiu jitsu style fighting. Ava liked that the women were trained alongside the men, and no one held back. The man didn't take it easy on her. Most of the women were smaller in stature, but as the woman aptly displayed, that didn't equal weak. She tapped him out after a few moves.

Several people clapped. The lady glanced in Ava's direction. Ava smiled and nodded her head. The lady smiled back. Ava hoped her title wouldn't make anyone hold back when it came time for her to start sparring. Where was Fulcinia anyway? Ava was instructed to be here at dawn to start training, but her trainer was late.

As if they were one, everyone in the yard dropped to their knees and bowed their heads. Serellina, dressed in fighting clothes, entered the training yard and strode confidently toward Ava. All the jewels and accessories were gone. She looked just like everyone else, stripped down to a tiny pair of shorts, a corset, and over the left shoulder, the same tight sleeve all the way down her left arm. This time she had shoes on, and the jingly anklet was gone.

She didn't look like a woman in her sixties. She was fit, strong, and walked with the lithe movement of someone thirty years younger.

"As you were," she said.

Everyone stood and resumed what they were doing.

"Good morning, Niece."

"Am I supposed to bow?" Thinking back to how she behaved in the throne room, she didn't want to make that mistake again.

"That was genuflection and no. Royals and council members do not need to bow, genuflect, or curtsy. We nod to each other as a sign of respect. Honestly, I wish we'd do away with the whole bowing tradition, but I can't seem to make everyone stop, despite having told them thousands of times. So, I just go with it. I don't think I'll ever get used to it though."

Ava laughed. "Fair enough."

"Today we're going to learn how to use our silver magic."

"Wait. You're training me?"

"Yes. You have a problem with that?"

"No. I just figured you'd have better things to do."

"I have a lot of things to do, and I don't want to do any of them." She smiled.

Ava smiled back. "Ok. Let's get started then."

"Mages have silver in their blood, as you've been told. The heirs are the only ones with silver and gold, but ignore that for now. We're concentrating on the silver."

Ava surveyed at her hands. "My blood is red."

"Yes. It's not literally silver. The magic is silver, but inside a Mage, it's invisible. But it's there, trust me." She held up her hands, a small unalome on the underside of her right wrist flashed for a moment before her aunt flicked her wrist and it disappeared behind the movement. That must be her mark from the Gods. It was much more subtle than Ava's silver hair, she noted with a twinge of jealousy.

"Will I get a Mage Guard tattoo?" Ava interrupted something that her aunt was saying.

"No. The unalome is our mark. It's the remnant of the passage of magic when the Gods chose us. The Mage Guard tattoo represents their vow to defend and protect the God's mortal kingdom. They get it on graduation day. Now pay attention." Serellina flicked her wrist again and a dagger reappeared.

"That's cool." Ava flicked her wrist. Nothing happened. She frowned.

Serellina laughed. "Don't rush. Hear the theory first." She flicked her hand and the dagger vanished.

"Magic cannot produce something from nothing. That cost me some of my silver. Not much, but it adds up. If you're in a fight and you conjure weapon after weapon, you can deplete your silver quickly. It's like a muscle. The more you work and exercise, the stronger you get. The more you practice your Mage magic, the more silver your body creates to keep up with demand. That's why all Mage Guards practice, a lot.

"There are four types of magic: innate, rune, tangible, and intangible. Innate magic is all around us. The lights that turn on and off at will, the water temperature, things like that. I'm sure you've noticed."

Ava nodded.

"Its existence is beyond our influence. We can only use it as it's designed. Runes are a type of blood magic that can influence intangible and tangible magic, but not innate magic. Intangible magic is telepathy, empathy, and the such. Druids, along with a select few other creatures, wield intangible magic.

"Then there's tangible magic. The gems provided to us by the God Trees are a form of tangible magic called elemental magic. That's where the silver in a Mage's blood comes from. Anything we can see, touch, or feel, a Mage can modify, manipulate, or transform.

"When a Mage transforms, we're changing the cells of our body to conform to another phenotype, but our soul and genetics will still be ourselves. You know this because you've done it, right? Fulcinia told me you already know how to shape shift."

Ava nodded.

"Good. Listen to the next parts very closely. There are limitations to what a Mage can do, and if you push the boundaries, you could suffer intense pain, irreversible injury, or even death." She gave Ava a stern expression.

"It's impossible to change from a living creature to an inanimate object. We're too different. A biological system is made up of cells sorted in a manner that brings us to life. We adapt, learn, and grow. An inanimate object is a collection of atoms in various arrangements that expresses a certain physical form based on pressure and actions exerted on it.

"Objects react to their environment and are formed, whereas living beings are created from other living beings, and we affect the environment around us. Got it so far?"

"Yes, I think so."

"If I attempted to make a rock a living creature it would just explode. Other than being entertaining, it wouldn't really cause any harm, and sometimes people do that just for fun. But, if a Mage attempted to make themselves an inanimate object, they would, at best, get a headache, or at worst kill themselves."

"Don't try to become a rock or something else not living. Got it. Wasn't interested in that anyway, so I'm good with that," Ava said.

"We also cannot transform another living creature, only ourselves. You cannot manipulate something that has a will to resist manipulation. All cells resist change and manipulation from an unknown source. If you attempted to transform another person or animal, the magic would rebound back onto you, causing severe burns."

Ava raised her eyebrows. "Don't try to shape shift anyone but myself. Check."

"Good. Let's talk about shape shifting then. Every Mage has a spirit animal that closely matches our soul. It's easy to shift to that creature, whereas other animals are more difficult."

"Wait. We can shift into other animals besides the one that just happens?"

"Yes. Any skilled Mage, or Therian, can become any creature they desire with enough magic and practice, but it's not usually worth the effort. Changing from one creature to another who are vastly different is also more difficult. If you shift into a tadpole, then wish to become an elephant, that would require a lot of silver, and exhaust you greatly. Only the most powerful Mages and Therians can switch between animals so vastly different, and it really expends an unnecessary amount of magic. So again, we usually don't.

"Most of us stick to our spirit animal or animals very close in relation to it. We rarely venture outside of that, except for fun or in great desperation. Once in animal form, it requires no silver to maintain. You just are, at that point. Be careful to leave yourself enough silver reserve to change back. There've been times when some of us have gotten stuck in animal form for hours or days while our magic replenishes itself.

"Also, if you're killed in animal form, your body remains that way." Serellina tapped her chin for a moment as if she was trying to remember what came next.

"Clothing. You can imbue your clothes to shift with you so it's far less awkward shifting between forms. Keeping up the shifter clothes requires constant infusion so be selective on your shifter clothes."

Ava nodded.

"Shifts must also be lateral, meaning you can't shift into a younger version of yourself, or something like a puppy, and keep living multiple lifetimes. Many have tried to delay their death by shifting into younger bodies. The universe demands balance. If you want to be in a youthful form for longer than what is natural, your body will pay the toll in seizures, or the years will be taken from the end of your life."

"Noted. Won't shift into a younger version."

"Lastly. Shifting to another human's likeness is forbidden. If you try, you'll get a massive headache. If you continue beyond that, your skin will melt, and you'd eventually die if you kept pushing." Serellina clapped her hands. "I think that's all."

"Sounds simple enough. Work out my magic on the regular. Don't shift to extremes, don't try to shift objects, other people, or animals, or change into another human. Save enough magic to shift back. Did I miss anything?"

"Don't shift to a younger version."

"Right. Got it. Ok, I'm good. Let's get started. Show me how to conjure weapons." Ava jittered excitedly.

"Ok, calm down. Let's not get ahead of ourselves." Serellina laughed.

"When conjuring something using the silver within your body, you must summon the magic to the surface. Take a deep breath, think of what you want, and pull it into existence." With a slight flick of her wrist, the dagger came back. She held it for a moment then it vanished.

"This is easiest done by using your hands at first. But you don't have to." She held her arm up, and a long sword appeared in the air above her head.

Ava was really amazed now. She definitely wanted to learn how to sword fight. Not the lame fencing style sword fighting, but real swords, with enough power behind every strike to be deadly.

"When you want it to go away, you simply release the silver magic, and it dissipates."

"Does the silver come back to you then?"

"No. It goes into the atmosphere, gets reabsorbed into the ground, and will bloom again on the God Tree, eventually."

"For the first attempt try to summon a small sphere."

"A small sphere? Like a marble?"

"Yes. Exactly."

"That's lame. Why?"

"The objects we conjure must be one hundred percent known to us. The weight, feel, shape, every single detail. The only limitation to what we can conjure is our imagination, but that can also be a hindrance.

"If you can imagine a giant sword but don't understand its weight, the length it must be to wield it, the balance of the tang, all the things that go into it, then it will be an ineffective fighting tool, and maybe even a disadvantage in a fight.

"You conjure what you know. As you improve and familiarize yourself with more weapons, you can conjure more. Eventually, you'll have an arsenal at your demand. But we start with something small when we're learning."

"So, I summon the silver to the surface by doing what exactly?"

"Imagine a marble. How does it feel, what's the weight, what does it look like? Picture it, entirely, and pull the image from your heart into your palm."

Ava did everything her aunt said, and nothing happened.

"That's ok. Let's try something different. How do you shift?"

"My mind commands and my body obeys."

"Try that same principle, except your body isn't going to shift. It's going to create a marble."

Ava pulled her anger to the surface and channeled it into the demand. Not only did the marble appear in her hand, but it exploded, almost instantly, in a loud bang. Everyone in the yard jumped, including her aunt.

Shaking her hand, she rubbed it on the side of her leg. "Shit. That hurt."

"Ok. I wasn't expecting that. What were you thinking exactly?"

"Like I said. My mind commands and my body obeys."

"Yes, but what is the context there? What does that mean?"

Remembering the night that Sarah tried to drown her, or kidnap her now that she learned about bubble transport, Sarah told her to channel her anger and use it to force her body to do what she wanted. That's what she did to master shifting. She had more than enough anger to use. She was never in short supply of that.

"Anger. I channel my anger and use it like a weapon to make my body do what I want. Before I learned how to use my emotions as a tool, I couldn't control my shifts. They happened whenever my feelings were too intense. As I got better at controlling my reactions and emotions, I discovered that anger was the most powerful emotion, so it's easiest to use."

"That explains that. Anger is one of the most volatile emotions, hence the explosion. Your body isn't something you should be angry at or use anger toward. We respect ourselves. Our mind, heart, and body work together, as a team, to produce a desired effect. Try again but without anger. Just relax and pull the silver out by coaxing it calmly. Use a positive emotion to yield a positive response."

A calm request. This was a first. She'd produced a marble once, so all she had to do was repeat the process, only calmly.

Taking a deep breath, she searched for the magic again. When she found it, she calmly pulled it into the form she pictured. A tiny, bluish-purple, translucent marble appeared in the palm of her hand.

"Excellent. You're as skilled as I thought you'd be."

"It's just a marble." Ava rolled it around in her hand then tossed it to her other hand.

"Yes. But many Mages take days, weeks, or months to produce anything the first time. You got it in just a few minutes, and it's perfect." Serellina picked it up and examined it closely. "Yep. Perfect."

Ava swelled with pride. "I can't believe it would take so long for someone to make that. It seemed easy."

"Don't get cocky. Not all Mages are created equal in their inherent abilities. As with any task, some things are difficult for some people and easy for others. Some people are good at painting, others are better at music, some excel at science and math, while others have a knack for politics. Some, like you, are good at conjuring.

"Even within a given skillset, there are those who seem far above the rest, like a savant or a prodigy, and of course, there are those that are at the other end of the spectrum, who struggle with basic things.

"The same goes for Mages. Some, like Fulcinia, Yilfin, and you, are inherently very powerful, while others lack power to such a degree they're basically human, but that doesn't mean we get overconfident or treat anyone differently." Serellina leveled a stern look at Ava.

"I wouldn't treat someone different just because they weren't as good at something."

"Good. Mage magic requires a lot of practice and skill. This is just a marble after all." She tossed it back and Ava caught it.

"Now, release it."

"What do you mean?"

"When you create an object. It will stay as long as you allow it. It will vanish when you will it gone. So, let it go."

Ava concentrated on the marble and thought the word *go*. Nothing happened. She furrowed her eyebrows. *Bye.* Nothing. *Retreat.* Same result.

"How?" she asked.

"Feeling the pull is easiest when the object is far away. Once you feel the tug of magic you can release it."

"What?"

"Throw it." Her aunt pointed to a section of the yard that was empty. "Throw it over there."

Ava threw the marble, and she felt a slight tickle inside her chest, like a ball of yarn unraveling.

"Do you feel it?"

"Yes." She put a hand on her chest, but nothing was there.

"That's the silver you used to create the marble. It's still being expended. That's why it's important to release the things we create. Every moment they exist, they pull magic from us. When you hold it in your hands, the amount it pulls is minimal, you could probably hold a sword for a century and never exhaust but a drop. But the further away the object gets, the more magic it consumes to maintain.

"Now, break the tether."

Ava concentrated on the magical tether. It took barely a thought to sever the connection.

"Good. Do it again."

Ava conjured another marble, threw it, and released it before it hit the ground. Her aunt smiled, and Ava's heart leapt.

"One more time, but this time, release it while it's still in your palm."

She performed the task almost perfectly.

"Great. Now, learning the opposite will be the true challenge. Holding onto what we've created when we're not paying attention. But, we'll save that for another day. Practice creating and releasing a marble as much as you can today and tonight. We'll advance to something more challenging tomorrow. Come with me."

Ava followed her aunt into an interior room off the Mage training yard. Going through a set of doors, Ava's mouth fell open. Hundreds of weapons hung on the walls. Swords, maces, bows, crossbows, knives, sais, and many others she didn't know the names of.

"This is our inspiration room. We've collected weapons from all over the universe so that we can feel them, study them, and know them by heart."

A woman stepped out from another room. She immediately bowed.

"Ava, I'd like you to meet Zenai. Our weapons specialist. She helps us determine things like draw weight and ideal poundage for bows, or best type of knife or throwing dagger suited to an individual. That ensures we can conjure the best weapons for ourselves."

"Nice to meet you." Ava shook the woman's hand and thought her fingers may break off. Zenai's grip matched her strong stature.

"Is there a particular weapon that you fancy?" she asked.

"Swords, like the really long, big ones," Ava said.

The woman laughed. "I like this one. She's got balls. We have plenty of swords to choose from. I usually recommend we fit you to a sword, shield, and throwing dagger. You can play around with anything you like, but spend several months practicing with those three things and you'll have most of what you need in a real-life situation. Beyond those, is specialty crafts that take a lot more time and skill to master. Unless it's a passion, I wouldn't invest much time into them."

"What about guns?" Ava asked.

"Guns are a complicated beast. We do have some, but those are the hardest of all," Zenai said.

"Why?"

Serellina conjured a sword. "A sword is a single object. It has the blade." She pointed to the blade of the sword. "A tang." She pointed to the bottom where a rim of silver ran along the length of the handle. "A handle and guard, and there are many other intricacies you could opt for such as a double edge, single edge, fuller, etc.

"As long as you get the portions correct, the weight right for you, and the edge sharp, you've got a solid weapon you can use." She slashed the sword around in an artistic sweeping pattern, then posed in a fighting stance before the sword vanished.

"A gun has a lot more parts. Firing pin, cock, handle, trigger, trigger guard, slide stop, and so many other pieces, I can't remember them all, but they move."

"You must create them all just right, plus ensure they fit together, and move as intended within the limits of the mechanical properties necessary.

"Then you need bullets. Are you going to conjure those as well? Every bullet will have a tether pulling your silver. If you don't do everything exactly right, it can misfire, just like a regular gun.

"There are maybe three Mages who can safely conjure a gun that is usable, but even they don't use them in real fighting situations. It's not a reliable weapon, and it pulls entirely too much silver to make it worthwhile.

"Traditional weapons work better. But making bullet proof armor is a good skill to learn, because sometimes the enemy will have a gun."

"Makes sense. So, when do I conjure a sword?" Ava smiled enthusiastically.

"Why don't we practice a little more and build up to that. Zenai can start figuring out what fits you best, though. I'm heading back. I'll see you tomorrow morning."

"Who do I work with in the meantime?"

"Whoever you want, just ask anyone." Serellina turned to leave.

"Where's Fulcinia? I kind of thought she'd be the one teaching me."

"She and Yilfin are gone on a mission."

"Where?"

"You worry about your training."

Ava spent the next couple of hours trying out dozens of swords, knives, daggers, and shields. They were all heavier than she'd imagined. Zenai said there was a balance between how heavy was necessary to be a useful weapon, and how light it needed to be to wield it. If you tip too far in either direction, it's a hindrance in a fight.

By the time lunch rolled around, Ava worked up quite the appetite, so she headed to the dining hall. Sitting down next to Sibyl and Cassie, she introduced herself to the two guards who were on duty to watch Sibyl.

Demetrius had caramel toned skin with a close shaven goatee. He was, as every other guard, very well-muscled.

Wilson was of a slimmer stature and had reddish brown hair, green eyes nearly identical to her own, and a short stubble that looked like it was one day past due for a shave.

Sibyl fidgeted in her seat and poked at her food, obviously uncomfortable. Ava couldn't blame her. It would suck to be followed around and monitored all the time, but Ava did kind of agree with her aunt. Sibyl needed to learn to control the magic. Ava could only imagine what would happen if Sibyl's magic reacted like Ava's had when she tried to conjure the marble for the first time. An idea struck her.

"Check this out." Ava flicked her wrist. Nothing happened. "Shit. It was working earlier."

"Do you have the osmium on you?" Demetrius asked Sibyl.

"Yeah."

"That's why it's not working. None of us around her can conjure anything. See why the Aruka wants it out of her court?" Wilson said.

"Damn. That does suck." Ava slouched and went back to her food.

"Sorry. My magic makes me unconscious. It doesn't do anything cool like...what were you trying to do anyway?" Sibyl asked.

"I wouldn't exactly say that it's cool. I can make a marble."

"That's where we all start," Wilson said.

"When did you do that?" Ava asked.

"When I was about six."

"Six years old!" She was shocked they started so young.

He nodded and shoved a bite of food in his mouth.

"What about you?" She asked Demetrius.

"Same."

"Well great. I'm only about twenty years behind. I've got a lot of catching up to do."

"You're the Arukas. You'll catch up fast. Heirs are way more powerful," Wilson said.

Poking at her food, Ava digested that piece of information. She was the heir which meant she received a larger portion of magic than everyone else, because she was destined to oversee these people.

Ava surveyed the dozens of people chatting, eating, smiling, going about their day, seemingly without a care in the world. She'd have to rule over them one day. Make decisions to make sure they were fed, sheltered, safe. Make decisions that may get some of them killed. She glanced back at the two men in uniform in front of her.

They'd be the ones on the front lines of defense. They casually ate their food and talked as if it was an ordinary day to be guarding someone.

All these decisions, and probably so many more she couldn't even fathom, would be hers to make one day. Suddenly, she wasn't nearly as hungry as she was when she sat down. "You guys want to have a movie night tonight?"

"Yes!" Cassie said excitedly.

"Not an Adam Sandler movie," Ava said.

Cassie groaned.

"Sure. After dinner?" Sibyl asked.

"Yeah. We can meet in your room." Ava shoulder bumped Sibyl, trying to get her to smile.

Sibyl huffed a faint smile, but it fell away almost instantly.

"Wait. We don't have a TV," Cassie said.

"We'll use Sibyl's laptop. Don't think I haven't noticed you watching movies on that thing. How does that work anyway?"

"I have no idea. It's the innate magic, I guess. Keeps our phones charged and everything," Sibyl said.

"That's cool. Well, pick us out something good to watch, ok." Ava took a bite of food.

Sibyl nodded.

Later that night, the three women curled up on one of the beds and watched "Bride Wars" while Sibyl's two guards sat in the hallway outside the door. Ava kind of felt bad for them. They had to be bored sitting out there with nothing to do. Were they listening in on them or ignoring them completely? Did they stay there all night?

Pushing the questions from her mind, she relaxed onto the bed between her friends. That's something she wasn't used to. Friends. Surprisingly enough though, she liked it.

CHAPTER 12
SIBYL
LEOMAR WANG-2/JULY 5TH

Sibyl turned another page and sighed heavily. More 'how to' on the Druid arts. This chapter was all on magic transfer, and it made as little sense as the first three chapters she already read. Sitting back in her chair, she stared begrudgingly at the four books on the table in front of her. That was it. Four total books in the entire library, which was a massive five-story tall collection of books, so the fact that it only contained four on Druids was disappointing.

Each book was an accounting of a previous Druid's life and magic, and their personal explanation of how they used the magic, which wasn't overly helpful because they were all different. Apparently, there was no one way to do the same thing. It's all based on feel and intuition. The way one person created a mental shield could be the complete opposite of the way another person did it.

The oldest book was over thirteen hundred years old and the newest was over five hundred years old. The Aruka wasn't kidding when she said Orlon hadn't seen a Druid in hundreds of years.

Sibyl pulled out her laptop. Orlon's magic provided a continuous charge to all their electronics, including cell phones, and, freakishly enough, the cell signal and internet worked too. Hopefully she wasn't racking up any out of the country charges on her phone, talking with everyone back home.

Searching 'Druid' was unrewarding. Earth lore was much different than Orlon's. It was mostly based on religious beliefs. There was no helpful or accurate information to be had there.

"Hey." Clark sat down across from her with a pen and paper. "Tell me your full name, date of birth, and when you first started feeling the effects of your magic."

"Why?" Sibyl didn't want to answer any of that.

"I'm making the next Druid book." The green flecks in Clark's eyes swam amongst the gray iris granting them a mystical shimmer.

"Druid book?" Sibyl questioned.

"Yes. Like these." Clark gestured to the books on the table. "Someone wrote these accountings so that the next Druid could learn from them. I'm going to do the same for you." She sat up tall, paper and pen at the ready.

"I don't think that'll be overly helpful for anyone. Unlike them, I wasn't born here. I'll be going home soon so you'll have nothing to write about once I'm gone."

Clark started writing furiously.

"What are you writing?"

"The fact that you weren't born here. That's a good point. Future Druids will want to know that. If there's another Druid who isn't born in Orlon, maybe this could help them."

"I'm more interested in why a Druid is born."

"Druids come along when they're needed. You were born when Ava was born. She was lost and we needed her back," Clark said matter of factly.

Sibyl pondered that. Their birthdays were two weeks apart. Ava was born first. They were both in North Carolina for the first eighteen years of their lives, then they moved to Georgia, then they both ended up in Florida. All parallel movements to each other. That couldn't be a coincidence.

But Sibyl had nothing to do with them finding Ava. Fulcinia and Yilfin found her. Sibyl just happened to be around when they did.

"Look at this." Clark turned one of the opened Druid books toward Sibyl. "It says that when a Druid channels their magic, their eyes turn white." Clark looked at Sibyl expectantly.

"How would I know if my eyes change color?"

"They do."

Ambrose's voice startled her. He was the guard from the throne room who looked at her like she was nothing more than a worrisome pebble in his shoe, and he was obviously less than thrilled to be assigned as her guard. In the last eleven days he hadn't spoken a single word to her. She'd heard his voice when he talked to others, but never had he spoken directly to her, until now.

He was, by all conventional standards, a very attractive man. Tall, over six feet by a couple of inches, and had the most beautiful eyes. A light mahogany brown outside fading to a deep red center around the pupil. The opposite of hers which started dark green-gray on the outside and faded to a lighter yellow on the inside.

His hair was light brown with a matching beard and mustache that were very meticulously trimmed, and he was very well built. He had the kind of muscles that he earned through physical work, not in a gym.

His partner, Rokesh, was just as good looking as all the other guards, but he was smaller in size and build. Like Ava said, Sibyl had an entourage of hot guys following her around all the time. It was annoying, uncomfortable, and distracting.

"How do you know what my eyes do? I've never been able to use my magic since arriving in Orlon."

"I don't know if they change when you channel magic, but I'd venture a guess that they do, because they change with your mood for everything else." He flipped a page in the book he was reading, not even bothering to look at her.

How had he noticed her eyes when he rarely ever looked at her? He always acted like he had better things to do than to even bother acknowledging her existence, but apparently, he'd noted the color changing habits of her eyes.

Sibyl huffed. She'd been told before, by friends and family, that her eyes occasionally changed, but that's not uncommon with hazel eyes. She looked it up years ago when people started commenting on it, but no one had ever noticed a correlation to her mood.

"They change with my mood? How do you know that?"

Ambrose flipped another page, ignoring her. She cleared her throat. He tossed a glance at her, those beautiful cognac eyes boring into her soul. She swallowed down the unwelcome feelings his gaze stirred inside her.

"When you're calm, your eyes are a grayish-green color, like they are now."

"It's called hazel," Sibyl corrected.

He narrowed his eyes. "When you're happy, the yellow center gets brighter and expands. And when you're angry, all the color goes away leaving only a dark gray. I haven't seen any of your other moods yet, but I'd hazard a guess they're a different color too." He resumed reading.

Sibyl's mouth fell open. What was she, a freaking mood ring or something? She hadn't even known that about herself. And the fact that *he* noticed was weird. He was arrogant, silent, serious, and had a giant stick up his ass. The only thing Ambrose was good for so far was being an attractive statue that followed her everywhere she went. She'd never even seen him smile.

Rokesh was polite but he didn't say much either. Demetrius and Wilson were chatter boxes though. As much as she hated to admit it, she enjoyed their company. Demetrius was funny and tried to help her research sometimes. He was betrothed to Clark, and they were disgustingly cute together, reminding Sibyl of Melissa and Trent. She'd come to a different planet and managed to become a third wheel again.

"Hey dude." Cassie plopped down loudly in the chair next to her. "What are you guys up to?"

"Researching Druid stuff. What are you doing?" Sibyl resumed flipping through one of the Druid books.

"I just came back from the fields. Have you seen them?" Cassie jittered her leg. Sibyl couldn't tell if it was from excitement, exertion, or something neurologic. It didn't quite fit into any one particular category of jitteriness.

"No. Not yet," Sibyl replied.

"Dude. There's got to be like ten football fields worth of crops, with tons of different fruits and vegetables I've never seen before." She picked up a book and thumbed through it for a few seconds before hastily throwing it back down on the table. Several people shot reproachful glares at the raucous.

"Hey. Treat these with respect. They're hundreds of years old. And be quiet. This is a library," Clark scolded.

"Sorry." Cassie's eyes widened in mock offense. "Isn't it weird that we all speak English?" Cassie asked.

"What do you mean?" Sibyl asked.

"Think about it. We're from completely different worlds and yet we all speak English."

"That is an interesting point. How come we speak the same language? I would have expected you to speak differently than us," Sibyl said to Clark.

"We do speak a different language, but the magic translates it for us," Clark explained.

"How? I mean, even the text is in English." Sibyl pointed to the open book in front of her.

"It's not. It's in Tearnish. The magic will translate, when it's willed to do so."

"When its willed?" Sibyl asked.

"If I don't want to speak with you, then my words will not be translated for you to understand. Orlon knows that I want you to understand. Same with the text. The head librarian has allowed you access to the books, so you see your words and I see mine."

"That's cool. Tell me something in your language. I want to hear what Tearnish sounds like." Cassie leaned back on her chair balancing on the two back legs.

"Sit down before you fall," Sibyl scolded.

Cassie grunted and let the chair fall to normal position.

"Nyob zoo, kuv lub npe yog Clark," Clark said.

"Whoa. Cool. What did you say?"

"Hello. My name is Clark."

"And you're saying the same thing in your mind both times?" Sibyl asked.

Clark nodded.

"Cool." Sibyl smiled.

"Your turn," Clark said.

"Ok. So how do I do it?" Sibyl asked.

"Just will me not to understand," Clark said.

Sibyl thought about trying to speak with someone else who spoke a different language and just assumed the person wouldn't understand. "Hello. My name is Sibyl."

A corner of Clark's mouth tipped up. "That sounds weird."

"I thought the osmium neutralized all magic around it. I have it in my pocket. So how does the translation magic still work?"

"Because of the hierarchy of magic."

"What's that?" Cassie asked.

"The five types of magic are innate, rune, tangible, elemental and intangible. Innate magic is ubiquitous in the environment, and it supersedes all magic. That's the translation capabilities, the fact that your devices work without the power source from your planet, and the limitations on our Mage magic. I'm sure you've noticed those things."

Sibyl nodded.

"Innate magic is immune to all influences, and works all the time. Once you drink the water in Orlon you will always possess the innate magic everywhere you go, even if not in Orlon anymore.

"Runes are the second most powerful of the magics. They're blood magic. They can influence tangible and intangible magic but not innate magic. If I put the osmium inside a box with a containment rune then its effects would be contained only within that box and have no influence on anything outside it. But if I remove the rune then the osmium will resume its regular magical properties."

"This is super confusing," Cassie said.

Sibyl shushed her. She wanted to understand this thoroughly.

"The rune must be drawn in blood to work. Even if you possess no magic at all you can still create a magical rune."

"Ok. That's kind of cool. I could actually create some magical stuff?" Cassie asked.

"Yes. But, unlike innate magic, someone without magic can only create runes while in Orlon, where the innate magic exists to power it. If you're outside of the magical realm then only a magical being can create a rune that will work. Also, anyone could counteract your rune if you don't lock it, which must be done with a fingerprint of your blood on the rune. Then it will always work unless you erase it."

"Interesting," Sibyl said.

"Then there's intangible and tangible magic," Clark said.

"This one I know. Solstice told me."

"Who's Solstice?" Clark asked.

"Her unicorn friend who talks to her sometimes." A corner of Ambrose's mouth creeped upwards making him look frustratingly more attractive.

"Talking unicorn?" Clark questioned.

"You were there in the throne room. Didn't you hear about her conversation with the unicorn who gave her the osmium?" Rokesh asked.

"No. I must have missed that. What are they talking about?" Clark's forehead creased.

"Nothing. Ignore them. Keep going," Sibyl grumbled.

"Elemental magic, which are the gems, have two categories. The tangible forms are the gems from the God Trees and the intangible elements are from unicorn horns or other random sources. Each element has different abilities. They can affect each other but have no effect on runes or innate magic.

"You can hold a gem and temporarily use some of its magic, or you can absorb it into your body, utilizing its full potential, but you deplete it that way. When we're in our human form, we carry them either on a cuff, or a necklace, or just in our pockets, but when we're in animal form the gems absorb into our body for holding, but not use. In that form we can pull magic from a gem with simply a thought.

"Some gems can only be used in their entirety a single time, like bubbles. Some are ingested for a one-time effect like em, and some are used passively, like diamonds. Each gem has its own unique properties, and many we don't fully understand, like your osmium. We know that it neutralizes all tangible and intangible magic around it, but it will not affect innate or rune magic. It also has no effect on dark magic, unless it's corrupted by dark forces."

"Dark magic?" Sibyl asked.

"Yes. That's the misuse of the magics. Curses, spells, poisons. We don't practice dark magic, so we don't know much about it. But we do know that there's always a cost. Dark magic usually takes away something, disrupts the balance in nature, or causes harm to someone. Light magic maintains balance, harmony, and order in the environment, and protects the world and its inhabitants."

Sibyl pulled the osmium stone from her pocket and placed it on the table. "So, this is an intangible elemental magic?"

"Yes. It neutralizes all tangible and intangible magic around it including their elements, but it will not affect innate magic, runes, or dark magic." Clark pulled a necklace from around her neck and set it on the table next to the osmium. A swirly rainbow-colored stone dangled from the chain.

"Wow. That's beautiful." Unlike most of the gems Sibyl had seen so far, it was more disc shaped rather than spherical.

"It's an intangible element called ammolite."

"Ammolite. The power of love and rejuvenation," Sibyl said.

Clark smiled. "Yes. How'd you know?"

"A friend told me." She eyed Ambrose who'd gone back to not

paying any attention to her. She didn't want to start another round of 'pick on Sibyl for talking to a unicorn' conversation so she decided not to tell Clark about Solstice's mate Emmaline who had an ammolite horn.

"When we're claimed or intended, we wear them. It'll absorb my love, then when I give it to Demetrius, on our bonding day, it will be embedded over his heart. He will give me the one he's been wearing that's absorbing his love and I'll embed it over my heart." Clark put her hand on her chest over her heart. "After that we'll always feel each other's love, even if we're not around each other. Even now. I can feel it when I touch the stone."

"That's pretty cool." Sibyl handed the ammolite necklace back to Clark. "But it's not working now because the osmium is here?"

"Probably not." Clark tucked the necklace back under her shirt.

Sibyl picked up the osmium stone and studied it for a minute. "So, this doesn't have any effect on dark magic?"

Clark shook her head.

"That's a shame. I thought we could give it to the demon queen once I finally learn how to control my magic and don't need it anymore."

Clark laughed. "That's a nice thought but it won't do anything to weaken her."

"We could throw it at her. If it hits her in the head hard enough, it could knock her out," Cassie said.

Sibyl and Clark laughed.

"I was thinking we could fashion it into a necklace and give it to her as a present, like a Trojan horse."

"That's an awesome idea, like Monty Python," Cassie said.

"Sort of." Sibyl chuckled.

"What's a Trojan horse and Monty Python?" Clark asked.

"Monty Python is a satirical movie about how the Greeks defeated the Trojans. They pretended to give an offering to the Goddess Athena by creating a giant statue of a horse and leaving it at the gates for the Trojans. Greek soldiers hid inside it. When the Trojans brought the statue in, the soldiers broke out when everyone was sleeping and conquered the city.

"Up until that point the city was deemed impenetrable. A large wall surrounded it like the one around Tearnanelle. It stood for a long time before they brought in that stupid Trojan horse."

"That worked?" Ambrose asked.

"It did for the Greeks, but I don't think it ever would again since it's such a well-known story now."

"Then why'd you think it would work here?"

"I don't know. It was just a thought."

"How'd you plan to give Alyssium the necklace? Were you just going to walk over and hand it to her over lunch and a cup of tea?"

"I don't know. It's just a silly idea. You don't have to be a dick about it."

"I'm not. I'm just pointing out the holes in your plan."

Sibyl opened her mouth to shoot out a sarcastic retort, but Cassie interrupted.

"Hey. Let's go do something fun."

Sibyl sighed. "What do you want to do?" She was thankful for the interruption from what was probably going to escalate into an extremely immature argument.

"I met the apprentice gardener. She's really nice. Her name's Tacey. She's got these gnarly scars on her face from being attacked by a werewolf when she was younger. But anyways, she's super nice and wants to meet you."

"Me? Why?" Sibyl asked.

"Because you're a Druid. That's like celebrity status or something. She's really nice."

"You said that already."

"Well. It's true."

"Maybe later. I really need to figure this stuff out so I can go home." Sibyl reopened one of the Druid books to where she left off and started reading again. Turning a page, she noticed a torn corner toward the top. Inspecting it revealed it wasn't part of the page she was reading. There was a missing page.

"Hey. This book is missing a page."

Clark took the book from her and inspected it. She leafed through several pages and found a few more missing. Another page ripped as she flipped through.

"Oh shit," Cassie said.

"Yeah. That's my thoughts. This is the oldest one. It's falling apart." Clark grabbed another one of the Druid books and leafed through that one. Several pages were missing from that one as well.

"They need to be flagged for restoration and preservation before they completely disintegrate. Be careful with them. I'm going to go talk to Osisi about this." Clark left.

"Well, that sucks. Hopefully there's nothing important on those pages," Cassie said.

"I'm sure, between the four books, I can piece together everything I need. Not that it's helping much so far anyway. I've never heard of half these terms before. It's all completely foreign to me." Sibyl closed the books. "Ok. Let's see these gardens."

"Really?" Cassie's face lit up.

"Yeah. I want to go for a run anyway. How far are they?"

Cassie's face dropped. "About half a mile. What do you mean, run?"

"Jog. I usually do about three miles, so we can jog until we hit three miles or until we're tired."

"That won't be far since I don't exercise," Cassie said.

"Well. It's a good time to start. But you'll have to change."

Cassie looked down at herself. "What's wrong with what I'm wearing?"

"Your shirt is three sizes too big and twenty years old, and you have jeans on. You'll chafe in jeans."

"This shirt is awesome. It's Pink Floyd." Cassie stood up and held her arms out to show it off.

"I know who Pink Floyd is. But it's faded and has silverfish holes in it."

"What's silverfish?"

"Bugs. Bugs have eaten your shirt."

Cassie frowned.

Twenty minutes later, after changing, Sibyl and Cassie jogged around the fields. Well, Sibyl jogged. Cassie whined, panted, and floundered around like an uncoordinated toddler.

"Come on! I'm dying. My heart is going to explode."

"We've gone three quarters of a mile." Sibyl slowed to a walk so Cassie could catch her breath. Ambrose and Rokesh slowed to a walk behind them.

"You guys don't have to come along, you know. You can wait at the path we came in on."

Neither one of them was winded in the slightest, but Sibyl hoped they'd give her some space. It was weird having someone follow her around all the time. This must be what having secret service detail was like.

"We're good. It's a nice day and it beats sitting in the library," Rokesh said.

Cassie fell on the ground gasping for air, arms and legs splayed out.

"What are you doing?" Sibyl asked.

"Dying. What's it look like I'm doing?"

"You're ridiculous." Sibyl shook her head, but a smile weaseled its way over her face.

"Come on. Get up." She kicked Cassie's shoe.

Cassie flailed a leg at Sibyl.

"We can walk the rest of the loop if you want."

"Oh. Thank God." Cassie pushed herself to her hands and knees, and with Sibyl's help, she got back on her feet. They resumed walking. Someone ahead of them ducked between a row of vegetables that were nearly as tall as they were.

"Hey. There's Tacey. I'll go get her." Cassie dashed off while Sibyl stopped to stretch.

A few minutes later Cassie returned with a woman with voluminous blonde hair that covered half her face in an elegant wave-like style, then came together at the base of her skull to form a long braid. She shuffled timidly, her head down in a perpetual submissive posture.

Cassie was kind in the description of Tacey's scars. Her left eye was an almost white pale blue, and smaller than its deep violet counterpart. A large gash divided the wounded eye in half then continued down her face to her lip. The eye moved like normal, but it wept continuously because the eye lids didn't quite meet up correctly anymore. Three parallel scars fanned outwards from the large one connecting her eye and lip.

"Sibyl, this is Tacey. Tacey, Sibyl," Cassie said.

"Hey," Tacey said, bashfully, barely raising her chin. She fluffed her hair a bit more to try and cover the left side of her face.

"Hi." Sibyl had to make a concerted effort not to look at the scars. "The fields are beautiful. I've never seen vegetables like these. What are they?"

They spent the next hour learning about the vegetables and how they grew. Tacey's knowledge was impressive, and the workload she managed even more so.

Most of the fruits and vegetables in the kingdom came from these crops. There were several helpers, but most of the work was done by Tacey herself and without any magic. When Sibyl asked why she didn't use magic, Tacey just walked off quickly.

Later, Rokesh told her that Tacey was a falta-mage which was a Mage who lost their magic. Ten years ago, she and four of her friends snuck out to go to Lemalome, the fluorite kingdom to the north.

Fluorite imparted water and color magic. There's an annual ceremony and competition to create rainbow rivers that flow through the skies and take on any shape the wielder desires. It was one of the largest celebrations in Orlon before the war. While it still goes on every year, it's not nearly as big anymore, since the roads were too treacherous to safely traverse.

The five girls were ambushed by a pack of werewolves and taken to Tearnanoak where they were beaten, tortured, and raped for days. Three were killed and one, Metriona, was never seen again. Tacey somehow stole a bubble and escaped. But right before she got away, she was injured badly and underwent O'lim which was when a Mage's magic sacrifices itself to save its person.

A werewolf's claws were infused with anti-gold, preventing healing no matter how much medicine, herbs, or magic were used. Even with the healing magic of gold, it could still mean death. Tacey was lucky to be alive.

She was the first falta-mage the kingdom had seen in at least two centuries. The healers wanted to study her to see if they could somehow find a cure, but she was too traumatized and wanted to go home. Her parents insisted they discharge her from the healer's care.

Tacey hid in her home for several weeks, until, one day, the Aruka came to her house and told her to report to the castle gardens at sunrise the next morning to start her apprenticeship.

"Have you enjoyed Orlon so far?" Tacey asked. The perfume she wore was overpowering. Sibyl figured that she must be sweaty working outdoors all day, so Tacey overcompensated with a heavy dose of perfume.

"I guess so. I'm pretty home sick," Sibyl said.

"Is Earth a lot different than here?"

"Yes. We have a lot more industrial technology and no magic. We use machines for a lot of things. We travel by cars, and we also have electronics like TVs and cell phones."

"What do those things do?"

"They make life easier, convenient, and allow us to do things we wouldn't otherwise be able to do."

"A world without magic. I could fit in there better than here probably."

"You can visit me sometime if you want."

Tacey's head snapped to her, a look of surprise in her big violet eye. "I'd like that. Thank you. Maybe I will one day."

Sibyl smiled.

"I have to get back to work. Come visit me again, ok."

"Yeah. Definitely."

Tacey bowed and walked off. Sibyl thought the bowing was weird, but she accepted the gesture and watched Tacey leave. Her braid dangled behind her with bits of dirt, sticks, and leaves tangled throughout it.

"She never goes anywhere except home and the fields," Cassie whispered.

"That's sad." This place may be her salvation, but Sibyl thought it was more like her hiding place.

On the way back to their rooms, Cassie chatted Sibyl's ear off about random things, but Sibyl wasn't listening. She couldn't stop thinking about Tacey. Everyone always talked about people who die in war, accidents, and tragedies, but we rarely considered the survivors of such incidents. Would it have been better for Tacey to have died? Was it horrible to think that? Sibyl thought that if it were her, she'd rather have died than endured what Tacey went through and lived to tell the tale.

Not just that, but everyone knew about it, and thought about it every time they looked at her. She was reminded every single day when she looked in the mirror or saw people's faces when they recoiled or stared. It must be horrible for Tacey.

Sibyl wouldn't have survived either the attack or the aftermath. If this was the type of threat she was up against then she needed every advantage she could get. Even when she returned home, she needed something better to defend herself than Ativan and a rock.

"Stop." Sibyl held out her arms. All three of them halted abruptly. "I want to try something."

Cassie, Rokesh and Ambrose exchanged apprehensive glances.

"I need to figure out how to shield my mind, so I'm never forced to do anything I don't want to do. Can you guys help me?"

Cassie nodded enthusiastically.

"I can try," Rokesh said.

Ambrose stared at her with a condescending scowl.

She handed the stone to Rokesh. He curled his lip, obviously displeased with having it.

"You stay there and don't move," she instructed.

Taking a deep breath, she backed up a step. Then two. Then four. She continued to back up slowly until pressure built up around her. She stood for a moment and let her body acclimate to the feel.

"What's happening?" It sounded as if Cassie spoke into a microphone, the words were so loud.

Sibyl backed up a half step and a tidal wave slammed down on her mind, drowning out the world.

"Sibyl." A voice echoed her name. It sounded familiar.

"Sibyl." Someone else's voice.

"Sibyl. Wake up."

Opening her eyes, she saw three concerned faces staring down at her. "Shit. I passed out, didn't I?"

"Yep." Cassie nodded.

Sibyl sat up. A wave of nausea made her sway.

"Take it easy." Rokesh handed her a flask of water, which she chugged greedily.

"Thanks. Well, that went well," she said sarcastically. She handed the empty flask back to him.

"What were you trying to do?" Cassie asked.

"Not pass out."

"It didn't work," Ambrose said.

"No shit, Sherlock." Ugh. He was so vapid. Sibyl stood. Her legs were shaky but strong.

Rokesh held out the rock for her.

She shook her head. "I want to try again."

"Really?" His eyebrows shot up.

"Yes." Embarrassment and frustration fueled her determination. She would figure this out come hell or high water.

Hell was what came next. After another five attempts with the same results, she finally gave up.

It felt like her head had been used as a tennis ball. Her legs were so wobbly, she could barely walk without assistance, and she'd vomited several times. Her body couldn't take another attempt. This was hopeless.

She should be studying for boards, not trying to learn about some stupid magic that she didn't have any hope in hell of ever being able to control. Her problems would be over if the Aruka would just let her keep the stupid rock.

"I don't think it's a good idea to do this anymore right now." Rokesh rubbed a hand through his hair, watching her double over and vomit again.

"Yeah. I'm done." She spit out the last bit of contents from her stomach then stood back up and nearly fell over. Ambrose caught her. She held onto his arms, which she noted were as strong as they appeared.

"Come on. Let's get you back to your room," he said.

She couldn't argue. She could barely stay awake. She let him lead her back to her room where she fell on the bed and thought about how much of a failure she was. This thoroughly sucked.

"You ok? Cassie asked.

Sibyl rolled over. "Yeah. I just need to rest for a bit. I'll be fine."

"Ok. I'm going to go get us some dinner. I'll bring you some food back."

When the door closed behind Cassie, Sibyl let the silent tears flow.

CHAPTER 13

AVA

VIRLEM WANC-2/AUGUST 10TH

The air nipped at Ava's exposed skin like tiny stinging insects, and the wind ripped tears from her eyes. It didn't hurt, in fact, it felt invigorating.

The ground approached quickly as she fell through the sky at free fall speed. In just a minute or so she would meet the terrain on fatal terms if she didn't intervene. Giving the mental command, Ava shifted. Ripples erupted all over her body, and dark brown feathers sprouted from every pore. Within a few heartbeats, beautiful plumes of perfectly lined and oiled feathers hid Ava's skin.

Where once there was a mouth now was a beak, and where once there were human feet now were thin orange legs with 4 taloned skinny toes. The eyes were still a bright jade green.

Large brown wings spread out and caught the updraft so intensely that her neck jolted, giving her a bit of whiplash. The quick descent abruptly stopped, she leveled off, and sailed effortlessly over the forest.

Ava started practicing shifting to different animals since learning about it in Mage training. The maned wolf, her spirit animal, came naturally and required no effort. But, just like her aunt said, the further away she got from canine form, the more difficult the shifts became.

So far, birds were the most challenging species she'd tried, but also one of the most sensational. Feathers sticking out of her thin skin and the light bone structure were only two of the pleasantly strange aspects of an avian body that she wanted to explore more deeply.

For the first attempt with shifting into an avian species she chose the ostrich because the size differential was easier to calculate. The ostrich could run moderately fast, but its bulbous body was awkward to maneuver on the tall skinny legs.

Next, she tried a turkey but the weight of its breast made walking cumbersome, much less flying. After she felt confident managing the species differentials, she tried a hawk.

She saw a Harris Hawk at a zoo once and thought the bird was wise and fearsome. The way it looked at her, as if it knew what she was, and chastised her for hiding it. She had a connection with the creature. So, the hawk seemed like the next logical step in her Mage apprenticeship.

She successfully shifted into the predatory bird within a few hours of tiresome attempts. After another three days she was able to consistently change back and forth between her human and hawk form almost effortlessly, similar in ease as her wolf. But the true challenge came next. Learning to fly. That proved to be a painfully laborious process.

Heeding her aunt's warnings, she shifted into an adult hawk since she was already an adult. Pin feathers would have caught more air and cushioned her falls, but nothing worth having ever came easy, so she was determined to learn to fly despite the ill-prepared body.

It took about a week for Ava to lift herself and hover a few feet off the ground for about thirty seconds. After another two days of hovering with no progress she became bored and frustrated, so she concocted the idiotic idea of jumping from a high point and gliding down. She reasoned that gliding down wouldn't hurt. That's what birds did when they learned to fly. They just jumped from the nest.

Her body was lighter than her human counterpart so even if she did fall from tree-top height, other than being sore, she shouldn't get seriously injured. *Shouldn't,* being the operative word.

In squirrel form, Ava climbed the tallest tree she could find, and without hesitation, she plunged outward. Within a split second, she shifted into the hawk and fell in a flailing ungraceful bundle of feathers, knocking herself unconscious when she hit the ground.

When she awoke, she had equal amounts of determination and pain. She hit the ground three more times before she figured out how to get her wings coordinated enough to glide down. Luckily, each sequential fall had gotten softer, so she didn't knock herself out again. Now it was time to try flying.

The first few flights were a flapping erratic mess that sent her spiraling in many directions, crashing into trees, and eventually plummeting to the underbrush. Every time she shifted between forms, the damaged feathers were replaced brand new again, but the bruises remained in all forms, until her healing magic kicked in.

She threw herself from that tree about thirty more times over the course of several days before she finally took flight. Now she soared confidently through the sky like she was born to do it.

The lightweight feathers and bones navigated between the subtle wind currents naturally. The sky was an invisible ocean of billowing winds. Her hawk body instinctively knew how to handle the changes in pressure, flow, and intensity of the air currents, but her human brain struggled to coordinate it all. She learned through trial and error that the less she attempted to control her wings, the more stable her flight became.

Flying was an art that consisted of letting the air filter between the feathers to push or pull her wings and body in directions necessary to maintain a straight flight path. The only time she really needed to interject on the process was to change the course of travel. In most instances, very small adjustments effected profound change, except when ascending, which required maximal effort to climb the skies.

With the wind and her thoughts pushing her along, she flew

deeper into the forest beyond Tearnanelle's wall until it fell from sight behind her.

Mage training had stagnated. She could now conjure nearly any object she wanted, albeit they still needed some tweaking to get all the details perfect, but it was good enough, and she was getting bored.

Fight training was improving as well. Just as she'd hoped, no one took it easy on her. In fact, most people acted as if it was a challenge to see who could kick the Arukas's ass the fastest. Luckily for her, she excelled under pressure and quickly ascended the ranks. She'd gained most everyone's respect and made many friends which was weird.

Everyone wanted to get to know her, and a lot of the guys wanted to get to *know* her. She wasn't used to all the attention. It made her uncomfortable. She didn't like having so many connections to people. That meant more people who could let her down or potentially get killed because of her. So, she kept most of them at arm's length, preferring Cassie's company most of the time, even though she could be super annoying sometimes.

Her aunt was overly controlling. Ava was only allowed to conjure what her aunt wanted and fight the way her aunt instructed. Ava was ready for more challenges, but Serellina held her back. She was obsessed with perfecting every tiny detail of every single thing which was preventing Ava from learning new things. Ava had to get away for a while.

She hadn't intended on going over the wall, but once you're a bird and can fly, it's easy to slip right past. The sky was safe. Werewolves couldn't fly, so she didn't see the harm in surveying the land from this vantage point.

Morbid curiosity pulled her toward Tearnanoak, the kingdom where she was born. She'd only take a quick look, then fly straight back. Each day she flew a tiny bit further. She wasn't stupid. She wouldn't fly right into Tearnanoak and announce herself. She planned to fly around its perimeter and use her enhanced hawk vision to take a quick peek. That was all. It was perfectly safe.

Ava flapped her powerful wings, ascending as close to the clouds as she could before the air became thin, and her lungs and wings hurt from the effort. Shifting into her human form again, naked Ava floated just beneath the troposphere as if gravity and time didn't exist. The cool air suspended her body like she was sitting on an invisible hammock.

After a few seconds, gravitational forces sussed her out and started their inevitable push, then she fell, again. Ava threw her arms out, spread her legs, and tossed her head back. Her red and silver hair flapped behind her like a cape. She fell for several minutes, reveling in the moment. This must be what a dog feels like when he sticks his head out of a car window.

Prying her eyes open, she checked her rate of descent. She was close to the ground again, so she transformed back into the hawk, and leveled off. She'd repeated this stunt about three times now, and like a kid zipping down a water slide, it wasn't losing its entertainment value. She could see why people enjoyed skydiving. The adrenaline rush of free fall was intoxicating. She didn't like the idea of relying on a parachute, but relying on herself; that, she could do.

Movement on the ground caught her attention. Two people walked through a small clearing about a mile away. Ava's precision hawk vision narrowed in on them. Two adult men of large stature wearing plain grey T-shirts and denim jeans. They didn't dress like anyone in Tearnanelle. Anxiety pulsed through her.

Tipping a wing down, Ava circled back toward Tearnanelle. She couldn't see the wall anymore. The castle tree was but a tiny spec jutting into the clouds. In human form, that would be at least a day's walk back to the castle, perhaps more. In bird form, it was about an hour flight.

Tearnanelle was roughly two-hundred and fifty miles in diameter, although the magic stretched or shrunk the acreage circumstantially, so it was difficult to be certain exactly how big Tearnanelle, or any kingdom in Orlon, really was. And that didn't include undefined land between kingdoms which seemed to be a gray zone of wild that no one claimed.

The Twin Kingdoms borders, however, backed up to each other which made it easy for someone to cross the boundary without even knowing it. She did know for certain, though, that she was still in Tearnanelle, so these men were trespassing.

Ava circled back around and flew toward the trespassers. Tucking her wings against her body, she dove from the bright blue sky. The sun disappeared behind trees, and the autumn warmth gave way to cool shade. She glided silently over the heads of the oblivious men to a nearby tree and landed on a branch. Craning her neck in the direction where the two men were, she tried to get a better look, but multicolored leaves blocked her line of sight. She could make out their words though.

"Don't do it man," a gruff male voice came.

"Why? You don't think I can?" The second man's voice was slightly higher pitched than the first.

"I love you man but...." He trailed off, not finishing his sentence.

"But what?"

The two men came into full view about twenty feet below her. They were tall, at least six feet each, with well-defined muscles bulging out of their shirts. Ava caught a whiff of their scents, confirming her suspicions, werewolves. Her heart rate increased, and her feathers ruffled. Narrowing her eyes, she watched silently as they continued on, completely unaware of her presence.

Once they were too far away for Ava to make out their words, she left the safety of her perch. Perhaps it wasn't the wisest move, but her curiosity overcame her sensibility.

She glided to the ground and shifted into her human form right as her bare feet silently touched down. She still hadn't learned to imbue clothing, so she was completely naked which was embarrassingly inconvenient. Making a mental note to learn that next, she took a courageous breath and peered cautiously around the tree.

The two men bobbed in and out of view between the trees. They smelled of wet dog and mildew. No rotting smell like with Sarah and the other one on the beach a couple of months ago. She conjured a dagger and clutched it so tightly that her knuckles turned white.

Leaning out a little more, she tried to get a better view. If she didn't have an animalistic olfactory sense, she would never know they weren't normal men. There were no distinguishing characteristics that set them apart from a regular human.

They headed in the opposite direction of Tearnanelle, getting further away from her. Slowly, her heart rate calmed down. Whatever they were doing here didn't matter anymore. They were leaving which was exactly what she should do as well.

Ava backed up into something solid. She didn't remember a tree right there. Before she could turn around, an arm wrapped around her shoulders and a hand closed over her mouth. Another arm slithered around her waist, grabbed her dagger hand, and bent it back in a painfully unnatural position that forced her to release the blade.

Reaching her free arm over her head, she grabbed for the person, but they snatched her flailing arm and folded it against her torso with her other incapacitated arm. The attacker shoved her into the tree, pinning her painfully against it.

She kicked backward, but the person jabbed their knee into the back of her legs, effectively immobilizing her. She pushed against the tree in an attempt to dislodge them, but it was no use. They were stronger and larger than her. She couldn't gain any leverage.

She screamed and bit the hand covering her mouth. They growled and yanked her head back into their chest. Bent at this painful angle, she could see part of her attacker's face. Male, taller than her by at least half a foot, brown beard that tickled her forehead.

"Shhhhhhh." His warm breath caressed her ear, sending chills down her spine. Panic washed over her when his scent hit her. Pine needles during the autumn mixed with werewolf.

Struggling more frantically, she tried to dislodge him, but that only made him tighten his grip and press harder against her. Bark scratched her bare skin painfully and it was difficult to breathe passed so firmly against the tree.

Heat flushed through her cheeks, suddenly remembering she was completely naked. The embarrassment only lasted a moment. The feel of his body pressed against hers sent her mind spiraling into a panic. Stories of what werewolves did to other Mages flooded her mind, mixing with images of the Hanson's mangled bodies.

Taking shallow breaths, the only type she was able to accomplish in her compressed position, she tried to stay calm. Panic would only worsen the situation and ensure her demise.

The man locked eyes with her then his gaze drifted over naked chest, hovered there for a moment, then he looked toward the two men. They babbled on, completely unaware that she was being held captive by one of their brethren a few feet away.

One shout from him and she was doomed, but he kept quiet. The two men's steps and voices faded as they got further and further away until finally, after what seemed like an eternity, they were gone. Another minute or two passed before the man at her back eased his grip. She couldn't feel her fingers anymore and various points of her front side throbbed against the tree.

Squeezing her eyes closed, she tried to block it out. She had to keep her wits if she was going to survive. How the hell would she get out of this? Why hadn't he killed her yet? Why didn't he call for backup? A horrifying thought crossed her mind. He wanted her for himself. She'd die before she'd allow that to happen.

"I'm going to let you go. Don't do anything stupid, like scream, or your friends will come back, and they won't be as nice as me."

He removed his hand off her mouth. He'd held her so long that their sweat melded them together and it felt like peeling duct tape off her lips. *Gross.* The moment his arms fell away, she whirled on him. Rolling the pain from her neck, she conjured a sword, and took up a defensive pose. He backed away slowly, holding his hands up.

Her vision tilted as the blood rushed back into her limbs, leaving her lightheaded. Stumbling backward into the same damned tree that he'd pinned her against, she used it for support while waiting for her head to clear and her limbs to become something other than noodles.

She slashed the sword aimlessly, trying to look at least somewhat threatening.

Finally, the scene stabilized, her arms and legs cooperated, and her vision focused on him. He leaned against a tree, arms folded across his chest, and an amused expression over his face. Ignoring the pins and needles in her legs, she took a step toward him, holding the sword in a strike position, trying desperately to keep her hands from shaking.

"I'm no threat to you." His eyes dropped, then back up again, a smile tugged at his lips.

Shit. Remembering her nudity, she conjured a shield and shortened the sword to make it a one-handed weapon.

"Touch me again and I'll rip your heart out, and squash it between my fingers before you even know what hit you."

"That's dramatic, don't you think? Especially considering I just saved your life and all."

Confusion and rage boiled inside her. "You did not. I was in total control of the situation."

"Were you now? What was your plan? Shock them with your sexiness then slash them to pieces with that tiny dagger?" He cocked an eyebrow, accentuating his beautiful mocha-colored eyes that matched his luscious brown hair, beard, and mustache. The sleeves of his grey T-shirt protested against his biceps, and his blue jeans were filled out nicely as well.

Ava shook off the thoughts. What was wrong with her? She pointed her sword at him and backed up a step. He cocked his head. Not taking her eyes off him, she thought furiously about her options.

Attack him? No. That was a terrible idea. Physically, she was no match, and based on his stealth and quick movements from when he snuck up on her, she was outmatched in combat as well.

Her best chance was escape. Yes. Shift and fly. She bent her knees, preparing to push off.

"Aren't your arms getting tired from holding that sword and shield?"

They locked eyes, and her mind went blank.

"No. I could do this all day." The only response she could think of. How lame.

"Really? All day? Well, that sounds boring. If you're not going to attack me then why not just put it away?" He took a step toward her. She backed up equidistant. He stopped.

"Who says I'm not going to attack you? Why aren't you attacking me? Are you waiting for me to let my guard down? Because that's not going to happen."

"If I was, I certainly wouldn't tell you. I wouldn't be very smart if I told my victim my plans, would I?" That damned eyebrow ticked up again.

What was he playing at? "Who are you and why did you attack me then let me go?"

He sighed deeply. "I didn't attack you. I thought we already settled this. I stopped you from doing something really really stupid."

Her anger flared hotter. "I'm not stupid. I know what I'm doing."

"Yeah. You look like you do," He smirked.

The anger overpowered her senses and she lunged. Recalling everything she'd been taught over the years and more recently in Mage training, Ava swung her sword with lethal grace at his throat. It sank deep into the tree that he no longer stood beside.

Her legs went out from under her, and she hit the ground. Spears of pain shot through her spine, zapping the wind from her lungs. Her sword and shield vanished, and he came in to view, standing over her.

"That was rude," he said.

The fury rose again. Summoning every ounce of strength she could muster, she scrambled to her feet, assumed an offensive position, and reconjured her shield and sword. He backed up, but this time, he took up a defensive stance. Good. He was taking her seriously. Or was that good? Had he been toying with her up until now?

His hands up and feet spread apart to distribute his center of gravity, he sidestepped. She matched the move. A wide smile took over his face, making him devilishly handsome. Damn it. She'd knock that smug smile right off his stupid face.

Shrinking her sword to a dagger, she pelted it right between his eyes. It spun through the air straight and precise. He dodged it at the last moment, but she was prepared for that. When he turned back around her foot was waiting.

The impact sent a surge of pain through her leg. She'd never kicked someone with a bare foot before. His large body toppled to the ground. She limped over as fast as she could and pounced on him before he had a chance to recover. Conjuring another dagger, she pressed it firmly against his throat.

He stiffened and looked at her coolly.

She smiled triumphantly. She'd taken down a werewolf.

His lip was bleeding where she kicked him. Good. Hopefully it hurt.

With her heart pounding so wildly that he may actually hear it, she pondered her next move. What now? Kill him?

He squirmed a little and she pushed the blade deeper against his throat. He swallowed, and a drop of blood welled on his neck. Her eyes widened and her hand started to shake. Could she actually kill him?

Flashbacks of the Hansons filled her vision. Blood. So much blood, everywhere. Her family ripped apart before she had a chance to create a life with them. A storm of rage tore through her. He may not be the one who killed them, but they were all the same. Yes. She could kill him. Right before she pushed the blade into his throat he spoke.

"Well. This isn't how I envisioned you on top of me for the first time, but it's still pretty sexy." He smiled.

Ava froze. Was he hitting on her when she held a knife to his throat?

"Kill me or fuck me. Whichever one it is, get on with it, but just so you know, I prefer the second option." His eyes grazed hungrily over her body and that stupid eyebrow cocked up again.

She sucked in a breath and glanced down at herself. She knelt on her right leg, and her left knee was wedged between his legs. Her bare breasts dangled over his torso.

She realized her mistake too late. In one fluid movement he

slapped the dagger away from his neck, tossed her onto her back, pinned both of her arms above her head, and sat on top of her. Both of her legs were trapped between his. The entire weight of him pressed her into the ground, and a morbidly satisfied expression played across his face.

Rocks and sticks jabbed into her backside as she struggled against him, but it was futile. He was a boulder on top of a hummingbird.

Remembering her plan to shift and fly away, she gave the mental command. The ripple started, but pain exploded on the back of her head when he lifted her off the ground then slammed her down, stopping the transformation before it started.

"No, you don't. You can't get away that easily."

Everything was foggy and her head throbbed. She couldn't think straight. She shook her head, and the fog thinned, but it was replaced with panic. She was in trouble this time.

Fighting back the only way she could at the moment, she yelled. "You fucking bastard! I'll rip you apart! Get off me!" She tried to pull her arms free, she kicked, bucked, thrashed, and yelled, but nothing worked. He didn't budge.

"You're really turning me on now." He smiled wickedly.

Her response was more thrashing, bucking, and yelling obscenities.

"Wow. Such a foul mouth for such a beautiful woman." He laughed. He actually laughed at her.

Ava yelled until her voice was hoarse and thrashed until all her strength was depleted. Finally, when she had nothing left, she stopped fighting and just lay there panting, her bare chest rising and falling with every defeated breath. Sweat dripped down her neck. She was completely exhausted and exposed.

Fearing the worst, despair seeped into her. He could take her, and she wouldn't be able to stop him. Tears pooled in her eyes and her hands shook. Squeezing her eyes closed and clenching her hands into fists, she willed herself to stay calm. She wouldn't give him the satisfaction of seeing her fall apart. She would not be a helpless victim, and she wouldn't go down without a fight.

"Are you calm now?" he asked.

She glared at him, willing every ounce of anger into her eyes.

He licked the blood away from his lip that was already healed. "That was a good kick. You could have had me, but you didn't secure my arms. That was your first mistake."

What was he doing? Giving her fight lessons or rubbing it in her face?

"And you hesitated. That was your second mistake." His chocolate eyes connected with hers. "I'm curious why? You could've killed me the moment you conjured that blade, but you didn't. Why?"

She gave him another stern scowl but said nothing.

"Ooooohhhhh. You've never killed anyone."

Her eyes widened and she swallowed the mountain sized lump in her throat. How did he know? Was it that obvious?

He nodded. "Well, as much fun as this is, I do need to get going. Surely, they will have heard your profane screaming and they'll be coming back this way soon. If I am to lead them astray, you'll need to abandon your foolish attempts to attack me and just fly on away pretty little hawk."

Ava sucked in a shocked breath.

"Yes. I know what you are, but what I don't know is why you're here, so far from the safety of your walls." He leaned in closer, his face only inches from hers. The warmth of his breath wisped over her cheeks. His pine and autumn scent was.... surprisingly pleasant. The werewolf odor was faint, but nothing like the usual death and decay smell that she'd come to associate with his kind.

He brushed away a strand of hair from her face. She flinched from the touch. His beautiful brown eyes locked onto hers.

"Why are you here, pretty little hawk?"

Ava tore her gaze away.

"Hmmm. The silent treatment. That's better than all the names you called me a few minutes ago, I suppose." His body lifted from hers. He moved like a wraith. To be so bulky yet so agile was a conundrum.

She rolled onto her side. The pins and needles resurfaced with a vengeance. Staggering to her feet, she conjured a sword and shield again, then faced him, feigning a confidence that could rival a pack mule refusing to be led up a mountain.

He shook his head and laughed. "You don't give up do you?"

"What's your deal? Why aren't you trying to kill me, or kidnap me, or do.... other things?" she asked.

"Wow. As tempting as that is. I generally prefer my women willing." His features morphed into one of disgust. Reaching down to the hem of his shirt, he pulled it over his head. Perfectly honed muscles rippled with his every movement.

It wasn't like she hadn't been surrounded by gorgeous topless men for the last couple of months. She wasn't innocent to men either, but the way his muscles contracted and expanded was mesmerizing. She didn't see the shirt until it landed at her feet.

What the hell was she doing? She was acting like a prepubescent teenager. Gripping her shield and sword tighter, she grounded herself, and balanced on the balls of her feet. She couldn't lose focus again. She narrowed in on his face, refusing to look at his body.

"You can have it, so you don't feel so exposed." He pointed to the shirt.

She wouldn't look down. She wasn't falling for that trick.

"Call it a show of good faith. A gift to prove that I'm not trying to kill you, kidnap you, or do *other* things to you, as you put it." He placed a hand over his heart. Small brown hairs that matched the ones on his head grew on his chest. Damn it. He was ridiculously distracting.

Her heart hammered in her chest, making her dizzy. She could shift in half a heartbeat, and be in the air within a few seconds. But was that fast enough? He seemed capable of impossible speed and agility, but he had the upper hand several times already and didn't do anything.

She let the sword disappear. He watched but made no move.

Reaching down, she tentatively picked up the shirt, never taking her eyes off him. He stood so still someone could mistake him for a statue.

Her hand closed around the shirt, and his scent wafted from it. She bit down on her bottom lip, snatched up the garment, then quickly ducked behind a bush.

She pulled the shirt over her head and asked, "why aren't you trying to kill me or kidnap me? I thought that's what your kind did to Mages."

Once the shirt was on, she made sure she was completely covered, then she glanced around the tree. She gasped. He was gone.

Her heart raced as she surveyed the forest. She half expected him to fly out from a bush just to finally take her down, like it was some game he was playing all along. Stretching her senses as wide as possible, she heard nothing and saw no one, but she smelled him. His lingering pine and autumn scent clung to the shirt that swallowed her, falling to just above her knees.

Ava stood dumbfounded for a few more minutes, thinking he may come back. Mixed emotions of relief and disappointment filled her when he didn't. Would it be so bad if he came back?

That's stupidity talking. Shaking off the thought, she turned toward Tearnanelle. With her head swimming in questions and confusion, she made her way back.

By the time she reached the wall, the sun was setting, casting the land in an orange hue. The balmy autumn evening was stagnant and hot, but she felt nothing but relief when she flew back into the safety of Tearnanelle castle grounds, but she still couldn't shake the questions.

Why did he let her go? Was he telling the truth of trying to prevent her from being seen by the other two? If so, why? Why was he in Tearnanelle? Why didn't he try to take her, or kill her, or worse? And the most important question: *Who was he?*

CHAPTER 14
SIBYL
VIRLEM FIROQ-3/AUGUST 18TH

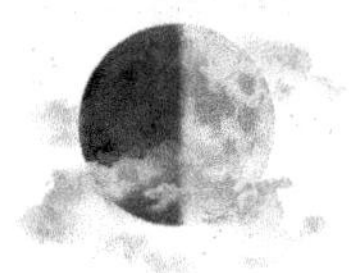

Sibyl's eyes were heavy but she couldn't sleep so she decided to read the Dragon book that was in her nightstand. Ava left a few hours ago after movie night ended, and Cassie fell asleep shortly after. Sibyl was nearly to the end of the book when commotion outside the door snagged her attention.

Laughter, voices, and stomping all grew louder, like dozens of people partied in the hallway. Sibyl was surprised the noise didn't disturbed Cassie.

Sibyl went to the door. Cracking it slightly, she peeked out. All four of her guards stood outside chatting. It was shift change, which meant it was midnight. Ambrose and Rokesh would leave, and Demetrius and Wilson would take over.

All around them, dozens of people in various states of drunkenness filtered by. Some stopped to chat with the guards. One woman was openly flirting with Wilson who put on his most dashing charm. Sibyl rolled her eyes and closed the door. There must be a party somewhere that just ended. Leaning against the door, she smiled broadly. An idea popped into her mind.

Grabbing her phone and the osmium stone off her nightstand, she got dressed and tip-toed to the next room which was now empty since Ava slept in the Arukas chambers. Sibyl opened that door just a crack. People still walked by.

Opening the door further, she poked her head out. Rokesh, Demetrius, and Wilson's backs were to her. Ambrose faced her general direction, but he was too immersed in conversation to notice her.

When a group of taller individuals walked by Sibyl ducked behind them and closed the door quietly. Sneaking between people, she headed in the opposite direction then scurried around a corner. Glancing back, she saw all four guards, completely unaware that their charge had evaded them.

Sibyl smiled triumphantly as she walked down the empty hallway and away from the constant surveillance. Finally, she had a moment to herself. For nearly two months the only privacy she had was in the bathroom and bedroom which barely counted as private since Cassie was in the room half the time.

Heading to the nearest exit, Sibyl went downstairs, through the dining hall, and stepped into the autumn night. A chilly wind blew in the smell of a storm, and heat lightning flashed above the clouds.

Walking leisurely through the gardens, Sibyl reveled in the tranquility of solitude. A few people meandered around the western gardens, but not nearly as many as during the day. No one gave her a second glance. Anonymity was wonderful.

She followed a pathway with fewer people until the smell of horses caught her attention. The stables were ahead and horses grazed in fields behind a fence. Hoisting herself onto the fence, she leaned over the top rail. One of the horses came over.

"Hey there." She rubbed his face, and he nuzzled her shoulder. Sibyl giggled when his whiskers tickled her cheek. Then he nibbled her fingers.

"Sorry. I didn't bring any treats. I wasn't expecting to meet a horse tonight."

He sniffed her hair.

"Don't take a bite. It's not hay."

A loud noise, like a stick snapping, spooked the horse. He bolted sideways and galloped off, tail in the air. Sibyl stared into the darkness where the noise came from but didn't see anything.

"Hello?"

The horse snorted loudly, and Sibyl's heart rate spiked. Putting a hand over her hip where the osmium stone was nestled securely in her pocket, she grasped it. A werewolf couldn't pop up when she had the stone, right? Wait, did Clark say that osmium wouldn't neutralize curses or dark magic? So, it couldn't protect her from werewolves? Her heart thundered louder.

"There's no werewolf. We're safe behind the walls. It was probably just a critter of some sort," Sibyl said to herself. The words helped to calm her nerves.

Thunder rumbled in the distance, wind rustled the trees, and branches rubbed on each other, making a creaking sound.

She laughed. The wind must have caused a branch to fall. The environment was similar to Earth so she imagined their wildlife would also be similar; bunnies, coyotes, opossums, raccoons, etc. It could have easily been a critter rustling around.

Feeling silly, she hopped off the railing, stuck earbuds in, shuffled the songs on her phone, then picked up a jog. She followed the path until she came to the last light post. Not caring that the night was becoming darker, she kept going. She passed green houses on her left and the castle towered behind her to her right. Numbness took over her legs. That's when she could really cover some ground. She picked up the pace and followed the path that was now barely visible.

She wouldn't describe herself as being afraid of the dark, but she also had no desire to venture out alone into unfamiliar woods at night, so she stuck to the path. The moon was nearly full, but it was blocked out by the storm clouds that started to leak. A few raindrops hit her face. She looked up to the sky and mis stepped.

Hitting the ground on her hands and knees, she slid to a stop in the gravel. Pain shot through her legs and hands. Her palms had few superficial scrapes but nothing major. Touching her knees, however, felt like razor blades being dragged across her skin. She got her cell phone and clicked on the flashlight. Yep. Her knees were covered in blood. That's just great. How would she explain that to everyone tomorrow? Guess she'd be wearing pants for a while. Running in the dark didn't seem like such a smart move now.

Pulling the ear buds out, she laid on the ground and stared up at the starless sky. A flash of heat lightning lit up behind the clouds.

She took the osmium from her pocket. Too bad it wasn't a chunk of gold that could heal her wounds. She rubbed its surface. The remedy she'd always wanted and the chains that tied her down all in one stupid object. Her resentment toward it had grown exponentially over the last several weeks which was stupid since it's an inanimate object. But she resented it, nonetheless. She was simultaneously thankful for it as well. If only she could take it with her, all her problems would be solved.

But, would they really though? The Aruka did have a point. Sibyl couldn't take it everywhere she went. It really would be best for her to control the magic without relying on drugs, manipulating her own mind, or some stupid rock. In an attempt to ignore the throbbing pain in her knees, she thought about all her failed attempts at staying conscious. What was she missing?

Maybe it was everyone watching her. She hated when all eyes were on her, and she was constantly being watched these days. Maybe she'd be able to control her mind better when no one was around, like now.

Setting the rock down, she limped to the perimeter of its nullifying magic. She'd learned the boundaries quite well over the last several weeks. There was a distinctive hum that grew more intense the closer she got to the limit. If she stepped through then tingling would erupt all over her body right before losing consciousness.

Putting a hand out, she pushed through the pressure and tingling consumed her hand. Pulling her hand back through, the tingling stopped instantly. She stuck a foot out, same result. Pulled it back, same result. She walked the perimeter of the magical forcefield, dragging a finger through it as if she hung her hand over the edge of a boat.

The rock was basically creating a forcefield around itself. She could create this same type of forcefield in her mind. But how? She needed to know what the pressure differential was made of so she could recreate it. Taking a deep breath, Sibyl stepped into the forcefield.

Something wet rubbed her face. It smelled pleasant, like cedarwood and earthy spices. Opening her eyes, the sky flashed in and out of vision as something rubbed over her face and eyes. Her head throbbed like a jackhammer pounded against her skull.

She pushed off whatever rubbed her face. Not rubbing, licking. A big brown dog with a spatula shaped tongue backed up and panted anxiously at her.

"What the hell?" She wiped the slobber off her face and sat up. Her knees screamed with pain. The osmium stone lay on the ground next to her, and the golden retriever type of dog whimpered beside her.

The memory hit her like a slap in the face. "Shit. I passed out. Did you bring this back?" She pointed at the rock.

The dog barked. She pet him between the ears. He leaned into it and groaned.

"Lucky you were here to fetch the rock, I guess, otherwise I'd still be laying there for someone to find me in the morning. That would be super embarrassing."

The dog cocked his head. She picked up the rock and her shoulders slumped. She didn't mean to go all the way through the forcefield. She was trying to stop within the pressure gradient to see if she could figure out what it was exactly. Another failed experiment. So much for that theory. She chucked the rock to the ground beside her.

"Guess I'm a failure when no one's watching too." A gust of wind blew in a cyclone of leaves, and with it came the heavy feeling of defeat.

"I can't do this. Everyone knows it. I know it. You'd know it too if you hung around long enough."

The dog gave her a curious expression.

An urge to throw the rock overtook her. She grabbed it and raised her arm. The dog stood up, tail wagging and body tense, he was fully prepared to fetch it if she threw it. How ironic would that be? She wouldn't even be able to rid herself of the stupid rock even if she wanted to. Lowering her arm, she rested her head on her knees for about a millisecond before the pain reminded her that she couldn't do that either.

Sibyl's frustration reached a boiling point, and she exploded. Stomping the ground with her feet, she scattered pebbles out in all directions. She screamed, then she threw bits of gravel into the night.

The dog backed up and whimpered.

"You picked the wrong person, you stupid ass holes!" she yelled at the sky. Tears welled in her eyes. With a few more stomps, and one last obscene shout for good measure, she threw herself onto the ground and curled into the fetal position. The disappointment, frustration, fear, and pain, all poured out. She sobbed so hard that her body undulated.

Another thunder vibrated the sky, but it was further away this time. The storm was skirting them. Maybe mother nature felt bad for her and decided to give her some space.

After the crying stopped, she was left with swollen eyes, scraped knees and palms, and a massively bruised ego. How did she get here? She had problems, for sure, but she was usually smart, collected, composed, and excellent at problem solving and working under pressure. But this challenge had truly defeated her.

She shouldn't have come here. She should have just taken her meds and continued on with her life like everyone told her to. She'd rather have Ativan than some stupid rock. That was the only way she'd be able to live her life, under the dulling effects of prescription drugs and meditation. It wasn't really that bad. Look at everything she'd accomplished with the medication.

"I give up. I'll just give the rock to the Aruka and then she'll let me go home."

The dog whined.

"What? You think I should stay?"

He perked up and barked once.

Sibyl laughed. "You'd be the only one who thinks that. You don't even know me." She huffed. "I don't even know me." Laying down on her back, she gazed at the sky again. The clouds followed the storm on its way out, and another round of heat lightning far away put in its last word for the night. She laid there until the throbbing her knees was almost unbearable.

"I should get back before my guards notice I'm gone."

The dog groaned.

"I don't like having guards either, but I don't want them getting in trouble if anyone finds out I snuck out. It's not their fault I'm a complete failure." Wiping away the last bit of tears, she pulled herself up and limped toward the castle. The dog trotted along beside her.

"You should go home. I doubt they'd let me keep a dog in the castle, besides I'm leaving soon, now that I won't be trying to be a Druid anymore, so go back to your family. I'm going back to mine."

A light breeze ruffled his fur, and he stared at her with an expression she could swear was chastising.

She bent over and patted him on the head. "Thanks for fetching the rock. You probably saved me from loads of embarrassment, and I don't know, maybe saved my life too." With one last pat she limped off. When she turned around, a few steps later, he was gone.

Once she was back inside, she went through the dining hall and perused the buffet of desserts. There was always a buffet of food available no matter the hour. The types of food changed depending on the time of day. Starting a few hours before sunrise to right before midday, the tables were filled with breakfast foods. Mid-day to early evening was soups, salads, sandwiches, and various assortments of nuts and berries. A few hours before sunset it switched to dinner foods which were much heavier meats, vegetables, and lots of breads and other carbs.

Sibyl's favorite, though, was when the moon first appeared in the sky. The buffet switched to sweets and desserts. She came down almost every night and feasted on the sugary delights the castle cooks offered up.

There was always someone in the kitchens and dining hall too. Guards switching shifts, people visiting for appeals or seeing the sights, occasionally the Aruka herself dined down here. It was never empty. But right now was an exception. It was completely empty. Probably because she was here much later than usual, or earlier depending on how you looked at it.

Grabbing a few chocolate chip cookies, she headed to her room. After a few minutes of walking, she realized she wasn't in the wing where her room was. She had somehow gotten turned around and couldn't find the stairwell to the guest rooms. She didn't recognize anything.

Hallways and offices were on the left and to the right was an elaborately decorated door. Curiosity got the best of her. She stuffed the last cookie into her mouth, pushed through the fancy door, and found herself in a room not nearly as large as the ball room but just as grand.

A fully stocked bar was on one wall, a fancy chandelier hung from the ceiling, an entire wall full of leather-bound books at the back, and a grand piano sat on a raised floor to her right.

"Wow. Fancy." Sibyl limped over to the piano and rubbed a hand down the beautiful grain. She'd taken piano lessons since the age of five. Music was another method of meditation, but one that didn't feel like a chore. Lifting the fallboard, she sat down and tested a few keys. The notes echoed beautifully in the room. It was tuned perfectly.

Recalling some songs she'd learned throughout the years, she started to play. After a couple of classical songs from Beethoven, Mozart, and others, she played some mainstream cover songs and a few Disney melodies. Playing and singing pushed out the remainder of the negative energy that bogged her down, and she could finally think clearly.

She felt rejuvenated, and ready for a challenge. She rolled her shoulders, popped her neck and knuckles, then set her hands down on the keys and started to play a song that won her first place in a recital several years ago. It was a difficult song that took her a long time to learn, but once Sibyl Murphy learned something, she never forgot it.

Her fingers moved instinctively across the keys. The music filled the room and swept her away. Closing her eyes, she let her hands chase the notes without thinking. The music flowed from the heart and time cease to exist. She didn't have any problems to face or challenges to overcome except for this one beautiful song.

When the song was over, she sat for a moment, enjoying the relaxing feeling of accomplishment. She'd forgotten what that felt like.

Someone clapped and Sibyl's heart jumped to her throat. She stood up so quickly that the bench fell over. Ambrose leaned casually against the doorway looking intimidatingly gorgeous. Smoothing her hair down and trying to cover her knees, she tried to cover up her insecurity with a smile. His face held an expression she'd never seen on him before.

"I'm sorry. I hope it's ok that I'm in here. I just saw the piano and wanted to play."

"Anyone who can play like that can use the room anytime they want as far as I'm concerned. That was really amazing." He picked up the bench and set it back right side up.

"Thank you. I didn't know anyone was listening. I don't usually play in front of people." She sat back down.

Ambrose took a seat next to her. He was so close that their knees brushed. The bench was too small to scoot over so she let her wounded knee rest against his.

"Well, I'm honored then. Where'd you learn to play like that?"

"I've taken lessons since I was a kid. I'm not that good. I fumbled with some of the lines I couldn't remember, and I hit a lot of wrong notes."

"Stop doing that."

"Doing what?"

"Talking down on yourself. You do that a lot, and you don't suck. You're really good actually."

She'd actually done something to impress him. Who knew it was possible? "Thanks." She chewed on her lip nervously.

"You want to try a new song?" he asked.

Sibyl gave him a questioning look. "I guess."

Opening the book that was on the music stand, he turned to a page then pointed. The notes and music cleft were the exact same as on Earth.

"It's the Tearnanelle Anthem." He hummed the tune.

Sibyl stared at him, disbelieving what she was hearing.

"What?"

"I never pictured you as the singing type."

He shrugged.

"And you're being nice to me. It's weird."

"You want me to be mean to you?"

"No. But you're usually kind of an ass."

"I am not. I just tell you when you're being dense, which is most of the time."

She laughed. "And there he is. The real Ambrose has returned."

"I'm not an ass. I'm direct."

"Fine. Let's compromise. You're a hard ass."

"I can live with that." He smiled.

"Wow. He smiles." She smiled too.

"Wow. So does she," he said in a mocking tone.

"Ok. Truce."

"Do you want to learn this song or not?"

"Yeah. Fine." She sat up tall and put her fingers on the piano keys.

"I know it by heart. Everyone in Tearnanelle does."

"I should definitely learn it then, since I've been here so long." Starting from the beginning, Sibyl played to his direction. Whenever she made a mistake, he slapped her hand playfully. A few times, when they hit a particularly difficult part, he got frustrated and impatient with her. She scolded him in response, but he kept directing and she followed along until they finally played the song all the way through. When the song concluded Sibyl smiled broadly. Ambrose's expression mirrored her own.

"I'm sorry I snuck out." She's not sure why she blurted it out, but she felt like she owed him an apology. "You guys aren't going to get in trouble, are you?"

"No." His expression was gentle. Nothing like the stern smug guard she'd gotten used to.

"That's good."

"Why did you sneak out?"

Sibyl sighed. "I just wanted some time alone."

"You were in your room alone."

"No, I wasn't. Cassie was there."

He leveled a reproachful look at her.

"I never consented to having an escort everywhere I go. In my world I'm a free woman to come and go as I please. I just needed some space to clear my head."

"And did you?"

"Yes. As a matter of fact, I did. I feel a lot better now."

He nodded.

"How'd you know I was gone? Aren't you off duty?" Checking her phone, it read 3:32am.

"Yes. I'm technically off duty." He cleared his throat and fidgeted a little. "I heard the music, so I investigated and I was surprised to find you, so I-"

"Eavesdropped," she finished.

"Something like that."

"Why aren't you sleeping like everyone else?" she asked.

"I could ask you the same thing."

"Fair point." She rubbed the back of her neck, trying to relieve some of the tension. "I couldn't sleep. I have a lot on my mind."

"You want to talk about it?" He asked hesitantly. He was being uncharacteristically nice at the moment, but that didn't mean she wanted to talk to him, did it?

Before she could answer herself, she pulled the rock from her pocket and asked, "do you know what this is?"

"The reason everyone hates you," he said, flatly.

"Ha ha. Very funny, smart ass. No. It's silence."

He furrowed his eyebrows.

"Most of my life, I've heard and felt things that I couldn't explain. At first, I thought it *was* other people's thoughts and stuff, but everyone told me that was impossible.

'You can't hear what other people are thinking, Sibyl. That's ridiculous,' she said in mocking tone.

"I believed them, though. How's that for irony?" She huffed a resentful laugh. "So, if it wasn't other people in my head then what was wrong with me?" She picked at a string on her shirt.

"The word schizophrenic was thrown around for a bit. That was scary, and that's when my parents put me in therapy."

"Therapy?"

"A healer for the mind, for crazy people."

His face fell.

"There was no other explanation for what was wrong with me, why I heard things that weren't real." She fidgeted uncomfortably. She wasn't sure why she was telling him these things. It was as if her mouth had a mind of its own.

"Sometimes it's so intense that my own thoughts get pushed to the side and I kind of disappear somewhere in my own head, like I'm trapped in a box with no doors or windows, with no escape. Then the panic sets in and I get pins and needles in my hands, and sometimes I pass out. You've seen that." She paused, trying to decide how much she wanted to say. Fuck it. She'd already told him most of it, so why not the rest.

"Then the visions started and that pretty much convinced everyone, convinced me, that I'm insane."

"You're not insane." There was no judgement or pity in his voice. He said it as if it was fact.

"Yeah right."

"Your biggest problem is you don't trust yourself, you have no confidence, and you're scared of the magic."

"Gee, is that all?" She huffed a fake laugh.

"I'm just saying that you should trust yourself and don't be scared of the magic."

"That's easy enough to say, but you've seen what it does to me. You have no idea what it's like, not knowing what's real and what's illusion. I can't control my own mind, and it's basically ruined my life. When I came here and found out I have some form of telepathy and empathy, I was so relieved. Then I got this rock." She held it between them.

"For the first time in my life, I was finally alone in my own head. I could hear myself think without interruption or confusion. And I realized that I have no idea who I am. I mean, I know who I am on a basic level, but I don't know how to handle my own thoughts and feelings. And I'm supposed to figure that out at the same time I'm supposed to somehow learn to control the magic. And there's always an audience to all my failures." She gestured to him.

"And you can somehow read my emotions based on what color my eyes are. Do you know how frustrating that is? I can hear and feel everyone so loudly, but I can barely hear myself. Yet you know what I'm feeling even when I don't." She shook her head.

"I don't always know what you're feeling. It's just a clue sometimes. A characteristic I've observed on occasion."

"I just want it all to go away and for me to have my thoughts to myself." She sighed. "That's why I needed to be alone. To know how it felt to have just me in my own head."

"How did it feel?"

"Peaceful. Lonely." She laughed. "Isn't that a bitch? I was kind of lonely. All these years I've been suffocated by everyone else in my head and when it was all finally gone, I was kind of lonely. Not that I want any of it back, of course. I just want the opportunity to get to know myself without outside influence or judgement."

He didn't take his eyes off her. Those eyes with hints of yellow flowing through beautiful brown that faded to red at the center. They were a magnet pulling her in.

Shaking off the trance, she said, "anyways. Sorry to unload on you."

"It's ok. I didn't know that you'd gone through all that. I understand now why you get so freaked out sometimes."

She wasn't sure what to say. She'd pretty much just dumped all her problems on him.

"You know what I learned about you tonight?" he said.

"That I'm a total nut bag?"

He laughed. "No. I've never seen you happy since you've been here, until you played the piano."

"Music is calming for me. It frees my mind of all the worry and stress."

"That's what's missing."

"What do you mean?"

"That feeling you get when you play. You're happy, calm, focused. You can learn to control the magic if you come at it like you do music. I can help if you want."

"That's different. I'm good at music. One of the only things I'm good at."

"Stop downing yourself. You're good at a lot of things."

"How would you know?"

"I've seen those test questions you study for and they're crazy hard."

"Thanks, but both of those things are the result of years of study and practice, and trust me, it wasn't always easy or happy."

"I didn't say it would be easy. I just mean that you can do it if your emotions are in the right place. You can learn to do anything if you just believe you can."

Sibyl scoffed. "What are you? An inspirational poster?"

"No. I'm just saying I know you can do this, and I can help if you want."

"You want to help me? You can barely stand me."

"That's not true."

"Uh. Huh." She rolled her eyes.

"Music is something I've practiced for over twenty years, and becoming a vet has taken me eight years. I only just found out about being a Druid less than two months ago. I don't have years to learn how to be a Druid, and even if I did, I don't want to. I have a life back home that I need to get back to."

"It won't take you that long. You just need a foundation of something to build on and then you'll whiz through the rest, just like you did with that song."

"A foundation of what exactly? It's intangible. It's literally called intangible magic. Nothing solid actually exists." She shook her head. "I'm done. I have this rock that will neutralize it, and at home, I have Ativan. That's all I need." She got up and headed to the door.

"Watch out," he yelled.

It was too late. She forgot that the piano was on a raised floor, and she stepped off the ledge, twisting her ankle. Crashing down on her knees, the pain was doubly bad this time. Wincing, she rolled to a sitting position. He offered a hand, but she waved it off. She needed to let the throbbing subside before she tried to stand.

"Your knees are bleeding again," he said.

"That's an old scrape."

"From when you fell outside?"

"Yeah."

He kneeled next to her, inspecting the wounds. "It's not deep. You scraped the first few layers of skin off. You just need some bandages and a gold poultice, and it'll heal up fine."

"Wait." Sibyl thought about his last statement. "What did you say?"

"Gold is a healing magic. If we put some on the wounds, they'll heal faster."

"No. Before that. How did you know I fell outside?"

He sighed and bowed his head.

Thoughts raced through her mind, recalling every step she'd taken that night. The branch snapping when she was with the horse. Was he following her? Then it hit her.

"The dog."

He didn't say anything. He didn't have to. The look on his face said it all.

A lump the size of China formed in her throat. She'd thrown a toddler sized temper tantrum, and called their Gods ass holes, and told him things that she'd never say to him otherwise. He licked her!

"You licked me!"

"I was trying to wake you up."

"You could have slapped me, like a normal human, as a human. But you were a dog, and you LICKED ME!"

"I couldn't shift because of the stupid rock. And slapping you is better?"

"YES! NO! I don't know, but you could have transformed back at any time. I said things. I..." She ugly cried for ten minutes in the fetal position on the ground.

Embarrassment hit her like a kick in the gut. Scrambling to her feet, she limped away. The pain in her ankle vying for the lead role in her torment.

"Sibyl wait." He grabbed her arm, pulling her to him. "I'm sorry. I didn't think about it when you passed out. I just acted. Then, it seemed like you needed to get some things out, so I just stood guard."

"I don't need your help."

"Yeah right." He winced after he said it, but it was too late to take it back now.

"What's that supposed to mean?" Her anger boiled to the surface, and she tried to yank her arm free.

His grip tightened, and his expression changed back to the stern, formal ass hole that she'd gotten used to. He leaned in so close that she could feel his breath on her face. He smelled just like she remembered the dog, cedarwood and earthy spices.

"If I wasn't there, you'd still be laying on the ground unconscious. What in Mokor were you thinking trying to do that when no one was around to help?"

"It's not your responsibility to manage what I do or don't do!"

"Yes, it is. It's my job, and you're making it harder than it has to be."

"Let me go!" She yanked her arm.

He released her.

She shoved him. He was barely pushed off balance in the slightest, which infuriated her even further. Fucking brute. "Go away!"

"Why? So, you can do something else really stupid?"

Sibyl slapped him. Sucking in a breath, she covered her mouth. She didn't mean to do that. The anger just lashed out uncontrollably. She was too shocked to move or speak. She'd never slapped anyone before, except her brother when they were kids. Her hand stung from the impact and his cheek was red.

His jaw ticked and a low growl rumbled from his throat.

Taking a deep breath, she steadied her nerves. "Leave me alone."

"I can't until you go back to your room." His voice was lethally level. He was definitely pissed. That was mildly satisfying.

"Fine." Doing her best not to limp, she walked out. Ambrose followed a healthy distance behind her. She turned down a hallway, then another, and another. Nothing looked familiar. She had no idea where she was.

"You don't know where you're going do you?" he asked.

"SHUT UP!" she snapped. Turning down another hallway, she sped up, her desperation to get away from him doubled. Another hallway, then another. Come on. At some point, statistically speaking, she had to find the damned stairwell.

Her knees hurt, her ankle throbbed, the humiliation made her nauseous. She needed this night to be over. She had no choice. Stopping, she folded her arms over her chest and asked, "which way is it?" Not bothering to turn around or look at him.

"Turn right at the next hall, then two lefts and you're back in the throne room. You should know your way from there I hope."

Ignoring the jab, she followed his directions, increasing the pace as fast as her injured body could go. Once she was in the throne room, she marched stiffly past the guards lining the hallways. She didn't acknowledge anyone despite their questioning glances. Once she was on her floor, she sped up even more, nearly running now.

Demetrius and Wilson jumped up when she came around the corner.

"What happened to you? How'd you get out here?" Wilson asked.

She ignored him and entered her room.

"What's going on?" Demetrius asked, right before she slammed the door in their faces.

Once on the other side, her legs gave out. Sliding to the floor, she heard them talking on the other side of the door, but she couldn't make out the words. Ambrose was, no doubt, telling them what happened and how pathetic she was.

"Hey dude. Are you ok?" Cassie asked.

She forgot Cassie was in the room. "I'm sorry. I didn't mean to wake you up. Go back to bed."

"What happened?" Cassie hopped out of bed and assessed Sibyl's wounds. She was too tired and defeated to reject the help, so Cassie dressed the wounds, gave her some ibuprofen, and got her in bed.

Once she was tucked under the covers, Cassie sat down next to her. "Do you want to talk about it?"

"No."

"OK. Well, when you're ready I'm here man." The lights blinked out then Cassie laid down next to Sibyl.

She wrapped an arm around Cassie's shoulders.

Cassie grasped her hand. "Good night."

"Thank you, Cassie. Good night." Sibyl was so tired, and the ibuprofen was already kicking in. It didn't take long for sleep to find her.

CHAPTER 15
AVA
VIRLEM WAXG-4/AUGUST 22ND

Ava stood outside the door to the Aruka's office listening to the conversation. Rubbing her fingers over the surface of the moonstone gem on her cuff, she drank in some of its magic and her hearing enhanced.

Each nation of Orlon had a magical gem that grew on their corresponding God tree. If a person was born of that nation, the magic ran through their blood like Ava's silver magic. But anyone could use silver for protection or to conjure items if they obtained a silver gem.

Moonstone was from the southeastern isle of Zurzura where it grew on the Angel Trumpet tree. Harpies, a weird bird-human hybrid type of creature with a short temper, oversaw that nation. Moonstone enhanced sight and hearing, enabled long distance communication, or granted the ability to leave spoken or written messages for one another.

Ava already learned how to use all the different gems in Orlon. Rubies provided heat, fire, and explosives. Diamonds provided light and temporary immobilization. Citrine modified the earth or structures, and built mountains and dams, or dug out valleys, etc. There were thirteen nations in Orlon, all offering different tangible properties like the moonstone she used now.

"We've interviewed everyone in the castle. No one knows anything about the patrol," Ziv said. The captain of the guard was similar in stature to most of the other Mage Guards. Large, muscled, dignified, and intimidating. The kind of man that demanded attention and authority every time he entered a room.

"How can you be sure no one is lying?" The Aruka asked.

"I can't be one hundred percent certain, but I feel very confident."

"Start questioning the guards."

"Are you sure that's a wise decision? People will think we don't trust our own guards. No one would be stupid enough to help Alyssium and the werewolves. They're all loyal. I'd stake my life on it."

"It's someone on the inside. Someone close to us who has access to sensitive information. I hate to think it as well, but until we find the traitor we can't trust anyone. No one can be excluded from questioning, even our most loyal guards. Question everyone."

"Yes Aruka."

"I have some leads I'm working on as well. Hopefully we'll find the culprit before we lose any more people. In the meantime, send notifiers out to the families and prepare a condolence stipend in honor of their service and sacrifice."

"Aruka." Footsteps sounded.

Quickly ducking around the corner of the hallway, Ava waited for Ziv to leave. Thankfully he went the other way. Leaning against the wall, Ava thought about what her aunt said. There was a spy in Tearnanelle, leaking information to the werewolves. What if that man in the woods was him? He certainly didn't behave like she'd expected of his kind. Maybe he was on his way back from spying when she ran into him.

"Ava! What are you doing?"

Her aunt's voice startled her. "Sorry. Hi. I was headed to your office for training. Are you ready?" Ava donned an innocent smile, hoping her aunt wouldn't question why she was hiding suspiciously around the corner.

"Yes. Let's go. Today you get to learn about the laws and how we handle anyone who violates them."

Ava's heart dropped. She wasn't interested in politics in the slightest. A bunch of rule breakers that she'd someday have to come up with fair punishments for. This was going to be a long, boring morning.

The first case was a dispute about a perceived unfair trade negotiation. Ten rubies for twenty opals. That did seem a bit lopsided. People selected specific stones and gems to wear, or use based on their magical needs, and what they could afford in trade. The actual value of a particular gem, stone, or other commodity relied heavily on supply and demand.

During certain times of the year or on another continent, some goods were harder to come by, making them more valuable. Many times, though, a gem's worth was very subjective and individualized to the seller or buyer. In those instances, the people relied on trust and fairness between negotiating parties to come to mutually fair terms.

Unfortunately, it also made it easy for people to get in disputes on what they each thought was fair. Ava didn't necessarily have a solution, but she wondered why someone didn't set a basic standard for what a particular gem was worth, in comparison to another, to remove a lot of the ambiguity.

Part of the Aruka or Aurko's responsibility was to settle disagreements in trade. That didn't mean they must oversee these disputes personally. Jameson, the commissioner of law, usually oversaw these types of things, but when there were a lot of cases, the duties were shared with the Aruka. Today, they were doing it just so Ava could learn.

Luckily, disputes didn't happen often because they were usually dealt with in a fairly severe manner. One or both parties always left displeased. Jameson assigned patrol guards to monitor the markets for any signs of problems or misconduct. This deterred most conflicts.

"I'm curious what anyone needs twenty opals for," the Aruka said.

Opal provided camouflage or invisibility. It was harvested from the willow God Tree that grew on tiny volcanic islands in the Kitezh oceans. Kappas were the guardians of Kitezh. They could render themselves invisible or take on any likeness they chose. It wasn't the same as shape shifting. They only created the illusion of change. Their normal appearance resembled a creepy desiccated turtle-looking creature.

"I'm trying to hide my flock of sheep," the man said. "Several of them have disappeared in the last few months. I've found the hollowed-out carcasses of a few, but most I've never seen again."

"Interesting. Do you have any ideas as to what's happening to your sheep?" The Aruka asked.

"None that make any sense."

"Indulge me."

"I think there's a creature eating them that isn't human and doesn't belong in Tearnanelle."

A creature? What does he mean by that?

"I do not think it's a fair trade to give only ten rubies for twenty opals," the Aruka stated.

"It's all I can afford. I was hoping he would see my plight and give me a deal."

The other man sneered. "This is business. I can't give my opals away just because you're in a difficult time."

"Mr. Sigra, keep your opals," the Aruka said. "There will be no trade. Mr. Fensy, you will be given fifty opals to protect your sheep, and I will send some Mage Guards to search the land around your farm for any suspicious activity. In the meantime, I'd appreciate it if you could report any findings to the guards. Is this something you can help us with?"

"Yes Ma'am. Certainly. Thank you for your generosity." The man smiled broadly. He bowed. Mr. Sigra wasn't nearly as happy with the outcome, but he lost nothing in the transaction so he simply frowned. They were both dismissed.

A woman in the corner wrote furiously on a clipboard. Their version of the court clerk, Ava presumed.

Two more people stepped forward for their dispute. After that, the next dispute came, then another, and another, and so the morning went. After the eleventh case, her aunt finally released her for the day. When Ava told her she was going to work on imbuing her clothes, her aunt said that it's best done in private since it can get a little awkward until it's mastered. That gave Ava the perfect excuse to do some spying of her own.

Following the trail from a few days prior, Ava arrived at the location where she met the werewolf man. She loped there in cheetah form to keep her clothes on. He wasn't there, but she was earlier in the day than last time. She decided to wait at a better vantage point so she could see him coming.

Removing her clothes, she folded them neatly, and laid them in a pile behind a tree. Underneath, she wore his shirt. She figured it may gain his trust to see her wearing it again. She removed that shirt as well then shifted into a squirrel and climbed a tree to one of its uppermost branches. Sitting there quietly, she waited.

She figured that if he was the spy then he must have a routine and normal path of travel going to and from Tearnanelle. She must have stumbled across it last time. So, all she had to do was wait and he'd come back by. That was the theory at least.

After an hour she got bored and decided to try a different tactic. She descended the tree, pulled on his shirt, and shifted into her maned wolf spirit animal. Shoving her snout into his shirt, she took in deep breaths, filling her nose and lungs with his pine needles in the autumn scent. Once his smell was committed to memory, the red lanky wolf padded quietly through the forest, following a stale scent trail.

Despite not being able to see the sky through the trees, she knew she was heading closer to Tearnanoak. It would be wise to turn around, but she'd made up her mind. She was going to be Aruka one day and there was a spy. It was her job to protect the kingdom, and she was better at that in the field, not in the courts. Pushing down the ball of apprehension, she pressed on.

After several miles, the scent converged with several others going in many different directions. The smell of werewolf was strong, but the woods were calm and quiet except for chirping birds and other forest sounds.

Ava sat on her haunches and stuck her nose in the air, sucking in a deep breath. His fresh strong smell hit her like a punch to the nose. He was here.

"Are you looking for me?"

She turned around so quickly that she tripped over her own feet and fell on her side. Scrambling to her feet, she lowered her head and growled at the man. With raised hackles, she curled her lips to show off her sharp teeth.

"Well, my feelings are hurt. You came all this way and that's the greeting I get?"

Ava sidestepped behind a bush and shifted to her human form. After ensuring his shirt fully covered everything necessary, she stepped out. This may be one of the dumbest ideas she ever had, but if it worked, she'd catch the spy.

"Well look at you. My shirt looks good on you. Better than on me, I think. Although I really like the outfit you wore last time. Especially when you were on top of me. If you want to do that again, I'm game." He smiled devilishly.

"Who are you?" she demanded.

"That's a pretty strong tone to carry, don't you think? Especially with how well we know each other."

"I don't know you at all."

"And yet, you're wearing my clothes." That eyebrow ticked up.

Mind games. He enjoyed toying with her. She wouldn't get flustered like she did last time. She checked her tone and asked politely, "who are you?"

"I'd think that you'd be a little nicer to me, considering I saved your life, gave you clothes, and was nice to you even after you shoved a knife to my throat." He ticked each point off with his fingers as he said it.

"You didn't save my life," Ava growled. "But, you didn't try to-"

"Kill you, kidnap you, or do *other things?*" he finished for her.

"Yeah."

He leaned against a tree, a smug expression on his face. Those caramel-colored eyes connected with hers.

"What do you want with me?" she asked, mimicking his flirtatious tone.

"I don't want anything from you. You're the one that keeps crossing my path."

"Oh my God. You're so frustrating. Can't you just answer a question seriously?"

He chuckled. "Fine, pretty little hawk, or should I say pretty wolf?" He tapped his chin playfully. "I will answer one question in exchange for one of my own." He cocked his head sideways.

"Fine. Who are you and what are you doing in Tearnanelle?" she asked.

"That's two questions. I only agreed to one, and as much as I enjoy you wearing my shirt, I have something for you." He reached behind a tree and presented a set of pants, a shirt, and some boots. He tossed them onto the ground at her feet.

"It's difficult to talk to you while I'm constantly distracted by your sexy body. I guessed at your size, but I'm pretty sure I got it right. I remember your body vividly." An arrogant smile tugged at his lips.

Ava blushed which frustrated her. She picked up the clothes and inspected them. They were normal clothing, no tricks or hidden elements to cause her harm.

"You know, most Mages remain fully clothed during their shifts. That leads me to believe that you like being naked around me. Is that the case?"

She didn't want to reveal that she hadn't figured out how to imbue her clothes yet, so she averted the answer with a question. "Are you going to run away again while I dress?"

"I didn't run away. I had somewhere to be." He turned around. The fact that he turned his back on her didn't go beyond her notice. He obviously didn't feel threatened, which infuriated her. She'd proven to be completely inadequate in self-defense. Something she planned to remedy soon.

Another baffling question rose to the forefront of her mind though. Why did he bring a change of clothes out here? Was he expecting to see her again?

Ava pulled the clothes on while watching his back from the corner of her eye. They smelled like him and fit surprisingly well. The pants were a little tight, but since they were soft leather, she was able to stretch the fabric over her form and button them up.

"The pants are too small," she said.

He turned back around and his brown eyes surveyed her now fully clothed body. "I disagree. They fit perfectly."

She rolled her eyes. "Now will you answer my questions?"

"I agreed to answer one for one." He walked away.

"Where are you going?"

"That's a question," he shouted over his shoulder. "Just walking. You coming?"

"That's a question too," she mumbled under her breath, and jogged to catch up with him.

"So, who are you?" she asked.

He cast a sideways glance at her. For a moment she didn't think he'd answer.

"My name is Redly." He marched on as if he was on a time sensitive mission.

Struggling to keep pace with him, she speed-walked through the underbrush. "Where are you going and why are you in such a hurry?"

"Nah uh. It's my turn."

Ava growled in frustration.

"Why are you out here, pretty little hawk?"

"I was just exploring."

He stopped so quickly she almost ran into his back.

"You have plenty of territory to explore within the walls of Tear-nanelle, do you not?" He chastised her like a parent scolding a child.

"It's none of your business where I go or don't go."

"No. It's not, but you should know better. You put yourself in unnecessary danger coming out here."

She bristled. "I can protect myself."

He laughed and resumed his previous path and pace again.

"What? You don't think I can protect myself? I got you to the ground before."

"Yes. You did. You got in a lucky kick because I underestimated you, which happens to be your *only* useful weapon."

"That's not my only weapon. I can conjure anything I can think of."

"And all those weapons are only as good as the person who wields them." He leveled a look at her that shut her up.

He had a point. She could conjure damn near anything, but she lacked the skills to use any of them effectively. Checking her temper, she asked, "how did you learn how to fight so well?"

"We're forced to fight," he replied, flatly, all the playful teasing left his voice.

"Who forces you?"

"Nope. It's my turn."

She growled. "Fine. What's your question?"

"Is that red wolf your spirit animal? Or is the hawk?"

"That's your question?"

"Yes. Is there something wrong with my question?"

"The wolf," she replied.

"Hm. I would have thought it was the hawk, but I did feel something different from you when you were the wolf. Very interesting."

"Why is that interesting?" she asked as they broke out of the forest into a small clearing. The midday sun shined bright and his mocha eyes gleamed mischievously.

"Is that your next question?" he asked.

She hesitated, looking around the meadow where butterflies and birds flitted around in the tall grass. When she finally met his gaze again, she said, "no. I have a different one. Will you teach me to fight like you do?"

His eyebrows shot to the sky. "That's a request, not a question."

"It's both." She squared her shoulders and stood tall.

He scratched his chin, pinching his short beard between his fingertips for a second. "I will, under one condition."

"What's that?"

He smiled broadly. His whole face rounded making him impossibly handsome. "You say please."

"Oh my God. Please." She put her hands on her hips and smirked at him.

"No. That was insincere. You need to mean it. I want to feel moved by your desire for me to help you."

"I don't need your help. I just want to add some of your offensive moves to my repertoire of fighting knowledge." *And extract information from you in the process.*

He burst out laughing.

She bit down on her tongue.

"That's some clever B.S. But B.S. none the less. Say please and mean it or I walk."

"Fine. I don't need your help. I'm leaving." Ava stormed across the meadow.

"Tearnanelle's that way." He pointed to her right about thirty degrees off from where she was heading.

"I know. This is a deer path. I was going to veer off once I hit the woods."

"Wow. You're really good at making up stories."

"You're so infuriating." She stomped in the direction he pointed.

"Why? Because I tell you all the ways you're wrong?"

"I'm not wrong. I just do things differently than you."

"Yeah. You do them wrong."

She stopped and glared at him.

"I thought you were leaving."

"Well, now I have to prove *you* wrong."

"Prove me wrong in what?"

"Let's fight. If I win, you apologize for insulting me. If you win, then I'll say please."

"You will say please in a sincere tone," he corrected.

"Yes," She ground out between clenched teeth.

"Ok. Deal." He stood in the middle of the meadow completely relaxed and lackadaisical.

"Well? Aren't you going to attack me like you did the other day?" she asked.

Now it was his turn to roll his eyes. "I didn't attack you." He tossed his head to the side and threw his arms in the air. "I-"

His words were cut off when Ava slammed into his side with a shield, knocking him off balance. He nearly fell to the ground. Nearly.

Catching himself at the last moment, he threw an arm out and pushed himself upright. Ava swiped at him with a large sword that she conjured, but he ducked under it at the last minute. Preparing another strike, she turned on him, but halted in mid swing when he wasn't there.

Out of her periphery, she saw him just in time to duck under his outstretched leg. Spinning in a circle, she thrust her own leg out and tripped him. He grabbed for her, but she backed up quickly, barely slipping through his fingers.

His large body stumbled to the ground, but instead of falling, he rolled with the movement and was back on his feet in a heartbeat. Once again, he was impossibly fast with reflexes that rivaled lightning. A ridiculously handsome mocking grin took over his face. Ava rolled her neck and shoulders preparing for her next attack.

"That was pretty good. Distracting me with your annoying yammering. Way to use your strengths to your advantage."

"I don't yammer," she spat. "How do you move so fast?"

"I channel my inner wolf. You don't have to be in your animal form to use their strengths and abilities."

Ava pondered that revolutionary detail, momentarily letting her guard down. Redly took full advantage of her mistake. An arm wrapped around her torso, and her legs were yanked out from under her all within a split second. She became weightless momentarily before slamming into the ground. Her sword vanished and her lungs spasmed from the impact.

He climbed on top of her, pinning her hands above her head just like he did before. Ava struggled against her paralyzed lungs. Trying not to panic, she waited for the spasms to pass.

"Calm down and breathe," he said, coolly.

After a few heartbeats, she sucked in a painful breath, and with the air came fury. "Is this the only way you can get a woman under you?" She spat between deep precious breaths.

He laughed then rolled off her and extended a hand to help her up. She slapped it away and tore herself from the ground as if it was made of lava.

They walked in a circle around one another. He sauntered arrogantly with a large smile plastered on his face. She seethed, her hands balling into tight fists at her sides.

"You get distracted too easily. Never take your eyes off your opponent, no matter what they do or say."

She stopped and stared at him.

He stopped and stared at her questioningly. "What? You wanted me to teach you to fight. That's my first advice for you."

She chewed on the inside of her bottom lip. "I didn't say please."

"Consider it a freebie."

Taking a deep breath, she said. "Redly."

As if he was blasted with a paralytic bolt, he froze. The smile dropped from his face.

"Will you *please* teach me how to fight like you do?"

He marched toward her with such fierce determination that Ava instinctively backed up. Her heart thundered as quickly as he advanced on her. What was he going to do? Did she piss him off or accidentally give away her plan?

She backed up until a tree stopped her retreat. Conjuring a dagger, she held it in front of her. He moved into her personal space so that their bodies were only inches from one another. The blade pressed against the same spot on his neck that it did last time.

Resting an arm beside her head, he bore those deep brown eyes into hers. He acted as if the knife at his neck didn't exist, fearlessly pushing into the blade. With his other hand, he reached for her.

She flinched and pushed the knife in harder.

His hand froze. Her eyes darted between his face, his hand, and her blade. Her heart beat at hyper speed as his hand resumed a slow approach for her.

He took a lock of her hair in his grasp. Confusion and fear fought within her. Should she stay or run away? Fight or give in? Push the blade deeper or release it? She wasn't sure which action to take, so she did nothing.

He gently rubbed the strands of her hair between his fingers. "I like when you say my name, Arukas."

Ava's heart fell out of her chest. She'd forgotten to bind her hair like her aunt instructed, again. Damn it. How stupid could she be?

"What are you talking about? I'm not the Arukas." She made an effort to laugh.

"You're not?" A challenging intensity burned behind his chocolate eyes.

"No. I dye my hair this color. It's fashionable on Earth to have streaks in your hair."

"So, the rumors are true? The lost Arukas has returned to Orlon."

Damn it. Another slip. She was a terrible spy. So far, she'd given him more information than she'd gotten from. He stepped away. She relaxed and released the dagger.

"I'm not the Arukas. I lived on Earth for a few years for a study abroad program."

"Study abroad program?" he asked sarcastically.

"It's so we can understand other worlds better." She feigned her best confident pose.

"Really? I've never heard of such a thing."

"Well, I bet you don't get out of Tearnanoak much do you?"

His face dropped. "Fine. I accept the possibility I'm wrong, however remote that may be. Do you want to resume fight training, *non-Arukas*?"

"Don't call me that."

"OK. What should I call you then? Pretty little hawk?" He arched that damned eyebrow that drove her crazy.

She considered telling him a fake name, but what was the point in that? They knew no one in common and there was no important information he could gain from knowing her name.

"Ava. My name is Ava."

He smiled and her damned heart skipped a beat. Her name on his lips sounded better than she cared to admit.

"Well, Ava. Let's begin training then." He waved an arm to the field behind him.

CHAPTER 16
SIBYL
LIBNYS WANG-1/SEPTEMBER 2ND

The music was so loud that Sibyl could barely hear herself think. The bluegrass sounds reminded her of Fleetwood Mac mixed with Twisted Pine. Cassie, Clark, and Ava sat next to her at the bar. Demetrius, Wilson, Rokesh, and Ambrose weren't far away, but only the latter two were on duty. Demetrius and Wilson were here to have fun.

Glancing at the two guards on duty, her eyes connected with Ambrose's typical arrogant expression. After sending him a stern scowl, she tore her gaze away.

"What's going on with you two?" Ava asked.

"Nothing. He's just an ass." Things between them were weird ever since their argument in the piano room. He'd reverted back to being a total prick all the time, arguing with her about every little thing she did or didn't do, and watching her so closely that he probably knew her cycle at this point. He also locked the door to the adjoining bedroom which was insulting on a whole other level.

Actually, he hadn't reverted back to his former arrogant self. He'd gotten worse. At least before, he was more of a judgmental bystander who rarely spoke. Now he couldn't keep his asinine comments to himself half the time.

He tried to micromanage her routine, demanding to know where she was going and what she was doing every second of every day. It also seemed to personally offend him that she stopped trying to make mental shields. He continually pestered her to keep working on it. She didn't understand why he was so invested in her magic. What difference did it make to him if she failed or succeeded as long as she wasn't a threat? He needed to back off.

Putting her hand up, Sibyl motioned for another drink. Once the bartender filled her glass, she took a sip. The beer in Tearnanelle tasted better than Earth, less bitter, more flavorful, and sweeter.

"Let me have some." Cassie took the drink and walked off with it. Rolling her eyes, Sibyl put her hand up again, but the bartender was on the other side now. It would be at least ten minutes before he returned. Great.

Sibyl swiveled around and surveyed the scene. The taproom was bursting at the seams with lively people, loud music, drinking, and bar games. People arm wrestled, played magical darts, cards, and of course, they danced. It smelled like a typical bar in the U.S.; beer, smoke, and sweat. But where there would be only humans in the bars on Earth, this establishment boasted a more diverse group of patrons.

A Kappa sat a few chairs down from them. He or she was the only one in the room who didn't appear to be having a good time, other than herself. Its skin was a leathery brown that resembled a lizard who'd laid out in the sun too long. On its back was a giant turtle shell with spikes. A stubby pointed tail poked out of its bottom, and water pooled in the bowl-shaped head.

Apparently whenever Kappas weren't submerged in water, they carried it on their head so they wouldn't dehydrate too much since they normally lived in water full time. Ava, Sibyl, and Cassie called them D.D.s, short for desiccated dinosaurs, until they learned what their actual name was.

Four elves sat at a table in the back corner. Their entire bodies were a weird shade of eggshell yellow, including the hair and ears which stuck straight off the top of their heads about five to six inches. The only part of their body with any pigment were their deep black eyes. Even their fingernails lacked pigment of any kind.

Elves were from Nysanok, on the western continent. They harvested Emerald from the Quaking Aspen God Trees. Everyone called it Em for short. Em distorted reality. It was used in battle as gas bombs to disorient the enemy, but it was mainly used recreationally to get high.

One of the Elves smiled at her and tipped its glass. Sibyl dipped her head and smiled back.

Pixies, Fairies, and other creatures the size of small birds flitted around above their heads. Shelves built into the walls above the doors and window frames held miniature chairs and tables. Many of the tiny creatures sat and drank while others danced within ceiling rafters flickering like lightning bugs. The dim lighting of the room and the fairies winking in and out created a mesmerizing pseudo-night sky.

Everyone was having fun for Sibyl's and Ava's birthdays. Everyone, that is, except Sibyl. She didn't want to be here. She should be at home, celebrating with her friends and family. She'd gone to the Aruka and offered to give up the stone in exchange for a bubble, but she let the Aruka manipulate her into staying until Dragon training. Sibyl was such a terrible push over sometimes and it drove her crazy that she couldn't stand up for herself better.

Ava and Cassie were thrilled she stayed. So were Clark and Demetrius, even Wilson and Rokesh seemed pleased that she was sticking around. But Ambrose acted as if her presence was a personal affront.

Her gaze shifted to him again. They locked eyes. His expression was apologetic. What the hell? That was a new one. Maybe he felt bad for invading her privacy or he sympathized with her desire to go home. Either way, she didn't care. She still hated him. Sibyl flipped him off. His jaw ticked and he looked away.

"Ok. I don't know what's going on, but obviously something happened between you two," Ava said.

"It doesn't matter," Sibyl said, glaring at the side of his head. At least he hadn't told anyone about her melt down in the gardens when she snuck out. She thought for sure he would have gossiped that shit all over the kingdom, but so far not a soul knew. She was grateful for that little bit of mercy at least. Maybe he did have some compassion. A teeny tiny little speck of it at least.

"Do you know what his spirit animal is?" Sibyl asked.

"A grizzly bear. I've seen him in practice. He's a beast."

Of course he is. "Really? Not a dog?" Sibyl asked.

"No. Definitely a bear. Why?"

"But you guys can change into whatever you want. It doesn't have to be only your spirit animal, right?"

"Yeah. Any skilled Mage can have multiple animals. I have three now." Ava smiled proudly.

"I guess he's pretty skilled then," Sibyl said, ignoring Ava's boast.

Ava sighed, an exasperated expression pulling her face down.

"Sorry. Good job on that. I know it's challenging and fun."

Ava set her glass down and faced Sibyl. "Seriously Sibyl. I know you want to go home, but it's only a few more weeks before the Dragons get here. And, come on. Don't you want to meet a real-life Dragon? How awesome is that going to be?"

Sibyl sighed. It would be cool to meet a Dragon. She'd researched a lot about them, and she read the entire book in her room. They're telepathic and empathic, just like she was. Other than the Gods and Druids, Dragons have the largest intangible magic spectrum of any other creature. If anyone could help her, it was probably them. They may have the answer to learning to live without the rock and Ativan.

That's ultimately why she gave in to the Aruka's request to stay, but it still pissed her off. She could have gone home then come back, but the Aruka didn't want to waste precious bubbles just for home-sickness.

"Ok. I'm back." Cassie handed Sibyl the drink she'd taken.

"Thanks for giving me *my* drink back." Sibyl took the cup and chugged it all down in one gulp.

"Jeeze dude. Slow down. You're going to get a head rush," Cassie said.

"I didn't want you to take it again." Sibyl set the glass down on the bar. The hairs on the back of her neck stood up. Throwing a quick glance over her shoulder, she caught him staring at her so intently that she was overcome by a surge of self-consciousness.

She smoothed her hair down, patted her front to make sure her dress wasn't tucked up on accident, and her boobs were secure in the low-cut corset. All was good. Whatever was up his ass, he could get over it.

"Ok. You're being a Debbie Downer. Let's dance." Cassie grabbed Ava's and Sibyl's hands, dragging them to the dance floor. On their way by Clark, Cassie grabbed her too, ripping her from a conversation with Demetrius.

The four women formed a circle and started dancing. Sibyl was stiff and unmoving at first, but after a few minutes the music ensnared her, and she started to feel happier and lighter. A ripple of calm washed over her, and all her stress and anger slowly faded away.

Throwing her arms up, she spun around. Everything blurred, the musicians glowed, the instruments pulsed in time with the beat, and the music morphed into an entity of its own. Melodious notes snaked through the crowd like fog rolling through a forest, serpentining through everyone's legs. The floor fell away and Sibyl floated into the twinkling pixies.

She grabbed Cassie's hand on her left and Ava's hand on the right, pulling them with her. Swimming through a pool of musical butterflies, Sibyl's skin tingled when their wings brushed against her. Radiant scribbles spiraled along her arms and legs where the music touched her.

Cassie pulled Sibyl in for a hug. Sibyl wrapped her arms around her friend and levitated.

"I can feel my blood flowing. I can see it. Does that mean I have translucent skin?" Sibyl stared at her hands, infatuated by the rivers of blood flowing within them.

She laughed. She was so happy. Everyone around her laughed too. Waves of laughter crashed into each of them creating a whirlpool of happiness. When the laughter echoes hit Sibyl, she laughed even harder. Each laughter ripple emitted, created another. Maybe that's why people said laughter was contagious.

The music stopped and the floor returned. Her tongue stuck to the roof of her mouth like tacky sandpaper. She needed a drink. Making her way to the bar, she got turned around in the crowd of people and creatures. Where was the bar? Someone tugged on her arm. Turning a full one-eighty, she found herself face to face with Ambrose.

"Sibyl?" His voice was thunder that rattled her brain. "I think you've had enough to drink for one night." Of course he wants to tell her what to do.

"I'll drink however much I want to," she retorted. The room jolted sideways. His hands gripped her shoulders, holding her upright.

"I think we should get you home," he said.

"Is that what you think?" She laughed. "You know what I think? I think you were watching me. I saw you."

"Yeah, because that's my job."

"No. You want to dance with me because I've got the sexy moves." Sibyl did her best sexy drop and fell on her butt at his feet. He pulled her up by the arms.

"Don't flatter yourself. You dance like a deranged duck."

"So grumpy. Mr. Grumpy pants." Sibyl poked her lip out making a pout face. She grabbed his lips and pushed them into a pout too.

He swatted her hands away.

"Grumpy. Grumpy. Grumpy," she giggled.

Someone bumped into her shoulder and the room dipped sideways again. She leaned against him, watching people zip by her, as if they were swept away on a river. One by one they all zoomed past until all the people were gone and the wall approached. If the room didn't stop moving soon the wall would crash into her. She backed up and fell straight into a chair.

The room reappeared and people danced around as if they hadn't just been swept away. How did that happen? Where'd they go and how'd they return so quickly? The walls expanded and contracted with every beat of the music.

"The building is dancing. It's happy too." She wanted to dance more. She got up to walk to the dance floor, but chains wrapped around her wrists, preventing her from leaving that spot. "What's going on? Why are my arms chained?"

Ava stepped in front of her. "Sibyl?" She grabbed Sibyl's chin.

Ava's touch ignited a burst of pleasant sensations. Sibyl leaned into the warm softness of her hand. They melted into each other, becoming one being.

"Jesus, how much did you drink?" Ava's voice again.

"What are you talking about?" Sibyl tried to concentrate, but it was so difficult. The music demanded her full attention.

She looked longingly at the dance floor. Plumes of black smoke swirled around the room between the flying pixies in the rafters. A dark cloud fell on the heads of the dancing people, but they didn't see it! They jumped and hopped around like drunken hyenas, throwing their hands in the air, spinning around, and flailing their heads. The floor buckled beneath them. The whole room was going to collapse. She had to warn them.

She tried to go to the possessed people, but she couldn't move. Her hands were tied to the chair. "What the hell?" Desperation seized her. The blanket of dark smoke descended on the dancing people, and her arms disappeared.

"Somebody help!" She looked around frantically, but she was alone. "Hello!"

Faint twinkles peeked through the darkness, and muffled voices penetrated through the depths of nothing.

"Sibyl, you're fine. You're just tripping. Ambrose is going to take you home," Ava said.

What!? No way in hell would she go anywhere with that asshat. Sibyl tried to get up but there was no floor, nor was there a chair anymore. She wasn't sitting or standing. She floated in absolute darkness. She couldn't even see her body.

It became hard to breathe. Something obstructed the airflow over her mouth and nose. Unlike when she'd traveled through the bubble when breathing wasn't necessary, this time her lungs demanded air.

Pain ripped through her chest as she struggled to pull in air, but found none. What was happening? She went rigid as the airless atmosphere suffocated her. Her body spasmed then a warm calmness enveloped her.

The emptiness held her in a strong embrace. Time didn't exist. It was peaceful. She could stay like this forever. It would be so easy to just fall asleep in the arms of emptiness and never wake up.

Air kissed her lips filling her with life, passion, and purpose. There was so much she wanted to do still. She wasn't ready for the end yet. She needed to get back to the real world now.

Pushing away the blanket of darkness, she forced her eyes open. Stars danced in a black velvet sky. She was suspended in space still, but now she could see. Trees skipped merrily by, waving branched hands at her. Sibyl waved back.

"Who are you waving at?" Ambrose's face was inches from hers. Her forehead brushed his stubbled jaw line. He had a good jawline. What makes a good jawline anyways? His was good, but why? And why was it so close?

"Why are you so close to me?"

"I'm carrying you home." His voice dripped with irritation and his eyes remained forward.

Following his line of sight, Sibyl recognized the road back to the castle then she looked back at him and noted that her body wasn't suspended in space like she originally thought. She was in his arms, her head on his chest.

She dove from him. He nearly dropped her in her clumsy effort to get away. The world stood straight up making her momentarily nauseous. She swayed but something strong wrapped around her waist. Tracing the arm back to its point of origin, she met Ambrose's gaze.

"Get off me." She pushed him. The ground rose up and punched her on the side of the head, hard.

"Ouch!" Sibyl slapped the dirt, causing another burst of pain in her hand.

His hands were on her again. Rolling to her back, she kicked out.

"Stop pushing me!" she yelled at him.

"I'm not. I'm trying to help you!" he yelled even louder. Emotions exuding from him like lava spilling over the lip of a volcano. Frustration, anger, resentment, and something weird, like guilt.

Idiot. You're so damned stubborn, he said.

"Fuck you!"

His red-brown eyes widened.

She kicked at him again, her right foot connected with his leg that time.

"Ouch." Hopping back a safe distance, he rubbed his shin and growled.

She's had a bit too much to drink.

Excellent, there's Em at this party. I can't wait!

He deserved that. He's such a prick.

"Yes, he is," Sibyl shouted.

"Who are you talking to?" Ambrose asked.

A group of women walked by heading toward the tavern. Locating a woman with long black wavy hair and an elegant dress that flattered her skinny frame, Sibyl pointed. "She said you're a prick."

The woman's dark eyes widened when Ambrose spotted her.

"Nice. Leabella."

"I didn't say anything." Putting a hand on her chest, the woman named Leabella feigned innocence.

"Yes, you did. I heard you, and it's true. He is a prick." Sibyl glared at Ambrose, kicking her legs again when he stepped too close for her liking. Leabella took the opportunity while he was distracted to walk away hastily.

Stupid Druid, now my thoughts aren't even safe anymore. The woman's irritation and embarrassment poured off her in waves, but underneath that, was an ocean of longing. Her physical and emotional desires reached toward Ambrose. She shot a few backwards glances at him, sadness in her eyes and heart.

"She has feelings for you," Sibyl said, sitting up.

"Not anymore, she doesn't. That's my ex."

"Well, she still wants you."

"That's a shame for her because it's not going to happen. She's a crazy bitch, just like you." His tone was mocking.

"Don't call me that! I'm not crazy!" Ire burned through Sibyl.

"Says the woman sitting in a mud puddle flailing around like a fish out of water."

Sibyl looked down at herself. Unfortunately, he was right. She was currently ass deep in a mud puddle in the middle of the road. The beautiful lilac dress she borrowed from Clark was completely ruined. People walked past, giving her a wide berth. Some tried to cover their smiles while others sneered.

Wow. Some people can't handle their liquor.

Poor thing. I hope she finds her way home safely.

Damn he's hot. He can do so much better than her.

Sibyl's cheeks flushed. She managed to get to her feet but nearly fell again. The world steadied. Not caring that it was Ambrose supporting her, she grabbed onto him. It was that or fall again. This was the least humiliating option at least.

You better not try to kick me again or I'm letting your ass fall.

"I won't kick you," she snapped.

"Thanks," he spat. The pair hobbled toward the castle in silence. Well mostly silence. He continued to exude frustration rivaled only by her own. Other people passed by, and she heard what they said but no one's mouth moved. Craning her neck at a group that walked by, she zeroed in on them. Their desires, emotions, thoughts, all of it cascaded into her mind in a jumble of confusion.

"I can hear their thoughts."

Fishing in her pockets, she searched for the familiar grey rock. "Where's the osmium stone?" Panic formed in the pit of her stomach as she frantically patted herself down like a cop patting down a criminal. The stone wasn't there.

"No. No. No. No." She looked back toward the taproom. They were already more than a mile from it. "I need to find it. I must have dropped it."

Ambrose grabbed her shoulders. "Sibyl, look at me."

She obeyed without thinking.

"You don't have the stone, and you haven't passed out." He raised his eyebrows.

She forced herself to think. He was right. She was awake, in Orlon, without the stone, and her mind wasn't overwhelmed.

"How? I'm not even trying."

"Probably the Em. Maybe it helps you or something."

"Em?"

"It's a mind-altering substance-"

"I know what it is. I didn't take any."

"There was more than alcohol in that drink," he said, very matter of factly.

Sibyl thought furiously, but her head was clouded. She couldn't remember much of the night. She remembered Cassie taking her drink then coming back a few minutes later.

"Cassie," Sibyl growled. She also remembered Cassie rifling through her pockets when she was dancing with her. "I'm going to kill her. Where is she?"

"She left before you did. I assume she went back to the room."

Sibyl stormed off in the direction of the castle. Ambrose on her heels.

"The Em is wearing off. You're walking straight again."

"How long do the effects usually last?"

"It depends on how much you take. Based on how you behaved, I'd say you took a lot. Most people who take that much would probably be out for days."

"How long was I out?"

"Maybe thirty minutes."

"How is that possible?"

"I have no idea." His face was unreadable, as usual, but she didn't need him to say anything. She felt it all. His anger was gone, replaced with sadness, curiosity, confusion, affection, and guilt. He felt bad for how he'd treated her.

"Thank you," she said.

He didn't reply, but he didn't need to. She felt everything. The one thing that surprised her the most was his concern. He wanted to make sure she got back to her room. Not just because it was his job, but because he wanted to ensure she was safe.

The lights of the small town faded behind them as the lights from the castle came into view in front of them. The God Tree stood tall, a mountain blocking out the black sky. The path between the castle grounds and town was never left in complete darkness, but they were right in the middle, at the darkest point of the journey, and they were alone.

Sibyl gazed at the stars. "Do you guys have the big dipper here?"

"What's that?"

"An astrological formation of stars."

"No. We don't have that, but we do have a constellation for each kingdom and the Empyrean Star."

"Really? That's cool. Can we see any?"

"Tearnanelle and Tearnanoak are the twins." He pointed almost directly above them to a group of stars that made what looked like a box.

"Silvermar is to the east. Aldwinelle north of Silvermar and Lemalome north of us that way." He pointed out each of them. Sibyl didn't see any special formations of stars, but she would take his word.

"You can't see the rest from here, but there's Nysanok, Annwin, Sarganar, and Baiyanelle to the west. Kunlan to the northwest, and Zurzura to the south of us in the Lemuria Sea and the Kitezh Ocean beyond the western continent. Twelve constellations in all, each representing the thirteen nations. Our nations are the only twin Goddesses."

Sibyl stopped dead in her tracks, which caused Ambrose to a stop.

"Wait. You guys have twelve zodiacs?"

"Yes. It's in relation to the sun and moon which affects the God Trees."

Sibyl's mouth dropped open.

"What?"

"We have twelve zodiacs on Earth too. I don't really know much about astrology, but I know it also has to do with the sun and moon's path. We also have one constellation that is twins. We call them the Gemini. That must be why your Mage Guard tattoos are the Gemini symbol. It makes so much sense now."

Ambrose nodded, seemingly unimpressed, and resumed walking.

"Don't you find that interesting? Our worlds have the twelve zodiacs in common?"

"All the planets in the living realm are extensions of Orlon's magic. Empyrean created the God Trees. The God Trees created Orlon, and their roots extend far beyond Orlon to create all the living worlds. We're taught that in our elementary learning."

She picked up the pace, wanting to get back to her room to kill Cassie as soon as possible. "Why do you call it the living realm? You're alive too."

"The magic gets thinner the farther away from Empyrean that you get. The magic is so thin in the living realm that the only gift the Gods are able to give is life itself, which of course, we could argue, is the best gift."

"What's Empyrean and the Empyrean Star?"

"Empyrean is the source of all life and magic. When we die, we all return to Empyrean unless you're evil then you go to Mokor to burn and be tortured eternally."

"Like Heaven and Hell. We say that when good people die, they go to Heaven to live in eternal grace. When bad people die, they go to hell where they're cursed to live in eternal damnation."

"Yeah, basically. I guess your world has different names for them. The Empyrean Star is there." He pointed. She followed the direction where he indicated and saw a really bright star shining.

"That's also how we keep track of time at night. By the placement of the Empyrean Star."

"That must be like our North Star on Earth."

"I guess so," he said, half paying attention. His head swiveled up and down the road and into the woods. An apprehensive expression strained his features.

"What's wrong?"

He didn't answer. Her senses became clearer as the Em wore off. Taking in a deep breath, the night air filled her lungs. It smelled so refreshing...Or did it? Taking another breath, she recoiled.

"What's that smell?" She covered her nose. "It smells like something died and it's rotting."

"Yeah. I smell it too. I have ever since...." He didn't finish the sentence. He stared at her with furrowed eyebrows.

A noise sounded in the woods to their left. His head snapped toward the sound, a predator narrowing in on its prey. Ambrose shoved her behind him and conjured a giant silver sword.

"What's going on?" she asked.

"Shhh." It wasn't a request. She snapped her mouth shut and stared at the back of his head. His Mage Guard tattoo glowed faintly. The smell was overpowering, and it was worse being this close to him. She gagged. What in the hell was it? It reminded her of the werewolf that attacked Ava on the beach.

"Let's move." He pushed her toward the castle, not taking his eyes from the woods.

A rush of voices and emotions swept over her. There were too many voices speaking simultaneously. They melted together into unintelligible gibberish. Her fingers tingled with hundreds of unfiltered emotions seeping into every pore. The tingling sensation coursed through her hands and up her arms, and it became difficult to breathe when it moved into her chest.

Her knees buckled. She grabbed the back of his shirt to keep from falling.

He caught her with his free arm without turning around. "What are you doing?" He sounded annoyed.

"I need the osmium stone. I think I'm going to pass out." Leaning on him for support, she tried to stay standing, but she was losing the battle.

"Shit." Ambrose turned around and grabbed her shoulders. Her knees gave out completely, and she fell. His arms wrapped around her waist, holding her up, their bodies pressed together intimately. If she was strong enough to stand on her own, she'd probably push him off her, but at the moment she was grateful for the help.

"Damn it. Look at me Sibyl."

She locked eyes with his beautiful cognac ones.

"Picture a wall like the one surrounding Tearnanelle and create one in your mind." His eyes darted around wildly then back to her, an urgency was hidden behind his words. Maybe having him this close wasn't so terrible. It felt good to be held. She leaned against him, and the periphery closed in around her.

"Come on. Sibyl, stay awake. I need you to stay awake."

"Ok." Her words came out breathlessly as she struggled to breathe under the pressure. The voices crescendoed, and pain surged into her head like she was punched between the eyes. Squeezing her eyes shut, she begged it to stop. Her head became too heavy to hold up anymore, so she laid it on his chest.

"Listen to my voice. Just me. Put a wall around us, Sibyl. A wall so strong that nothing can get past it, not even a whisper." He sounded desperate and distant. Something warm caressed her cheek. She opened her eyes. His hand was on her face.

"Don't lick me again." She tried to laugh but she was too weak.

"You got jokes." He huffed a desperate laugh. "Good. Then you're awake enough to build a wall. You can do this, Sibyl. You *need* to do this right now."

"It hurts." Her voice cracked.

"It won't if you block it out."

Ok. Concentrating, she tried to picture a wall. The darkness closed in. An earthquake shook her head.

"No. Wake up damn it. Build a Gods damned wall, Sibyl!" he yelled, but his voice was distant. Fighting against the heaviness of the world, she heard his warped voice, but she couldn't make out the words anymore. She was supposed to do something. What was it?

Build a wall. That's right. Something solid held her, giving her strength. Holding onto that strength, she focused on her task. A foundation of imaginary bricks appeared around her. She touched one of the bricks. It felt real. Mimicking what her therapist taught her about grounding, she rubbed her hand along the edge of the brick. *Real.*

Another layer of brick fell over the first one. A sharp spear of pain throbbed inside her head. She hissed and buckled over.

A voice echoed inside the ankle high wall, but she couldn't make out the words. Someone was here with her but in another dimension.

What was I doing? She tried to remember. A small speed bump-like structure surrounded her. An unfinished wall. That's right. She was building that wall. She added a few more layers of bricks until it was waist high. Walking alongside it, she dragged a finger across the rough surface, adding another layer of brick as she passed by. Then a few more layers. It was as tall as she was now.

"Sibyl?"

She recognized his voice. It was time to go back. She could bring the wall with her if she finished the last few rows first. The pressure in her mind lessened when she added another row. The voices went away with the next row. The tingling dissipated with the next, and when she placed the last brick, it transformed into a solid barricade of brick and mortar that surrounded herself and Ambrose.

Voices scratched along the outside, but nothing got through. Her mind was light and free, and her body was sentient again. Something wrapped around her tightly, not something. Someone. He held her as if their lives depended on it.

"Are you with me?" His voice was a breathy whisper within the silent cocoon she'd created.

"Yeah. I'm here." Opening her eyes, there he was, so close she breathed in his scent. Cedarwood and earthy spices mixed with rotting smell. Her strength came back in a surge of electricity. Pushing out of his arms, she took a deep breath.

"You smell terrible."

"I know. Something got on me when I wasn't paying attention."

"You weren't paying attention? I don't believe it," she said, sarcastically.

"I was kind of distracted at the time."

"By what?"

He looked at her with a weird expression. "Don't worry about it. Let's just get back to the castle, and don't get too far away."

"I did it." She smiled at the realization. "I actually did it."

"We can celebrate later. Let's go." He grabbed her hand and pulled her into a speed walking pace that was so fast she tripped over a tree root and nearly fell to the ground. Ambrose grabbed her and pulled her upright, again.

"You're very clumsy. You know that?" A grin played across his face.

Her heart skipped. Then the smell hit her, and her heart rate reestablished itself. "Yeah. Well, you smell like death. You know that?"

"Just keep moving and try not to fall."

She picked up a light jog and was pleased that the wall not only stayed strong, but it followed her as well. When she closed her eyes, she saw it, but when she opened her eyes it was invisible, like it existed in an alternate reality. She couldn't believe she'd finally done it and now that it was up, it was effortless to maintain. She didn't have to concentrate at all.

They approached the eastern courtyard and continued quickly

through the gardens and into the eastern terrace of the castle, then through the west wing, through the throne room, and up to the guest rooms in the east wing. Once they were back to her room, she slammed the door open. Cassie wasn't there.

"Where is she?" Grabbing her phone from the nightstand, Sibyl dialed Cassie's number. A buzzing sound on the other nightstand got their attention. Ambrose picked it up and showed it to her. Cassie's phone.

"Damn it," Sibyl growled.

"You don't need the stone anyway. You're doing fine without it."

Sibyl sighed. She wasn't sure what to say or feel. On one hand he was right, but on the other hand, she was really mad at Cassie and she wanted to know why Cassie did that to her?

Rokesh, Demetrius, and Wilson showed up at the door in a panicked state, breathing heavily like they ran the entire way here.

"Oh, my Gods. Thank Empyrean. There you are. I turned around and you guys were gone. You weren't answering your moonstone. I couldn't find you anywhere. Where were you?" Rokesh asked Ambrose.

"You didn't see us leave?" Sibyl asked.

"No."

"Gods. What in Mokor is that smell? Did someone shit themselves and then die?" Wilson wafted a hand in front of his face. Sibyl must have gotten used to it because she didn't notice anymore. It wasn't nearly as bad as when they were near the woods.

"We smelled something on the way back. Ambrose got-"

"Ok. Well, have a good night, Sibyl. See you tomorrow." Ambrose ushered the three men out the door.

"Hey Ambrose," Sibyl said.

He turned.

"Thanks." She smiled sincerely.

He nodded and walked out quickly, like he was embarrassed to be seen in her room or something.

"Ok. Well. We'll be out here. Are you sure you're ok?" Demetrius asked.

"I'm good. Thanks. Good night."

"Glad you're ok but take a shower. You both smell horrendous. What kind of dirty things did you two to do?" Wilson laughed.

"Shut up," Ambrose growled.

"Good night, Wilson." Sibyl rolled her eyes and closed the door on them.

Changing out of her mud-covered dress, she got a shower, just like Wilson suggested, and scrubbed extra well to remove all traces of the stench.

After checking that the wall was still in place, she climbed into bed. Satisfaction and relief flooded through her. She'd finally accomplished building a damned wall, and Ambrose helped. She probably shouldn't get used to it. He'd probably be an ass again tomorrow. That seemed to be a pattern with him. Maybe he was some sort of emotional vampire. Only nice at night and cranky during the day.

No matter how uptight he could be though, she was thankful he was there tonight otherwise there's no telling what could have happened to her once she'd passed out.

Pulling the covers up, her mind flashed back to his arms around her, his body against hers, his touch on her face. So gentle, yet so strong. Butterflies tickled her stomach. Sibyl smiled and closed her eyes.

CHAPTER 17

SIBYL
LIBNYS WANG-1/SEPTEMBER 2ND

Sibyl awoke under the starry sky for the second time in one night. This time she stood on her own two feet in the middle of a meadow of waist high grass. A chilly breeze pried goose bumps from her exposed skin underneath the skimpy nightgown. The only light was that of the nearly full moon.

Movement to her right caught her eye. A large figure approached. Sibyl looked around for something to defend herself with. Spotting a fist sized rock, she snatched it up. Hoisting it above her head, she posed ready to launch at the first sign of threat.

Are you going to stone me now?

"Solstice?"

Yes. I'm happy to see you. It took you long enough to get your emotions and magic under control.

Tossing the rock aside, she said, "I wouldn't say I've got it all under control yet. I drank Em."

So, you traded one mind altering drug for another?

Solstice's disapproval hit her like a smack across the face. "No actually, Cassie spiked my drink." Rubbing her arms vigorously, she attempted to fend off the cold.

Why would someone you call a friend do that?

"I have no idea. She and I will have a talk about that when I find her. Where are we?"

Don't worry about where we are. The reason you're here is more important.

"Ok. Why am I here?"

You tell me. You summoned me. The horse towered in front of her like a majestic statue. Only the right side of him was visible under the moon, his fiery red fur was a shimmering tide pool of brown. His left side was completely engulfed in darkness.

"I did? How? I didn't mean to."

You must want to talk to me about something.

"Yes, actually. I'm curious about a few things about mental shields. Ambrose, one of my guards, helped me build the wall that I'm using right now, but I'm afraid to remove it because I might not be able to build it again. And how do I allow some thoughts through and not others?"

The first advice I have is to take it one step at a time. Once the wall you build is up, there is no need to take it down. You just create a door for those you want, like you've done with me now.

"But I don't know how I did it. I didn't even know I did until I fell asleep."

Sometimes our subconscious knows things we haven't figured out yet. Yours knew it wanted to allow me in, so you did.

"Well, how do I do it when I'm awake?"

Every individual has a signature. My mind recognizes certain signatures that I will always allow access to, while there are others who will never be permitted. And unfamiliar ones are alerted to me so that I can judge if I want to let them in.

You'll also begin to recognize signatures that are created against you. You can construct your shield to have a pattern recognition that will dissolve or intensify automatically to your subconscious preset signature guidelines, which, of course, you can change with just a thought, at any time.

"That sounds confusing and difficult. How do I sort all that out?"

You start with one at a time. Find one signature you know and trust then practice letting them in and pushing them out again. And if they are willing, see if you can get beyond their mental shield.

Druids reflect the magic of those around them, so the more powerful someone is, the easier it will be for you to manipulate the magic. I will caution you against unwelcome intrusion into someone's mind though. Use only willing participants to practice on. Everyone values their privacy, and many will not take kindly to you barging in on their personal thoughts.

"Will they know if I do?"

At first, probably so. When a foal first learns to walk, we're clumsy and fall down a lot. You'll stumble around their head and prop yourself up on their mental infrastructure which can cause pain, anxiety, or anger. One day, though, I imagine you'll be as silent as a wraith moving undetected by even the most skilled telepaths. Until then, just be careful you don't go traipsing around the wrong person's mind.

"You underestimate how clumsy I am." Sibyl's entire body shivered uncontrollably, and her toes went numb. "I thought I couldn't speak or feel anyone who doesn't have magic. How come on Earth I was over-stimulated a lot?"

On Earth it would be difficult to hear or feel anyone who doesn't possess a little bit of magic. I think there is more magic or magical beings on Earth than most people realize.

Whenever you were in close proximity to someone who possessed magic, you felt it. Also, if you're under the influence of an enhancement type of substance you may occasionally sense or feel a non-magical being's thoughts or emotions. If someone is in an intense or heightened state of emotion, you may be able to feel them as well. Everyone has some magic in them since life itself is magical.

"Why does everyone think I'm nuts because I told them I spoke to a unicorn?"

He chuckled. *Unicorns are endangered. Many believe my kind are already extinct, which I have purposefully propagated by hiding my herd out here. You're the first human I've seen since Tearnanoak fell, and I am the only one who can talk to you.*

"Why?"

Don't bother yourself with such things. Concentrate on mastering your Druid magic. It's of the utmost importance.

"Yeah. Ok." Sibyl's teeth started to chatter. "I need to get back before I freeze to death."

I think that's a wise decision. He smiled. She couldn't see it, but she felt it.

"How do I go back?"

Just think of where your body currently rests and will yourself to return there. Your spirit can travel anywhere it pleases while in dream or meditative states, but your body will remain where you left it.

"That sounds easy enough I guess. Hey. I forgot to ask. How's Oberon? Is he ok?"

He's fully recovered, and his horn is already partially grown back.

"Good. I was so worried. Tell him thank you for me and I'm sorry. I didn't realize that would make him so weak and sick, but I really appreciate the stone."

I will tell him, but only if you promise not to let the stone turn into a crutch. He lowered his head to her eye level.

"I'll work on that."

Good night, Sibyl.

"Good night, Solstice."

Dipping his majestic head, he turned and walked into the darkness, leaving her alone.

"Well shit. No pressure Sibyl. You just have to figure out how to get yourself back to bed before you die of hypothermia." Closing her eyes, she thought of her warm soft bed, bundled up all cozy under the blankets.

Within a single breath, the silky sheets brushed against her skin and warm relief engulfed her. Tentatively, she opened her eyes to find herself in her bedroom in Tearnanelle castle. Pulling up the covers, she cocooned herself into their warmth and went back to sleep. For real sleep this time.

—— Libnys WanG-2/September 3rd ——

The throbbing pulsed in time with her heartbeat. It felt like the seven dwarfs were mining in her head, each one throwing their pickaxe down at the exact same moment over and over and over again. Sibyl groaned and pressed her fingers into her temples.

"Drink this." Ambrose shoved a foul-smelling concoction in front of her face.

"What is it?" She scrunched up her nose.

"It's a tea formula of herbs that promote diuresis with a bit of gold dust to help with the hangover."

"That sounds wonderful." She took the cup from him and set it down next to her untouched plate of food. Wilson and Demetrius sat down next to Rokesh and Ambrose and started chatting about something that Sibyl tried not to listen to. All she heard was fingers down a chalkboard whenever anyone spoke.

When she woke up this morning, she found a small wooden box on her nightstand. A rune in the shape of a square with a circle inside it was etched on the box. Cassie had created a containment rune and put the osmium inside.

Sibyl was surprised and impressed that Cassie had paid attention during their magic lecture in the library. The osmium stone was cut in two pieces. One piece was rounded and polished into an elegant swirly grey gem and placed in a gem bracket so it could be attached to the necklace that was also inside the box. The loose rope type chain was a beautiful silver that Sibyl envisioned was what a Mage's magic looked like in its raw form. The other piece of jagged rock was also in the box and that's where it would stay for now.

That's why Cassie took the stone last night, and why she got Sibyl shit faced. To prevent her from being overwhelmed by the magic while the stone was gone. Thoughtful gesture, horribly executed. Sibyl's anger toward Cassie was significantly less now that she knew it wasn't for nefarious reasons, but she was still pissed.

"That was quite the party last night. Almost as crazy as summer solstice." Demetrius's voice cut through Sibyl's head like a knife. She groaned and rubbed her temples.

"Not quite the good time as that but it was pretty fun until she drank herself stupid," Rokesh replied. Everyone laughed.

"Yeah. That wasn't my fault. I was roofied." Sibyl glared at Cassie.

"How else were we supposed to make sure you didn't pass out or notice the stone was gone?"

"We?" She looked at the group.

Wilson and Demetrius shoveled food into their mouths pretending not to listen. Rokesh scratched his head and Ambrose looked at her sheepishly. Clark stared at her plate of food, avoiding all eye contact. Sibyl couldn't believe it. They were all in on it.

"For the record, I didn't know she was doing that. The last plan I heard was that we were going to take you to the market today and get the stone fashioned," Ava said.

"But we wanted to get both of you a present, so we had to keep you out of the loop too," Cassie said to Ava.

"That's the plan I was told for you," Sibyl said to Ava. They'd gotten Ava a tiger's eye stone which was an intangible element that promoted inner strength and cleared negative energy and stress. Ava added it to the cuff she wore around her arm.

"I don't care what your intentions were, that was so incredibly irresponsible and dangerous. I can't even begin to tell you how not ok that was. You don't do that to a friend no matter the reason. I would never do something like that to you. It's just not ok at all," Sibyl scolded Cassie.

"Sorry dude, but nothing was going to happen. They were watching you. No one will fuck with them." Cassie pointed to the four

Mage Guards. "Besides, it's basically like pot and you've done that before, so I knew you'd be ok with it."

"That was *my* decision to smoke pot. You took away my decision. It doesn't matter who's around to watch me. I don't want them watching me. I can take care of myself when I'm not inebriated beyond all recognition."

"It was only supposed to be a small dose. Just enough so you'd feel good and relaxed. That way the magic wouldn't bother you. That's all. I swear. Something got messed up with the dose. I'm sorry," Cassie said. Everyone else at the table was quiet.

Sibyl clutched the necklace around her neck. She was grateful. The smaller stone was a huge improvement over the cumbersome rock and its radius of neutralizing effects had shrunk to only about two feet, so she didn't hinder anyone around her anymore. That was probably an ulterior motivation for them to have it made for her as well, but it was still a nice gesture, nonetheless.

Shame trickled through her. She hadn't really done anything to earn the necklace or their friendship. In a weird fucked up way this proved that they considered her a friend and all she'd done since she arrived was try to leave.

"I really do appreciate it, but next time just tell me what you're doing instead of drugging me. You're supposed to be protecting me, not getting me high," she said to the four men.

Ambrose was apologetic but Demetrius, Wilson, and Rokesh sniggered, barely holding in their laughter. Clark smacked Demetrius on the shoulder.

Sibyl rolled her eyes. "You're a bunch of children."

Picking up the fork, Sibyl poked at the food. A wave of nausea made her think better of it and she set the fork back down. Taking a sip of the horrible tasting tea, she figured it couldn't be any worse than her headache. After a few gagging gulps, she set the empty cup back on the table, pushed the plate of food out of the way, and nestled her aching head into the fold of her arms.

"Well. I'm going to take a nap before our shift starts," Rokesh said. "Happy Birthday ladies."

"Thank you," Sibyl said from beneath her arms.

"Yeah, I should too. Happy birthday Sibyl, Ava. See you later." Ambrose stood and left.

"Bye," Sibyl said, not bothering to look up.

The healing power of the tea acted quickly. Within moments her head cleared, and the queasiness ebbed. She lifted her head and was pleased to find that the light no longer attempted to stab her eyes out.

"Wow. This stuff works quickly."

"Yes. It does," Clark said.

Pulling the plate of food closer, Sibyl took a bite. The sugary jelly coaxed her hunger to the surface like a beast who'd been freed from a cage. She devoured the eggs, fruit, and a bowl of oatmeal like she hadn't eaten in days.

"Jeeze dude. Slow down. You're going to get indigestion," Cassie said.

"I'm so hungry, I could eat a horse," Sibyl said between mouthfuls.

"That's the Em hangover wearing off." Clark giggled. "Get your fill. We'll start practice when you're done."

Sibyl groaned. "I thought I could use today to recover from last night." She donned the best puppy dog face she could muster.

"You finally built a mental shield last night. You need to practice. I'm glad you like the necklace we got for you, but you need to learn to do this on your own."

"Yes mom. Jeeze. You're starting to sound like Ambrose and Ava."

"Hey, I take offense to that." Ava stood up from the table.

"Where are you going?" Sibyl asked.

"I have things to do. Sounds like you do too. See you later."

"Bye." Sibyl wondered where Ava went every day. After Mage training and lunch, Ava disappeared, and no one could find her again until dinner. She said she was practicing imbuing her clothes and shifting which was better done in private, but something didn't quite add up. Ava advanced so quickly with everything else, why were these two things holding her back for so long now? There was something else going on. Sibyl could feel it.

"My shift starts in thirty minutes. See you in the library?" Clark also got up.

Sibyl nodded.

"I'm going to the fields to hang out with Tacey." Cassie stood up and Sibyl noticed that she was wearing Orlon style clothing. She'd gained some weight too. Her skin was a healthier color, and her hair was growing in evenly. Orlon was good for her.

When Sibyl and her guards finished breakfast, they went back to her room. Sibyl washed up and decided to try the Orlon style clothes. Ava looked really good in them. Maybe Sibyl would too. Pulling out the clothes that she had ignored since the day they arrived, she held them up. The red corset style shirt and black pants looked like something straight out of a medieval steampunk movie, but it's what everyone wore here. If she wanted to fit in, then she may as well try to at least look like everyone else.

Once she had the outfit on, she surveyed herself in the mirror. Sibyl barely recognized herself. She'd always had a child-like appearance with her freckles, blonde unruly hair, and weird hazel eyes. In this outfit, with her hair plaited into a tight braid, she looked more mature and refined. She hated to admit that she liked it. The clothes flattered her body in all the right ways.

Feeling a little self-conscious, Sibyl took a deep breath and stepped into the hallway.

"Whoa," Wilson said.

"Shut up. All my clothes are dirty," she lied.

"You look good," Demetrius said.

"Thanks." Her face heated as led the way to the library. Everyone they passed looked right over her as if she didn't exist, except a few who gave her a second glance, but not for the usual reasons. Their smiles were more flirtatious than suspicious.

For nearly three months she'd been stared at, glared at, thrown suspicious looks and curious gazes. The entire time she thought it was because everyone knew she was *the inadequate Druid,* but now she wondered if her foreign clothes made her stand out. She felt uncomfortable in this attire, but it did allow her to blend in better.

Go figure. The anonymity she'd wanted since she arrived could have been achieved a lot quicker if she'd just tried on the stupid clothes like everyone kept telling her.

"Hey. Look at you! You look good!" Clark's smile was huge.

"Thanks." Sibyl nervously smoothed down the front of the corset style shirt.

They spent the next couple of hours researching signature patterns for telepaths before trying to conjure a shield again. Her brain needed a break from intangible magic. Residual shadows of Em hangover still lingered under the surface, an angry animal ready to pounce with a healthy dose of pain if poked.

Flipping the page in one of the Druid books, she found a passage on signature recognition. Unlike shield building. The instructions for this were all basically the same, at least in these two books. The two oldest books weren't available at the moment, because they were being restored and preserved. Clark said it could take a couple of months then they'd trade them out for these two. Apparently, Clark had begged to keep at least two of them in circulation as long as they promised to be extremely careful with them.

Sibyl read the passage again.

Find the tether of consciousness and memorize who it belongs to. It can be a scent, feel, sound, color, etc. Every individual has a different signature that is unique, like a fingerprint. Once you know who's who then it's easy to let them in or push them out accordingly.

"Why do you need a book to tell you how? Just go practice it. It already worked once." Wilson propped his feet on the table, flipping through a book about strategies for winning card games.

"Because I like to research and study my craft before I go blundering into something like an ignorant baboon."

Demetrius chuckled. "I think she called you an ignorant baboon."

"Yet. I'm the one who can erect a mental shield like that." Wilson snapped his fingers.

Sibyl closed the book. "First of all, I have doubts that you can erect anything with substantial proficiency."

Demetrius laughed loudly, earning a few glares and shushes from other patrons nearby.

"Secondly. I may have only done it once, but I bet it's better than any shield you've ever created."

"You want to make that a bet?" Wilson closed the book he was reading, put his legs down, and stared at her challengingly. Clark and Demetrius stared at the pair with eyes wide.

"You're on." Sibyl stormed out of the library. She really hoped she hadn't just over played her hand. This newfound confidence may bite her in the ass.

They went to the courtyard behind the library. People were scattered on the lawn or under trees immersed in studies or pleasure reading. Out here there were no noise rules so they wouldn't disturb anyone if things got ugly. Sibyl went to a spot far enough away from everyone so they could talk and practice without being overheard.

"OK. Mr. hot shot. Show me what you got." She faced Wilson.

"How am I supposed to *show* you? None of it's visible," he said.

"Actually. That's not true. I can see my wall, so I have a theory that I can see others if I know how." She paced back and forth tapping her chin. "I think that's part of people's signature patterns I'm supposed to recognize. If I know what your signature, tether, aura, shield, whatever, looks like or feels like, I can either block you or let you in. That's in theory of course, but I need to try and see it. If you're ok with it. I'd like you to form a mental shield and I will try to see it. That's all. I won't try to trespass over it."

"Yeah. Ok," Wilson said.

"Cool." Reaching into the collar of her shirt, Sibyl pulled the osmium necklace over her head and dropped it into Clark's hand. "When I tell you, back away from me with the stone, but this time *I* will control when, how quickly, and how far you go, so be ready for my instruction."

"Got it." Clark waited for direction.

"Ok." Sibyl took a deep breath. She was a bit nervous now. *What was I thinking? I'm going to look so ridiculous when I pass out again. Not like they haven't seen it before. Fuck it.* Sibyl marched up to Wilson with feigned confidence and stood a few feet in front of him.

"What now?" he asked.

"Ok. Clark. Take two steps back." Sibyl's heart hammered violently and she closed her eyes. Letting all the noise from the outside world fall away, she concentrated on the warm sunshine against her skin, the cool breeze rustling the leaves, the ground beneath her feet. She slowly fell into a meditative state.

"One more step."

Whispers grazed her consciousness.

"Stop!" This was it. Pressure pushed in on her. Another half a step and the world would crash down on her. Standing on the precipice of the osmium's perimeter, she concentrated. She was out of it enough to use the magic but not so far out that she was overwhelmed.

Finally, a literal step in the right direction. She made quick work replicating the mental wall from the previous night. Once she was satisfied that it was solid, she asked Clark to back up five steps.

Voices pressed in on her, but none broke through. Sibyl swelled with pride. She'd finally done it. Completely on her own this time, without drugs. This was all her.

"How are you doing?" Even though he spoke softly, Wilson's voice echoed loudly. The wall undulated, and a voice broke through.

He caressed her center gently between his fingers sending fire through her soul and pleasure burst between her legs.

Sibyl's mouth curved up in a smile. "Someone's reading a very naughty book nearby."

"Are you eavesdropping on people?" Wilson asked.

"No. Whenever you speak my wall falters, and some voices get through. I don't know how to stop it. It didn't do that last night."

"So can you see it?" His voice was a wrecking ball, punching holes through the wall creating avenues for the voices and emotions to rush in. The pressure pushed her down and she fell to the ground. Darkness moved in on her periphery. *No! No! No!* She pushed back, throwing her arms out. The onslaught of magic stopped abruptly.

"Are you ok? What happened?" Clark stood right next to her.

Damn. Clark had rescued her. Sibyl sighed. "Well. It's an improvement, but I don't know what happened. Whenever you spoke it caused my wall to get damaged and then it completely collapsed. I never even got a chance to see if yours was up or not."

"Give it time. It'll get stronger as you get better. That was awesome though. You didn't pass out!" Clark beamed.

"It doesn't feel like much of an accomplishment," Sibyl said as she got to her feet with Wilson's help.

"Are you coming to Dragon training?" Wilson asked. "I think you'd get a lot out of it. More than the guards for sure."

"The Aruka told me about it. Dragons come here once a month to help train you guys in mental shields, right?"

Wilson nodded.

She was so close to figuring this out. Maybe the Dragons would have the pieces of the puzzle she was missing. "Yeah, I'd definitely like to come to that. When's the next session?"

"It's every Newm week," Demetrius said.

"Newm week?"

"The fifth week of every month."

"What about the months that don't have a fifth week, like February?"

"What's February?" Demetrius asked.

"The second month of the year? Which is also the shortest month of the year. It only has twenty-eight days, or twenty-nine during leap year. But it only has four weeks so when would they come when there's no fifth week? Do they just skip those months?"

They all stared at her as if she lost her mind.

"Every month has eight weeks no matter how many days are in the month," Clark said.

"Oh. Earth keeps time differently. Our weeks have seven days, so the number of weeks in a month varies depending on how many days are in the month. How do you guys keep time here?"

"By the moon," Clark answered. "The moon has eight phases, and each phase is anywhere from three to five days. So, the length of each moon phase determines how many days are in that week."

"That makes so much more sense than how we do it. Ours is based on religion, which is really stupid actually, because it's basically just made up, but the origins are loosely based on the moon and sun and stuff. The way you guys' tract time is way more logical."

They decided to quit for the day and headed to lunch. When she got to the table, Ambrose and Rokesh had already arrived for shift change. Ambrose gawked at her as she walked up.

"What?" she asked.

"Nothing. I've just never seen you wear normal clothes."

"These aren't normal where I'm from." Sibyl laughed.

His head cocked sideways, like a playful dog trying to figure out his next move.

"Why are you looking at me like that? Is there something wrong with the outfit?"

"Yeah. Why are you looking at her like that, Ambrose?" Wilson asked with a large grin.

Sibyl's cheeks heated.

"Shut up. You're making her uncomfortable. Sibyl, he's a moron. Just ignore him," Demetrius said.

"I learned to disregard pretty much every word that comes out of his mouth within the first twenty minutes of meeting him," Sibyl said.

Demetrius burst out laughing, so did Rokesh and Ambrose.

"Ha. Ha. You're a riot today," Wilson said, mockingly.

Clark sat down next to Demetrius, and they whispered to each other as if no one was around.

"Get a room," Wilson said.

Sibyl smiled. She liked seeing them together. She suddenly realized that she hadn't thought of her ex in weeks or months. Also, thinking of him didn't hurt anymore.

"What are you smiling about?" Wilson asked.

"Nothing. Just thinking about some things." No matter how hard Sibyl tried, she couldn't wipe the smirky smile off her face. With the newfound sense of accomplishment, came a confidence that she hadn't felt in a long time. And finally feeling like herself again, she was bursting with energy.

Thinking back to what Ambrose said, she hated to admit it, but he was right. Ever since she arrived, she wore outsider clothes, had a magic neutralizing stone, and made no effort to get to know anyone. She basically had a sign on her head that said, 'fuck off' to everyone around her, but now, a new curiosity bloomed inside her.

"I want to explore Tearnanelle this afternoon. I've been here nearly three months and I've never seen much outside of the gardens and west wing of the castle. I'd like to see more of your kingdom."

"I think that sounds nice. Let's do it. Ambrose and I can show you around. Can't we?" Rokesh elbowed Ambrose who nodded.

"Yeah. Of course we can." Ambrose looked at her with a soft intensity that made her heart skip. She averted her eyes and went back to her food.

They spent the afternoon visiting different shops in the market. Sibyl sampled some of the foods that were freshly cooked by a few street venders, selecting ones that didn't exist on Earth.

At Ambrose's insistence, she got a few more shirts and pants to make her wardrobe now four sets of clothes. Ambrose told the storekeepers to charge it to the palace account. Sibyl wasn't comfortable with that, but he assured her it was fine and the Aruka would rather have her blend in than continue wearing her Earth clothes, so she relented.

After that, they went to the stables. Sibyl met Travinia, the stable hand. Travinia was very chatty and introduced Sibyl to each horse. She learned that the horse she met a few weeks ago in the middle of the night was named Raka. When they got to the last stall at the end of the barn, Sibyl's jaw dropped. An extra-large stall with no ceiling housed a Pegasus.

"Oh my God. It's a Pegasus!"

The animal was huge. Nearly the size of Solstice and she was a beautiful chestnut color with four white socks and a big blaze down the center of her face. Her wings were the same color as her body, a brilliant brick red.

"They're temperamental and flighty." Travinia smiled. "Pun intended."

Sibyl laughed.

"Not many people ride them because getting bucked off in midair is problematic. Most Mages who ride them are ones who shape shift into birds, so they have a backup plan in those scenarios. This beautiful lady is Voler."

"Makes sense. I'd love to ride one, but I think I'll stick with regular horses for now." Sibyl pet Voler's face. The mare snorted loudly and rubbed her head aggressively on Sibyl's arm. Once she had her fill of pets, Voler resumed eating hay.

Sibyl helped Travinia do the evening feed. Rokesh and Ambrose hopped right in and helped with barn chores. Ambrose's family owned a horse farm, so he was used to farm chores and Rokesh was basically an adopted brother in his family, so he was accustomed to the work as well.

They decided to go for a walk on a trail through the woods behind the castle after that. Ambrose and Sibyl chatted about horses, stories from their childhood, and other subjects that the conversation natu-rally led them to. He was easy to talk to and funny at times. It shouldn't have surprised her, but it did.

They didn't talk about magic, their responsibilities, work, school, or anything that had been stressing her out since she arrived. For the first time in months, she was happy. She enjoyed being a normal person having a carefree day.

Rokesh stayed silent most of the time. He was never a big talker even despite Sibyl trying to include him in the conversations. The more effort she made, however, the more he hung back. The distance between them grew the further down the trail they went. It seemed like he wanted some time to himself, so Ambrose and Sibyl let the distance between them expand until they were basically alone.

By the time dinner rolled around they made the entire loop of the walking trail. The woods in Orlon were similar to the forest surrounding her family's cabin except for the occasional strange creature that scurried by.

Ambrose waited patiently while she chased after a few of them to get a closer look. She swore she saw a chupacabra at one point, but after losing it, she meandered back to the main trail. Ambrose did confirm that there were, in fact, chupacabras in Orlon.

By the time they got to dinner Sibyl was starving. She scarfed down her food and told Cassie and Ava to give her thirty minutes to shower then she'd be ready for movie night. When she got out of the shower, Ava and Cassie were already waiting on the bed with a bowl of some sort of chocolate rice ball.

"Sorry to keep you guys waiting." Sibyl grabbed a handful of the familiar looking food and shoved it in her mouth. She chewed for a minute then asked, "is that Cocoa Puffs?"

"Yes!" Cassie said excitedly.

"Where did you get Cocoa Puffs?"

"I brought a couple of boxes with me and was bummed when I was running out, so I gave one box to the cooks in the kitchens, and they recreated it!" Cassie said, excitedly.

"You're kidding." Sibyl sat down next to them and took another bite of the Orlon style Cocoa Puffs.

"I don't kid about Cocoa Puffs," Cassie said, seriously.

"So, what did you do today?" A grin spread over Ava's face.

"Explored the kingdom."

"You were pretty chummy with Ambrose." Ava tossed a few pieces of Cocoa Puffs into her mouth.

"It's not like that. He was just being a tour guide."

"Uh huh." Ava smiled broadly.

"Seriously. That's all," Sibyl persisted.

"What's the movie pick tonight?" Cassie asked.

Sibyl was grateful for the change of subject. "Beautiful Disaster."

"Oh. That's a good one," Ava said.

"I've never seen it. What's it about?" Cassie asked.

"It's one of my favorites. You'll like it." Sibyl pressed play on the laptop, thought about something for a moment, then pressed pause.

"What's up?" Cassie asked.

Sibyl looked at the door then looked at them. "Do you mind if I invite them in?"

"You mean Rokesh and *Ambrose*?" Ava said his name in a mocking manner, her green eyes gleaming playfully.

"I just kind of feel bad. They sit out there every night. It's probably really boring and uncomfortable. Don't you think?"

"Definitely. Yes. Invite them in." Ava's shit eating grin got larger.

"Don't make it weird." Sibyl got up and opened the door.

The two men looked up in surprise when she stepped out.

"Have you guys ever watched a movie?"

They both shook their heads.

Holding the door open, Sibyl gestured them inside. Everyone settled in around the tiny laptop screen. With five people on a bed made for two, they were pressed really close against each other. Ambrose ended up sitting next to her. She was hyper aware of his leg brushing against hers the entire time, but if he noticed, he didn't let on.

He was enamored with the movie, as was Rokesh. They had to pause the movie about every three minutes to explain things. What is a car? What is a train? How come people walk on rivers of hard rock everywhere? So many things that Sibyl took for granted in her society were completely foreign to them. It took them twice as long to get through the movie as normal.

By the time the guys went back to the hallway and Ava left for the night, it was nearly midnight. She climbed into bed next to Cassie feeling happy for the first time in months.

Cassie was already snoring away, but Sibyl couldn't turn her brain off. Her mind was crowded with thoughts of Ambrose. He was so nice to her today and he was easy to talk to. Like the Ambrose from the piano room before he went ass hole on her again, and he did help her build a mental wall.

Her mind wandered to his eyes. The beautiful red and yellow colors coalesced into a mesmerizing brown that pulled her in like a moth to a flame. The way he looked at her practically stripped her down to her raw self. What was he thinking when he looked at her like that?

She rubbed her fingers gently over the smooth surface of the osmium stone. If she learned to control her magic, she could look into his thoughts and find out. Sibyl shook that off and rolled over. No. Solstice warned her to not go traipsing into people's minds. Private thoughts were private for a reason. If Ambrose wanted her to know what he was thinking, he would say it. He was never shy about what he thought about her. There was nothing to be curious about. He was just doing his job, and his job was easier if they were amiable toward one another. That's all it was. Nothing else.

CHAPTER 18

AVA

LIBNYS LASQ-4/SEPTEMBER 11TH

Ava tugged at the collar of her shirt. It was unusually hot for this late in the year. The forest was changing into a beautiful tapestry of yellows, oranges, and reds, and even through the heat Ava smelled autumn in the air.

Picking her way through the underbrush, her footsteps crunching loudly on the leaves, Ava reflected on the last two weeks. Mage training was progressing sluggishly slow. She was learning how to run a kingdom, working on the primary weapons forms, imbuing her clothes, and sparring.

In fighting and sparring she was advancing quickly. She discovered that Mages relied too heavily on their magic, which put them at a disadvantage in hand-to-hand combat. The werewolves had the upper hand in that department. It was no wonder Tearnanelle was losing so many guards. All a werewolf had to do was survive long enough for the Mage's silver to run out and it was game over for the Mage.

Ava started teaching the Mage Guards what she learned from Redly. She told them it was techniques she learned on Earth, and they bought it, even her aunt.

Despite advancing to one of the most skilled fighters in Tearnanelle in such a short time, Redly still kicked her ass most days. She'd get a lucky shot in every now and again, but relying on luck wasn't her goal. She needed to figure out how to gain the upper hand on a werewolf opponent and that was proving to be substantially more difficult than she'd anticipated.

Ever since the Hansons were murdered, she'd taken martial arts and self-defense classes. While it provided her a solid foundation, Redly still out fought her and outsmarted her by a lot. He made it look so easy. It was infuriating.

Weaponry wasn't going any better either. Primary weapons were a sword, shield, and dagger. Every Mage Guard must learn to master all sword forms and dagger kali drills before they're allowed to advance to specialized weaponry. Since she still sucked at them, and her forms were deplorable, she was stuck.

Plenty of guards were enthusiastic to help her learn, especially since she'd started teaching them different fighting techniques, but she wasn't making much progress. She feared weapons may never be her forte.

So far, she preferred the sword because it allowed her to keep a safer distance from her opponent, but she hated that she couldn't throw it like a dagger. She also had a bad habit of switching between the weapons during a fight then getting confused about what she had at any given time and using the weapons incorrectly.

Another problem she had was unintentionally releasing the weapons. Redly was right. She got distracted too easily and every time that happened, she let go of the magical tether then had to reconjure it which cost time and silver. There was a balance between being aware of your surroundings and being distracted by everything, and she hadn't figured out that balance yet.

Imbuing clothes was finally progressing. She figured out how to do it, but the monstrous amount of magic it required was limiting. She was depleted and weak after just a single article, and it took several hours for her body to replenish the lost silver. She imbued one item per night then ate a huge dinner and went to bed, so she'd be fully recovered by morning.

The imbuing didn't last forever either. One imbuing lasted about twenty to thirty shifts then it would need to be repeated. Now she understood why Mages had specific sets of clothes they wore for shifting and fighting and didn't imbue everything they owned. It would take years to have a full wardrobe of imbued clothes. It was a laborious and silver consuming process, but unless she wanted to go everywhere naked it was necessary.

Between Mage training in the morning, Aruka training in the early afternoon, fight training with Redly in the late afternoon and imbuing her clothes at night Ava was thoroughly exhausted. She could barely hold her eyes open these days.

She fell asleep at the last movie night. She'd already seen the movie before, so she didn't miss out on anything except hanging with her friends. That was weird too. It wasn't just Cassie and Sibyl anymore. Last time it was all four of Sibyl's guards, Clark, and the three of them. Her friend circle was becoming quite large. That would take some getting used to, but she thoroughly enjoyed being around everyone.

Although when she fell asleep, they did spray shaving cream on her hand and tickle her nose. It didn't work out as planned because she scratched her face with the other hand then rolled over smearing the cream onto Sibyl's pillow. They thought it was hilarious. The thought brought a smile to her face. Her extreme exhaustion wouldn't keep her from movie night.

Stepping into the meadow, she saw Redly basking in the shade of the fruit tree they met at every day.

"Hey." She sat down next to him.

"If you were any louder, they might hear you in Tearnanoak." He didn't even bother opening his eyes.

"You're one to talk. Sitting here with your eyes closed, anyone could sneak up on you."

"Not you." He peeked an eye open. "Maybe our lesson today should be in stealth, or how to walk without sucking."

"I wasn't trying to be quiet. Besides, no one can walk quietly on a bed of crunchy leaves."

"I can."

"Yeah right." She leaned her head against the tree and closed her eyes too.

"You ready to start training?"

"No. Let's just chill for a bit. I'm exhausted."

"Aww. Are they working you too hard in Tearnanelle Arukas?" he teased.

She growled at him. She hated it when he called her that. He did it just to irritate her.

"Looks like you got some shifter clothes."

"Yeah. We make them using our silver magic."

He grunted.

"What?"

"I liked your outfits." His eyes scanned her body before returning to her face. "Or lack thereof." A mischievous smile took over his face.

"You would." She rolled her eyes.

He put his head back against the tree again, but the smile stayed plastered to his face.

"Do you guys imbue clothes too?" she asked.

"Not anymore."

"What do you mean?"

"I'm not Therian anymore. I'm a werewolf. We can't imbue anything." He sounded resentful.

"Oh." She paused for a moment then asked. "Can I ask you a serious question?"

"Even if I said no, you would anyway, so go ahead."

The corners of her mouth ticked up. "What's the demon queen like?"

He groaned. "Why do you want to talk about her?"

"Just curious."

"Well, you probably know as much about her as I do."

"I don't know anything. Come on, you have to know something useful."

"Why Ava, are you trying to spy?" he asked, teasingly.

Shit. She'd blown her cover.

"You are trying to spy!" He laughed deeply.

Ava's face dropped.

"I'm sorry to disappoint you, Arukas, but you picked the worst person to spy on. I'm the lowest rank in Tearnanoak, except for maybe seamstress or guardian. Shit, they may even know more than I do. I purposefully stay out of the politics as much as possible."

"What are your ranks?" She picked at a blade of grass, trying to act casual.

He looked at her sideways, an amused expression on his face.

"What?" She did her best to act innocent.

"Ok. I'll tell you what I know, but don't be too disappointed when you realize I don't have much useful information for you."

"Wait. You're really going to tell me?"

"Yeah. If it'll help Tearnanelle take Alyssium down, I'll tell you anything you want to know, but like I said, I don't know much."

"You *want* to help Tearnanelle?"

"Yeah."

"Why?"

"You haven't figured it out yet?"

"Figured what out?"

"I'm a slave, Ava."

"What do you mean?"

"I. Am. A. Slave. I have no allegiance to a demon who destroyed my home, killed my family, and cursed me into...the monster I become. Do you think I want to serve the demon who destroyed my life? Who in their right mind would choose this for themselves?" He huffed resentfully and put his head back against the tree.

Ava felt silly for not seeing it before now. When Tearnanoak was destroyed Alyssium cursed the Therians. She stupidly assumed everyone who lived there was willing participants. Or, at least, if they weren't then, they were now. But that's an incredibly asinine assumption. Like he said, who would want those things to happen to them?

"Whatever information you want, if I know it, I'll give it to you."

She wasn't sure what to think. He could be lying to gain her trust and feed her false information in an attempt to weaken Tearnanelle. "How do I know you're not lying?"

He shrugged. "You don't, but, for the record, I would never lie to you." His expression became melancholic. "Before you came along, I lived everyday waiting for it to be the last or waiting for an opportunity to...." He didn't finish his sentence. His mocha eyes connected with hers. "Spending time with you has been the only good thing that's ever happened in my life. Anything you want from me. I'll give it to you. I'll never lie to you, Ava."

She swallowed the lump in her throat. She didn't know how to respond to that, so she chose not to for now. Finding her voice, she asked "what's it like? Living in Tearnanoak?"

He fidgeted. She'd never seen him uncomfortable before. He didn't answer right away. She thought he may not at first, but he finally said, "I'll tell you in exchange for something."

He usually flirted, joked, and teased about everything, but now he was serious. This version of Redly would take some getting used to.

She was nervous about what he would ask for. She hoped she'd be able to meet his demands because the information could be vital, assuming he'd tell the truth like he said he would.

He hesitated then finally said, "teach me to read."

Ava's mouth dropped. That was not what she was expecting. "You don't know how to read?"

He shook his head. "Reading is banned amongst the cursed slaves. Only Alyssium and her top-ranking officials can read."

"Why would reading be banned?"

"Easier to control the masses if they're ignorant and illiterate. Plus, it's less resources to allocate. She wants expendable weapons and decoys, not people who can think for themselves, solve problems, and potentially organize against her. If one of us gets too smart, we disappear. We've lost virtually everyone who knew how to read. The few who remain keep their knowledge hidden, so they don't jeopardize themselves or their loved ones. To read in Tearnanoak is a death sentence not only to you, but everyone you're close to."

Throwing a rock across the meadow, he watched it disappear. His eyes that were normally vibrant and playful were full of sadness.

"What if you get caught?"

"I've got nothing and no one to lose. They're all already gone."

She didn't point out that he could lose his life. Even if he didn't care, she did. She didn't want to put him in jeopardy. *Shit. What was she thinking?* She shouldn't be worried about him. Regardless if he wanted to be a slave or not, he was on the side that killed her family, and she needed information. Her interest was revenge and figuring out who the spy was, not protecting him. He was perfectly capable of handling himself, and he wanted to help. If he wasn't worried, then she shouldn't be either.

"OK. Deal," she said.

He smiled. "So, what do you want to know?"

"Everything."

"I thought you might say that."

"What's the military command structure? Who's in charge?" she asked, barely holding in her excitement.

"I don't know the command structure, but the one in charge is Abigor. He's a piece of work, just as bad as Alyssium. He's a demon too. He and his generals are the masterminds of everything that happens in Tearnanoak. Alyssium doesn't usually get involved in the inner workings of those things. She likes to keep her days free for *other* things as you'd put it."

His meaning was clear. Ava didn't want or need to know any of those details.

"You said before that you're the lowest rank. What are the ranks?"

"We call them postings. When we turn sixteen, we have nine options for how to serve Tearnanoak. Servant in the castle ruins, private slave to the queen, soldier, trainer, hunter, seamstress, guardian, or patrol. The two most coveted posts are private slave and trainer. They're also the most difficult and deadly posts to obtain.

"Everyone is put in the guardian's care at six years old which is when we start our education; fighting and combat. Those of us with no parents go into the guardian's care from the beginning and we start training earlier.

"I've been fighting since I was four years old. Every single day for twelve years I was trained to fight, injure, kill, and most importantly win at all costs with no mercy given. We win or we die. We don't lose. I slept, ate, trained, and survived. That was my life."

"Wait. Children fight to the death?"

He nodded.

Ava's heart dropped. When she was in kindergarten learning the alphabet, how to count, and playing hide and seek with friends. Redly was literally fighting to survive.

"There's only one exception. Every year Alyssium selects the most beautiful six-year-olds to go live with the retired private slaves to be trained in the arts of sexual pleasure. She usually chooses about fifty males and fifty females. They're still required to fight but they have a private trainer away from everyone else and their time is split between fighting and pleasure training. The queen doesn't want them scarred up too much before she gets them."

A nauseating pit formed in the bottom of Ava's stomach. Making children do those things was deplorable. The man who tried to molest her when she was six flashed in her head. At least she was allowed to fight him off and he went to prison for his crimes. These kids had no one fighting for them. Ava was angry for them.

"On their sixteenth birthday they, along with any others who feel they're worthy enough, step before the demon queen for selection. Every year several hundred apply for the post, but she only selects the most attractive twenty-five males and twenty-five females to compete to the death until only three from each sex remain. The tournament is called sekkusu and it lasts about a month. The winners are given the title and *honor* of becoming her private slaves for a year until the next batch of fresh recruits are ready.

"It's a tough assignment. Her second favorite thing to do after sex is to torture people, and those two things aren't mutually exclusive. You've got to be strong to survive. Most private slaves survive the year, but they don't retire unscathed. Her ever-changing whims and desires make it difficult to predict what she'll want on a given day."

"Why would anyone choose that?" Ava asked.

"Because they're treated like royalty. After a year, their service is done and they're allowed to remain in the luxurious suites where they never have to worry about food, shelter, or any threats outside of the queen. She gets bored of the same partners for too long, so she rarely goes back to the retired slaves after she gets fresh pickings. She only returns to the ones she likes the most.

"There's a balance in Tearnanoak. Be good enough to survive, but not so good she notices you for too long. A year of sexual servitude for a lifetime of living in safety and the lap of luxury is worth it for many people. It's very competitive. People kill for the chance, literally."

Ava would rather have taken her chances in the masses where Redly was.

"The other two highest-ranking posts are trainer and soldier. The trainers are hand-picked by the queen and Abigor, and the soldiers are selected by the trainers. They're usually the strongest, most loyal, and violent ones of us. The trainers teach us to fight. What I'm teaching you, I learned from them.

"About thirty percent of pups don't survive training. Most die within the first year. The queen accepts no weaknesses and culls the pack early on. Those of us skilled enough to survive are kicked out of the guardian's care at sixteen and assigned a post."

"I don't get it. If she doesn't want you guys revolting against her then why train all of you to fight? Couldn't you just team up and take her down? There's only one of her."

"While the soldiers are her primary military force, any of us can be called at any time to serve. When that day comes, she wants us to be effective weapons. She's not scared of the masses. She has her officers and highest-ranking soldiers. They are very loyal to her and are happy with the curse and their post. They'd die to protect her.

"Also, she's a demon. Demons are immortal. We're not. Even though we're hard to kill, it's not impossible. Plus, she can control us. Not all at once, especially not in our human form, but enough to keep us subdued."

Now Ava understood why Tearnanelle was losing so badly. Most of the population in Tearnanelle was civilians and families. There were only maybe ten to twenty thousand trained Mage Guards and Tearnanoak had.... "How many people live in Tearnanoak?"

"I don't know. Two to three hundred thousand maybe."

"And they're all trained fighters?"

"The sick, injured, very young, and very old aren't good fighters, but if you're alive in Tearnanoak you went through at least ten years of fight training, so yes everyone is trained fighters."

Ava swallowed down her anxiety. Tearnanelle was outnumbered ten to one and outmatched in combat. The only reason they'd survived as long as they have was because of the werewolves' silver allergy. How in the world was she supposed to tip the scales?

"What did you have to go through to get your posting?"

"The remaining postings of castle servant, seamstress, hunter, guardian, and patrol guard can be requested or assigned. I requested patrol, figuring it required the least amount of work and it's far enough from the queen that I'm safe from her ever changing and unpredictable influence." He smiled but it wasn't real. She knew his smile by heart and this one was fake.

"My request was granted and with it I was awarded the shittiest accommodations in the kingdom. The lowest ranking posts sleep beneath the eroding foundation of what remains of Tearnanoak, while the higher-ranking officials sleep above ground in what remains of the real castle barracks.

"Most of the castle was destroyed when Tearnanoak died. Her root system withered away leaving what little foundation remained to slowly erode over the years. Now it's barely more than a hovel held together by mud motor, infested with rats and bugs, and leaks everywhere causing mold to grow. That's what I call home. It's great. I get stale food, a rickety bed, cold showers, and sleep in an open room with about a hundred other men. Total lap of luxury.

"It is better than being tossed outside to starve and freeze to death though. That's what happens to anyone who's injured or ill beyond the help of our innate golden blood. There's no healer for the cursed slaves. You survive on your own or you die on your own."

Ava's heart sank. She'd slept in a lot of shit holes throughout her life, but he'd never slept anywhere else.

"The honored officials, and other chosen, sleep adjacent to her throne room surrounded by cushions, decadent food, a shower with actual rubies, and diamonds for lights. That's what I'm told at least. I've never seen it."

That explained the robberies on the roads outside of Tearnanelle. Alyssium was using the stuff they stole for her own pleasures and amenities.

"Hunter is what I would have wanted if I hadn't been given patrol guard post. Anyone can transition to hunter post at any time, but once you become a hunter you're stuck there. You can't transition out. We always need more hunters since our population is growing exponentially, despite all the fighting and culling.

"Hunters can come and go as they please and make their own schedules so long as they bring food back every day. That's the only rule. A hunter cannot return empty handed. If they do then they're sacrificed, quartered, and fed to the masses."

"That's cannibalism."

"Like she cares. The only reason she ensures that we're fed at all is to keep her army strong, otherwise she'd probably let us starve."

The more he talked, the more disgusted Ava became. It dawned on her; the nine postings that Alyssium had created were his only choices in life. There was no education, doctors, boring jobs, hobbies, teenage shenanigans, meaningful relationships, nothing. No luxuries in life at all. They do their assigned work every day and survive. That's it. Ava thought her life was shit, but she was spoiled compared to him. She knew it was bad in Tearnanoak, but she never imagined it was this bad.

"I didn't know any of this. I'm sorry."

"All of you Mages think we're evil, violent, blood thirsty animals, right?"

Ava bit her lip. She couldn't defend that point. It was true. Everyone in Tearnanelle did think that, as did she up until a few minutes ago.

"It's fine. I'd think that too if I were you. How would you know otherwise? It's not like you guys can come over for a visit. No one other than werewolves and demons step foot into Tearnanoak and live to tell."

He was wrong about that. There was one survivor. Tacey. She'd lived, barely. If you called that living. She didn't talk about what she went through, but she didn't have to. It was literally written on her face.

Redly was uncharacteristically forlorn. Her heart broke for him. How did he live every day acting as happy as he did when this was his life? She couldn't take any more depressing discussion. Deciding to change the subject she asked, "what do you eat?"

"What?"

"What do you eat?" she asked again.

"Um. Food. Why? Are you going to make me a fancy meal or something?"

She laughed. "No. I can't cook for shit. I just want to know what you eat normally?"

"Regular food just like you, unless you eat something weird. Is that why you're asking? What do you eat?"

"I eat normal food like fruits, vegetables, meat, cooked meat. But I don't eat raw meat like sheep."

"I'm glad. I don't like to eat sheep either." He squinted his eyes.

"But you do eat sheep raw sometimes?"

His face fell. "You want to know what a cursed werewolf eats?"

"Yeah."

"First thing I want you to understand, Ava, and I cannot make this more clear. I am not that beast. That's a cursed monster that uses my body and I cease to exist when that thing comes out." He looked at her with such intensity. She'd never seen this side of him before, even when they sparred.

"If that monster ever comes out, you run. Do you understand?"

Ava nodded.

"I'm serious, Ava. I won't be me anymore. I'm gone and I don't want to wake up and find you.... Just run. Promise me you'll run."

"OK. I promise." It wasn't a difficult promise to make. She was scared to death of a werewolf. He was the only one she knew, and she sometimes forgot that he was one. She never considered that the person behind the werewolf was a slave to the curse with no choice in what they did.

"And to answer your question; Yes. The monster may eat a sheep if one was around when the werewolf came out. When we shift, it's like being trapped in a dark, silent room. True darkness. True silence. You perceive nothing. My voice, my breathing, my sight. It's all gone, but I feel what's happening and it's never good. I know I do things, but it's not me. I have no control over the beast."

"So, you... I mean, a werewolf would eat a sheep and leave the carcass in the field?"

"Yes. Why are you asking this?"

"Sheep are getting attacked in Tearnanelle. We also think there's a spy leaking information to your side."

"That can't be a werewolf. We transform every newm night, uncontrollably, and it's a free for all. I think you'd notice a werewolf on the loose. It would have killed more than just sheep. It sounds like whatever's in Tearnanelle is selectively hunting sheep. Werewolves are not selective. They fight, feed, and fuck just about anything in their path."

"Ew."

"Yeah. Try being the one who wakes up in the aftermath trying to piece together what happened. It's as bad as it sounds. The only time we're able to remember what happened in werewolf form is when Alyssium allows it. She can bring light and sound to the prison inside us. We're still not able to control our actions, but we can watch the events as they happen, completely helpless to stop it.

"Not only that, but we enjoy it. She plants false desires into us so that we want to do the things she forces us to do. Until she lets us go and we get our own feelings back." His gaze became distant like he was recalling something.

"I felt everything. I saw what I did. I wanted to do it." His fists clenched. "I'd much prefer to stay ignorant to what I do or what is done to me than ever live through that again."

Without thinking Ava grabbed his hand. It startled him. She'd never seen him rattled. She squeezed his hand. His shoulders relaxed and he gripped her hand tighter.

"When we're in our cursed form she can manipulate us very easily. She can control one of us or all of us at the same time. She'd know if one of her werewolves was in Tearnanelle. Besides, what good would a werewolf do her? We're the front lines. The fighters. The sacrifice. If she was going to send someone over there to spy, they'd need to be able to read and steal information and always stay hidden and in control. That's not a werewolf."

"What else eats sheep then?"

"Demons. They need fresh blood. That's part of our role as well. She eats us, alive. Demons eat regular food just like the rest of us, but they need fresh blood to survive."

Ava was getting used to being shocked by how horrible Alyssium was, but that little fact pushed her disgusted knob up another notch.

"What does a demon look like?"

"They could be anyone. Once they've possessed someone they'll look like any normal person on the outside."

"How can I tell if someone is possessed?"

He thought for a minute. "The smell is the only way I can think of."

"Smell?"

"Dark magic smells bad, like something is dying."

Ava thought back to the times she'd encountered a werewolf. It always smelled like rot and decay.

"You..." She bit her lip.

He nodded. "Yes. When we shift, we smell like death. Even when I'm me, it's always there, faintly under the surface. Never letting me forget that I'm cursed. It's like a disease and we're infected. Infection smells bad."

"I know the smell. It shouldn't be too hard to find the person in Tearnanelle who smells like that."

"It's a good clue, but it won't be consistent. Alyssium rarely smells like that. I don't know why sometimes they do and sometimes they don't. You could be standing right next to them and never know it."

"Once I find this demon. How do I kill it?"

"I don't know. If I did, I would have killed Alyssium years ago. Or died trying."

Ava had to figure out who the spy was and how to kill them somehow. She also wanted to find out who killed the Hansons and kill them.

"Do you know how to figure out who Alyssium assigns to do her work?"

"What kind of work?"

"Leaving this world to hunt for the missing Arukas."

Redly pulled his hand from hers, got up, and stretched. The bottom of his shirt rose up enough that his hip lines peeked out. Butterflies danced in her stomach. He dropped his arms and the lower section of his abs disappeared under his shirt.

She tore her gaze away then got up and leaned against the tree.

"How long ago are we talking?" Redly asked.

"Fifteen years ago."

He grimaced. "I don't know, but I can look into it for you. Why?"

"That's when my family was killed. My adoptive family. The only people on Earth who ever loved me. Alyssium sent werewolves after me and whoever it was, killed them instead."

Redly's face dropped. "I'm sorry."

She shrugged. "That's what she does, right? Destroy homes and families."

"I'll see what I can find out, but they may already be dead. If they came back without you then that's a failed mission. She executes failures."

"I don't want to put you in harm's way."

"Aww. Are you worried about me?" He stepped closer until he brushed against her propped up knee. The butterflies in her stomach flitted around like they'd taken Em.

"I just don't want my spy getting killed or captured. What good are you to me if you're dead?"

He smiled, and her heart leapt. She put her foot down and stood to her tallest height which was still shorter than him by at least half a foot.

He moved closer. "Of course that's all it is. Don't you worry. I won't let anything happen to your spy." He leaned an arm against the tree caging her in.

Her heart raced as their eyes connected.

"I'm going to bring a surprise for you tomorrow," she said.

"What kind of surprise?"

It killed her to hear about how horrible his life was. She wanted to bring some happiness to him.

"I'm going to borrow Sibyl's laptop, and we'll watch a movie. I think 'The Princess Bride' is the perfect first movie for us to watch together."

"I have no idea what most of that is, but if it involves you then I'm in."

"You don't even know what it is, and you agreed to it? What if it's some form of torture?"

"Is it?" His eyebrow ticked up.

"Some men on Earth might think it is."

"Why is that?"

"It's kind of a chick flick. Most women like it, but men don't always. Worst case scenario, you'll be bored out of your mind for an hour and a half."

"I'll be with you. You're never boring." His hand caressed her cheek.

Her breath hitched. This was a bad idea on so many levels. There were advantages to getting close to your enemy, but too close was reckless. But was he the enemy? She put her hand on his chest, over his heart. It beat just like any ordinary man's heart. A man who had no choice. A man who survived the horrible things that had been done to him and still found the strength to fight back and even be happy sometimes. She was lucky to get out of Tearnanoak before the curse took her, otherwise, she'd be in the same position as him.

His calloused thumb rubbed over her lips, and a flame ignited inside her. Shit. She was in trouble. She lost herself in his deep brown eyes. Fuck it. She could keep physical attraction separate from what she had to do. Besides, he wasn't the enemy. He was a slave of the enemy. That made them allies.

She leaned into him. The moment their lips touched a ripple started inside her. Not the kind of ripple she was expecting.

He pulled away. "Do you feel that?"

Ava held up her hands. They were gone. In their place were wolfish paws. "What's happening?"

"Ava. Run!" Redly doubled over as his body started to change. "RUN!" he yelled again. His face contorted into a half man-half monster version of himself.

She moved away quickly but she fell. Her legs were mid shift, fighting to stay human but losing the battle. Pain ripped through her entire body as it fought with itself, unable to decide which form it was supposed to take. She hadn't lost control since she was fourteen years old, and this had never happened before.

The shifts were never painful. Even when she didn't want to shift, it was smooth and painless, like putting on a silk nightgown. But this felt like someone poured scalding hot water all over her. She screamed.

When her body finally succumbed to the wolf, she looked up and her heart fell to the bottom of her stomach. Redly was gone, and in his place was a nine-foot humanoid beast. The eyes that were kind and sexy a moment ago now stared down at her with a venomous rage, and the stench of rot and death filled her nostrils.

Ava panicked, thinking back to what Redly said, *Werewolves are not selective. They fight, feed, and fuck just about anything in their path.*

She was in his direct path.

CHAPTER 19
SIBYL
LIBNYS LASQ-4/SEPTEMBER 11TH

A mild tingling sensation coursed through Sibyl's hands. She intertwined her fingers trying to quell the nervous energy, but it did little to help. It wasn't her magic overwhelming her this time, but rather her anxiety.

Her mental shield was holding with little effort, thankfully, but she tip-toed on the edge of mental anarchy. One wrong move and she'd fall into insanity. She should probably be used to the feeling by now since that's how she'd lived most of her life.

Taking a few deep meditative breaths, she followed a few steps behind Rokesh and Ambrose as they led the way to the throne room. She felt like a prisoner marching down death row.

Ambrose glanced over his shoulder and she met his gaze. He held his normal unreadable expression, but his eyes were soft. At least he didn't talk because she still hadn't mastered the art of holding a conversation while simultaneously maintaining the mental barrier.

She twisted her fingers around each other until she hit the painful end range of motion. Any further and she may actually dislocate a finger. That little bit of pain helped keep her grounded and calm.

Ambrose's eyebrows creased. *What are you doing?* His voice startled her. Solstice was the only other person she'd ever spoken to telepathically.

Nothing. Sorry. It's a nervous habit. She shoved her hands into her pockets.

His eyebrows shot up and he turned around quickly. Did he mean to talk to her? Was she supposed to hear that? Was that considered trespassing into his private thoughts like Solstice warned against? Great. She was already screwing this up.

Swallowing nervously, she tried not to think about the humiliating experience from the last time she was in the throne room. At the Aruka's request Sibyl had stayed away from the woman for the last three months. It wasn't a difficult request to fulfill since Serellina scared the shit out of her, but she couldn't decline a royal summons. So here she was, on her way to speak with The Aruka.

All she'd been told was that the Aruka wanted to see her, 'without any tools to detract from your magic,' the guard had said. Sibyl knew what he meant even though he didn't. There was only one tool she possessed.

Reaching for her neck, she grasped at the empty space. The necklace had become a calming tool. Without it, she felt vulnerable. Maybe Solstice was right, it was becoming a crutch.

She squared her shoulders and walked ahead, feigning a confidence that she'd never had. *Fake it until you make it.* She didn't need the stone. She was just fine without it.

Descending the last steps, they turned the corner and entered the throne room. Its magnificence still overwhelmed her. The Aruka sat on her throne as regal as the first time Sibyl saw her. Fulcinia and Yilfin stood by her side to the left, but they weren't who made Sibyl's mouth fall open.

On the right of the throne taking up a third of the entire dais stood a large brownish-red Dragon. The beast was about four times the size of an elephant, and its skin had an iridescent scaly texture like a snake. Dozens of horns jutted off its head. The two on top twisted upwards about four feet and three sets of medium sized horns stuck off the sides of the face. Rings with dozens of different gems encircled the horns. That was definitely a safe place to store them. No one would dare take a gem off a Dragon's face horn.

The creature's long neck had a beautiful light blue colored sail with spines transecting it every two to three feet. The sail moved fluidly to stand erect or lay neatly against the Dragon's neck. Swirly shimmering lines spread all over the lizard-like body and throughout the massive webbed wings that rested against his barrel. A large sapphire was embedded into the Dragon's forehead. The Aruko of Silvermar was marked by the God with a sapphire because the hottest flames burned blue. All other Dragons contained rubies within their foreheads or so she read in the book from her room.

Deep black eyes with no discernable pupil, sclera, or iris looked directly at her as if he could see straight into her soul. Sibyl withered under the Dragon's imposing gaze. The book also stated that Dragons were gentle creatures. She hoped the text was accurate because this Dragon was one of the most beautiful and terrifying creatures Sibyl had ever laid eyes on.

Once they were at the base of the dais, Rokesh and Ambrose dropped to one knee and bowed their heads. Tearing her eyes away from the Dragon, she mimicked their genuflect. After a few seconds all three rose. The Aruka narrowed her eyes at Ambrose before her gaze flicked casually to Sibyl.

"Sibyl, I'm pleased to see you standing here. It didn't take you long to get control of your abilities. I hear you're making excellent progress." The words didn't sound sincere and despite the smile, the Aruka's expression was strained.

The words bounced off Sybil's shield. Unfamiliar consciousnesses seeped through the cracks hitting Sibyl like locusts flying into her on a summer night. Flinching, she closed her eyes and repaired the wall where it faltered.

"I'm starting to get the hang of it….but I wouldn't qualify it as excellent progress. I still struggle to carry on conversations such as this." Squeezing her eyes closed again, she pinched her nose between her fingertips. The wall buckled and toppled in several places, letting a few voices propel into her. Working quickly, she attempted to repair the structure, but it was a sinking ship. For every hole she plugged, two more popped up.

If I may. A dominating male voice broke into her consciousness bypassing her wall, without disrupting it. Her eyes shot to the Dragon.

A telepathic conversation is much easier to have for ones like us, especially when learning to multitask. He didn't say so, but Sibyl knew everyone in the room could hear him.

So, this is normal? she asked.

Yes.

Relief and hope swelled inside her.

"I'm sorry it's difficult, but don't downplay your achievements. You've made a lot of progress in a short amount of time with very little useful support or help for one with your unique gifts." The Aruka stood and descended the dais. Even though the words were kind the tone was dripping with contempt. "That's why I've called you here today actually.

"Once a month, Dragons visit Tearnanelle to help my guards, and other Mages who wish to learn, with their mental shields. This month Aiden, the Aruko of Silvermar, has come early to work with you individually. Isn't that nice?" The Aruka made a strained smile.

"Yes. It is." Sibyl's heart fluttered with an equal mixture of excitement and apprehension. No matter how the Aruka felt about her they all wanted the same thing. Sibyl would prove that she could control her magic and in doing so she'd eventually get in the Aruka's good graces.

Serellina walked up to Sibyl and ushered her away from Ambrose and Rokesh, turning their backs on the men. She spoke quietly so that only Sibyl could hear. "Listen, Sibyl. I know you've been invited to attend the training sessions, and I know you're excited. And while you've made excellent progress, I just don't think you're ready." The Aruka grabbed one of Sibyl's hands and gripped it tightly, like she was trying to be supportive and comforting.

It was similar to how Chris treated her when he dumped her. How one would placate a child. Sibyl's lips turned down. The tingling in her hands intensified as more and more voices broke through the wall that was now half of what it was just a few moments ago. The weight of the magic pushed in on her, but for now, the wall remained a somewhat effective barricade against the bulk of the magic.

"You can barely stand here and speak with me. You're sweating darling. I think we should hold off another month or two until you've gotten even better. Don't you think?"

Sibyl slumped with disappointment. It wasn't a bad idea. She could study for the boards anywhere. By staying in Orlon, she could study and practice the Druid magic at the same time. Maybe she'd be more prepared next month.

"If I may, Aruka," Ambrose interjected. He'd walked up to them at some point. "I think she can do it. Most of her problems are due to lack of confidence, not lack of skill. Just give her a chance and I think you'll see she's perfectly capable of mastering the magic and becoming an asset to Tearnanelle. Besides, what harm is it for her to try?"

As if someone snapped a string through her spine, the Aruka went rigid. "I appreciate your input, but I don't think she's ready. She needs more time for some things to be sorted out." The Aruka glared at him.

His jaw ticked as if he wanted to say something, but he didn't.

Sibyl felt the conflict between them. They'd had a disagreement about something. Her. They'd argued about her before they came here. She couldn't tell exactly what the conversation was about, but she knew that it happened, and they hadn't come to an agreement.

It was mildly insulting that they were arguing about her. Whatever problem they had with her they should discuss with her and not behind her back. This wasn't high school.

Ambrose dipped his head, submitting to the Aruka's authority. He went back and stood next to Rokesh. Sibyl stared at his back. She could practically see the anger boiling off him like a pot of steam. What was he so angry about?

I have no intention of teaching Sibyl here.

Everyone's heads snapped to the Dragon as if they'd forgotten he was there. As if that's possible. He took up an entire corner of the room. Sibyl's heart sank. She thought that's why he'd come. To help her. That's what the Aruka said a few minutes ago.

I'd like her to return with me to Silvermar where she would have the advantage of training with many different skilled telepaths. I think this would greatly reduce her learning curve.

The Aruka's anger flared. Sibyl could actually see it, kind of like the fumes over a fire.

Since she wasn't wearing the osmium stone as much, Sibyl saw these phenomena more frequently. Instead of people's emotions physically invading her, when the mental shield was in place, she watched them as a bystander.

She'd learned that everyone's aura of emotions looked different, even if they were the same feeling. One person's happiness looked and felt different than another person's. Like with the Aruka and Ambrose right now. They were both angry, but each had a different look and feel to them. She could tell who was who, even if she closed her eyes.

"Absolutely not. That's out of the question. She's not leaving Tearnanelle. It's too dangerous," the Aruka yelled at him.

It's dangerous everywhere, Aruka. She'll be perfectly safe. I'll ensure it myself. She'll be an honored guest. That is, of course, if she wants come with me to Silvermar.

"Yes," Sibyl blurted out before she could even give herself time to think about the offer.

A smile creeped over Ambrose's face. He was proud of her. Sibyl swelled. It felt good to win his approval. *Wait.* She didn't care about his opinion, did she? One minute he hated her, the next he was nice and helping her, now he defended her. He probably just wanted her to learn the magic and leave so he could be done with her once and for all.

Ambrose glanced back. His expression was confused. Did she think that out loud? Is that possible? Sibyl was getting really confused.

"It doesn't matter what she wants. I'm the Aruka of Tearnanelle.

She's my subject and she cannot go." Serellina crossed her arms. Fulcinia and Yilfin came to stand at her side, both carrying concerned expressions.

With all due respect Aruka. I'm the Aruko of Silvermar, and I have the authority to extend an invite to anyone I choose, and unless I am unaware of a change in your laws, or the laws of Orlon, I believe she is a free person to make her own decisions and come and go as she pleases. Is she not?

Serellina's green eyes narrowed at the beast.

Sibyl admired the woman's courage. Serellina was a fraction of his size, but she was a force to be reckoned with. She stood her ground against the massive Dragon without the slightest hint of fear.

"You cross a line, Aiden. She's perfectly free to come and go as she pleases, but she is unaware of the dangers of our land, and unfamiliar with its inhabitants, traditions, and cultures. She's a target, and it's my job, and yours, to protect her, which is why I restrict her movements for now. I question your motive for wanting to remove her from the safety of my walls."

Ambrose scoffed.

If looks could kill, then Ambrose would be dead under the Aruka's lethal glare. Why was he so confrontational toward her? What was going on between them?

Aiden countered her argument, but it was drowned out by the voices that were now catapulting themselves over Sibyl's mental wall. She'd gotten so distracted by the conversation that she'd forgotten to check the status of her wall.

The tingling in her hands swept through her body. Closing her eyes, she inspected the damage. It was falling at a rate she was unable to keep up with. The voices of thousands pummeled her as a flash flood of magic flooded her mind. Shielding her head with her arms, she attempted to stave off the voices. That did nothing to prevent the onslaught. Panic seized her. She fell to her knees, and the wall dissolved into barely more than a speed bump as more magic poured in.

The room swayed and Sibyl became queasy. Her head desperately needed a reprieve, but she refused to back down this time. She would fight to stay conscious. It was time she took control of her own mind.

A monsoon of voices bore down her. She pushed back. The magic responded ever so slightly, providing a flicker of relief. It was enough to ignite an intense determination. That was the first time she'd gained any ground, and that tiny bit of triumph fueled her desire to keep fighting for control.

Sibyl threw her arms out. The pressure receded briefly then fell on her like a tidal wave. Her head took the brunt of the force, as if someone punched her in the face. Rocking back, she grabbed the sides of her head, and a piercing scream erupted in the room. She didn't recognize it at first, but it belonged to her.

"Stop!" she yelled, as fear took over.

Rokesh and Ambrose cautiously stepped toward her but halted in their tracks a few feet away.

"STOP!" she yelled louder.

Buckling over, the men grabbed their heads.

A voice slithered through the cacophony of emotions and consciousnesses.

Sibyl. It's Aiden. Just breathe and filter out everyone else but me. You can do it. You're so close. His black eyes met hers. He was a calm in the midst of a hurricane. *Listen to me. Come to me.*

Rising to her feet, she stared at the Dragon, but didn't move. Ambrose and Rokesh writhed on the ground on either side of her. Was she doing that? She saw Fulcinia and Yilfin shielding Serellina behind them.

The Aruka's shocked face poked around Fulcinia's shoulder.

Sibyl took a tentative step toward the Dragon and reached her hand out. It was immediately swarmed by a stinging pain. Emotions and voices climbed up her arm, to her chest, and dove into her head in a rush.

"No." She grabbed the sides of her head.

Look at me, Sibyl. Push them out.

She closed her eyes. The wall was gone. Her senses were

completely open to everyone and everything. People and creatures surrounded her in an endless chasm between the physical and meta-physical world. None of them noticed her. They talked to themselves or with each other. Some prayed, others worked on various tasks, mumbling to themselves. Some made love, held their babies, cooked, cleaned. They were everywhere.

Sibyl pushed against them, trying to force the magic back and recreate the failed wall. They all fell to the ground, just like Ambrose and Rokesh.

Aiden walked through the mass of strangers as if they didn't exist. *Filter it all out, Sibyl. Just concentrate on me. They don't know you're there. You've accidentally stumbled into their consciousness.* The Dragon stood only a dozen feet away, but she couldn't get to him.

"It hurts. It's too much," she sobbed.

Everyone's thoughts and emotions are invading you at once. It's too much for your mind to process. You have to push it all out.

"I can't." She shook her head.

You can.

"Who are you?" a heavy-set middle-aged woman asked. The woman was sweeping previously, but now she stared at Sibyl. "How'd you get in here? What do you want? Get out before I get my husband." The woman waved the broom at Sibyl.

The woman's fear filled Sibyl, mixing with her own until she over-flowed her body and mind. Sibyl backed away from the woman.

Calm down, Sibyl. Aiden's voice was distant. She could barely hear him over all the other voices that started yelling at her.

Just relax and let all the voices fade away. They're as scared as you are right now. Someone spoke to her. Wise words, but who was that? She couldn't remember.

A mixture of shock, awe, fear, and confusion swirled together creating a hurricane of paralyzing feelings in her mind. Bile rose in her throat and the edge of her vision darkened. Wolves howled in the distance. People screamed. Sibyl covered her ears. The diabolical howls crescendoed into a deafening roar as more and more wolves joined the chorus. Many of the humans in the void and everyone in the throne room changed form.

Ambrose became a grizzly bear. Rokesh was a honey badger. Sibyl recognized Fulcinia and Yilfin in their wolf forms. The Aruka was missing. Most of the people in the chasm had shifted into ordinary animals, but some were beasts like the one from the beach that night when Fulcinia and Yilfin came to their rescue. Werewolves.

The scent of decay and rot filled her nostrils. Fear and terror collided with anger and confusion. It was complete chaos in the metaphysical chasm she'd fallen into.

Who are you? What's happening? a male voice asked. He was out of breath and sounded exhausted, like he was fighting for his life.

Sibyl? Ava's voice broke through the chaos.

Sibyl searched for Ava, but she didn't see her. "Ava! Where are you? Help me!" Sibyl fell to her knees.

You are ready, another voice interrupted. It sounded familiar, but Sibyl couldn't place it. This being was full of malice and hate. Chills climbed up Sibyl's spine.

A faint chuckle emanated. *It's time to go to Tearnanoak. You can leave anytime, just like the Dragon said. I can take you there. Come outside. I'm here, waiting for you. I'll show you the way.*

Sibyl's mind went blank. The mental anarchy was obliterated, and peaceful tranquility flowed through her. She stood in a white room that had only one door. She took a cautious step toward the door.

Yes. That's right. Come on child. I have the answers you've been looking for. A way to make it all go away permanently. This voice. This being could help her. They had the answers she needed. The answers were in Tearnanoak.

*Yes. Come on. Keep coming. We will go together. I....*whoever was talking to her stopped mid-sentence and screamed. *NO!*

The white room winked out and the world went dark as Sibyl lost the magical battle within her own mind.

CHAPTER 20

AVA

LIBNYS LASQ-4/SEPTEMBER 11TH

Fear paralyzed Ava to the spot. She stared at the beast that was once Redly. Some of the fear was her own, but most of it felt extrinsic, like bugs crawling all over her skin leaving terror in their wake.

The beast took a step toward her.

STOP! Sibyl's voice shouted.

The beast obeyed.

Howls erupted all around Ava. Looking around frantically, she searched the forest for the source, but saw no one. The howls and yips coalesced with screams. Ava covered her ears. The meadow was completely empty sans the two of them, but it sounded like there were thousands of people and werewolves right next to her. The scent of decay and rot settled into the atmosphere.

The werewolf version of Redly whimpered.

Ava turned to him but came face to face with Sibyl, or at least a version of her. She was transparent like a ghost. The diaphanous version of Sibyl looked around desperately, her normally hazel eyes were completely taken over by an emerald green. Even though Ava stood right in front of her, it was as if Sibyl couldn't see her.

"Ava! Where are you? Help me!" Sibyl cried and fell to her knees.

Ava reached for her friend, but her fur covered paw went through the apparition as if it were mist.

You are ready. Another voice spoke.

Chills climbed up Ava's spine when the voice chuckled.

It's time to come to Tearnanoak. You can leave anytime, just like the Dragon said. I can take you there. Come outside. I'm here, waiting for you. I'll show you the way.

A tendril of fear slithered throughAva's head and spine. *Don't do it, Sibyl,* she pleaded softly, but her words were lost in an empty atmosphere of pain and terror. Trying to calm the rising storm inside her, she took a few deep breaths then opened her eyes.

Red mist as hot as a furnace surrounded her. It was so hot the hairs on her body singed. Ava tucked her tail between her legs and whimpered as the fiery mist blocked all routes of escape.

The werewolf version of Redly was trapped in the circle of red mist with her. She wasn't sure which would kill her first, but there was only a few seconds until she'd find out.

With a sudden poof, the mist vanished, and Ava's body shifted to her human form without a moment's thought. This time was painless, unlike the forced shift from a few minutes ago. Luckily her imbued clothing held up, so she was covered. She gulped down the fresh air as if she was starving. Redly was back in his human form as well. Thank the Gods.

"What the fuck was that?" Redly asked, sitting up.

"I have a feeling that my friend just came into her power," Ava said.

"What does that mean?"

For a moment, Ava wondered how much she should say. Had she already given him too much information? She stood up, surprised to find her legs just as strong and steady as normal. Redly followed her example but his clothes did not survive the experience.

Ava turned around quickly. The rest of his body was just as attractive as the parts she'd already seen. After a moment of hearing him move around she glanced over her shoulder. Her eyes dropped instinctively. Turning back around, she swallowed nervously. Yep. He was gorgeous.

"You really have a thing against nudity, don't you?" He gave a half-hearted laugh.

"No. It's just generally understood that we should all remain clothed while in public."

"We're in the middle of the forest, and it's not like I purposefully stripped down."

"True but we're basically strangers. I should leave, so you can collect yourself in private."

"I'm hurt. You still consider me a stranger."

"Fine. Acquaintances. I still don't go gallivanting around naked with my friends."

"That's a shame. You should try it sometime. It's so freeing. Similar to what I expect you feel when you do your bird free fall stunts in the sky."

Ava snapped around. "You saw me?"

He stood proudly in his birthday suit and smiled at her. That eyebrow ticked up flirtatiously.

"Jeeze." Ava covered her eyes and turned back around again.

He laughed.

"Do you enjoy making me uncomfortable?" she asked.

"Yes. Actually, I do. There. I'm decent-ish."

Ava cautiously turned and found him holding a bit of torn fabric over his groin area. It barely hid anything except for his manhood. She could see every sculpted muscle on his torso, pelvis, and the muscled thighs that tapered to a teasing lustful point. The flush in her cheeks deepened.

He smiled mischievously. "If you're going to have the same response with me holding this bit of fabric, I can just discard it and save myself the trouble of holding it."

"NO! Just keep holding it there please." She squeaked out the words in a raspy tone and cleared her throat.

Redly walked around the clearing searching the tall grass. "That was intense. It felt similar to newm night when I'm forced to shift, only a lot more fear." He picked up a torn bit of clothing that laid across a clump of weeds.

"What do you mean the shift didn't feel normal?" Ava asked.

"We're forced to shift once the invisible moon rises. It's the height of dark magic's influence on the world and the most dangerous time of the month for us. Most pups are the result of newm nights, which is also why most don't know who their fathers are.

"Also, if *my queen* wants to, she can force us to shift at any time, which is one of the reasons I make it a point to stay off her radar, but this was something or someone else. Alyssium feels more confident and maniacal. This was reactive and fearful. It wasn't purposeful." He curled his lip before bending over to pick up a piece of fabric, which gave Ava a brief glimpse of things as they dangled into sight.

Pulling herself back to the conversation, she said, "I think I know who it was."

After he collected all the fabric pieces lying around, he walked in the direction of Tearnanoak. Ava watched him, mesmerized by his backside.

"Are you coming, or are you just going to keep staring at my ass?"

Embarrassment washed over her as she quickly shuffled to follow along. She tried her best to pay attention to the conversation and not his ass, which was an almost impossible task.

"So, who was it then?" Redly asked.

"My friend, Sibyl. She's a Druid and. She-" Ava was cut off midsentence when Redly wheeled around so fast, her head could have spun off her neck.

"What did you say?"

Ava stumbled backwards. "My friend. Sibyl. She's a Druid. She's been practicing her magic which hasn't been going well. That was her though. I saw her searching for me."

His eyes widened. "Are you telling me that you have a Druid in

Tearnanelle and you're out here traipsing around the forest every day like you have no care in the world?"

"What does a Druid in Tearnanelle have to do with me being out here?"

"Keep your voice down," he scolded. "The future Aruka shouldn't be out here at all, especially if she has a Druid on her counsel. For Empyrean's sake." He brushed his free hand through his already jostled hair. "Unbelievable," he mumbled to himself.

Ava shoved him. That surprised her as much as it did him. He rocked back losing his balance for a split second then gawked at her in disbelief.

"I know what I'm doing. I have my reasons for coming here. Don't talk to me like I'm a child. I'm not stupid."

"Well, you certainly do a lot of stupid things for someone who isn't stupid."

She made to smack him, but he caught her wrist before it connected with him. She tried to wriggle her wrist loose, but his grip was unyielding.

"You make unwise decisions, Arukas. And now *my queen* knows you have a Druid. She's going to send an army into Tearnanelle after that Druid, and you."

Ava snorted.

"What? You don't believe me."

"Yes. I know. My aunt told us about how Sibyl could be used as a puppet for destruction, but you don't know her. She's strong and we'll protect her."

"Oh. I know she's strong, and now, so does Alyssium. You said it yourself, she just came into her power. It's the perfect time to strike while she's weak enough to be captured, but strong enough to be useful."

"We will protect her," Ava said through clenched teeth.

"We?" he asked.

"Me, my aunt, my friends, and Tearnanelle." Ava massaged her wrist after he let go of her.

"You don't understand. There are some of us who will want to do exactly as their queen demands, capture her and bring her back. But there are others who will want to kill her."

"Kill her? Why?"

"So, she can't be used to subjugate and enslave us further."

"What do you mean?"

"Remember I told you that Alyssium can force us to shift and do her bidding at any time she chooses?"

Ava nodded her head.

"Well, she can only control a few of us at a given time, and only over a certain distance. Her control is limited. With a Druid she could control more and see more through us. She'll use us in more horrible ways than she already does."

"How could she do that?"

"Think about it. Demons possess people. Your friend would be an amazing person to possess with her mind control capabilities. Alyssium could control everyone, not just those of us who are cursed, and not just on newm nights.

"While there are thousands of werewolves who are very happy with this arrangement and vie for her attentions and affections, there are just as many, if not more of us, who try desperately to stay away from her and would stop at nothing to ensure she doesn't gain more power."

"Then they should ban together to stop her. Sibyl can help."

"Years of servitude, torture, and brain washing have a way of making people dangerously subservient. Many probably would want to join your cause, but most would be scared enough of losing what little control they have that they'd destroy the one thing that may actually save them."

"That's stupid. It wouldn't help them in the long run."

"You and I know that, but most are so afraid that they can't think straight half the time. Scared people do stupid things." He walked off and started looking at the trunks of random trees. She followed along, watching his every move.

"I know you're watching me," he said, without even turning toward her.

"What are you doing?"

"Ah ha!" He pulled out a shirt and pants that were tucked under a tree root. The clothes smelled like mildew and were full of holes where wild critters had torn bits of the fabric away.

"You keep random clothes hidden in the woods?"

"Yes. Like you said, it's generally recommended that one should wear clothing while in public. And, like I told you before, Therians have lost the ability to imbue clothes. Sometimes we shift so quickly that our clothes don't stand a chance. I've got them hidden everywhere." He dropped the bit of fabric he was holding and began to dress. Ava stared at the unobstructed sight of him.

"Could you turn around please?" he said, playfully.

She spun around so quickly she nearly fell.

After a minute, he said, "ok. I'm decent now."

Turning slowly, Ava found him fully clothed now. A surge of relief and disappointment flooded her.

"Which one are you?" she asked.

He furrowed his eyebrows.

"Do you want my friend to help, or do you want to kill her?" The answer to this question could change everything between them.

"I don't know," he answered.

Ava sighed. "Fair enough."

"I do know beyond the shadow of a doubt though, that you shouldn't be out here. It's too dangerous." He moved closer to her. "You're too valuable to both sides to risk being captured or killed. You have no idea what Alyssium would do to you if she got you." He brushed the silver streak of hair behind her ear.

Ava didn't shy away. "I can take care of myself."

"So you keep saying."

"If you're really that worried about me then you'll keep teaching me to fight."

"You need to leave, pretty little hawk, and don't come back," he whispered.

"I'll be back tomorrow," Ava said pointedly.

He let out an exasperated sigh. "Ava. You've got people who can teach you to fight. You don't need me."

"I promised I would teach you to read, and you said you'd watch a movie with me, and you made a deal to teach me to fight." She couldn't believe what was coming out of her mouth. She was begging him to keep meeting her. What was happening? He was right. She should walk away. She could have died today. He was a monster. The same kind of monster who'd killed her family, but his words echoed in her mind.

I am not that beast. That's a cursed monster that uses my body and I cease to exist when that thing comes out.

She saw the struggle behind his eyes. He was trying to convince himself to leave her. To not come back. She didn't want him to not exist and she didn't want him to leave. He was a good man. She wasn't going to let someone else in her life get taken away because of the stupid demon that calls herself a queen.

"I'm the Arukas. You made a deal, and you will uphold your end. I will be back tomorrow, and I expect you to be here." She poked her chin out, daring him to argue.

His eyebrows shot up and a smile creeped over his face. "Is that so?"

"Yes."

He didn't respond. He just stared at her with those beautiful chocolate eyes that made her insides twist in knots.

"Will you be here tomorrow?" Her voice cracked a little as she tried to maintain the façade of authority.

"This is my patrol. I'm here every day."

Ava smiled and held her head high. "Well, I'm leaving for now. Sibyl probably needs me. She was calling for me, after all. See you tomorrow?"

"Yeah. See you tomorrow." Even though his expression was that of a boy who'd been grounded for misbehaving, his voice sounded relieved.

CHAPTER 21

SIBYL

LIBNYS LASQ-4/SEPTEMBER 11TH

"Hello Solstice."

The brick red horse jumped to the side. *Sibyl. You startled me.*

"Sorry." Sibyl dangled her legs over a large bluff.

You're getting really good at Druid Dreaming. Usually, I can tell when you arrive. This time you were so quiet one would think you were invisible. Is everything ok?

She shrugged and stared out at the wilderness that prepared for sleep. Locusts and frogs sang their lullabies to the world as the sun sank lower and lower on the horizon. They both watched the world slowly change colors from the bright blue of day to the deep violet hues of dusk. The silence drew out peacefully. Solstice stood for a long time, patiently waiting for her to speak.

Finally, Sibyl asked, "what am I supposed to do?" A tear tickled her cheek. "I can't do this. I can conjure a shield that's as flimsy as a sheet and apparently, I can sneak up on you in a Druid Dream but that's about it. That's all I've managed to learn in three months. Oh. And I almost destroyed the entire world. I forgot about that." Sibyl shook her head.

You didn't almost destroy the world. You finally embraced the magic and stood your ground against its torrent. It was a good thing, albeit a bit heavier than any of us predicted. But it's still a step in the right direction. Now you just have to manage your emotions and the magic will fall into place.

"How was that good? I couldn't control any of it. I've tried, but I just can't. I'm right back to square one of passing out. I've made no progress. Actually, I've regressed which is impressive since I wasn't that good to begin with."

When we're young, we cannot control our legs. It seems so difficult to walk. Running is completely out of the question. My legs wobbled and barely held me up. But the more I used them, the stronger they became and now I'm one of the fastest and strongest unicorns in existence. He arched his neck proudly.

It takes time to master a difficult task. You crawled and now you're stumbling around trying to walk. Tomorrow you will stand and the day after that, you'll take your first step. Then you'll progress one step at a time. But Sibyl, you must get your emotions under control.

"You make it sound so easy. Walking only affects me. No one gets hurt by walking. What I can do, what I am, can hurt people."

It can also help them.

Mixed emotions swam inside her. Self-doubt, perseverance, determination, fear, anxiety. All these feelings vied for the lead position in a dance she didn't know the steps to.

Your biggest problem is you don't believe in yourself, and you let your insecurities overwhelm you.

"I'm getting really tired of everyone telling me what my problems are. I already know what they are." Pulling her knees to her chest, she wrapped her arms around them and rested her chin.

Solstice snorted. *Remember I said that magic is a reflection. If you attempt to read a telepath who is weak, you'll get a weak reading. If you read a telepath who is powerful, you'll get a powerful interaction. This is also true of yourself. If you're emotionally unstable then the magic will be unstable. Believe in yourself Sibyl. You're strong. You saw how strong you are. So, believe you can control it and you will.*

Sibyl closed her eyes. A breeze jostled her hair. "But what if I can't?" she whispered into her knees.

Tearnanoak fell twenty-seven years ago. A God fell. Many died. Thousands were enslaved. No one ever thought that was possible, but it happened. There's always the possibility of danger and even death. With anything that is great and powerful comes risk, but that doesn't mean we give up. You've been chosen by the Gods to receive this gift because you are worthy of it. Nothing worth having is easy. If the Gods didn't believe you could handle it, then they wouldn't have given it to you.

"But I don't want it? I just want to have a normal life. I have friends, family, a career, a life back on Earth. I'm supposed to be studying for boards, not pretending to be a Druid. I don't belong here. I don't want to have to manage this thing inside me that could potentially destroy me and all those I love. I can't handle the pressure of not knowing if I'll be a savior or a destroyer. I don't want this. The Gods chose wrong."

You do understand that even if you didn't have this magic, you still need to get your emotions under control, right?

She glared at him. What the hell was that supposed to mean?

Anything that you try to do in life will be affected by your fears and anxiety. It's holding you back from everything. The magic is a reflection of what you feel. When it exploded earlier what did you feel?

"Afraid," she mumbled.

Exactly.

Sibyl pressed her forehead into her knees. "What do you want me to do? It's not like I can just say 'Hey. Don't be afraid to die or hurt people or become enslaved.' Those things are worthy of being afraid. I'm scared. I don't know how not to be."

Being scared is normal. Letting it control you is the problem.

"That's easier said than done," Sibyl snorted.

No one can stop you from going home. You have the osmium stone. I just don't want you to leave because you're running away otherwise the anxiety will just be waiting for you everywhere you go. You can't outrun yourself, Sibyl.

She sucked in a deep breath, inhaling the refreshing forest scents. "Serellina won't let me leave."

She doesn't want to put you or anyone else at risk. That's not the same thing as not letting you leave.

"You think she'll really let me go home?"

Yes.

"Even after what happened?"

Yes.

The mental turmoil started to simmer down as Sibyl thought about her options. The osmium stone could suppress everything. She could live a normal life. She stared at the half-moon that became brighter with every passing moment.

For as long as she could remember her fingers and hands tingled whenever her anxiety spiked, and the most debilitating experience of all, the panic attacks. Everyone, including herself, thought she was crazy. Ever since she found out she was a Druid, she assumed that the magic was the cause of her anxiety, but what if it was the other way around? What if it was really her inability to control her emotions and the Druid magic just reacting to it?

The stone wasn't a cure, but it was a containment. It would allow her to have a normal life and then she would only need to manage her anxiety disorder. Plenty of people lived with anxiety disorder and managed it just fine. She could too. Her mind was made up.

"I want to go home, Solstice."

He dipped his head. A mixture of relief and disappointment flooded her. She couldn't wait to see her friends and family. She missed them so much, but she'd miss her new friends too, and this wonderful world.

Sibyl stared into the night that had fully awakened. The majestic unicorn scanned the horizon pensively. A breeze jostled the black curls of his mane. Stars twinkled in the sky above him. He was a fantastical portrait, like something out of a story book. She would never see it again if she gave this up. A pang of regret and doubt reverberated through her.

"I've worked for years to become a doctor. Just because I'm backing down from this doesn't make me a failure."

No one believes you're a failure.

"Yeah right." She kicked the rock ledge with her heel.

Solstice nuzzled her shoulder. *You should get back now.*

"Yeah. Time to face the music." Standing up, she dusted off her bottom. Not like it made a difference. She wouldn't be in this form much longer anyway. "Goodbye Solstice."

Whatever decision you make, don't be a stranger. You can visit me anytime you need.

"Thanks." Sibyl closed her eyes, took a deep breath, and when she opened them again, she was back in the throne room.

Everything was foggy. She rubbed a hand over her eyes, trying to force them into focus. The scene cleared slightly and Ambrose's face came into view.

"Sibyl?" His voice was warped, as if he was talking under water. His eyes slowly came into focus, concern brewed behind the beautiful cognac colors.

She laid on the floor, her head in his lap, and voices argued all around her.

"What the fuck did you do that for?" he shouted.

"Guard! Watch your tone when speaking to an Aruko." Serellina's voice boomed.

The voices bounced around in Sibyl's head like a pinball clanging bells every time it hit her skull. Sibyl pushed herself up to sitting. Ambrose jumped to his feet. Rokesh stood nearby and the Dragon was a few feet away towering over them all. Everyone was a bit shaken and disheveled, but unharmed. The weight of their stares settled on her and the pain in her head was worse than the hangover from being drugged on Em.

It's ok. His concern is genuine, Aiden said.

"What happened?" Rokesh asked more calmly than Ambrose had.

Cassie and Clark came running in from a side door.

"Here! I brought this for you." Clark handed the necklace to Sibyl.

Pulling it over her neck, the pain inside her head eased. Sibyl dabbed the back of her head. It felt like someone was driving a hammer through her skull. There was a palpable dent.

"What do you mean?" Serellina asked the Dragon. "Are you insane?" the Aruka yelled at him.

"Does anyone want to fill me in on what's being said about me?" Sibyl said flatly.

All heads snapped to her. She picked up the necklace and dangled it so they would see she had the osmium which rendered her deaf to their telepathic conversation.

"He says that you opened yourself up to your full potential which was brave but stupid because you weren't ready. It scared you and you let your fear and insecurities over power you." Fulcinia answered. "He says that was a Druid in full power having a panic attack."

"Awesome. Everyone gets a front row seat to Sibyl's crazy. That's just perfect." She tried to stand, but her legs were jelly.

"Be careful. You're not ready to stand yet." Ambrose gave her a hand.

She pushed him away. "Let me be. I'm getting really sick of people telling me what I can and can't do. I know what I can handle, and I've told you all the entire time I've been here that I can't do this!" Her voice got louder with every word.

"Well, for once we're in agreement," the Aruka said.

"Fuck off!"

"Don't you speak to me that way." Serellina pointed a finger at her.

"Or what?" Sibyl challenged.

Serellina's green eyes widened.

Sibyl didn't care that she was speaking to the ruler of a magical nation on a different planet. How much worse could it get? Maybe her ticket home would be to piss Serellina off enough that she got banished to Earth. Win, win.

"You've basically held me prisoner since the day I got here, and I don't know why. You obviously don't want me here. I'll make it easy for everyone. I'm leaving." She tried to get up again, but a wave of nausea made her think better of it. She sat back down. "As soon as I can stand up."

"That's not going to happen. You said it yourself. You can't control it and from what I can tell, you're not even trying," Serellina spat.

"She is trying. She's had no one to help her. He can help." Ambrose pointed to the Dragon.

Sibyl tried to stand up again. Her head spun. An arm wrapped around her waist. This time she welcomed the help. It was better than sitting beneath everyone.

"No one asked for your opinion." Serellina crossed her arms and glared at Ambrose.

He returned the glare with twice as much animosity. "I think you did. You just don't remember."

"Watch your tone with me, or you'll find yourself looking for a new job."

"Ok. Let's all calm down." Rokesh put a hand on Ambrose's shoulder.

The Aruka and Ambrose stared at each other, some silent argument playing between them.

"Aruka." Yilfin stepped in. "I agree with the Aruko. She needs to learn to control it. If she doesn't, she'll be a prisoner under the subjugation of osmium, hiding until the day she dies."

The words sat in her stomach like sour milk. He had a point.

"And now the demon queen knows there's a Druid in Tearnanelle. She'll be searching for her," Fulcinia said.

"OK. First of all, stop talking about me like I'm not here. Second of all, Alyssium already knew."

"What? How do you know that?" Serellina asked.

"Someone was here. They tried to get me to go with them. They were outside." Sibyl turned toward the large archway to the throne room. "They knew I was here and said I was ready to go to Tearnanoak now. I might have done it if I hadn't passed out."

"You mean if you hadn't been knocked out," Ambrose corrected.

Sibyl touched the back of her head sending a renewed spear of pain into her skull. A large welt was forming. "I was knocked out?" That explained the knot.

"Yes. Aiden hit you in the back of your head with his tail," Ambrose explained. His tone was anything but understanding.

Sibyl's heart sank. What would have happened if the Dragon hadn't stepped in? Would she have gone to demon queen and be turned into the puppet they all feared?

"You see. She admits it. She nearly turned on us," Serellina said. "At least untrained she would probably just die before she was able to be used against us."

Several people gasped. Serellina fidgeted nervously.

"Now who's letting their fear take over their better judgment?" Ambrose said.

For once the Aruka averted her eyes rather than arguing. She put her shaking hands into her pockets.

"I agree with him Aruka," Fulcinia said.

Serellina turned on her advisor. "What? Are you serious? After what just happened?"

"I agree too." A black-haired woman walked into the room from behind the dais. She wore a long, elegant nightgown, and her hair was down. It looked as if she'd just woken up.

"Bekora. I'm sorry I wasn't there. I tried to get to you, but I couldn't."

The woman grabbed Serellina's hand, and they intertwined their fingers together.

"I felt whatever happened in here. Everyone felt it. It was intense. I couldn't control my own thoughts or body. I knew what it was, but most importantly, I knew where it originated."

"What do you mean?" Fulcinia asked.

"I knew that it was the Druid, and I knew it came from this castle, in this very room. I apologize for eavesdropping but if Alyssium felt even a portion of what we did then I suspect she now knows where to find her, not just that she exists, and she knows how powerful she is too. We have no choice, my love. We must train her."

Bekora shifted her gaze to Aiden. "And if I'm being completely honest, I'd feel a lot safer if she wasn't here until she was fully in control and sworn allegiance to our cause."

Serellina wrapped an arm around the woman's shoulder and kissed her forehead.

"Alright." Serellina took a deep relenting breath. "I think we have no choice at this point. She can go with you. I hope she'll be what you all hope of her, and not what I fear of her."

Sibyl stuck her chin out. "I changed my mind. I don't want to go to Silvermar. I'm going home."

"Sibyl." Ambrose's words were laced with exasperation.

"Don't," she spat. "None of you have any right to stand here and dictate my life. I never wanted any of this. I'm not swearing allegiance to anyone. I'm going home and you can't stop me." Turning on her heel, Sibyl stormed out and headed to her room, her anger seething hotter than it had since the night Ambrose licked her. At least she knew the exact route to her room from here. It only took five minutes.

"Sibyl, wait," Ambrose called from down the hall. Sibyl growled. Why couldn't he just leave her alone.

"GO AWAY!" She entered her room and slammed the door behind her, but he caught it and pushed his way through, closing it behind him.

"What part of go away don't you understand?" she growled.

"Just calm down. Let's talk about this rationally."

"I am rational. I see perfectly clear. I nearly took down the entire kingdom. Remember? You were there. How did it feel, having someone else fucking with your mind? Is that something you want?"

"No, but it proves what you're capable of."

"I DON'T WANT TO DO THOSE THINGS!"

The door opened slightly, and Cassie stuck her head in. "Is everything ok?"

Ambrose shook his head and motioned her away. Cassie nodded and closed the door quietly.

Sibyl took a deep calming breath. Her hands shook and her head throbbed. Once she was composed, she said, "I help people and animals. I'm a doctor. I repair wounds, perform surgery, administer medicine. I don't fight magical battles and control people's minds and bodies and speak telepathically." She grabbed her backpack and started hastily stuffing all her things in it.

"Obviously you do. You've done all those things."

"I don't want to, and with this-" She held up the necklace. "-I won't have to."

"I don't want to wash dishes or do laundry, but I have to," Ambrose said.

"That's not even a remotely close comparison, and you know it."

"Ok. Ok. Come here. Just sit down for a minute please." He grabbed her shoulders.

She jerked away, but he gripped her tighter.

"Let me go!"

"Would you just calm down? You're acting like a petulant child."

"I hate you! Let me go!"

He put his hands up. She went back to stuffing things in her backpack.

"You're just running away because you're scared." He raised his voice.

"I'm not running away. I'm going home where I belong. I was never going to stay anyway. I came here to get a solution to my problems, and I found it, so now it's time to leave."

"That stone isn't a solution. It's a Band Aid."

"Everything will be normal again. I'll pass the boards, get a job, and live my life like I'm supposed to, like I worked for. Everything was going perfect until I made the stupid decision to come here."

"Your life was perfect, really?"

"Yes," she spat.

"With your anxiety, failed relationships, hearing voices, and seeing things?"

"Fuck you! You have no idea what you're talking about. I love my family and friends, and I worked hard to get to where I am. I'm not going to throw it all away for this bullshit."

"What's your plan Sibyl? You don't even have a bubble."

"I'll go to the market and get one. I'll trade everything I own if I have to." She stuffed the last of her belongings in the backpack, threw it over her shoulder and headed to the door. He rushed in front of her and blocked it.

"Get out of my way." She was about to lose her shit on him.

"Sibyl. Please just talk to me for ten minutes."

"No. Move."

"Here." He held up a hand and between his fingers was a bubble. Sibyl froze, staring at the bubble.

"I'll give this to you if you just talk to me for ten minutes. If you still want to leave after that, you can have it and I'll walk you out myself."

She had absolutely no desire to talk to him, but she wasn't quick enough to take the bubble from him either. His offer was a good one. Here was a bubble for free and all she had to do was endure his insufferable company for ten more minutes and it was hers.

"Fine." She tossed her backpack on the chair in the corner and sat down on the bed. He sat next to her. She sidled away.

"I'm not going to lie. That was scary. I've never experienced anything like that ever."

"Nine minutes and forty-five seconds."

He sighed. "When I was twelve, I nearly cut my arm off when I tried to conjure this ridiculous samurai sword that my dad told me not to. I thought I was a bad ass waving it all around until I sliced through my arm all the way to the bone." He pulled his sleeve up and showed her a scar across his arm. She glanced at it from the corner of her eye. It was gnarly. She believed it went to the bone with as gruesome as it looked.

Pretending to pick at a hangnail, she said, "Eight and a half minutes."

"All magic can be dangerous. I've been learning to control mine since I was six years old. You've been hiding from yours for about the same amount of time. Everything new is scary. It'll just take a little time and practice, and it won't be so scary anymore. I promise."

"So? It doesn't matter. I want to go home." Her voice cracked, the anger finally giving way to despair. "I don't belong here. I have people who love me, and I love them, and I miss them. This is your home, not mine. Could you imagine being somewhere completely different and having no friends and this uncontrollable force inside you and no one to help?"

"No. I couldn't." He scooted closer to her and pulled her chin to face him. She met his eyes. "But you do have friends here, and you have people who can help, and an entire civilization of Dragons who want to help." He took a breath. "I want to help."

"You say that now but tomorrow you'll want me gone again."

He slumped and dropped his hand. A minute or two went by. How long did he have left? Maybe six minutes? She'd say six minutes, that sounded fair.

"I'm sorry for the way I behaved when you first got here."

She stared at him in disbelief. Ambrose was apologizing?

He shook his head. "I made some stupid decisions, and I'm sorry. You're not the only one who messes up sometimes. I made some mistakes based on snap judgments." He rubbed a hand through his hair. It was spikey from the dried sweat. He turned to her. Those beautiful brown-red eyes pulled her in like a sunrise on a spring morning that you couldn't help but stare at.

"Please stay and figure this out. If you leave now, you'll just be running away and hiding again. Nothing will change. You told me you felt crazy and alone. Those feelings will be right there waiting for you, and you won't have anyone to help you over there." He grabbed her hand.

Something stirred inside her. She shoved it down, whatever it was.

"Ignore the Aruka. What Aiden said is all true. Rokesh, Demetrius,

Wilson, Clark, Ava, everyone who knows you believes in you. They're your friends." He swallowed. "I believe in you." His thumb brushed her hand. The sensation tingled up her arm but not the normal anxiety ridden sensation that scared her. A warm peaceful energy seeped into her soul.

"Stay." His voice was low and soft.

"Why do you want me to stay so bad?" It was getting harder to breathe. Her heart hammered furiously. What was going on?

His expression was conflicted, like he was trying to figure out what he wanted to say. She could look into his mind, see what he was thinking. All she had to do was take the necklace off.

She clutched the pendant.

His eyes fell to her hand then flicked up to her face again.

That wasn't the answer. He needed to put words to whatever was going on inside that head of his. Prying into his thoughts wasn't the way to figure this out.

"Ambrose?"

Finally, he said, "you came here for a reason. You know this is where you need to be even though you keep saying otherwise. It's just not as straightforward as you thought it would be."

She was acutely aware of his hand still holding hers, his thumb rubbing in tiny comforting circles.

"And I think you can help us," he said.

She gave him a questioning look.

"I think you may be the key to this war."

Sibyl groaned and fell backwards onto the bed. Not this again. She had no obligation to help anyone but herself. She didn't owe them anything and she certainly didn't want to participate in a magical war.

"I know that's not what you want to hear, but we could really use your help if you're willing. And if you're not willing, that's fine. But for yourself, you should get this under control and that alone will help Tearnanelle. Help yourself and it will help us too, but if you do want to be part of Tearnanelle, there's a place for you here." He tucked a stray lock of hair behind her ear and caressed her cheek.

A cascade of thoughts and feelings erupted under his touch. At least they were all her own, but they were almost as difficult to sort out. She closed her eyes and leaned into his hand. The texture of his rough fingers was tantalizing. Opening her eyes, she followed the contour of muscles in his arm to his shoulders, then to his neck, and then his face. She met that intense unreadable expression, and she melted.

Emotions she hadn't felt in a long time rose from the depths of her heart. He was impossibly good looking, but he was as emotionally volatile as she was. Hot one minute, cold the next, overbearing, demanding, arrogant. But he was also kind, loyal, strong, protective. So, he acted before thinking sometimes and he drove her crazy routinely. She was familiar with that neighborhood. She practically grew up in crazy town.

His thumb rubbed her cheek similar to how he had rubbed her hand. Hummingbirds flitted inside her belly. Their eyes collided like two hurricanes in the ocean. She lost herself in the storm behind his eyes. He leaned down and kissed her gently. She remembered his smell vividly from when the dog version of Ambrose licked her and the night he carried her from the tavern. He tasted exactly like he smelled, earthy spices mixed with cedarwood. It was amazing and familiar.

He pulled away and looked at her with those stormy cognac eyes. They were so captivating, even when he was being completely insufferable, they had a way of pulling her in.

"Is this a trick to convince me to stay?" she whispered.

"No, but if it was, is it working?" He smiled mischievously.

She scoffed and sat up, pushing him to the side.

"Maybe." She smiled. Her thoughts were so jumbled it was difficult to figure out what to do. If she stayed, was it because of him or because it's what she wanted? Now she was so confused.

As if he'd read her mind, he said, "stay for you, Sibyl. I'll admit I want you to stay for selfish reasons, but that can't be why you decide to stay or go. I think it's best for you, but you have to make the decision yourself."

He pulled something from his belt. Taking her hand, he dropped the bubble into her palm. "It's yours. I gave you my word I'd escort you out if you decided to leave, and I will. You just tell me what you want to do."

She stared at the vast ocean that rippled within the tiny sphere. She swore there were two cyclones swirling side by side. Closing her hand around the bubble, she thought about her options.

She could leave right now. That's all she'd wanted since she arrived. Go home to her friends and family. Then what? She clutched the osmium necklace in her other hand. It was her salvation and her crutch, just like Solstice said. It would work, but only while she wore it. She'd be dependent on it for the rest of her life.

What if the werewolves found her? They'd already showed up in her dreams. She wasn't like Ava. She didn't move around a lot. It wouldn't be difficult to find her eventually. But, if she gave in now and stayed, was she being manipulated or was it her choice? Did it matter as long as it was the right choice?

She looked at Ambrose. He sat patiently waiting for her to tell him what she wanted. How cliché, a man waiting for a woman to make up her mind.

It didn't matter if their desires aligned as long as it's what was best for her. She wanted to be free and independent from any influence or control. That included all medication and magical objects. She needed to be the master of her own mind.

"You're right," she said.

"I'm sorry. I don't think I heard you. Did you say that I'm right?" He smiled.

"Oh my god. You're going to be impossible after this." She shook her head. "You're right. Ok. I can't hide behind a rock for the rest of my life, figuratively or literally."

She rubbed a hand over the osmium stone around her neck. "It's a tool, not the answer. Everyone's been saying it from the beginning. I just didn't want to hear it."

"Here, I don't need it after all." She held the bubble up for him.

"Keep it." His gaze was one she'd never seen on him before. Hope, relief, satisfaction? Probably smugness in actuality. He loved being right.

"Thanks." She set the bubble on the nightstand. She'd have to get another bracket to hold it on the necklace next to her osmium. She was starting to look like she belonged in Tearnanelle.

He cleared his throat. "So, are you going to go to Silvermar now?"

"I think that makes the most sense, if I have any hope of learning to control this so I'm not afraid to live life anymore."

That's what it boiled down to. She was afraid to live. That's why she'd hidden behind the medication for so long. There were times when she used her anxiety as an excuse to not try new things because she was scared. She didn't want to be that person anymore. That person was weak. She wanted to be strong like Ava, Clark, even Cassie, and Ambrose.

He took one of her hands in his and their eyes collided. He pulled her to him. This time, she didn't fight it. The kiss wasn't gentle.

A hand wrapped around her waist and his lips stole her breath as he morphed into an aggressive affection that threatened to undo all her propriety and composure. His tongue swept inside her mouth in an erotic flutter sending her head spinning. She wrapped her arms around his neck and climbed onto him, straddling his lap. He pulled her into him firmly, holding her there as if his life depended on it.

With their bodies this close he would surely feel how hard her heart was beating. The world fell away. The only thing that existed was him, his tongue, his hands that strayed lower and lower until they grabbed her ass.

She exploded into a desperate desire. Pressing into him harder, she nibbled his lip, pulling a groan from him. He pulled her into him even harder. His arousal pressed between her legs. Pressure built up inside her. She took small breaths between the direction of his tongue and grabbed a handful of his hair to brace herself otherwise she may fall into oblivion.

He spun her onto her back and he laid on top of her. His pants struggled to contain his desire. She wanted it, and him, so bad. She had to have him or else she may die. He pressed into her forcing all her breath out in a moan.

"Sibyl." He was as breathless as she was. He pushed his hips into her again and her body instinctively thrust against his. It was his turn to groan.

A knock sounded on the door about one second before it opened.

"Sibyl? Oh. Shit," Ava exclaimed.

Sibyl rolled out from under him so fast that she kneed him in the groin. He curled into the fetal position, growling in pain. Sibyl fell off the side of the bed landing on her ass.

"Ouch." The sensual fervor from a heartbeat ago was replaced with pain literally in her ass and soul deep embarrassment. She sat on the floor waiting for this moment to be over so she could go hide under a rock somewhere.

"Wow. I can't say that I'm surprised." Ava crossed her arms.

"I told her not to come in." Cassie came into the room followed by Rokesh and Clark.

"What do you want?" Ambrose yelled.

"I was coming to check on Sibyl. I wanted to make sure you were ok, but I can see you're fine." Ava smiled widely.

"Dude, did you punch him in the dick?" Cassie laughed.

Ambrose growled, rolled off the bed and limped to the bathroom. Ava snorted trying to hold in her laughter. Rokesh followed Ambrose to the bathroom.

"This is awesome. Let's just have a party in Sibyl's room. You guys do remember that this is *my* room, right? Do any of you know how to knock?"

"I did knock," Ava said, between laughs.

"Technically this is my room too, you know." Cassie flung herself on the bed.

Ava was trying desperately to control her laughter and losing the battle. Clark stood in the doorway covering her mouth with a hand which did nothing to conceal the smile behind it.

Ava's shit eating grin infected Sibyl and she started laughing too. This entire situation was absolutely ridiculously embarrassing, but it was kind of funny.

CHAPTER 22
SIBYL
LIBNYS WANC-2/SEPTEMBER 13TH

Aiden was even more intimidating out in the open. Sibyl swallowed down her anxiety. It wasn't too late to back out. *No!* That was the old Sibyl talking. The new Sibyl was brave and confident.

The Dragon yawned and she got a good look at the giant razor-sharp teeth. There had to be at least a hundred of them. Ok. Maybe the new Sibyl was stupid. She backed up a step. A hand found the small of her back. She glanced over her shoulder and met Ambrose's encouraging eyes. A sudden urge to kiss him took over all her thoughts. His fingers tickled her back.

Her cheeks flushed, not out of embarrassment, but from other feelings that had been awakened. That's all she'd thought about for the last twenty-four hours. His hands, his lips, his body. Kissing wasn't all she wanted.

"Are you guys ready to go?" Rokesh asked, pulling her from her lascivious thoughts.

"Ready as I'll ever be. Are you sure we can't ride horses?"

Silvermar City cannot be reached on foot. It would be a two-day journey on horseback to reach the coast then a two-day journey by boat. Flying is quicker. The flight is less than three hours, Aiden said.

"A bubble would get us there in seconds. We could do that," Sibyl argued.

Waste of a good bubble. My wings can get us there. The exercise and the open air will be good. Aiden stretched out his wings to show off how large they were. Sibyl swore she saw a toothy grin on the Dragon.

"Dude, you get to ride a Dragon. I'm jealous," Cassie said, excitedly.

"Yeah. It's something," Sibyl said, with mock excitement.

"Oh, come on. It'll be fun." Ambrose grinned widely. She wished she had half the courage he possessed. Cassie, Ava, and Clark gawked at the beast with equal amounts of awe and uncertainty in their expression. Clark held the osmium necklace. Sibyl didn't need it because Aiden would shield everyone around him. A trick she would apparently learn in the next couple of days.

Aiden kneeled so they could climb on to his back. Even when kneeling, he towered over them. Sibyl scrambled up ungracefully and settled in behind Rokesh who'd already mounted the beast. The Aruka insisted two guards accompany her, for Sibyl's protection, of course.

Serellina wasn't thrilled it was Ambrose and Rokesh. She tried to assign someone that Sibyl hadn't ever met before, but Ambrose and the Aruka nearly came to blows arguing over it. Sibyl stepped in and said she'd go with Rokesh and Ambrose or she wouldn't go at all. The Aruka begrudgingly caved.

Ambrose hoisted himself up and settled in behind her. He nestled in so close she could feel every curve and angle of his body against her back which aroused many thoughts that were wildly inappropriate, especially considering she was sandwiched between two men. Ambrose put his hands on her waist. She sucked in a breath.

"Is this ok?" His breath on her neck sent chills down her spine. This was going to be a long ride.

"Yes," she choked out.

"Are you sure?" he whispered in her ear and slid a hand over her stomach just low enough that his pinky brushed under the hem of her pants. Shit. The asshole was doing it on purpose.

She elbowed him. He chuckled and moved his hand back to a safer location. She grabbed Rokesh's waist who then grabbed two horns on the base of the Dragon's neck just behind the sail.

Everyone ready? Aiden asked.

"Let's do this," Sibyl said, sounding braver than she felt.

Ambrose and Rokesh gave their approval, and the Dragon spread his massive wings. The webbing was more translucent than she originally thought. She originally thought they were decorative designs, but from this vantage point she could see that it was the blood supply. A spider web of vessels laced through the wings in a beautiful pattern.

The Dragon's back muscles shifted, they dropped several feet, and her stomach flipped on itself when they launched into the air. Trees and bushes bent sideways from the disturbance of his massive wings. She grabbed Rokesh so firmly she may actually squeeze him to death.

Flying straight up, they gained altitude higher and higher. Looking down, Sibyl watched her waving friends become smaller and smaller until they were indiscernible within the landscape. The bright mid-day sun popped in and out of her vision between the flapping wings confusing her eyes, so she closed them and pressed her head into Rokesh's back.

She rode horses throughout her adolescent life. She only stopped when she went to vet school, but this was nothing like that.

The cold wind pelted the side of her face, but she remained warm nestled between the two men. Once they reached cruising altitude height, Sibyl braved a look. The Dragon's wings leveled out, catching the wind allowing him to silently maneuver in the sky like a catamaran in the ocean.

The level of quiet surprised her. In a plane there was always some form of white noise, other people, or engines, but his wings sliced through the wind making him the perfectly silent predator. Cruising smoothly along the firmament road, Rokesh and Ambrose chatted intermittently, but Sibyl was too busy taking in the scenery to listen to them.

Eventually tree tops and meadows transitioned to rocky terrain and snowcapped mountains. The same ones that were on the cover of the book she'd found in her room.

The flight time, in total, was about two and a half hours before an ocean appeared. Dark blue waves crashed against steep rocky cliff sides, spraying the air with plumes of white mist. Salt and ocean scents collided with cold mountain air. They followed the coastline for a few miles before a red maple tree sprouted up between two steep cliff faces at the edge of the ocean.

Up until this moment, the live oak tree castle in Tearnanelle was the most magnificent sight she'd ever seen, but this God Tree was a close tie. The maple towered majestically into the sky so tall that she couldn't see the top. Roots dangled into the canyon and over the cliffs on both sides. Giant branches fell in sweeping fashion to the rocky beach below. Sparkling red ruby leaves that reflected the sun's light adorned every inch of every branch making it appear as if the tree was on fire.

Despite the changing of seasons The God trees didn't lose their leaves like all the other trees in Orlon and the deciduous Earth trees.

Aiden descended until they were level with the base of the tree that spanned a deep crevasse. Dragons of various sizes, colors, and shapes flew all around, in and out of the tree, and over the large ravine. Flying straight toward the center of the canyon, Aiden tucked his wings and dove smoothly through the sky through an opening between two roots just big enough to fit a single Dragon.

Sibyl ducked instinctively, but they cleared the opening with several feet to spare on all sides. Once beneath the maple's trunk base, they entered a cave large enough that the Dragon was able to spread his wings once again.

The ride through the cave was a lot more turbulent. Cave formations jutted out on all sides and drafts blew in many directions. Cold and hot air mingled, confusing her senses. One second a blast of ice-cold air pelted her, the next, it felt like a sauna. There must be lava beneath the cave somewhere to emit that amount of heat.

Diamond lights embedded into the cave walls illuminated the tunnel which led deep into the crevasse. Sibyl's ears popped as they went deeper and deeper into the lithosphere. She heard water running below them, but she couldn't see it. There was no telling how deep the cave went. She looked behind her. The opening was gone. The only light now was that of the diamonds.

Ambrose must have sensed her anxiety because he wrapped his arms around her a bit more snugly. She leaned into the embrace that was more comforting than arousing in her current borderline state of claustrophobia.

An archway that could easily fit a creature four times the size of Aiden came into view ahead of them. Enormous rubies that resembled a bed of embers surrounded the entrance. Two Dragons, similar in size to Aiden, stood on either side of the entrance. They were the same basic build as Aiden except their heads had less horns and one didn't have a sail on his back. That one was more like a snake. The gems on their foreheads were rubies instead of a sapphire.

Aiden landed in front of the entrance. The two Dragons bowed to their Aruko as he passed through the archway and into Silvermar's throne room.

The interior was nothing short of incredible. The floors were a beautiful swirling mother of pearl, and the walls were black agate marble. A large diamond chandelier, almost identical to the one in Tearnanelle, hung from the ceiling. Ten circumferential balconies cascaded upwards. Each balcony was tall and wide enough for at least two Dragons to walk side by side. There were no stairs. Sibyl assumed they had no need for stairs since Dragons could fly.

There are stairs to access the upper levels through the interior entrance, Aiden answered. She must have thought that out loud. That was something she would need to figure out as well. How to keep her thoughts she wanted read separate from the ones she didn't.

At the back of the room was the largest pillow Sibyl had ever seen. Aiden stopped in the middle of the room and kneeled for them to dismount.

A few audible pops echoed in the room as Ambrose and Rokesh worked the kinks out of their necks and shoulders. Sibyl stretched the cramps from her back and legs.

"Hey, Aiden, I have a question. I thought elemental magic couldn't affect innate magic, but the other day, in the throne room, I couldn't hear you talk when I had the osmium. I thought the translation magic was innate, so why did the osmium neutralize it?"

You are very clever to make that observation, but also very lacking in awareness not to realize that you created a mental shield and blocked me out.

"What? That doesn't make sense. I would know if I created a shield."

You don't know the half of what you're capable of, nor how to control it. Do you think it inconceivable that your mind would create something without your knowing? Aiden admonished.

"Oh." Duh, of course that made sense. Her mind did things all the time that she wasn't aware of, much less in control of. That's why she was here.

The Dragon walked to the cloud-like pillow, circled a few times, fluffing it up in certain areas then nestled down comfortably.

"Your throne looks way more comfortable than Serellina's," Sibyl said.

Aiden chuckled. *Yes. We are creatures of comfort.*

A small Dragon about the same height as Sibyl entered from an archway to the side of the room. It walked on two legs, just like a human.

Hello. My name is Zassun. I'll show you to the human rooms, if you follow me. Not waiting for a response, the Dragon walked past them and out the same way they'd entered.

Zassun was all black, and just like the others, he had a ruby embedded into his forehead. Feathered wings that drug the ground folded neatly behind his back which had no sail. His head lacked horns too. He looked more like a lizard with wings than a Dragon.

His front legs were nearly the same as human arms with 4 dexterous fingers and his tail was just as long as his body was tall. They followed behind him, careful not to step on it.

Once they were outside the throne room in the large cave mouth they turned right and went through a smaller tunnel that Sibyl hadn't noticed when they first arrived. It was dimly lit but not completely dark in the tunnel.

They came to an intersection where the tunnel split into three paths. Zassun stopped and pointed to the tunnel on the right. *That's the way to the feeding lair. We'll be sure to have some human food available for you at sunrise, mid-day, and sunset. If you do not eat it all, just leave it on the offering table. The other Dragons will eat it. Also, if you're late they may eat it, so don't be late.*

"Thank you," Sibyl said.

He dipped his head.

That way- He pointed to the tunnel that went straight. *-Are more guest quarters for other creatures. There are currently no other guests right now. This way-* He pointed to the left. *-Are the human quarters. Follow me.*

He went into the tunnel and down a staircase. They descended at least two levels before a small hallway opened up to five doors. Two on the left, two on the right, and one straight at the end of the hallway. He walked to the one at the end.

This is the royal suite. Since it's only you three and no royals, it has been decided that you are honored enough guests to occupy this suite for the duration of your stay. He sounded slightly perturbed about that. Opening the door, Zassun ushered them in.

It wasn't luxurious by normal standards, more of a rustic cabin in the woods feel. Running water sounded close by. The bed was a giant red pillow that sat on the floor similar to Aiden's throne. Sibyl jumped on it and several blankets toppled off the sides. Zassun picked up the blankets and set them on the rough-cut table, next to the backpack that Ambrose set down. Two ramshackle chairs were pushed under the table as well, but that was it for furniture.

The bathing chambers are through that door. Zassun pointed to a door to the side. Ambrose opened the door and looked inside like he was scoping it out for threats. After a minute he nodded to Rokesh.

"Thank you. This is very nice," Sibyl said.

You're free to explore Silvermar and go wherever you please, but it's easy to get lost, so try to pay attention. I don't want to rescue you all the time.

After breakfast tomorrow, Aiden would like to see you back in the throne room to start your apprenticeship. If you need anything just say my name and I will assist you. He turned to leave then paused at the door. *You do realize you have to speak my name telepathically for me to hear you right? If you speak with your tangible voice, I can only hear you when we're nearby.*

Sibyl hadn't considered that. She'd only spoken twice telepathically, but it hadn't been that hard. *Like this?*

Zassun nodded his head. *Yes.*

What if you're far away? Sibyl asked.

Anyone you wish to speak to will hear you while you remain within the borders of Silvermar as long as they are open to communicate with you. I will leave a path for you open all hours during your stay.

Thank you. Sibyl smiled.

Zassun left and closed the door behind him.

"Did you know there were miniature Dragons?" Rokesh asked.

"No." Ambrose surveyed the ceiling. He knocked on the wall with his fist. "It's as if they bored tunnels into the mountain." He studied a wooden beam that went up the wall, across the ceiling, then down the other wall. "It's some amazing architecture."

"Just as impressive as Tearnanelle," Sibyl said.

They nodded.

She went into the bathroom. "Whoa. I wasn't expecting this."

The men came in behind her. She pointed to a waterfall in the back of the room splashing down into a large pool of water. Sibyl knelt over the small ledge and dragged a hand through the water. "The water is perfect."

Rokesh walked over to a spot in the corner. "It's a latrine style toilet."

Sibyl peered through the hole in the floor. There was running water in there, but it was so far beneath the surface that she couldn't see it.

"I guess you just relieve yourself in there and clean with the bidet over there." Rokesh pointed at a water fountain type of structure. They looked at each other and laughed.

"This will be interesting," Ambrose said.

"How long are we staying?" Rokesh asked.

"I don't know. A few days maybe," Sibyl answered.

"There's only one bed," Rokesh said. The men looked at Sibyl.

Her cheeks heated. She'd brought shorts and a T-shirt to sleep in, but they weren't exactly company appropriate. She assumed they would sleep in separate rooms and when Zassun showed them in, she hadn't thought about asking him for additional rooms. Now it seemed like it would be rude to ask him back to open up more rooms.

"We're going to take shifts so only one of us will sleep at a time. We can sleep on the floor," Ambrose said.

Rokesh nodded, but she could tell they weren't keen on the idea. They were just being gentlemanly. Sibyl stomped the floor. It was hard stone. There was no way anyone would be able to sleep on that.

"Why are you sleeping in shifts? You don't think we're safe here?"

"Just a precaution," Ambrose said.

"There's no need for anyone to sleep on the floor. It's fine. I can share the bed, but I get the side closest to the bathroom."

"You sure?" Rokesh asked.

Sibyl nodded, but refused to make eye contact with either of them. This didn't have to be awkward. They were all adults and friends. She could control her hormones around them. She had been for months now. This was no different....except she'd kissed Ambrose and whenever he was near her she got butterflies and...she looked at him. He watched her, those cognac eyes stripping her down to her soul. Her heart fluttered nervously.

They'd be sleeping next to each other with a chaperone in the room. Ambrose was correct. This was going to be an interesting few days.

"I'm starving. Do you guys want to get dinner?" she asked, trying to diffuse her heated thoughts.

They took the tunnel that led to the feeding lair. This one ascended through the mountain at least five stories. It was hard to tell exactly how far they climbed as the stairs were narrow and spiraled tightly. It could have been 10 stories for all Sibyl knew. Good thing they were all in shape.

The feeding lair was a large cave that opened on the cliffside overlooking the ocean. Sibyl stood at the edge of the cave mouth. The sun dipped below the horizon at the edge of the sea. Ambrose and Rokesh stood next to her, and all three stared out at the ocean.

It's beautiful isn't it? An unfamiliar green Dragon about the size of an elephant came up next to Sibyl. Her wings were similar to Aiden's, but her body was more like a snake with legs. Unlike Zassun, she walked on all fours.

It is, Sibyl said. She ensured that Ambrose and Rokesh were in on the conversation, at least from her end. *I don't remember seeing it when we flew in earlier.*

It's concealed by runes. The Dragon's long neck craned up. Sibyl followed her gaze. All around the cave's archway were markings that resembled double X's.

I'm Brigid.

Nice to meet you. I'm Sibyl.

I know who you are. We all do. The Dragon turned and faced the center of the feeding lair where dozens of Dragons now stared unabashedly at her. Three tiny humans standing in a Dragon feeding lair. This could, quite possibly, be one of the dumbest decisions she'd ever made.

As if Brigid read her mind she said, *don't be uneasy. We don't eat humans. There's not much meat on you.* She chuffed in a manner that Sibyl assumed was a Dragon laughing. *You're welcome here. We haven't had a human guest in a long time, and we're honored the Druid has come to visit us.*

Of course they read her mind. She didn't have a barrier preventing it. There were private thoughts she'd rather no one know. Could they hear and see everything or just some things?

By this time tomorrow we won't be able to, but yes, we can hear everything you think right now. You think very loudly.

Sibyl blushed.

Don't worry. Your thoughts are safe. No one will judge you here. Follow me. I'll show you where we put the human food for you.

Since the Dragons hunted and ate fresh raw kill, their food was not meant for human consumption, but they were kind enough to have a completely intact cooked hog and some apples and other fruit, that Sibyl didn't recognize, available to them.

Here you are. I hope you find it to your liking. I fire roasted it myself. Brigid arched her neck and snorted a puff of smoke.

"Thank you," Rokesh said.

The Dragon dipped her head and walked off to join a group of Dragons on the other side of the room. The three of them sat down and studied the large pig.

"I guess we just use our fingers?" Sibyl said.

"Here." Ambrose conjured a carving knife and handed it to her.

Rokesh dug in without hesitation. "It's actually quite good," he said between mouthfuls as grease poured down his arms.

Sibyl laughed and carved a piece off. He was right. It was delicious.

After eating their fill, they sat and spoke with several Dragons for a few hours. Sibyl asked them about some of the stories she'd read in the book in her room back in Tearnanelle. They corrected some of the myths that apparently were recorded wrong and told a few stories she didn't know.

By the time they left, the moon was high in the sky. Sibyl thanked them all for the hospitality and the three made their way back to their room where Sibyl planned to take full advantage of the waterfall shower pool.

After soaking in the pool for more than an hour, she finally got out, dried off, and put her PJs on. Running a hand through her hair, she tried to make it look as natural as possible yet elegant. An almost impossible task.

Standing at the door to the bedroom, she twisted her fingers around nervously. This was silly. Why was she so nervous? It's not like she hadn't slept in the same room with many people of various states of sobriety and propriety. She'd been to countless fraternity parties with tons of friends and strangers. Why was this so nerve racking? It wasn't. She was making it weird.

"Just be cool. Act natural," she whispered to herself. Opening the door, she walked into the room confidently.

Rokesh sat on his side of the bed with a thin white T-shirt and boxers, and Ambrose was shirtless in sweatpants that hung dangerously low on his pelvis with his arms in the air, and his legs stretched apart in some sort of a yoga pose.

Sibyl tripped over her own feet. Stumbling a few steps, she managed to grab the edge of the table and prevent herself from falling all the way to the floor. So much for acting natural.

"Are you ok?" Ambrose asked.

"Yes. I'm fine." *No. Is anyone else finding it difficult to breathe?*

"Has anyone ever told you that you're clumsy?" He smiled and she swore her heart stopped beating.

"The rug corner is sticking up over there." She pointed to the corner of the rug where it was clearly flattened down perfectly. "Watch your step coming out of the bathroom." Sibyl rushed to the bed and climbed in, pulling the covers up to her waist.

"I'm taking the first shift." Ambrose resumed his stretching. All the muscles in his back moved appetizingly slow as he shifted from one pose to another. His arms stretched out to his side, and he stepped a leg up twisting around to face her. The lines on his hips disappeared into his pants.

Her eyes roamed over his chest, his hands, his arms, shoulders, neck, face. She met his eyes that were looking right at her. Her face heated. Pulling the covers up, she turned her back on him and laid down. Rokesh lay in bed next to her, a knowing grin on his face.

"Shut up."

He chuckled.

She closed her eyes. *Shit.* She was in trouble.

CHAPTER 23
SIBYL
LIBNYS WANC-3/SEPTEMBER 14TH

Sibyl, Rokesh, and Ambrose made their way to the center of the throne room and sat down on three small cushions they assumed were put there for them. Sibyl tucked her knees under her in a meditative stance.

Aiden was on his cushiony throne, his head tucked under a wing and his tail wrapped around his body like a dog curled up. He breathed in a gentle sleeping rhythm in synchrony with the rise and fall of his chest. Sibyl wondered if he slept here last night.

No. He has a nest in the upper most part of the tree with his mate, but he was here early waiting for you, Zassun answered.

Sibyl searched the room but didn't see him.

Wait there. I'll wake the Aruko and call the council.

She twisted her fingers around on each other nervously. She hoped this event wouldn't be a repeat of what happened in Tearnanelle a couple of days ago.

On either side of the room, behind the throne, Dragons entered single file, a ruby in the center of each one's head, but none as grand as Aiden's sapphire. The Aruko's head rose and he yawned, showing off the hundreds of lethally sharp teeth.

Three of the Dragons were nearly as small as Zassun, an orange one and two dark green ones. Only one had wings, but all three had too many horns to count. Five of the dragons were as large as Aiden. A blue one that resembled a snake. One was as black as tar with wings tucked elegantly against its body in a manner that made them nearly invisible. The remaining three were as red as fire with a build similar to Aiden and just as many horns. The remaining four dragons varied in size from a small horse to a large elephant and were an assortment of colors.

The dragons surrounded the three humans. Even the small ones were intimidating, causing Sibyl's anxiety to spike. Rokesh and Ambrose stood up and put their backs to her in a protective manner.

No need to worry gentlemen. We mean you no harm. I'd like you to meet my council, Aiden said.

Neither man let down their guard. Apprehension poured from them.

"Aruko. With all due respect. I know you say you're an ally to Tear-nanelle, but it's our job to protect Sibyl, and if you try anything you will be met with hostility." Ambrose's audacity surprised Sibyl. It probably shouldn't, but he was either exceptionally brave or incredibly stupid, perhaps both, to speak to an Aruko in that manner, especially when surrounded by an entire thunder of Dragons.

I understand and I would expect nothing less.

The sincerity of Aiden's words was palpable. He held no ill intentions toward them.

The men exchanged a look, and relaxed. An entire conversation with just a look. They'd known each other since they were kids. They were practically brothers. Rokesh grew up with his aunt and uncle next door to Ambrose's family. They went to school together, signed up for Mage Guard together, trained together, and were put on assignment together. They basically knew what the other was thinking without the need for telepathy.

Ambrose took a seat. Rokesh looked around for a minute before he finally sat back down.

Do you know how a Dragon learns to fly? Aiden asked, pulling Sibyl's attention back.

"No, but I'd hazard a guess it's similar to how a bird learns. The mom just pushes them out of the nest, and they fly or fall."

Aiden nodded. *That's the gist of it.*

Sibyl didn't like the way this was going already.

This is how a Dragon learns to create a mental shield. When we're young, our parents protect us with their shields, but as we grow, we must learn to do it ourselves.

"Are you doing that right now? Shielding us all?"

Yes. That stone is a very useful tool, but you've become too dependent on it. Even though you're good at creating a shield against passive intrusion, you've never been challenged with purposeful attack which is why your shield is so flimsy. That's where we will start.

Today, Sibyl, you will learn to fly, metaphorically speaking. We've found that the best way to learn is to be forced into it. There really isn't a gentle way. You just push through until you've got it.

"Will it hurt?" Sibyl asked.

Probably.

Sibyl deflated.

It's not a physical pain. It's intangible, and it will go away the moment you learn how to command the magic. You've felt it before, I imagine. The pain in your head that happens when the magic is out of control or there are too many thoughts pushing down on you.

"Yeah. I know it well." This was going to suck.

Are you ready?

Facing the Dragon, she mustered as much courage as she could. "Let's do this."

Without warning, tingling ripped through her hands, arms, and into her abdomen like a punch to the gut. Toppling backward, she hit the floor so hard the room vanished.

"Sibyl!" Ambrose shouted a moment before silence engulfed her.

Sitting up, she took in her surroundings. She was in a strange room with bleach white walls, floor, and ceiling. It was similar to the room she was in a few days ago, only this time there was no door or windows, just a small eight by eight box. She got to her feet and pressed a hand against the wall.

Odd. It felt like glass, not drywall with paint. Sibyl picked at it. Her fingers slipped right off. There was no texture to gain a grip on. There was no paint that she knew of that was that smooth.

"This isn't real," she whispered. Dragging her fingers along the surface, she walked the perimeter. There were no seams or cracks, even in the corners. It was a perfect cube-shaped glass room.

"Hello?" Her voice was muted under the deafening silence. The walls started closing in which should be impossible since there were no cracks or seams. Sibyl spun around frantically as all four walls advanced on her. She tried to think of how to get out of this, but panic closed its talons around her mind, muddying her thoughts.

She didn't have much time. The walls were nearly on her. Backing up against one wall, she put her foot against the opposite one trying to push it back. That was useless. When her knee was at full flexion, she put it down so her leg wouldn't snap. When the walls were so close she had to turn her head, she sucked in a breath, making herself as small as possible. She had but seconds to live before she'd be nothing more than a Sibyl pancake.

Coming to terms with her end, she inhaled one last breath and closed her eyes, waiting for the pain to start. When it never came, she opened her eyes to see the beautiful chandelier of the ceiling in the Silvermar throne room.

"Are you ok?" Ambrose rubbed a hand over her forehead and down the side of her face.

"What happened?"

You were hyperventilating and about to have a seizure, so we put our shield back in place.

Ambrose helped her sit up. Aiden and the circle of statuesque Dragons stared at her with an heir of disapproval.

"I wasn't ready for that."

Yes, you are, and an enemy won't give you warning before they attack.

The tingling in her fingers started again.

"Wait!" she said, but it was too late. Within one blink she was back in the white room. "Damn it, Aiden."

She made her way quickly around the room, searching for a hidden exit. None was evident. Water seeped in from the edges of the floor.

"Oh. Great. This time I get to drown." The room filled up impossibly fast. Within thirty seconds it was waist deep. Another thirty seconds and Sibyl treaded water, her head pressed against the ceiling. Taking a deep breath, she ducked beneath the surface. She pounded on the ceiling, hopeful there may be an exit up there that she couldn't reach before. Nope.

Her lungs screamed for air. She'd be forced to take a breath soon. Why weren't they pulling her out? Surely, they wouldn't actually let her drown, would they? But they may let her stay in until she was forced to breathe.

A near drowning experience didn't sound appealing in the slightest. She'd inhaled water once before when she was a kid. It hurt a lot. She didn't want to go through that today. Flailing her arms and legs frantically at the ceiling in futile effort to find a way out, she lost control, opened her mouth, and took a breath.

Fresh air dove into her lungs as she crouched on the floor of the throne room. She coughed up the invisible insult. "STOP IT!" she choked out.

"That's too far," Ambrose yelled.

You can do this.

Savoring every breath, she tried to calm her shaking hands and slow her heart rate, but before her body came to homeostasis again the tingling started.

"NO!" she coughed out, but it was too late. She was back in the white room. "DAMN YOU!" Sibyl backed up against one of the walls, waiting for whatever came next, accepting defeat before the challenge even started.

Again and again, they sent her to the white box. Each time with different obstacles or situations to overcome and every single time, she failed. She was subjected to hornets, poison gas, snakes, fire, and countless other methods of cruel and unusual forms of torture. Even though it scared her and hurt in the moment, nothing ever caused her any real harm.

After coming out of the room when it had spun around like a Gravitron amusement ride for what felt like hours, she laid on the floor of the throne room panting. The pain in her head was unbearable. Sweat dripped from every part of her body and her vision still spun.

Ambrose and Rokesh knelt beside her, arguing about something, but she couldn't understand anything they said. Squeezing her eyes closed, she fought the nausea that broiled in her stomach.

Sibyl. What's going on? Aiden's voice was fingernails down a chalkboard.

"I can't do this," she whimpered.

Yes, you can. You're letting your fears overtake you instead of thinking logically.

"I don't know how to get out of that room. What's the point of putting me in there?"

What room?

"The white room you keep sending me to."

We aren't sending you to any room.

The scene stabilized enough so that she could sit up without vomiting. "What do you mean? Every time you attack me, you send me to that stupid white room with no doors and torture me until I can't take it anymore. Then I come back here right before I die. Then you do it again and again and again. I can't go back to that place. Please don't send me back there. I won't survive it." Her voice cracked, and tears streamed down her face.

A hand rubbed her back. She didn't know if it was Rokesh or Ambrose. She didn't have the strength to figure it out. She slumped to the floor again.

Interesting, Aiden replied. *The only thing we're doing is intruding into your mind. We're only telepaths. We can't create anything like you're describing. It sounds like your mind has developed a way to hide from attack instead of protecting you against it. A coping mechanism, if you will, but it's a dangerous one. You're vulnerable in that state.*

"Why would my mind create a torture room for myself?"

I don't know. Maybe part of you wants to hide and another part of you is trying to force you to fight back. Once you're in this white room, what do you do?

"Try to escape. What do you think I do?"

Well, try something different.

"Like what?" she snapped.

I don't know. Change your mindset. Whatever you feel when you're there, try to feel something different.

"Oh. Is that all?" She was too exhausted to argue anymore. Laying on the floor, she relished in the cold mother of pearl tile against her sweat soaked skin.

"Can you give us a minute?" Ambrose knelt beside her.

Aiden backed away, along with Rokesh and all the other Dragons.

Once they were out of ear shot, Ambrose brushed the sweat soaked hair from her face and neck.

"Go away." She rolled back over and hid her face under her arms. She didn't want him to see her like this. Weak, pathetic, ineffective. Not to mention she probably looked like shit.

"Hey. Come on. Sit up."

She pushed against him as he tried to lift her from the floor.

"Stop being obstinate," he growled.

She relented and let him pull her up. There was no fight left in her. She sat on her knees, her head slumped down, trying to hide her face. He pulled her chin up, forcing her to look at him. When she met his eyes, tears started. Damn it. Why couldn't she control her stupid emotions? Everyone was right. She was a complete mess.

"Hey." He wiped away the tears. That's not the touch she wanted from him.

"We've been here before. Do you want me to lick you?"

Sibyl laughed. "No."

"There's that smile." He sat down and folded his legs in front of him so close that their knees touched. Taking one of her hands in his, he started to massage it.

She nearly melted. "That feels so good."

"You twist your fingers all around. Sometimes I think you're going to break them off. Why do you do that?"

"It's just a nervous habit."

"No. There's more to it than that. Tell me why you do it." His strong hands worked over her sore palms and fingers. The pressure bordered on pain but never crossed the line. The tension in her body slowly eased.

"My fingers and hands tingle like thousands of needles poking me. Stretching them like that drives the blood back into them and relieves the pain."

He switched to her other hand. She shivered as a chill climbed up her arm and down her spine. His touch was lightening.

"Why do you think you get that feeling?" he asked.

"My therapist says it's my anxiety manifesting as a physical symptom."

"I don't think so. I think it's a side effect of not listening to your magic."

"What do you mean?"

"When you feel your magic or try to use it, what's the first thing that happens?"

"My fingers tingle."

"What if that's not the first thing that happens? What if there's things that happen before that, but that' just the first thing you notice?"

"I don't understand. Nothing happens before that."

"When I conjure anything, it starts in my head." He pointed to his temple. "I picture what I want then I pull the magic from here." He pointed to his chest. "And I siphon it to my hands." He held out his hand and a beautiful blue shimmering object appeared. He handed it to her.

"What is it?"

"It's the rune for heart, which is where the magic originates. You should feel it there first. Remember that night you snuck out?"

"Yes. When you licked me."

"Yes, that night, but I'm talking about when you played the piano. You were calm, happy, relaxed. I've never seen anyone so engrossed in something. It's like you were gone somewhere else and everything you did was instinctual and beautiful."

Beautiful? Her eyes were swollen from crying, her knees were skinned up, her hair was a complete mess. Similar to now sans the scraped-up knees. Was his type pitiful and pathetic? Because she was nailing it.

"When you played the piano, you played from the heart, and it moved through your body and manifested in your hands and fingers. Not the other way around, right?"

"That's different."

"No, it's not. It was hard to learn that. That's what you said, right?"

"Yes, but-"

"It took a lot of practice and failed attempts before you achieved it, right?"

"Well, yeah."

"Whenever you let your hands lead, is it as good as when you let your heart lead?"

Sibyl thought about what he was saying.

"What if your magic is whispering to you, but you're not listening, so it starts to scream? Quiet your mind and open your heart. When you hear it, don't be afraid of it, don't hide from it, just direct it. Play the magic like you would play an instrument. From the heart."

Sibyl's mind reeled. What if he was right and she was missing the first signals? The heart pumped blood to the hands, and they tingled when the blood flow was compromised, which was why she twisted them on themselves; to pump the blood back into them.

"Will you try that? Listen to your heart and see if you can hear and feel the magic there."

"If I get trapped in that stupid room again, I'm done."

"You won't if you just listen." He caressed her cheek.

She leaned into the touch. She knew everyone was watching, but she didn't care. She needed to feel something real, something good.

When he pulled his hand away, she felt the loss deep inside her. She wanted it back. If she said she was done for the day, she could run into his arms, forget about everyone else, make Rokesh stay away, and just let it be the two of them. Their eyes connected. That unreadable expression that said so much, yet so little, stared back at her.

No. She couldn't do that. That's just another form of running away. She didn't come here to hide behind yet another protective force, even one as good looking as him. She'd master this or she'd die trying. Then when she went to him, she'd be worthy of his affection.

It wasn't just that though. She needed to feel worthy for herself. She wanted to be strong, and that started by being able to protect her mind on her own.

"I want to try again."

"That's my girl." He smiled.

My girl. Did he mean that the way it sounded?

Are you ready to try again? Aiden asked.

She faced the Dragon. "Yes, I'm ready." She took a deep breath and let everything in the room disappear from her mind. Time slowed down as she honed in on her heart, feeling it beat rhythmically in her chest. Closing her eyes, she listened. Lub dub, lub dub. A slight flutter interrupted the pattern a split second before her hands started to tingle. Opening her eyes, she was back in that stupid white room, and her heart sank.

"Shit." Walking around the room, she buffeted her shirt in an attempt to get some air flow. It was stiflingly hot. After a minute or two, it was so hot that sweat soaked her.

"Heat exhaustion this time. Great." Sibyl pressed her head against the nondescript white wall. The temperature rose quickly until it became difficult to breathe, and she became light headed.

Thinking about what Ambrose said, an idea came to her. Sitting down with her back against the wall, she closed her eyes and breathed in deeply through nose and exhaled slowly out her mouth.

Her habit of twisting her fingers on top of themselves was overwhelmingly tempting. Instead, she pretended to play a piano song on her knees. Recalling the notes to a song she'd memorized, she tapped her fingers on the imaginary keys on her knees and lost herself in the music. It echoed in the room as if she was actually playing.

The song siphoned from her heart and into her fingers, directing them to play the fake notes. She fell into the music completely, forgetting where she was and what she was doing. When she played the last note, she inhaled a deep breath of fresh cool air. Goosebumps erupted on her arms.

Opening her eyes, Sibyl found herself in the middle of the woods. Not just any forest, her home forest in North Carolina. Birds chirped all around her. The sun peaked in and out of trees in full summer bloom. It smelled and felt like home. Relief flooded her.

"There you are," Aiden said.

She jumped.

Adien strolled up through the woods to stand in front of her. "Your mind is beautiful."

"This is my mind?" Sibyl looked around in awe. "It's my home."

"That seems appropriate."

Other Dragons meandered causally throughout her mindscape forest.

"Hey. You're talking, like for real talking? I can see your mouth move."

"It's not telepathy if we're inside our minds. It's only when we're outside that we have to speak telepathically.....Well, Dragons do, since we don't have vocal cords. You can do both."

"What do I do now?"

"As much as I've enjoyed exploring this beautiful place, I think it's time you push us out."

"How do I do that?"

"Will it so."

"It's that simple?"

"Yep."

She thought for a minute then came up with an idea. A giant oven mitt manifested in the sky, reached down, and scooped each of the Dragons up one at a time. It was comical to watch Aiden disappear into the clouds in a giant gloved hand.

And just like that, she was alone in her own mind. She breathed in the forest air, allowing her fatigued mind a moment of respite. The headache melted away and her tired muscles relaxed. After a few minutes she decided it was time to go.

Willing herself back to Silvermar, she blinked once then reopened her eyes and to find herself kneeling on the cushioned pillow in the middle of Silvermar throne room.

Dragons didn't have facial expressions, but if they did, Sibyl imagined Aiden was smiling at her.

In a moment of unfamiliar confidence, she said. "I think you should try it again."

Are you sure? Aiden asked.

Sibyl looked over her shoulder at Ambrose who held a smug expression. He knew he was right, again. Damn him. Somehow it made him hotter.

Turning back to Aiden, she said, "yes." All she had to do was listen and direct. It was the difference of an eighth of a second.

Pulling the magic into a ball inside her, she let it build for a few seconds until it became a large sphere of raw inertial magic. The moment her heart fluttered she released it.

The force catapulted her backwards and the entire circle of Dragons slammed against the walls of the room. A large earthquaking rumble reverberated through the throne room. The chandelier shook, making the lights flicker, and small pebbles fell from the stalactite ceiling all around her. Sibyl threw her arms over her head. Ambrose dove over her protectively.

Rokesh ducked out of the way of a large piece of rock that crashed right next to him. "Holy shit. What did you do?"

"I just meant to push them out of my head, not knock them down."

"You didn't just knock them down. You knocked them on their asses!" Ambrose smiled widely and helped her up.

"I'm so sorry. Really. I didn't mean to do that," Sibyl said with as much sincerity that she could muster. "I really hope you're not pissed because you could literally stomp us to death."

The Dragons collected themselves and returned to the circle. The heavy weight of Aiden's gaze fell on her like a mountain. Shit, she pissed them off. They were about to die.

Nice to finally meet you, Sibyl Murphy, Druid of Orlon.

Rokesh grabbed her shoulder and squeezed. "You did it."

All words failed her. She only managed a smile. She met Ambrose's eyes, a gentle smile tugged the corners of his mouth and pride surged through her.

That night, she could barely hold her eyes open at dinner. Once her belly was full, she made her way back to the room, got a quick shower, then fell into the bed in an exhausted heap. She's not even sure if she spoke to either of the guys. She fell asleep the moment her head hit the pillow.

The next four days were basically a repeat of that day. She never worked with the entire council of Dragons again. She spent the mornings working with two or three of them, and then a few different ones in the afternoon.

They worked on refining her mental shield, developing signature patterns, learning how to protect her private thoughts, learning to discern when someone was accidentally sharing their thoughts versus when it was purposeful. She learned to listen to the fluttery whisper of her heart, but she was still a bit behind the beat on that, so her magic continued to be mildly reactionary. She also learned how to tether her mental shield to her subconsciousness so it would stay in place without thinking about it constantly.

Every day she grew stronger, and every day she was fatigued so thoroughly that she was barely able to drag herself into bed at night.

Ambrose said that was normal when strengthening your magic. It was the same as if a person had physically worked out. By the end of the fourth day, she was mentally and physically spent. Luckily at the end of that morning's session she was told that her training with them was finished. That was the extent of the Dragons' knowledge and abilities. Now she was on her own for the more advanced Druid magical arts.

She was too tired to leave right away, so the Dragons agreed to let them stay one more night so she could rest. She ate lunch then went to bed and slept for the next twenty hours at which she woke up feeling fully restored. She was strong, confident, capable. Things she hadn't felt in a long time.

Sitting between Rokesh and Ambrose, eating breakfast on their last day in Silvermar, Sibyl chatted quietly with a small Dragon.

"Well, I don't know about you two, but I'm ready to go home," Rokesh said, after he finished the last of his breakfast.

Ambrose wiped his hands and leaned back. "Yeah, me too."

Sibyl was the only one still eating because she was slow, distracted by thoughts and conversation. Rokesh's words jarred her.

It was time to go *home.* That word was more complicated than it used to be. Her eyes connected with Ambrose and her heart fluttered, but not from magic.

CHAPTER 24
AVA
SCORPLEM NEWM-1/OCTOBER 3RD

As autumn fell upon Orlon, the sun slept longer, and the air became colder with each passing day. In the early mornings Ava could see her breath now.

Her friends were starting to ask questions about where she went every day, so she decided to spend this morning in the library researching demons with them to deter some of their suspicions.

Sibyl agreed to stay a little longer to help them research and suss out the spy since Ava had gotten nowhere on her own. Libraries and research weren't really her forte. She needed book smart people like Sibyl and Clark. Surprisingly, Sibyl didn't take much convincing. Her time in Silvermar must have been productive because she came back with a renewed sense of confidence and eagerness. It probably helped that she had a thing for Ambrose that was so obvious to everyone even though she tried to hide it.

"Here's something," Clark said. "Demons are in constant need of either mental, physical, or emotional attention. When they aren't sated, their cursed souls will start to fester, and a putrid odor arises."

"So, it's when they need something," Sibyl said.

"That makes sense, like when they're hungry, horny, or angry, they'll smell bad," Clark said.

"That's a sucky trait. Nothing will turn someone off more than when putrid odors start," Demetrius said.

Wilson laughed.

"Do you think that's what followed us on the way home from the tavern that night?" Sibyl asked.

"You guys reeked when you got back to the castle," Demetrius answered.

"Yeah, Ambrose said it got on him when he wasn't paying attention."

"Ambrose not paying attention?" Wilson snorted.

"That's what I said," Sibyl replied.

"Shit, It's getting late. I need to go to Mage training." Ava stood from the table and pulled out a stack of books from her bag. "Clark, can you return these for me please?"

"Sure." Clark grabbed the books, but not before Sibyl snatched the book on top.

"Put that back," Ava yelled.

Several people shushed her. Ava rolled her eyes.

"The Little Elf Who Grew a Tree." Sibyl read the title then flipped through a few pages. "Aww. It has about four words on each page."

"I will throat punch you if you say one more word," Ava said.

"Look at the picture of the cute little elf." Sibyl held the book up for everyone to see.

Wilson started laughing. Clark bit her lip trying to hide a smile.

Ava snatched the book out of Sibyl's hands and put it back on the pile. "Not one word to anyone."

Wilson and Demetrius sniggered.

"You're all acting like children."

"I mean, we're not the one reading children's books," Wilson said.

Ava threw a pencil at him.

"Hey, that was mine," Sibyl exclaimed.

"Good. Go fetch then." Ava walked off.

"You're never borrowing my laptop again," Sibyl whisper yelled.

"I already have it in my bag." Ava put up a middle finger and left the library. Shit. She was going to have to come up with a convincing story about why she had children's books and other literacy learning material. She didn't want word getting back to her aunt. Maybe it was time to let her friends in on her secret.

Friends. Ava stopped at the door and glanced back to the table. Sibyl was back to being engrossed in a book. Clark put all the returned books on a cart. Demetrius and Wilson chatted about something she couldn't hear from her spot at the door.

Friends. She could get used to that.

After dropping her backpack off in the lockers, she made her way to the training yard while wrapping her hands in preparation for sparring. Fulcinia was there today. She hadn't been around much since she'd gotten back. She was always in meetings with the senior council.

Ava was allowed to join the appeals and was learning a lot of other mind numbingly boring shit, but her aunt locked her out of a lot of meetings lately. Serellina never did tell her about the spy. Ava wasn't sure why her aunt was keeping that bit of information from her, but it didn't matter because she didn't want her aunt knowing she was spying on the enemy anyway so not bringing it up made it easier to hide.

"Good morning. You're late." Fulcinia crossed her arms.

"Sorry. I was doing some research in the library with Sibyl."

Fulcinia raised her eyebrows.

"Seriously. I was. You can ask them." Ava conjured a sword. If you want to call it that. They used dull stick-like swords. It made sense. She sucked at sword form. She didn't want to accidentally injure or kill someone.

"Ok show me the Dragon's flow form," Fulcinia said.

Ava started going through the motions. In the middle of a movement Fulcinia pushed her and she nearly fell.

"What the hell?"

"Place your foot further outside of your hips to widen your base of support. Don't worry so much about what your sword is doing. Concentrate on foot placement. Once you feel balanced then worry about the sword. Then maybe you won't get knocked down." Fulcinia smiled mockingly.

Ava resumed the form, making sure to place her feet wider apart this time.

"When you slice the sword, your pelvis should initiate the movement, and the arm follows naturally behind the rotation of your hips." Fulcinia performed the movement in a slow exaggerated manner so that Ava could see what she meant. When she finished Ava repeated it.

"Better." Fulcinia circled her as she went through the next movement. "Again, your pelvis should move first. It's the origin of all movement and generates the strength and energy needed to support the form and the weapon. Do it again and slow down concentrating on that."

Ava did as she was instructed.

"Keep your arm movements within your frame. If you extend your arms beyond your frame, then you're exposed and weak."

Ava pulled her arms in more. When she made the next move, Fulcinia slapped her wrist with a stick she'd conjured in about half a heartbeat.

"Ouch." Ava shook her hand.

"Never expose the inside of your wrist to an opponent. Always move the weapon so that the outside of your arm is toward your opponent, and if you expose the inside of your wrist your other arm should be blocking."

"Ok." Ava shook the pain from her hand and started again. After about the tenth correction in as many seconds, Ava released the sword and put her hands on hips. "This is stupid. None of these movements make any sense for real life."

"The forms help with your fitness level and improve your mechanical and tactile conditioning. Precision in forms training increases our accuracy, depth of posture, power, and speed. If you take this seriously it will help with combat sword fighting. It's an art to be calm while in the heat of fighting. The only way to accurately control and wield a weapon in a high stress life and death situation is to have a solid foundation and training to fall back on."

"Fine." Ava restarted the form. When she was done, she was sweating, her arms shook, and she counted no less than one-hundred and twenty-three corrections. Considering there were only sixty-four movements in the form that meant she was messing up each movement at least two different ways. Awesome. She still sucked.

Fulcinia kept her late since she showed up late, so she had to run from practice back to her room. Changing quickly out of her sweaty clothes, she headed to meet her aunt for Aruka training. Once she got to her aunt's office she was out of breath from running, but she made it only two minutes late.

"Sorry. Mage training went over."

Her aunt sat behind her desk. "It's ok. I think we will take a break today. I'm not feeling well." Heavy bags hung under her aunt's eyes and she was paler than usual.

"Are you ok? Want me to call a healer?"

"No. I think I'll go to my room. Bekora will get the healer. You enjoy a free afternoon." Her aunt smiled weakly, then got up from the desk and headed out.

"I'll walk with you to your room," Ava said.

"That would be nice."

After she left her aunt safely in Bekora's care, Ava headed to meet Redly. She'd gotten really good at carrying the heavy backpack without being noticed. She transformed into an albatross and carried it on her back over the wall then transformed into a horse and galloped through the woods with it on her neck. She got to their tree a little early, so she sat down and waited.

After a while when he didn't show, she became concerned. He was at least an hour late. That was out of character for him. She checked under the rock where they kept a moonstone for communication just in case they missed each other. The moonstone held no message.

Ava's concern increased. The few times he couldn't be there he always left a message. She gazed over the meadow. All was quiet. Tapping her fingers on the trunk of the tree, she contemplated waiting or searching. She wasn't a patient person, but he'd warned her against crossing the border into Tearnanoak. She chewed on her lip.

"Fuck it." She set out toward Tearnanoak.

After a mile or two, the forest became more eerie. The tree canopies weren't as dense, the forest floor had more underbrush, and there weren't as many animals scurrying about. Ava stopped a time or two and thought about turning back, but decided she was just being paranoid and pressed on.

Suddenly, she was thrust backwards and slammed into a tree. Her back exploded with pain. Redly stood in front of her, ire burning in his mocha eyes.

"What the fuck are you doing here?" he whispered.

"Looking for you."

"Keep your voice down." Redly glanced around, eyes maniacally darting in every direction.

"You didn't show up, so I came looking for you." This time she whispered.

"It's newm. You can't be here right now." He was disheveled and dark bags similar to her aunt's dragged his eyes and face down. "Remember? I told you we aren't in control of ourselves during newm. You've got to go. *Now.*" He grabbed her arm and dragged her in the direction from which she came. He walked so quickly that she struggled to keep up.

"You're hurting my arm. Let me go."

Redly seemed startled by her voice. "Oh. Sorry." He dropped her arm.

She rubbed it, trying to massage the pain out. He had a grip like a vice.

"I know my way back. You don't have to escort me."

"Yes, I do. You were stupid to come this close to Tearnanoak. Did you know there was another patrol only thirty yards away from you?"

No. Actually she didn't know that.

"You're lucky I found you. You're not leaving my sight until I know you're safe. Don't ever come looking for me again."

Her anger flared. "Maybe if you plan to not show up, you should let me know. You don't stand someone up then expect them to not investigate."

Redly rounded on her. "It's newm. Can you not see the sky? You should've known better."

"Yes. I can see the moon," she retorted.

"Really? You can?"

"Well. I mean. I see the lack of the moon." She put her hands by her sides.

"Don't be smart with me."

"Lower your voice. There may be others around, remember."

Redly curled his fists. "Woman, you're infuriating. You're supposed to rule over a land you know almost nothing about, you shove your nose into places it doesn't belong, and expect others to keep rescuing you whenever you make stupid decisions. I hope you choose a good council because you're going to need smart people to counterbalance your stupidity."

Ava made to slap him, but he caught her wrist in midair again.

"Stop doing that. You deserve to be slapped."

Redly snorted."Yeah right. I tell you the truth, yet I deserve to be slapped?"

Ava yanked her arm away and stormed in the direction of Tear-nanelle.

"Ava. Wait. I'm sorry."

She stopped, but didn't turn around. Redly came up behind her and wrapped his arms around her waist. Lightening shot through her spine. Ever since the fiasco with Sibyl's magic explosion, they'd kept everything strictly business, but she wanted him now more than ever. The brief tease of his lips on hers only made her desires grow stronger.

Leaning into him, she breathed in his scent. Pine needles and autumn mixed with......musty sex. Ava whirled around and sniffed his shirt, channeling her wolf senses.

"You smell like sex."

Redly deflated. "I told you. We don't have control of our mind or bodies during newm. I don't know what I did or who I did it with but yes, I believe sex was involved."

Ava pushed him away.

"What do you want me to say? I don't want to do these things. I hate it. I'm coerced into being with someone I don't even know or remember, and I can't be with the one person I want to be with."

"Who is that?" Ava glared at him.

He put his hands on his hips and returned the glare. "You have to ask me that?"

"You haven't made a move on me since the day we both turned so what am I supposed to think?"

"Of course I want to be with you, Ava, but you shouldn't want to be with me. I'm a fucking werewolf!" He threw his arms up.

"Not by choice and one day we'll get the cure to the curse."

"When that day comes, I'd love to have a chance with you, but until then, you need to leave and not come back. It's too dangerous."

"Oh my god, not this argument again."

Redly sighed. "I don't want to argue. I just want you safe."

"And I want to be with you!" She couldn't believe she'd just said that out loud. Redly's eyebrows shot up. It was true. She was falling for him and maybe it was the worst decision ever, but when it came to the heart was there really a choice in the matter? The heart wants who it wants. They were silent for a minute or two.

"I'll walk you back. Come on." Redly walked toward Tearnanelle. Ava fell in step beside him. When they finally got back to their tree, his eyes were sad and tired. There was no hint of his usual playfulness.

"I have information for you." He scraped the ground with his boot. "Alyssium plans to attack during winter solstice. That gives you two months to plan."

"What? Are you serious?"

"Yeah. She plans to kidnap you and the Druid and kill anyone who gets in the way." He looked at the ground. "You know I can't help you during that time, right?"

"Because it'll be newm again?"

"It's not just any newm. It's the darkest time of the year. That's when Alyssium's magic is strongest and for three straight days we will shift and be totally out of control. Not only can I not help you. I'll be the enemy, Ava. You need to stay away from Tearnanoak and me."

"My aunt said that winter solstice is a time of celebration. She said it's when the land goes into a restorative sleep and then wakes up three days later renewed. She never mentioned anything about you guys being permanently transformed during that time."

"She probably doesn't know. We never leave Tearnanoak during those days. Alyssium has her own celebrations which usually consists of orgies, fighting, and consuming massive amounts of food, alcohol, and Em. But this year is different because you and the Druid are here."

"I wish I was the Aruka now so I could take back Tearnanoak."

Redly's face contorted into one of confusion. "What makes you think you can take back Tearnanoak? Don't get me wrong. I'd love for that to happen. But Ava you have to know that it's virtually impossible. Tearnanoak is dead."

"Well, that's a shitty attitude. As soon as I ascend, I'll restore Tearnanoak, take my rightful place as Aruka, and banish Alyssium. That's why I'm training so hard every day."

Redly's eyes widened.

"What?" Ava asked.

"Ava. You're the Arukas of Tearnanelle. You know that right?"

"No. I'm the Arukas of Tearnanoak."

Redly shook his head. "Why would you think that?"

"Because my mother was Aruka of Tearnanoak and I'm marked by the Goddess to inherit the magic and the throne." Ava pointed to her hair.

"You have silver hair, Ava." Redly grabbed a lock and looked into her eyes, waiting for her to understand. "Silver hair for the Silver Kingdom. Tearnanelle."

Ava's mind reeled. So many thoughts rushed into her. Why her aunt and Fulcinia had treated her weirdly whenever they mentioned her hair. Why some people looked at her with sadness in their eyes.

"There is no heir for the Gold Kingdom, Ava. You're proof that Tearnanoak is dead."

"Ok. Stop. I can't follow what you're saying." Panic and confusion threatened to undo her. She was supposed to save them. "If I restore Tearnanoak we can be together."

"Only the heir of Tearnanoak can restore the Goddess. You aren't that person. Tearnanoak didn't have a chance to choose an heir before she died. We all thought there was someone out there. For my entire life, Alyssium sent hunting parties to find you and they got close a few times, but no one realized until you got here that you're the heir to Tearnanelle."

"How do you know I'm the only one? There may be someone else out there."

"No one else was born in Tearnanoak for several months before you. If there was someone else, we'd know. You were the last person born before Tearnanoak fell and you're not marked with gold. There is no one else."

"Well. Even if I can't restore Tearnanoak, I could defeat Alyssium or send her back to..." She couldn't remember the name of the realm the demon came from.

"Mokor," Redly provided.

"Yes. Mokor. Somehow, we could banish her back to Mokor or trap her. Something."

Redly cupped her face in his hand.

"It's time to go home now, pretty little hawk. We can talk about this later." He kissed her hand. The gesture made butterflies dance in her belly.

"I'm not finished discussing this."

"The sun is getting lower. I can feel the curse pulling at me, Ava. I can't stay. As much as I want to, I can't."

"Will I see you tomorrow?" she asked.

He shook his head. "Two days from now then we'll be done with newm."

Ava nodded. Redly caressed her cheek one more time, then turned and walked away. She couldn't help but worry for him. He'd said that many werewolves die on newm because of the fighting. How would she know if that happened? They had no way to communicate for the next forty-eight hours. This was going to be a long two days.

Her mind roiled the entire way back home. Concern for Redly, anger that her aunt lied to her about what she was, anxiety over the impending attack. The pressures of ruling a kingdom were building and she wasn't even in charge yet. How did her aunt do this all the time?

When she got within a couple of miles of the wall, she shifted into an albatross again and before she could get to cruising altitude, she was nearly taken out by dozens of birds flying in a squawking panic away from Tearnanelle.

What the hell? Something smelled off. Smoke. Transforming her eyes into the precision accuracy of the hawk, she looked toward Tearnanelle. All of Ava's worries were temporarily forgotten as concern for Tearnanelle rocketed to the forefront of her mind. The sun was almost fully set, dusk swept over the land, but it was bright as day in Tearnanelle because of a large fire behind the God tree that originated from the field crops. *Cassie!*

Flying as quickly as her wings could go, she sailed over the wall, dodging all the other birds who were making their escape. The smoke was overwhelming now that she was within Tearnanelle proper. Diving to the ground, she shifted into her human form, ditched the bag, and ran toward the field crops.

Rounding a corner, she was nearly run over by horses. The barn was on fire, but that's not what made her breath hitch. Behind the barn was a blaze the size of a small mountain. She ran to the fields, trying not to let her fear get the best of her.

Hundreds of Mages ran frantically about, weaving fluorite gems, creating waves of water in an attempt to douse the blaze. Ava had never seen a fire this monstrous. Even from dozens of feet away, she could feel the heat radiating off it like a furnace.

The flames traveled over the crops, being pushed by the wind and leaving a wake of devastation behind. This late in the season everything was already naturally dying off, creating the perfect blanket of kindling. It wouldn't take long for the fire to consume every last crop and then set on the forest. The leaves were so dry there'd be no stopping it if it got to the trees.

A man in the middle of one of the fields yelled out orders, ushering people in different directions. Mages created a new fire in a field that wasn't hit yet while others ran up and down rows of crops filling up baskets, wheelbarrows, pockets, armfuls, whatever they could with the remaining food that they could grab. A line of cattle and horses pulled plows creating large rows of freshly churned dirt. Ava assumed the animals were Mages since any ordinary horse or cow would probably bolt from this situation. Dozens of others sprayed everything with water. It was organized chaos.

Heading to the man yelling orders, Ava asked, "what is everyone doing?"

"Creating a backfire and a fire break!" he said, barely paying her any attention.

"What?"

He appeared annoyed for a moment then recognition took over his features. "We're making a fire break here." The man pointed to the freshly plowed dirt. "The backfire will burn off anything on the other side so the fire can't jump it and spread further."

Ava surveyed the small fire that slowly made its way across the field, carefully controlled and directed by dozens of Mages wielding rubies and fluorites. Everything between it and the wildfire was burned to ash and dripping wet making it no longer flammable.

"We need more Mages to wield fluorite or pull a plow. Which are you better at?" He waited impatiently for an answer. The truth was she'd never done either of those things.

"Fluorite is easy to wield!" He obviously picked up on her inexperience, so he chose for her. He pointed to a wheelbarrow a few yards away. "Get a fluorite and just will water to pour from it."

She nodded and ran to the wheelbarrow. The gems were beautiful. They weren't shaped into round spheres like the ones that were used for trade. These were raw harvested large cylinders with streaks of blues, greens, and purples running through them. She picked one up that was about two feet long and as big around as her hand could grip. Pointing the fluorite, she willed the magic to work. As if she'd turned on a spigot, water sprayed out.

"Cool." Too bad she didn't have time to appreciate the magnificence of the magic. Running to the line of Mages who were already spraying the ground, she jumped in and did the same. A lot of the water evaporated before it even hit the ground. It was so stiflingly hot. It felt like the middle of summer in a desert. The water was helping, but this method seemed inefficient. If they could somehow drop the water from above it would probably be more effective. She had an idea.

Searching her gem cuff, she found an amethyst and pulled it free. She'd never used one of these either. Amethysts granted the user the ability to manipulate air. It couldn't be that hard. So far, she'd found elemental magic to be fairly easy to wield, so she pulled magic from the gem and created a sphere of fresh air around her. It worked. She was instantly relieved from the suffocating heat and smoke.

Now the real question was, could she use two gems at once? Testing out the possibility, she aimed the fluorite and water sprayed out again.

Satisfied that she could handle the task at hand, Ava shifted into a hawk, took the fluorite in one taloned foot and the amethyst in the other and took to the sky. Within a few wing beats, a solid black fortress of smoke surrounded the sphere of protection she'd created, making it impossible to see anything.

The air was so turbulent that her body was pushed violently around, and she nearly fell. That would be tragic and embarrassing. After a few minutes of fighting the fiery drafts, she finally found a smooth spiraling current and let her wings filter through it naturally. Leveling off, she watched the inferno dance around her in a powerful storm of violence.

She couldn't see anything except the fire and smoke swirling around her. Letting the air sift through her feathers she dropped until she could see the ground beneath her, then she found another draft and sailed around smoothly. Once she was over the fire break, she opened up the spigot of magic from the fluorite and rained down a storm of water. Cheering erupted from below.

Others took to the sky, following her example and soon dozens of Mage birds circled around the fire break soaking the ground and everyone below them.

When she exhausted her fluorite, she retrieved another. She repeated the process until the wheelbarrow was empty then she and the others landed. Shifting to her human self, she stumbled for a moment. She was dizzy and her legs were shaking. She'd expended a lot of magic.

"Need a hand?" Someone she didn't know grabbed her arm and pulled her away with the crowd. They all gathered a safe distance away and turned to watch the fiery show. The flames were within a dozen feet of the fire break now and the backfire was extinguished. Now they waited.

"AVA!" Wilson and Demetrius pushed through the crowd and came up next to her. Demetrius was a naturally dark-skinned person, but right now he was black as coal and Wilson matched. Everyone around them looked like that. She probably did too. They were covered in sweat and soot.

"Have you seen Cassie?" she asked.

"Yeah. She's in the healer's quarters. She's in pretty bad shape," Wilson said.

Oh Gods. Ava hoped Cassie would be ok.

"What about Tacey?" she asked.

Demetrius shook his head. "No one's found her yet."

"What started it?" she asked.

"I don't know." Demetrius wiped his face, smearing even more black soot over his features. The fire was only a few feet from the fire break now. As if it knew they were trying to kill it, the fire started to spin around itself. A giant tornado siphoned the flames into the air. Ava shielded her eyes. Everyone stepped back.

"Oh my Gods." Wilson tilted his head back following the blaze up until it disappeared into black clouds.

"What's happening?" Ava asked.

"Fire whirl," said the man who was giving orders earlier. "Fires suck in cool air from the bottom. As it heats up, it rises then starts to spiral. Beautiful and deadly." He watched with a look of awe on his face.

Everyone's attention turned back to the fire tornado that lit up the sky with intimidating intensity. When it hit the fire break, everyone backed up even further from the surge of heat. Ava's heart thundered in her chest. Hundreds of people and creatures stood as still as statues, watching, waiting, hoping, praying.

"Look." Wilson pointed. The fire was getting smaller.

"I think it's working." Demetrius smiled. Over the next few minutes, the fire tornado slowly whittled away until it was nothing more than a skinny tube and then with a flicker it fizzled out completely. All that remained were small patches of fires and beds of embers sporadically around the ruined fields.

Cheers and screams erupted from everyone. Wilson grabbed Ava and spun her around in a stinky sweaty hug. She didn't care. The relief flooded her, but she didn't have time to celebrate. There was still a pressing concern. Cassie.

Running through the hall, Ava made her way to the healer's wing of the castle. When she got to the giant oak double doors, she pushed them open and saw Sibyl, Ambrose, and Rokesh standing at the foot of one of the beds.

Sibyl's face was strained with concern. Ava ran to them, and her heart dropped. Cassie was bandaged up nearly head to toe.

"She's sustained severe burns. They've wrapped her in a gold poultice," Sibyl said. "Good news is she gets the benefit of magical healing. On Earth she'd be in critical condition and probably wouldn't survive."

Ava found it difficult to breath. She brought Cassie here because she thought her friend would be better off. Ava sat down on the bed and grabbed her chest. It hurt to breathe.

"Are you ok?" Rokesh asked.

Her chest tightened as if someone squeezed it. What if they hadn't found her? What if she died? The room spun.

"Ava?" Sibyl said.

Her fingers went numb. She held up her hands and stared at them, trying to figure out what was happening to her.

"Oh. I know that look. Sit down." Sibyl directed Ava to a chair.

Ava felt nauseous and dizzy. What was happening?

"Ava, just breathe in through your nose really slowly, and out through your mouth. Close your eyes and imagine you're somewhere else. Anywhere that makes you calm and happy," Sibyl said.

Ava closed her eyes and tried to take calming breaths, but it hurt. She had nowhere to picture herself being happy. Or did she? The fruit tree in the meadow. She pictured it.

"What do I do now?" Ava asked.

"What's the temperature like? What's the weather doing? Is there a breeze? Is anyone there with you? Can you get a glass of ice water?" Sibyl asked someone else.

Footsteps walked away. Ava thought about the questions and pictured herself laying in the grass on a sunny summer day. Redly watched her with those beautiful mocha eyes. A smile on his face and that eyebrow ticked up. He was being obstinate about something.

She smiled and the pain in her chest loosened its grip. Taking a breath, she relaxed and the feeling in her fingers returned.

"What was that?" Ava opened her eyes.

"You were having a panic attack," Sibyl said.

"What? No. I don't panic."

"We all panic sometimes. I'm just a professional at it," Sibyl joked.

Ambrose returned with the glass of water. "Here." He handed it to Ava. She was so parched. Taking the glass, she gulped it all down.

Sibyl took the empty glass, handed it back to Ambrose. "More."

"What am I, your servant?"

"Just get some more water please," Sibyl scolded.

Ambrose huffed and walked away again.

"Wow you've tamed the bear," Ava said.

"Yeah. He's nearly housebroken now." Sibyl laughed.

"I'm standing right here. I can hear you." Ambrose returned with a pitcher of water. "The healer gave me this. Here." He refilled the glass and handed it to Ava.

"Thank you." Ava took the glass but this time she just held it, absorbing the coldness from the condensation. She took in Cassie's full state and her eyes started to burn. Tears. She hadn't cried in years. "Do we know what happened?"

Sibyl's face fell. "It was Cassie."

"What do you mean?"

"Cassie caused the fire," Rokesh said. His expression showed a lot more sympathy than Ambrose did.

"I don't understand," Ava said.

"The fire started in one of the green houses. Apparently, Cassie brought some drugs with her when we left Earth, and she snuck away to get high. She must have accidentally passed out and the greenhouse caught fire." Sibyl shook her head.

There was nothing more to say. Cassie caused a fire so devastating there may be food shortages through the winter and possibly costing some people their lives. Ava hadn't paid close enough attention to her friend to see any signs of drug use. How could they not have noticed? Ava was a terrible friend.

"What's going to happen to her?" she asked.

"She'll be brought in front of the Aruka for judgement and punishment as soon as she's healthy enough." Ambrose crossed his arms over his chest. Definitely no sympathy there.

"Oh Cassie." Ava looked at her friend bandaged up so completely that you could barely see her face. "What have you done?"

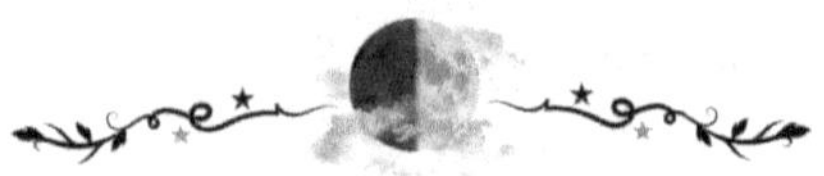

—— Scorplem Firoq-3/October 11th ——

Ava sat across from her aunt on the other side of the desk. As far as offices go, this was a nice one. Floor to ceiling library on one wall, a giant tapestry on another, a small hearth to help warm the office on cold days or nights, an old looking couch and, of course, the giant wooden desk. It was just elegant enough to be intimidating, but not so gaudy to be over the top.

Serellina was still weak from whatever illness had afflicted her for weeks, but she still found the energy to perform her Aruka duties. Fulcinia stood by her side, and they both held stern expressions.

"I cannot be lenient on this matter. Cassie has put everyone in jeopardy. We're still cleaning up the mess days later. People died."

"She doesn't belong in the cells. She needs rehab," Ava pleaded. The guilt sat on her so heavily. Tacey was missing, presumed dead, and two other burned corpses were recovered from the ashes. They were identified as garden attendants and had families who were mourning now. Along with dozens injured and a few horses even got injured and burned when the barn caught fire.

"Rehab isn't something this world offers. We can send her back if you would rather."

"Give her one more chance, please," Ava begged on behalf of her friend.

"No." Serellina didn't even consider the request.

"So that's all a person gets around here? One chance? I guess it's nice to be so fucking perfect."

"This isn't about chances or being perfect, which no one claims to be. It's about actions having consequences. She chose to partake in something that not only harms herself, but potentially others as well, as proven by this event."

"What's the consequence of lying to your family?"

"What are you talking about?" Serellina's tone became exasperated.

"Would you explain to me again what this *silver* streak in my hair means? I've been told that I was to inherit Tearnanoak, restore the fallen Goddess, and save the fallen kingdom, but that's funny don't you think since Tearnanoak is the Kingdom of Gold and I have a SILVER mark. Interesting right?" Ava smirked.

Fulcinia and Serellina exchanged a look.

"That's what I thought. So only you guys get to get away with being deceitful?"

"We didn't burn down half the kingdom," Serellina countered.

"You purposefully withheld information about me and my life. She was just trying to do something that made her feel good and had an accident."

"I'm sorry I misled you. I....We all truly thought you were going to be Tearnanoak's heir. When Fulcinia found you, we were shocked your mark was silver. We spent the last twenty-seven years searching for you, thinking you would restore Tearnanoak and when we finally found you, we all knew what it meant. We just weren't ready to face the truth yet, so we withheld some information. That's not the same as lying and it's certainly nowhere near as devastating as burning down our food supply and causing the death of innocent people."

Serellina laced her fingers together and leaned her elbows on the desk. The dark red sleeve of her left arm contrasted with her bare right arm beautifully. She bowed her head. "We are officially defeated. My sister's kingdom is lost, and I am obsolete."

Ava's heart wrenched. They'd fought for so long against the demon queen. They had one last hope, and that was dashed when they found her.

"That's one reason I've tried so desperately to keep Sibyl here. Alyssium knows I'm going to weaken soon. She'll come for this kingdom when it starts. Ava, I'm afraid you may be inheriting a doomed kingdom."

"Jeeze," Ava said. "You guys are all doom and gloom today. Just because Tearnanoak is gone doesn't mean all hope is lost, but if I'm going to be Aruka one day then let me help now with some things, at least in little ways. Please pardon my friend. I will take full responsibility for her from now on."

Her aunt gave her a sympathetic look. "Ava. That's not practical. You can't babysit a grown woman with a debilitating ailment."

"Yes, we can. Put guards on her like you do with Sibyl."

Her aunt chewed on her bottom lip. Ava could tell she was thinking about it.

"If you send her back to Earth, she will fail. There's too much temptation there. There's none here now. I searched her room and confiscated everything. It's all gone now. She has no choice but to get clean. It'll be hard for a few weeks or months, but it'll get easier for her as time goes by, and since she doesn't have access to anything anymore, she's not a threat."

Serellina's face softened. "Fine, but I'm not using any additional resources. She stays with Sibyl, and they can share guards."

Sibyl was going to hate that. She was already trying to get rid of her guards, now she'd basically have Cassie around all the time too.

"Speaking of Sibyl. She's gaining control of her magic and getting stronger every day. Do you think she really needs guards all the time?"

"Yes. She's shown no allegiance to us or our cause. She could easily get taken or turn to the enemy. Until we know for certain where her loyalties lie, she will be under watch at all times."

Well. She tried. That wasn't a hill worth dying on, since she'd just won Cassie's freedom. She'd take what she could get, but there was one more thing she should tell her aunt so they could start figuring out what to do about it.

"Alyssium plans to attack Tearnanelle during winter solstice."

Serellina's and Fulcinia's heads snapped to her.

"How did you get this information?" Fulcinia asked.

"Where I got it isn't important, but there's more. She plans to kidnap me and Sibyl. You can probably guess why."

"We can't let her get either one of you or we're truly doomed," Serellina replied.

"Trust me. I know. So, what do we do?"

"No one knows how to kill a demon," Fulcinia said.

"We've been researching that, and we haven't gotten closer to figuring it out either."

"Who's been researching that?" Serellina asked.

"Me, Cassie, Sibyl, all her guards, and Clark. We wanted to know how to kill the spy once we found out who it was."

"What?" Serellina exclaimed.

"Oh. Yeah. About that. I overheard you telling someone that we have a spy in Tearnanelle, so I've been trying to figure out who it is, and we determined it's a demon, so we've been trying to figure out how to kill a demon, but we haven't found anything useful."

"I'm not even going to address the fact that you were eavesdropping on a private conversation. How do you know it's a demon?" Serellina asked.

"The missing sheep and the smell that people have reported," Ava said.

Fulcinia and Serellina's faces contorted with confusion.

"Seriously? You guys don't know that demons smell bad?"

"Yes. We know they smell bad, but no one has reported a smell to me," Serellina said.

"Sibyl and Ambrose smelled it when they were coming back from the tavern one night. Ambrose was nearly attacked by this demon and was covered in the smell."

Serellina's eyebrows furrowed. "Ambrose smelled like it?"

"Yeah. He got it on his clothes or something."

"I think I underestimated you, niece." Serellina pulled herself to her feet. "Thank you for the information, although I'm going to want a full accounting of how you came by this information. Let's call a council meeting for tomorrow to discuss our plans for winter solstice. We need to come up with a defense strategy."

"And the spy?" Ava asked.

"I'll handle that. You concentrate on your training. There's a chance you may need it soon."

She meant Ava may need to fight to defend herself and her future kingdom soon. That was a large pill to swallow. Was she ready to rule a kingdom? Would there be a kingdom left to rule in two months? Would she be alive? Not if she kept sucking at the primary weapons. She needed to step up her game. She had to figure out who the spy was, and figure out how to kill a demon.

Ava's head fell into her hands. She'd been Arukas for four months and she was already crumbling under the weight of it all. How was she supposed to do all of this? If she failed, thousands of people would die and Tearnanelle would fall to the same fate as Tearnanoak.

All her friends, Redly, and countless others were all in real danger. She'd brought Cassie here thinking she'd be safer and that turned out horribly. Maybe she should send Cassie back. Maybe Ava should go back too.

No. This was her home. She wouldn't be chased out of it again. She would stay and fight, even if she died in the process, but Cassie and Sibyl had a choice. They should be informed of what was happening. She didn't want anyone else getting hurt or dying on her account.

CHAPTER 25
AVA
SCORPLEM WAXG-4/OCTOBER 15TH

Even though it was cold outside Ava was sweating. She spun lightly on her feet, swinging a dull dagger around in a twirling pattern she'd been practicing for weeks. No one was around to critique her, but if there was, she was sure she'd be told how horrible she was doing.

Moving her arms quickly in a strike combination blocking pattern, she leaned forward then swept her arm in a circle outward.

"What are you doing?" Redly walked into the meadow.

"Practicing a sumbrada kali drill." She didn't break form.

He watched as she went through several movements. When she finished, she met his gaze. He was his normal self again, which was to say gorgeous.

"Aruka training was cancelled again. My aunt has been sick. We were supposed to meet with the council to come up with defense strategies for the attack, but she hasn't left her bed in days."

Redly furrowed his eyebrows. "That's not good."

"Yeah. I'm worried."

"Well, let's take your mind off that. Tell me about that kali drill you were doing."

"I suck at it. I suck at all the primary weapons forms and drills actually."

"Primary weapons?"

"Sword and dagger. We're not allowed to advance to any other weapons until we have those two mastered because they're the simplest to conjure and learn, but I'm stuck."

"Why?"

"How long do you have?" she said sarcastically.

He chuckled.

"One of my many problems is I accidentally release my weapon when I get distracted, which as you know, is quite frequent."

"I have some ideas about that. May I?" He gestured for her to hand him the dagger. She did.

"It's dull," Redly smirked.

"We practice with dull weapons so we don't accidentally hurt ourselves or others."

He shook his head. "We both have enhanced healing. Give me a real weapon."

She released that one and conjured a new dagger that was sharp, and handed it to him.

"We don't practice with weapons, but we have claws which are kind of the same thing." He held up his hand which now contained five deadly six-inch daggers on each finger.

"They don't retract until I release them, but it's second nature. I don't have to try too hard to keep them."

Ava reached toward him. He pulled his hand back and the claws retracted into his fingers so quickly it was as if they disappeared.

"Why won't you let me see them?"

"They have anti-gold in the tips. I don't want you to get hurt."

"So. My dagger has silver in it." She pointed to the weapon he held. "I want to see them. Show me."

"Fine. Just be careful." He put his hand out again with his claws exposed.

The skin around the nail bed was black and smelled faintly

necrotic. She rubbed a finger down the length of one. The surface was rough like a jagged bone.

"Does it hurt when they retract in and out?"

"Not really. It feels like someone squeezing your fingers for a split second. That's all." She flipped his hand palm side up. Fading burn marks marred the skin. Within a few seconds they were gone and his hand was perfectly normal again, except for the claws.

"What were those marks that disappeared?"

"Burns from where I touched the silver."

"Does that hurt?"

He shrugged. "It's not too bad on the surface. It's when the silver gets into our blood that's a problem."

She turned his hand back over. The claws disappear into his fingers leaving behind a normal human hand.

He stepped closer to her. "Guess what?" he whispered.

Still holding his hand, she looked into his eyes and her heart fluttered. "What?" She tried to keep her voice level and casual. A gentle breeze wafted in the smell of pine needles in the autumn. She inhaled deeply and stepped closer until there was only inches between them.

He held up his other hand. "You forgot your weapon."

"Shit." She threw his hand down. Stupid hormones.

At least in a real fight, that was one less distraction she'd have to contend with. How was he in so much control? Did he feel things for her like she felt for him? He said he wanted her, but he never made a move except to endlessly flirt and tease her. It was frustrating as hell.

"This is a simple problem of multi-tasking. Conjure another."

She did what she was told and handed it to him. He flung it a few feet away into the dirt.

"Can you recall it, or do you have to physically go grab it?"

"I can recall it." She held out her hand and summoned the blade back. It spun through the air and into her outstretched hand where she then made an exaggerated strike pose and smiled.

"Ok. Show me your throwing skills." He pointed to a tree. She threw the knife. It spun through the air and stabbed into the bark with a satisfying thud.

"Your aim is good, and your recall is good. Leave that one there and conjure another."

"I've never conjured more than one at a time."

He raised his eyebrows. "Well, it's time you learn then. I can conjure one at a time or all ten. It should be similar for you, I would think. It's not that difficult."

She pulled another blade out. It wasn't difficult to conjure, but it was a bit challenging to maintain the split focus. He took it from her and hurled it into the ground a few feet to the right.

"Another."

After she conjured that one, he took it and flung it into the dirt to her left. That one sank to the hilt.

"Another."

"I don't know how many more I can hold."

"They're all still here. Another." He held out his hand impatiently.

They did it four more times before three of them disappeared when she tried to conjure an eighth weapon.

"Seven seems like your limit right now."

"There's only five," she corrected.

"You had seven until you tried the eighth, so we'll say seven. Conjure two more."

Her body protested at the strain of seven blades. It took a lot of concentration to hold them all.

"Now recall them one at a time."

Two were already in her hand so she turned to one of the others nearby and summoned it. When she caught it, she went to summon the next one and it was gone. Looking around, she confirmed her suspicion. They were all gone, except the three in her hand. "Well shit."

"Hmmmm." He put his hands on his hips. "What does it feel like once you conjure something?"

"There's a slight pull in my chest. The further an object gets away from me the weaker the pull. One reason I prefer the sword. I don't usually release them on accident if I physically hold them. Only when my opponent gains the upper hand on me."

"Ok. Why don't we try something different? Can you tie the tethers together?"

"What do you mean?"

"Release two and keep just one."

She did what he said.

"Now using that one, can you create another blade out of it, but maintain this one in its original capacity? Like two daggers stacked on top of each other."

"I have no idea. I've never tried."

"Let's find out," he said.

"Ok." She pulled the silver from her heart, siphoned it into her hand where the other dagger was, and pushed the magic through the handle, into the blade, then out the other side where it melded together with the other one to create a longer dagger with a seam halfway up the blade.

They both studied it.

"Can you throw the second one as if it were a separate weapon?" Redly asked.

She flung the blade at the tree, and it flew out of the initial blade and sank deep into the trunk. It didn't have a traditional handle, just a tang.

"Wow. That's kind of cool." Ava stared at the one in her hand. There was a hole on the end where the tang would interlock into it if she recalled it.

"Does it feel like two weapons or one?"

"One."

"How many can you stack?"

She smiled. "Let's find out." Six was the magic number to still be a functional weapon. She basically magically welded six daggers together to create a sword that she could wield but when desired throw the end dagger off while still having a sword to defend herself.

Since it was technically one weapon, she didn't have to concentrate on maintaining them all.

"This is badass. I've never seen anything like it." She admired her weapon.

"Me neither. May I?" He held his hand out.

Ava handed it to him. Inspecting it closely, he waved it through the air a few times then handed it back. "It feels and looks nice, but the question is, can you use it?"

Ava went through a few sword form movements then sliced the blade through the air releasing the end piece into a nearby tree where the dagger embedded itself to the hilt.

They smiled. She twirled around and swiped the blade down in a circular pattern releasing another piece that flew through the air and into another tree. One by one, she released the individual daggers with each movement in the sword form she'd been learning until only one piece remained. She was pleased that all the pieces remained tangible, and she didn't have to use much effort. Now she wanted to show off.

Doing the sword form backwards, she recalled each piece individually. One by one the daggers flew back to her weapon in hand and reattached themselves. Within a few seconds she'd recalled all the pieces in reverse order and now she had a full-length sword again.

"I think you've figured out the trick to conjuring more than one weapon, but now the question remains-" He marched straight up to her, determination burning in his eyes.

She swallowed nervously.

Without warning he swept her feet, and she fell on her ass. Pain shot through her spine.

"What the hell?" Frustration boiled through her. He was the second person today who tried to knock her down. At least Fulcinia was kind enough to just give her a nudge.

He stared down at her, a smug expression over his face. "Your weapon is gone, Arukas."

She glanced at her empty hand. "Damn it."

"Now, let's see about this focus problem. No weapons. Let's spar." He offered a hand.

She got to her feet and took up a ready stance. He did the same. They danced in a few circles then she attacked. It went quickly from there. She faked a jab and followed up with an overhand right. Easily deflecting her strikes, he came in with a powerful jab of his own.

Pain sliced through her nose. Falling to the ground for a second time in less than five minutes, she cupped her face. "I think you broke my nose." The metallic taste of blood seeped into her mouth. She groaned as she cupped her face and nose. "Just because I have enhanced healing doesn't mean I don't feel pain, ass hole."

"I know. It's the same for me, but better to break your nose in practice than break your neck in battle."

He was a blurry silhouette behind a shield of tears. If she could use any of her face muscles right now, she'd send him a death glare, but all she could manage was a pathetic squint.

"Let me see." He knelt beside her. She moved her hands away. He cupped her face. A cattle prod of pain zapped through her when he touched her nose. She growled, but before she could protest, he smashed her nose between his fingers.

"OUCH!" Pushing him away, she rolled over shielding her face.

"It was crooked. You didn't want it to heal that way. Now it's straight, so you'll be just as beautiful as you were originally." His voice was teasing, which made her want to throat punch him. That's a good idea. As soon as she was able to get up, that was her next move.

She was grateful that he set her nose. She didn't want it to heal crooked, but she wasn't going to tell him that right now.

"Something to keep in mind in this situation, is you won't be able to see for a few minutes. You're vulnerable after a strike to the nose so you may want to think of a better plan than writhing on the ground."

She really wanted to beat the shit out of him right now.

"Ok. Get up. Let's go again," he said, after a few minutes.

The pain was subsiding already. She cautiously touched her nose. It was still swollen but didn't feel broken anymore. Enhanced healing did have its perks. She got to her feet, rolled her neck, and wiped the blood from her face on the back of her arm. This shit was about to get real. If he wanted to play for blood, then she was up for the challenge.

"Watch your opponent's hip position. The hips tell you what's coming next. Likewise, if you hinder an opponent's ability to move their pelvis, then you cripple their ability to fight, defend, and attack."

That was similar to Fulcinia's instruction about the pelvis leading her strikes. Guess there was a point to the sword forms, like Fulcinia said.

Watching him closely, she tried to notice the movement of his hips before he attacked. That was insanely counterproductive. Now all she could think about was his package. Damn it. Forcing herself to concentrate, she side-stepped carefully, keeping her frame balanced. She'd wait for him to make the first move this time. They circled each other a few times before he finally attacked.

She blocked, spun around, and tried to land a punch. He blocked, and when her guard faltered, he elbowed her on the temple. She went down again. The world spun and the ringing in her ears was deafening. Could she actually sustain a serious injury? She physically healed faster than most, but what if she got a concussion or brain damage, or other type of mental damage, would she heal from those types of injuries?

A wave of nausea roiled in her stomach. Redly said something, but she couldn't hear him over the ringing. She tried to crawl away on her hands and knees, but she stumbled and fell. She couldn't even crawl.

His hands were on her. She knew he was trying to help, but it pissed her off. She tried to push him away, but she couldn't see him. The world spun around so quickly that it confused her senses. She closed her eyes and just laid there.

He rolled her over and inspected her head. He was talking, but his voice was warped. Opening her eyes was a mistake. Another wave of nausea gripped her, but she managed to hold in the contents of her stomach. He rubbed her back in slow soothing circles.

After a few minutes, the ringing ebbed and the spinning slowed.

He came into focus where he knelt beside her, his mocha eyes serious and unapologetic.

"What's your problem today?" she asked.

"What do you think about when you fight?"

"I don't know. Kicking your ass, which obviously I'm failing at. What do you think about?"

"Nothing. My mind goes to a different place. All I see is my opponent. I don't see them as a person, just an obstacle. I watch them, listen to their breathing, study every step they take for any weaknesses or inconsistencies. Once I find their pattern and way of movement, I wait for an opening. You have many openings. It's time we close them up."

"How can you see all that while you're fighting?"

"I call it the fog. My brain doesn't do anything else except that one task."

"What if someone comes at you from the sides or behind?"

"I don't forget my surroundings. There's always one ear and eye listening and watching for any threats, but the majority of my focus is on whoever's in front of me. That becomes even more important when you're fighting more than one opponent, which is a whole other level that you're not ready for. That's my concern, Ava. You need to be ready and there's not much time."

She hadn't considered that. In a real battle, it was very likely that she'd face more than one enemy at once. She could barely manage to defend herself from just him. What if there were two, three, or ten werewolves? She sat up. The meadow was finally level and still.

"Everyone has a pattern. You have a tendency to drop your right elbow, which makes your shoulder vulnerable. That's why I'm able to get you in an arm lock on that side as often as I do. An enemy won't put you in an arm lock, Ava. They're going to try to kill you."

"You said Alyssium wants me alive, ergo they probably would put me in an armlock."

He glared at her.

"I get what you're saying, but you don't have to beat me up to prove a point."

"I'm not trying to prove a point. I'm trying to see what it takes to get you in that fog. It's time to use sharp weapons, Ava. We all go through a transition period in our fighting. In the beginning it's just learning the stances and steps, but at some point, your brain needs to connect all that to an actual fight. Once the stakes are higher and you get hit a few times, you're more aware and have better instinctual defenses. Nothing makes you focus more than getting punched in the face a few times."

"Fine. But do you have to hit so hard?"

"That was only a fraction of what I'm capable of." He smiled arrogantly.

Ava rolled her eyes and got to her feet. The side of her head still ached a little, but most of the effects from the hit were gone now. Touching her nose, she found it to be perfectly normal.

Magical healing certainly had its benefits. Another reason werewolves probably held the upper hand when fighting. They weren't nearly as concerned about getting hit. If she could learn to fight through the pain, she could be virtually unstoppable.

When they started again her instincts and reflexes were much more sensitive now that she knew he was actually going to inflict real pain. Her body automatically moved faster, and her senses were sharper, but what if her instincts could be even sharper?

Recalling one of Redly's very first lessons, she channeled her inner wolf. Time slowed down and she saw his intentions seconds before he moved. A simple shift in weight or the glance of an eye.

He came at her with a right hook, and she turned her head at the last moment, just enough so the blow wasn't as direct or heavy. She stumbled from the force of the impact, but it didn't send her to the ground.

Using the momentum of her evasion, she dropped her hips, pivoted her rear foot, and redirected her force into an uppercut. Using all her strength, she struck him under the chin. He stumbled backwards but didn't fall.

That was it. Her opening. Before he regained his balance, she kicked low, clipping his knee. He fell to one knee, and she charged. He grabbed her neck with one arm. Her air was instantly cut off under his vice-like grip. Adrenaline surged through her body, preventing her from panicking.

Recalling a move in self-defense classes from years ago, she punched his elbow causing his arm to unlock, and using all her weight, she pushed into the hold, forcing him backwards until he fell on his back. He tried to dislodge her with his other arm, but she elbowed him on the side of the head, just like he'd done to her. His head rolled like one of those little bobble toys people put on their dashboards. That gave her just enough time to conjure a dagger and press it to his exposed neck, and that's when he finally stilled.

Panting, she made eye contact and couldn't help but smile triumphantly. She'd never managed to take him down without some sort of an advantage he granted her. This was a real win. He smiled and her breathing hitched.

He was completely vulnerable, his arms up, his chest and neck exposed. If he was a real enemy, she could kill him easily. Her original plan, should she succeed in subduing him, was to return the jab to the nose, but that's not what she wanted anymore.

Throwing all her inhibitions out the window, she kissed him with as much aggression and intensity as when they were fighting. He matched her aggression. His hands grabbed her waist and he pulled her closer to him. They melted into each other as their tongues fought for the dominant position in each other's mouths.

Taking a break to breathe, she locked eyes with him. He caressed her cheek with his thumb. The gentle contrast of his touch lit a firework inside her. Once the flame reached the black powder in her core, she exploded into a kissing frenzy.

Spinning her around, he threw her flat on her back. A satisfying pain temporarily knocked her breath away. Pinning her arms above her head, like he'd done dozens of times before, he looked at her hungrily. That eyebrow ticked up. Infuriating and sexy at the same time.

"Just like I said the first time we met; this is the only way you're able to get a woman under you, isn't it?" Ava smirked.

He smiled that smile that always sent her over the edge, then he kissed her with such fierce intensity that she lost all her control. She tugged her arms, but his grip tightened. The restraint tortured her in all the right ways. He pressed harder into her, and she went limp, completely giving in to his control.

The world fell away. He was the only thing that existed. His lips, his tongue, his body. Weaseling himself securely between her legs, he pressed into her. She arched into him. When he finally released her arms, she grabbed his back side and pushed him down harder.

A growl escaped him. He nibbled her ear then her neck then down to her collar bone. A hand slid under her shirt. His touch on her stomach undid her. She raked her hands under his shirt and dug her nails into his back. She reveled in the feel of every tantalizing movement of his muscles under her grip. His hand traveled further under her shirt and squeezed one of her breasts. She needed to feel more of him.

She pulled his shirt up, and Redly rocked to his knees and tossed it aside. She marveled at the sight of his body where he knelt between her legs. He was perfectly still, as she traced the contours of his torso, then his abs, then a hip line until it dove into his pants. He held his breath.

She'd wanted to do that since the first time she saw him. Running a finger along the hem of his pants, she watched him watch her. The appetite in his eyes mirrored her own. Pulling her shirt over her head, she tossed it aside. Then she removed her bra.

She'd dreamt of his body against hers for months now. She reached for his pants, but he grabbed her wrist. She froze. With his other hand he grabbed her chin and directed her face to his. His lips attacked her again. She had no choice but to let him dominate her mouth. After he got his fill, he let her go and wrapped his arms around her body, pulling her onto him.

Pressed against each other as close as humanly possible, Ava reveled in the feel of him between her legs. She couldn't take much more. There were still layers between them, denying her what she really wanted.

She clumsily tugged at his pants. It was difficult to concentrate when his tongue teased her so erotically. His arms wrapped around her, enveloping her in his strong embrace. One hand crawled up the back of her neck, grabbed a handful of hair and yanked her head back. She braced against the hold as he kissed her neck then traced his lips down to close around a breast.

Her breath left her, and all sense of reality evaporated as his tongue worked over her nipple and his other hand wrapped around her backside. Grabbing his shoulders she held herself to this reality, to this moment, to him, so she didn't lose herself completely.

When he was done with that breast, he moved to the other one and goosebumps erupted all over her skin at the tickling of his tongue. When he finally let her go, she collapsed into him, and dug her nails into his back. His mouth returned to hers. He pushed her onto her back slowly, carefully this time.

His kisses changed from an aggressive dominating force to a sensual slow tease as he eased his body onto hers. She couldn't take much more. A pressure built inside her that unless it was released, she would implode. He undid her pants then snuck a hand under them. His fingers found the epicenter of her desire and started to massage in tantalizing circles. That was it. She was done for.

"Redly." She couldn't get out any other word. That was the only word that existed in her world. His mouth crashed into hers again, and his fingers worked a magic that she'd never felt before. She thrust in timing with his hand and his fingers sank inside her. Energy pulsed through every nerve in her body. She held onto him, but it didn't do any good. She'd lost all sense of reality. Nothing existed but the feel of his fingers tickling inside her.

"Come for me, Ava," he breathed onto her neck.

She was obedient. She always did what he told her, and she knew in that moment that she always would. Her mind, her heart, and her body belonged to him.

The eruption overtook her. Wave after wave in synchrony to the movement of his fingers inside her. She held onto his arm refusing to let him stop. Not that he would, but she had to hold onto something, otherwise she may completely disappear into an erotic oblivion. That wouldn't be so bad, would it?

When the ripples of pleasure finally wore off, her head fell to the ground, and he removed his hand, finally bringing an end to the release she'd wanted for so long. He kissed her softly. She could barely remember to breathe, but his scent flooded her. She loved that smell. It was strong, mixed with a desire of his own that had yet to be sated.

Opening her eyes, she met his beautiful brown ones. His expression was carnal, unyielding, demanding.

"You're as beautiful as Empyrean," he whispered.

"I can't form words right now."

"You don't have to. Just relax." He kissed her cheek, then her nose, then the other cheek, then her lips.

"I don't want to relax. I want more." She wrapped one arm around his shoulders and with the other hand she stroked his pants. His breath hitched and his eyes rolled. He was barely contained. Fumbling with the buttons, she undid the last layers that stood between them. He kicked his shoes and pants off and finally she took him all in. He was just as amazing as she remembered.

She undid the laces of her shoes and kicked them away then she let him take over the rest. Unlike her clumsy desperate finagling with the buttons, he smoothly removed her pants. His eyes swept over her body in a predatory manner. She waited patiently for him to take in all that he wanted. Luckily, he didn't keep her waiting long.

When their lips met again, she finally felt all of him against her. Skin to skin, nothing between them now. He pressed against her, but it still wasn't close enough. She needed him closer, inside her.

"More," she whispered.

"Yes ma'am." He gave her what she wanted, filling her so

completely that it took her breath away. With every thrust he grew stronger and harder, and the world around her wavered, but it still wasn't enough. She grabbed his ass and pushed him deeper.

It was hard to breathe under the weight of him. He pressed his forehead into the crook of her neck and gave her more and more and more, sending them both closer to the edge.

Finally, his body spasmed and his breathing became erratic. She arched into his movements and with a final thrust, he found his release. She kissed his neck, teasing everything out of him. She wanted it all.

He gave her everything he had until he finally relaxed. He shuddered a few times then his body became heavy. They both lay there just concentrating on breathing as that's all they could manage to do at the moment.

After a few minutes he rolled off her. She snuggled up to him and rested her head on his chest. His fingers trailed over her side, tickling out goosebumps. She twirled a few of his chest hairs in her fingers. Listening to his heartbeat, her head rising and falling in rhythm to his breathing, she reveled in the feel of him, the smell of him. She didn't want this to end.

The sun was already below the tree line. Closing her eyes, she told herself that if she couldn't see the sun sinking, then she didn't have to acknowledge the fact that they would have to leave each other soon.

"It's getting late," he said.

She put a finger over his mouth. "Don't say it yet. Just lay with me for a few more minutes."

"Ok." He kissed her head and pulled her closer. Just a few more minutes was all she wanted. Really? Who was she kidding? That was a complete lie and they both knew it.

CHAPTER 26
AVA
SCORPLEM WANG-3/OCTOBER 21ST

A leaf tickled Ava's ear. She swatted it away. A few seconds later another one tickled her. Swatting that one away, she turned on her side.

"Why aren't you reading?" she asked.

"I'm stuck on this word." Redly held the book up for her to see.

Peeking an eye open, she read the word, "ground."

He scrunched his eyebrows. "That's stupid. It doesn't look anything like it sounds."

"The language barrier isn't helping us out any. It may look and sound completely different to you than it does to me, but in my language, we just accept that it's spelled funny and memorize it." Ava closed her eyes again.

Silence met her again. Another leaf tickled her ear. She swatted it away. Why wasn't he reading? The damned leaf tickled her again. She opened her eyes and saw Redly leaning over her with the stupid leaf.

"Get off me!" She laughed and sat up. "You're supposed to be reading, not goofing off."

"You're so cute laying there all unaware. I couldn't help myself."

She snatched the book from him and tossed it to the side.

"You are impossible, Redly Alder."

His thumb stroked her cheek causing her heart to flutter.

"I like when you say my name."

"I know." She smiled. "Your reading is coming along really well. We could probably step up our books to something more challenging."

"I have a good teacher. Oh, speaking of." He grabbed his pants, which were in the pile with hers, so it took him a moment to find them. Pulling out a piece of paper from his pocket, he handed it to her. "How's my writing?"

She read the note. "It's one word."

He nodded.

"Your e's are backwards otherwise it's good. What is Benelli?"

"It's not a what. It's a who. That's who you wanted me to find. That's who killed your family."

Her heart momentarily stopped beating. He'd actually done it. How much had he risked getting this information? And he wrote it down. What if he was caught?

"Thank you." She pulled her pants on then tucked it into her pocket.

He groaned and grabbed her arm, pulling her back down. She fell into his embrace, her back against his chest. He planted kisses along her neck and shoulder. "You're sexy when you're getting dressed," he whispered into her neck. "And undressed." He pushed a hand down her pants.

Her skin was on fire where he touched her, which was everywhere.

"I don't want you to spy anymore."

His hand stopped moving.

"It's too dangerous. We're already putting ourselves at risk enough. Don't read or write things down and don't get yourself noticed. You said you've spent your whole life trying to be invisible to her. It'll be weird if you take an interest now."

"Don't worry about me. I'll be fine." His hand resumed its original trajectory.

She grabbed his arm and spun around to face him. "I do worry about you."

"Aw. You really do care," he teased.

"Stop it. I'm serious. I don't want you to spy anymore, ok."

He huffed and got up. He didn't say anything while he dressed. She followed his lead and when they were both fully clothed, they finally faced each other. They knew that was the only way they could have a serious conversation.

"I won't take any unnecessary risks, Arukas." He put his hands on his hips.

"Don't call me that."

He grabbed her arm and pulled her back to him and kissed her. Her spine turned to lava. He held her tight, ensuring she wouldn't fall, which was good because her knees were weak from sparring and from the effect of his tongue.

When they pulled apart, she asked. "What would happen if you got caught?"

"I'm not going to get caught."

"Humor me. What would happen if you were?"

His jaw ticked. She could tell he didn't want to tell her.

"Tell me." She tugged on his shirt.

"I'd probably be tortured for a few days before being beheaded or sentenced to Bestiari for someone random I don't care much about, so it's no big deal."

Tortured, beheaded. That's a big deal. Ava swallowed down her fear. What was the third thing he said? "What is Bestiari?"

He bowed his head, then took a seat under their tree. She sat down in front of him.

"Anyone who commits an infraction that is subjectively serious enough to warrant death, she usually prefers Bestiari." His eyes were melancholic.

She hated when he got this way. Her heart hurt already, and she didn't even know what he was going to say.

"She seizes control of our mind, filling us with such intense hatred toward the person we care about most so that we mistake them for an enemy. She brings out the most primal animalistic nature and enhances it until we're consumed with violence and the need to kill. That's all there is. The person you are disappears completely and you become a monster." He didn't look at her.

"It's not a quick death. You draw it out and torture the person you love, painfully and slowly. Then right before they die, Alyssium relinquishes control, so that you can hold them in your arms while life leaves them. You get to see all the carnage you ravaged on her in her final moment. Alyssium makes sure you don't forget that." Redly stared at the ground.

"I can't remember anything I do on newm nights, but I remember every detail of the Bestiari. She has that ability; to remove, replace, or enhance memories."

"She did that to you?"

He nodded.

"Who was it?"

He hesitated. "My sister, Selaney."

Ava's eyes widened. She could barely breathe. What he must have felt? What he must still feel now?

"She was only eight. I was ten."

Ava swallowed down the bile that rose in her throat. They were children. She was the same age when her family was killed, but she wasn't forced to kill them.

"She was beaten nearly to death for failing at something during fight training. I don't even remember what it was. It doesn't matter. The injuries were so bad, she was healing too slow. She needed more food to heal faster. If you don't show up on time for fight training, you're punished, and she wouldn't survive another beating in the shape she was in.

"After I took the bread, I was caught and taken to the queen. She never even asked me what happened. She just extracted it from my mind. Then they retrieved my sister. She had to be carried in because she was so weak." His gaze drifted away as if he watched the scene play out in his mind. "Alyssium doesn't tolerate weakness, so it was the perfect opportunity to cull and exact a punishment.

"She implanted the death lust in me so intensely that I *wanted* to kill Selaney. I wanted nothing more than to hurt her. I hated her, detested the sight of her. I took satisfaction in slicing open her neck.

"Right before the spark of life left her eyes, Alyssium released her hold on my mind. I watched my sister take her last gurgling breaths and die in my arms." He closed his eyes. His chin quivered a little. "My sister was my first kill."

Ava sat silently, unsure what to say.

"I nearly took my own life that day. The only reason I didn't was because I want to take Alyssium down more than I want to escape the permanent guilt I feel every day. I trained harder and got stronger and I've been biding my time. That's all that's kept me going, until now."

"What changed now?"

"You." He stared at her so intensely that she thought he might actually see her soul. "You keep me going now."

Ava put her hand over her heart trying to will it to be still. He pulled her so close that their faces were only inches from each other.

"You could ask me to do anything in the world and I would do it for you." He kissed her. "Except give up trying to kill Alyssium. I've been waiting for this opportunity my whole life. I don't care if I die trying. I will help you in any way I can, even if it puts me in jeopardy. You're going to have to accept that."

Ava sighed. She couldn't argue with that. She understood completely.

"I know it's not the same, but she killed my family too. I was the same age as you when they were killed. I wasn't the one who did it, but the fact that the Hansons took me in and loved me, that's what got them killed. And seeing their bodies like that, their faces. They were so scared. I'll never get those images out of my mind. I still have nightmares about it."

"Me too," he said.

"I won't ask you to stop spying then, but just be careful. I don't want you to go through Bestiari again because of me, and your sister wouldn't want that either."

He flinched at the mention of his sister.

"There's no one else alive that I care about except you, and Alyssium can't get to you here, so it doesn't matter if I get caught as long as you're safe."

"But I don't want to lose you."

He caressed her cheek. "I'll be fine." He smiled, but it didn't meet his eyes. He kissed her. "It's time to go," he whispered.

She gripped him tighter and pressed her forehead into his. "Five more minutes."

He chuckled. "Ok. Five more minutes."

She took advantage of every minute in his embrace.

—- Scorplem Lasq-2/October 24th -—

The shocked expressions were unanimous. She'd expected it. I mean, how do you tell someone you're sleeping with the enemy without them getting a little freaked out? Ava was still a little freaked out by it herself sometimes, so she wasn't surprised they would be too.

"Well. This is a lot to unpack," Clark said. She sat next to Demetrius at the dining room table of Ava's room. They decided to meet in Ava's room since it was larger than Sibyl's room and now that Sibyl didn't have to wear the osmium, she was permitted into the royal quarters.

"That explains the children's books at least," Wilson said, from the couch. "We were beginning to worry a little."

"I suspected you were seeing someone, but I didn't think that's who it was." Sibyl actually smiled. "Is he hot?"

Ava smiled back and nodded.

They both laughed.

"I'm glad you two think this is funny," Ambrose chimed in. He held up the door frame to Ava's bedroom. Never one to sit and relax. "Our future Aruka is gallivanting around the countryside with the enemy. Do you know how dangerous and stupid that is?"

"You sound like my aunt."

"Well, I agree with her," Ambrose said.

The entire room collectively sighed.

"What?" Ambrose threw his arms out and actually had the audacity to look confused.

"Come on. She's smarter than that. If she was in any real danger, she would've known." Sibyl came to Ava's defense.

"Thank you," said Ava.

"She left the safety of the walls, alone, and was intercepted by a werewolf patrol. Guards have been getting killed by werewolf patrols for months and you're telling me that you happened to meet a *nice* werewolf?" Ambrose said.

"Yes. I got lucky, I guess. He saved me from one of the patrols that weren't the *nice* werewolves. They're not all bad. They're regular people who've been cursed into slaves and forced to do things they don't want to do. I'm telling you there are way more of them who'd be on our side if they could, and Redly's one of them. He'd rather die than see Alyssium win this battle. He puts his life at risk every day to help us."

"You mean to help you," Ambrose said.

"What difference does it make? He hates Alyssium. He cares about me, and he wants to help the good guys. That's us."

Ambrose finally shut his mouth at that.

"Let's get back to the real question. What are we going to do about the impending attack?" Sibyl asked.

"We?" Ava asked. "I thought you'd be on the first train out of here now that you got your magic under control."

Sibyl fidgeted nervously. "Well, I already pushed the boards to spring. I didn't know there was going to be a battle. I thought I would just help you figure out who the spy was and then I'd leave. I still plan to do that, so I can help with this too if you want."

"No way." Ambrose shook his head. "You need to go home for this."

"Excuse me? You asked me to stay, so I'm staying. Did you change your mind all of a sudden?"

"I asked you to stay before I knew war was coming to our gates. This changes everything."

"How? You were the one that said I could be the key to this war."

"Yeah. The key, not a fighter."

"I have no intention of fighting. I'll stay behind the walls and help the healers."

"And if they breach the walls, you'll be in danger."

Sibyl opened her mouth to reply, but Ava interrupted. "I agree with him on this, Sibyl."

Sibyl's mouth dropped open.

"You have friends and family on Earth. If something happens to you here, how am I supposed to explain that to them? I can't tell your mom you were killed in a magical war on a different planet."

"Wow. Thanks for your vote of confidence that I'll survive," Sibyl said.

"You know what I mean."

"I am so sick of everyone telling me what I can and can't do for my entire life! I'm finally getting my shit sorted out and now you guys are pushing me out because you think I can't handle it."

"That's not what we think at all," Ava said.

"Well then what do you think, because I don't see you sending Cassie back home." Sibyl narrowed her eyes.

"She's in a coma, Sibyl! The battle hasn't even started yet and she's almost already dead! I brought her here and she nearly burned down the entire fucking kingdom and cost some people their lives, and nearly died in the process!" Ava shouted.

Everyone got quiet. Ava took a calming breath. "I don't want something to happen to you on my account. You're my friend and I don't have many of those. One of my friends is laying in the hospital and may never wake up again. I couldn't live with myself if something happened to you too."

Sibyl's expression softened. "I appreciate the concern, but I'm a grown woman. I'm staying because it's where I want to be. You guys begged me to stay all summer, and now you're telling me to leave. I appreciate the sentiment, but it's my decision and it's final."

"I'm glad you're staying," Clark chimed in.

"Thank you. At least one person is." Sibyl rolled her eyes at Ambrose.

He tossed her an exasperated smirk.

"So, back to the subject at hand. Have we gotten any closer to figuring out who the spy is?" Demetrius asked. "Does this Redly guy know who it is?"

Ava shook her head. "He's pretty low ranking in Tearnanoak, so he doesn't know much. Just big picture stuff like the attack Alyssium's planning, but he doesn't even know any details about that."

"And you're sure we can trust him?" Ambrose asked.

"Yes," Ava hissed.

"And you're thinking clearly about this?" Ambrose asked.

Sibyl threw a pillow at him. "Shut up. Sometimes you're so dense."

Wilson sniggered.

Ambrose glared at him.

They stayed up until the wee hours of the morning discussing ideas about the battle, arguing about stupid things, and throwing out names of people they had suspicions about being the spy. By the time they all left for the night they'd come to no solid conclusion or plan on anything. Ava hoped they'd have something to bring to the council meeting tomorrow, or in a few hours actually, but it would appear they'd arrive with no more information than everyone already knew.

As everyone was leaving, Ava pulled Sibyl aside. "Can I talk to you alone for a minute?"

"Sure. What's up?"

"So, you're getting pretty good with your mind stuff, right?"

"I guess so. Why?"

"What if someone you didn't know came walking around the corner right now. Could you tell who they were?"

"Um. Theoretically, yes."

"What do you mean theoretically?"

"Unless they grant me permission, I shouldn't just trespass into someone's mind."

"Shouldn't? But you could if you wanted to?"

"Technically yes. Why?"

"How close do you have to be?"

"I don't know. Do you have an idea for the battle or something?"

"Kind of. It's more personal." Ava chewed on her lip. "Did you know that my adoptive family was killed when I was ten?"

"I know it happened, but I don't know any details. I'm so sorry."

"They were killed by werewolves who were looking for me." Ava tried to keep her voice level. Any time she thought of that day, anger and pain threatened to consume her. She could still smell, see, and feel everything as if it was yesterday.

Sibyl fidgeted uncomfortably. "That's awful."

"I know the name of the werewolf who did it, but I don't know what he looks like. I kind of thought you could help me with that, during the battle. Like, let me know if I happen to run into him."

"Ok. I'll do some research on that sort of thing and see if I can figure out something."

"Thank you."

"Sure. See you in a few hours at the council meeting?"

"Yep. See you."

— Scorplem Lasq-3/October 25th —

Ava took a seat at the head of the table next to an empty chair reserved for her aunt. This was the first time she'd been in the council room, and, in keeping with everything else in the God Tree castle, it was nothing short of spectacular. A giant oblong shaped oak table took up the majority of the center of the room. Thick ornately carved legs resembling tree branches growing out from the floor held up the table as if it blossomed from the tree itself. It wouldn't surprise Ava if it actually did.

Wooden chairs with red velvety fabric seats and backs surrounded the table and lined the walls of the room. A giant vine wrapped diamond chandelier hung over the center of the table, and if that wasn't enough light. Diamond sconces decorated the wall every few feet.

Sibyl, Ambrose, Rokesh, Wilson, Demetrius, and Clark all sat on one side of the table. Ava's junior council members.

Yilfin, Fulcinia, Ziv, who was the captain of the guard she'd overheard in her aunt's office a couple of months ago, and seven other people she hadn't met before sat on the other side of the table.

Bekora and her aunt entered the room. Serellina was pale and had lost a significant amount of weight, but the good news was she was on the mend. Everyone stood up. Yilfin offered a hand to help her to her seat.

"Thank you." She sat down. "Isn't this exciting? Our first official meeting with two councils. The regime is officially close to switching over." Serellina smiled.

Ava's pulse increased slightly. She wasn't ready to take over. Did that mean her aunt was close to dying? Is that why she was getting sick? Did she have to die in order for Ava to take over? Ava was suddenly a bit panicky. She didn't want to lose her only remaining family member, and she certainly wasn't ready to take over the responsibilities of running a magical kingdom.

"Let's get started. I don't have the energy to sit here all day. Why don't we all introduce ourselves? I don't think everyone here knows each other. My side will start." Serellina motioned to Bekora who stood up.

"My name is Bekora. I am the queen consort and comptroller for Tearnanelle. Basically, I oversee all the commerce and trade in the kingdom to make sure we can sustain ourselves and our people." She took her seat again. Ava didn't realize the council members had specific job duties and titles. She thought they were just a soundboard to help make decisions.

Fulcinia stood up next. "I handle foreign affairs." She sat back down. Always a woman of few words.

Yilfin stood up. "Magical coordinator. I ensure that magic is being used properly, not abused, or mishandled."

Next was Ziv. He was a clean shaven very fit man in his late forties or early fifties from what Ava could ascertain. In Orlon it was difficult to be completely sure of someone's age since the water kept everyone looking younger than the equivalent age of people on Earth. "I'm captain of the guard. I develop the recruiting and training program for the Mage Guard. Assign Mage Guards to their job duties, and organize our military for defense and offense if needed."

The next lady stood up. She had to be at least eighty-five or ninety years old, and that was a for real estimate. "My name is Osisi. I'm the head librarian and historian." She smiled and sat down. Clark was her apprentice so at least those two had an existing rapport.

The next person to introduce himself was Jameson, the commissioner of the law. He was medium height and build with black hair and a strong jawline. Then Runar, a public service representative who oversaw infrastructure and construction projects. Then the superintendent of education, Isola, introduced herself, the medical director,

Melinda, who they'd already met, then Lucas, the chief executive officer who oversaw the jobs in the kingdom, and last was the spiritual director named Sef. She apparently helped ensure the Gods were properly interpreted to the civilians so that everyone could live harmoniously within the magical realm. Ava really didn't understand her job at all.

Once Sef sat down, everyone looked at Ava expectantly.

"Well. Um. My council isn't organized into titles yet so I guess you guys can just say your name." How were they going to take her seriously if she didn't have a serious council? She was going to prioritize this after the battle, assuming they survived.

One by one they each said their name. When Clark sat down, Ava's heart dipped a little. Everyone she cared about was sitting in this room, sans Cassie and Redly.

A year ago, she had exactly zero family and friends and now she had more than she could count on both hands. This was new territory, and she wasn't sure how she felt about it. Caring for this many people was a huge responsibility and risk to themselves and herself.

"Let's get to it then," Serellina interrupted Ava's anxious introspection. "Ava has gained information that the werewolves plan to attack us on winter solstice." Serellina just blurted it out like it was another Tuesday luncheon.

"How did you come by this information?" Ziv asked.

"I have a source," Ava supplied.

"You have a source?" He narrowed his dark blue eyes.

"Yes."

"Would you like to share who this source is?"

"No," Ava said, pointedly.

His face fell.

"There's a spy among us. I'm not going to risk divulging my source because of that fact. They're putting their life on the line every day to get information for us. Until we figure out who the spy is. They will remain a secret."

"You think that someone on this council could be the spy?" Ziv asked indignantly.

"I'm not saying that, but I'm not willing to risk unnecessary exposure."

"Fair enough," Serellina said before anyone else could argue.

Ziv's expression was anything but pleased. "What other information has this *source* given you?" he asked sarcastically.

"Only that the werewolves aren't all bad. They're just Therians who are cursed. They want to be free of Alyssium just as badly as we do."

"So, you're saying they won't attack us then?" Sef, the spiritual director asked.

"Well, no. They will, and they will be our enemy, but they don't all want to be."

"I'm confused. You just said they're cursed people, but now you said they're our enemy and some don't want to be, which implies some do," Ziv said.

"When the Therians are in human form, they're just like me and you. They're not our enemy, most aren't at least. When they're in werewolf form, however, their minds are hijacked. They're forced to do what Alyssium wants, and she wants me and Sibyl alive, everyone else, she'll probably kill. She's breeding an army. They have two hundred to three hundred thousand trained fighters ready to dispatch at a moment's notice."

Everyone's head snapped to Ava at that.

"Are you sure about those numbers?" Ziv asked.

"One hundred percent," Ava said.

He leaned back in his chair. His expression changed to one of concern.

"Regardless that many of them may not want to be our enemy and don't want to hurt us, they will when they're in werewolf form, and that's another thing. Alyssium can only control them as an army when they're in that form. In human form she can only control a few at a time. That's why she's choosing newm solstice on the darkest night of the year."

"Because they'll be forced to shift at newm, and winter solstice is when light magic is at its weakest point," Clark said.

Osisi nodded. "Exactly."

"Ok. So, we know when it's going to happen and where and how many. Now, what's the plan to defend ourselves?" Runar asked. Everyone stared at each other blankly.

"No one has any ideas?" Fulcinia asked.

"We have the walls that are laced with silver," Sibyl said. "Put Mages with the best archery experience at the top of each battlement to defend the field below. All we have to do is last until morning, right? Then they'll shift back."

Several heads nodded.

"That's a good idea. Just wait it out," Jameson said.

"But that many werewolves will exhaust our Mages' silver pretty quickly. Do we have enough guards strong enough to last that long?" Osisi asked.

Ziv's expression was grim. "I don't know." He spoke in a way that made Ava believe he did know the answer, he just didn't want to voice it, because it wasn't what they wanted to hear.

"What about using arrows that are already made so the Mages don't have to always use their silver?" Sibyl asked.

"That's not a terrible idea. We can spend the next couple of months making silver arrows and imbuing them with even more silver to make them more powerful," Ziv said.

"Organize it and get it started immediately," Serellina said.

"And if they do breach the wall? What then?" Ambrose asked.

"We pray," Sef bowed her head. The gems woven within her long dreadlocks clanked on the table.

"That's not helpful," Rokesh said.

"I don't hear you coming up with any better ideas," she countered.

"How many unoccupied S-cells do we have?" Rokesh asked.

"A hundred maybe, why?" Jameson answered.

"We can fill them up with civilians for the night. As many as we can cram in there. Children primarily. Anyone who's most vulnerable who can't defend themselves. That way if the werewolves do break through, they won't be able to get to them behind silver."

"What are S-cells?" Sibyl asked.

"Prison cells made of silver. We have O-cells for Mages, which are made of osmium and I-cells made of iron to contain dark magic creatures or wielders," Ambrose answered.

"That's not a bad idea, but we can still only hold maybe two thousand people in the S-cells. We have two hundred thousand civilians at least," Jameson said. "What about the rest?"

"We have silver caves below the castle. They'll hold at least twenty thousand. We can bar it with silver too," the Aruka said.

"And the rest of our people? How do we choose who gets to be safe and who doesn't?" Jameson asked.

"Like Rokesh said," Ava chimed in. "We start with the children and then whoever's weakest. Anyone else will have to either fight, escape, or hide."

The room became silent. They were condemning people to die if the werewolves did get through, but they didn't have a choice.

"And what do we tell the people?" Runar asked.

"Nothing for now. Let them live in peace. Continue the plans for winter solstice party as usual. I won't let the werewolves ruin everything. We will announce our plan one week in advance. Maybe by then we'll have come up with something better." Serellina coughed.

She took a drink of water before she was able to resume talking. "Let's all think on this and meet again in two weeks to see if we have anything better. In the meantime, does anyone have any information about the spy?"

"We're pretty sure it's a demon," Clark said.

"A demon? How do you figure that?" Ziv asked.

"The sheep," Ava said. "Demons need blood to survive. They can eat regular food, but they eventually must feed on fresh blood, and we have sheep that are getting massacred."

"That's nothing new. Sheep have been getting slaughtered for years. Only recently it seems to have gotten worse. That's just a coincidence."

"It's not. When a demon is growing in power or impatience, their appetite will increase, and so will the side effects of their dark magic. Whoever this demon is, they're becoming more powerful as solstice gets closer."

"That's why the smell is happening more now too," Clark added.

"What smell?" Runar asked.

"Dark magic smells like death," Osisi answered.

"There have been several reports of rotting smells," Jameson said. "I assumed it was the wind blowing in the butchered sheep."

"It's not. It's the demon," Ava answered.

"There's got to be a way to figure out who it is. I think we'd notice a demon running around?" Bekora said.

"They'll look like anyone if they possess us," Clark said.

"How long can they possess someone?" Fulcinia asked.

Clark shook her head. "I don't know. I'll research that and get back to you at our next meeting."

Osisi nodded her head, approvingly.

"Please do. Anything else to discuss?" Serellina asked.

"The wall seems to have stabilized but we're still repairing sections that were crumbling. I think we need to assign more people to help us with repairs to ensure it's as strong as possible if and when the enemy arrives," Runar said.

"What do you mean the wall was crumbling?" Ava asked.

"The wall is twenty-seven years old, but has always been in pristine condition, until recently. We're not sure what's caused this sudden deterioration but thankfully it seems to have stopped, and we're now getting ahead with repairs."

Serellina shifted in her seat. "Yes. We will assign more workers for that. However many you need. Recruit Mages who are particularly gifted with citrine and azurite elemental magic as well as silver. That will be the best and quickest way to reinforce the wall."

"Yes Aruka." Runar took some notes.

"Until then let's call this a wrap. I'm tired. I need to rest again. I'm finally getting over whatever was getting me down, but I'm still not a hundred percent yet. I apologize for not being present the last few weeks."

Everyone began to disperse. Ava followed her aunt to the hallway. "Can I speak to you for a moment?"

Her aunt was obviously tired, but she stopped to give Ava her full attention.

"What happens to you when I ascend?"

"What do you mean? Why do you ask?" Serellina looked a little nervous.

"Do you die?" Ava asked.

"Die? No. Why would you think that?"

"Because you're sick, and I thought maybe it's because I am stealing your magic or something."

Serellina laughed weakly. "No. This is just a sickness. Nothing more. It has nothing to do with you becoming Aruka." Serellina smiled. "That process is peaceful and almost imperceptible to either of us. No need to worry about that now." She stroked Ava's cheek with the back of her fingers, vanquishing all of Ava's concerns.

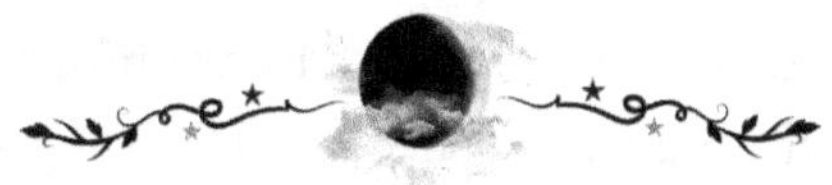

— Sasgar WaxC-5/November 12th —

It was difficult to spar with Redly now that their relationship had evolved. No matter how hard they tried to keep things serious, it usually ended up becoming intimate.

She'd finally started to progress in her training. Now that she knew how to zone in, she'd become a much more effective hand to hand fighter. And with her new weapon of choice, she'd even managed to pry a compliment out of Fulcinia at her last Mage training session.

Ava wouldn't say she was prepared to fight in a battle, but she was training as hard as she could every day. An hour or two distracted by matters of the heart wouldn't change her overall odds of survival enough to deter her from his touch. Besides, she wanted to soak up as much time with him as she could since there was a chance either of them could die soon.

Pushing that thought from her mind, she rested her head on his chest under the blanket she'd brought with her. It was growing colder by the day as November, or Sasgar is what they called it in Orlon, pressed on.

Redly kissed her head. "It's getting late. I need to head back." He shimmied out from her embrace and pulled his pants on.

"Noooooo. Stay a little longer."

"You say that every day." He cocked that eyebrow up.

"And I mean it every day."

He knelt down and kissed her.

She wrapped her arms around his neck and pulled him down. He lost his balance and fell over her. Giggling, she plastered kisses all over his face and neck. He pretended to struggle playfully for a moment then stiffened suddenly and his head shot up.

"What's wrong?" Ava asked.

Redly put a hand over her mouth. "Shhhhhhhh."

She stilled. Voices came from the far side of the meadow.

"Stay," he whispered. Rolling off her, he dashed into the forest.

Stay? What was she? A dog? Fuck that. Dressing quickly, she snuck in the direction he went, following the voices.

"-burn," an unknown man said. Ava hid behind a tree several yards away behind the backs of two men. Redly faced her.

"We have new orders," the man said. "Everyone must have a partner and we have to rotate patrols now."

"Since when?" Redly asked.

"Since this afternoon. You weren't at the shift meeting. Come to think of it. You haven't been at any meetings for a while now. You always leave early for patrol. That's a little weird. Who actually wants to work more than they're assigned?" the man asked.

"Maybe it's so he can jack off all the time." The other man laughed.

"Shut up, dip shit."

Redly's eyes widened when he saw Ava. Schooling his expression, he stepped sideways so that she couldn't see him anymore.

"What do you do out here all day?" one of the men asked.

"Patrol. That's what we're supposed to do," Redly answered.

"But way out here? You're in Tearnanelle."

"What? No way. This isn't Tearnanoak?"

"Don't act stupid. What are you doing?"

"Damn it. You caught me. Patrice and I play a game, kind of like strip hide and seek, and you guys are going to ruin it if you don't go soon," Redly said.

Who's Patrice? Ava thought.

"Patrice? No way. I never would have pegged her for the type," one of the men said.

"That's because nobody's pegged her," the other man said.

"Watch your mouth." Redly's temper flared.

The man threw his arms in the air. "I guess we'll leave you to it then, but starting tomorrow, you better take your foreplay somewhere else because you'll be assigned a partner."

"Noted," Redly said.

"See you later man."

Ava hid behind the tree as the men left in the direction of Tearnanoak.

"I cannot believe you came over here." Redly came from around the tree.

"Who's Patrice?" Ava asked.

"Are you fucking kidding me right now?" he snapped.

"You said you play strip hide and seek with Patrice. Who is she?"

"That was a lie to get them to leave."

"I know, but Patrice obviously exists because they know her and judging by your reaction to the way they spoke about her, you care for her." She knew it was childish at this particular moment, but she wanted to know if he was sleeping with someone else.

"She's a friend and now I've brought unnecessary attention to her. She's going to be pissed. What were you thinking coming over here?"

"I wanted to see what was going on?"

"Damn it, Ava. That was stupid. What if they caught you? If they were actually good patrol guards, they would've smelled you a mile away. Luckily it was the moron twins who couldn't smell a rotten carcass if it jumped out of a tree and fell on top of them."

"I'm not stupid. I was careful."

He scoffed. She made to slap him, but he caught her wrist in midair. Her anger flared. How did he do that?

"Let go of me."

He dropped her wrist, and she swung again. This time he ducked. She growled and pounced. The game was on. She threw a punch, and he dodged it. She swept his legs and he jumped. She was determined to take him down. Throwing all her weight into a punch, she swung her arm at him. He grabbed her arm, twisted it around her back then knocked her knees out. She slammed to the ground. Pain shot up her legs.

Puffing furiously, she fought to break free. After a few futile attempts, she slumped in submission.

Redly leaned over her. "You're letting your anger get the best of you. Control your emotions when fighting."

Seizing the moment, she grabbed his neck and yanked him as hard as she could. His feet flew over his head, and he landed on his back with a satisfying thud. A heartbeat later she straddled him holding a silver blade to his throat.

"I let you think you got the upper hand so I could take you down." She smiled. "Now, don't move." She slapped him. Her palm stung when she hit his cheek. "You deserve that. Don't call me stupid."

Fast as lightning, he rolled her over until she was face down in the dirt, and he slapped her ass.

"Get off me!" she squealed.

"Have you had enough naughty little hawk?" He let her roll to face him. Brushing a stray lock of hair from her face, he kissed her gently. He tasted so good. She leaned in for more, but he pulled away.

"You need to go before they circle back." A red handprint flushed over his cheek where she slapped him. "We won't be able to see each other for a while."

Ava's heart sank. "What are we going to do? How will I know you're ok?"

"I'll leave messages on the moon stone when I can, but be very careful when coming here from now on. There may be different patrols coming this way. Don't transform into your human self. Stay hidden, be safe."

Ava nodded. She was struggling to hold in her emotions. What if he died in the battle? She may never see him again.

"This could be the last time...." Her voice cracked. She couldn't finish the sentence.

"Don't think about that. As long as I still breathe, I'll never stop trying to get back to you. I love you."

Ava stopped breathing. Did she just hear him right? No. She'd obviously misheard. Their eyes collided. He was dead serious. Shaking her head, she got up.

The last time she'd heard those words was sixteen years ago, two weeks before the Hanson's were killed. Her head spun. No. She wouldn't say it. She wouldn't hear it.

"Hey." Redly reached for her, but she sidled away.

To love her was a death sentence. Anyone who loved her died. They all died.

"You can't love me." She shook her head vehemently.

"You can't tell me what to feel, and I do love you." Redly was so calm. How was that possible? Did he not hear himself when he spoke?

She tried to respond but her voice failed her.

"Come here." He held his hand out.

Ava stared at it, remembering a day many years ago when another hand was extended to her just like this. Ava went shopping with Mrs. Hanson, and she'd held out her hand, inviting Ava to hold it, while they walked across the parking lot of the mall.

Ava had refused. She hated herself for that. She should've just taken Mrs. Hanson's hand, felt the security of her grip, the tenderness of her skin, the meaning behind such a benign gesture. Why didn't she just take her hand? A missed opportunity that she would never have again.

Looking into Redly's mocha eyes, she saw the strength behind them, the assuredness, the certainty. He held no misgivings about what he said or the meaning behind it.

The Hanson's were unsuspecting, unprepared, and out matched. He wasn't any of those things. Anyone who loved her would have to be strong and she would have to be strong to allow herself to be loved. He knew all the reasons he shouldn't love her and yet he stood here with his hand out offering his love just like Mrs. Hanson had. Ava didn't want to look back on this moment and regret not taking his hand like she regretted it with her foster mother.

She took his hand. He pulled her to him. The world stabilized. She loved being held by him. She loved his smell. She loved his kisses. She loved the taste of him on her lips. She loved the look in his eyes when he was inside her. She loved his smile. She loved the look on his face when he was angry with her.

She loved him. It wasn't a revelation, but rather a coming to terms with herself. She was in love with him. It was that simple. The fortress around her heart crumbled away.

"I do love you," she whispered.

"I know you do. What's not to love? I'm pretty awesome." That eyebrow ticked up and he smiled.

She couldn't help but laugh. She loved his smart mouth too.

CHAPTER 27

SIBYL

SASGAR FIROQ-2/NOVEMBER 15TH

A hand gripped Sibyl's arm and pulled her off balance. She yelped from the initial startle, but the feeling was immediately replaced with something more sensual when earthy spice and cedarwood scent engulfed her. Ambrose always smelled so tantalizing this time of day, right before lunch, after his morning workout and shower.

Ducking behind a corner at the end of the hallway, she fell into his arms, and he kissed her so deeply that her toes curled.

Ever since returning from Silvermar things between them skyrocketed to a frustratingly marvelous level. With each day her attraction and desire for him grew, but their stolen moments were few and far between. When the opportunity arose, she pounced like a starved lioness.

Huddled strategically behind a decorative vine in a dead-end corner on the west side of the hallway between the dining hall and the library, she savored the feel of his hands roaming over her. Sensuous pressure rose to a boiling point inside her. She needed more of him.

"Now that I have control over my magic, do you think the Aruka will decrease my guards to one at a time, or maybe no guard at all?" she asked between kisses.

He shrugged. "I don't know who'd be more successful asking, you or me?"

"I'm pretty sure she hates me, so probably you."

"She's not exactly pleased with me right now either." He rubbed a thumb over her cheek.

Chills rippled down her neck. "Why do you say that?"

"I defied an order," he said, simply.

"What? I don't believe it." Sibyl smiled mockingly.

His eyes bore into her so intensely that she practically melted.

"Wait. It has something to do with me, doesn't it? I don't want to cause problems. I'm sorry. I-"

He put a finger over her mouth. "Stop over analyzing it. I made my own decisions and I'm happy with how things turned out. Just because she's Aruka doesn't mean we have to agree with everything she does and says." He removed his finger from her mouth, and she licked it. He smiled and rubbed his finger on her sleeve.

"Payback for licking me, which by the way I was covered in dog drool all over my face. So, your tiny little finger lick isn't even close to the slobbery assault you plastered on me."

"You are so hung up on that. Are you opposed to me licking you again if I'm human and it's not your face?"

A lightning rod of shock and pleasure shot through her.

He leaned in like he was going to kiss her then licked her nose.

"Stop it." She giggled and wiped her nose off.

He nibbled on her cheek, then her chin and down her neck, then the nibbles turned to kisses, then to something more. "You want me to stop licking you?" he whispered as he flicked his tongue over her ear.

"No." She could barely get the word out.

"Is there somewhere else you want me to lick?" His hand moved down, and his fingers trailed along the hem of her pants. To form thoughts or words at this moment was damn near impossible. He didn't wait for an answer. It was rhetorical anyway.

His mouth connected with hers and their tongues twisted over each other until all concept of reality vanished. There was only the feel of him pressed against her, his tongue in her mouth, and his hand moving under her clothes to a dangerously sensitive location.

Someone laughed nearby catapulting Sibyl back to reality.

A group of women walked by. Two of them held hands over their mouths, trying to hide their smiles. One woman glared at Sibyl with an expression of pure unadulterated hatred. She was vaguely familiar.

Ambrose removed his hand from the inappropriate place he was working toward.

No! she pleaded.

He looked at her sideways. *To be continued.*

Shit. She forgot to control her thoughts.

Turning his gaze toward the staring woman, he said, "Is there something we can help you with Leabella?"

Ambrose's ex. That explained the death glare. Leabella turned on her heel and walked away rigidly.

"See. This is why I need my security detail absolved. No privacy."

"We'll ask. It would be nice to have you all to myself sometimes. We could revisit this licking phobia you have. I think I have a cure for it." He smiled devilishly.

"I don't have a phobia. I just, I..."

He laughed. "I love how squeamish you get over this. What else makes you squirm?" He kissed her lightly.

The thoughts that went through her mind were anything but proper. She wanted to know what he'd do. All the things he would do, but not right now. "We have to get going or they'll come looking for us."

"I don't care if they find us."

"I don't want people to think I'm some sort of floozy."

"What's a floozy?"

"A woman who sleeps around."

He laughed. "No one thinks that and even if they did, who cares?"

She shrugged. "Everyone already hates me. I hear the whispers, even now. Some of them are afraid of me, most hate me, not many like me. If they think I'm sleeping around, it won't help my cause."

"Ignore them. They don't know you." He rubbed a thumb over her cheek, sending chills down her spine. "If they did know you better, I'd have too much competition to keep you to myself." He kissed her one last time then laced his fingers with hers and headed toward the dining hall.

When they reached the entrance, Sibyl let go of his hand and headed back to the table while Ambrose got food. Everyone was silent when she sat down. She resumed eating as if all was normal.

Ambrose made his way to the table and sat down beside her.

Wilson snorted a laugh.

"What's so funny?" Ambrose asked.

"We were just noting how long Sibyl, here, was in the bathroom. We were concerned you may be having some digestive problems. Is everything ok? Do you need a healer?" Wilson smiled mischievously.

Demetrius sniggered. Ambrose sighed heavily.

"I'm fine." Sibyl's cheeks heated.

"That's good." Wilson took a bite of food then added, "so, Ambrose. You seem exceptionally chipper lately. Did one of the healer's finally manage to remove the stick from your ass?"

Everyone laughed.

"Shut up." Ambrose shook his head.

Sibyl couldn't help herself. She laughed too.

"Not you too." He shot her an affronted look.

She smiled innocently.

"Hey guys, what are you up to this afternoon?" Ava came up to the table and sat down across from Sibyl and Ambrose. Sibyl could've kissed her, but that would probably start an entirely new and embarrassing conversation, so she just pretended as if the last two minutes never happened.

"Now that I've figured out how to keep everyone out of my head, I'm going to work on entering people's minds," Sibyl said.

Apprehension took over everyone's faces.

"Willing participants. I'm not going to overstep where I'm not supposed to. I'll get volunteers," she clarified.

They all relaxed and resumed eating.

"You can use me and Wilson," Demetrius said.

"Thank you, Demetrius. That's nice of you, but I'm not sure Wilson will be a great subject for me."

"Why's that?" Wilson asked.

"You need to have a brain in order for me to read it," Sibyl said, completely straight faced.

This time they all laughed really hard. Demetrius actually choked on his food. Ambrose grabbed her hand under the table and squeezed approvingly.

That's what he gets, she said.

"Alright. I see how it is," Wilson said.

Demetrius fist bumped her. "You get like a thousand points for that one."

Sibyl blushed, but she couldn't stop the smile that took over her face. She couldn't remember the last time she had this much fun just hanging out with friends.

After lunch, she spent the next few hours lounging in a corner of the library, telepathically scouting the premises. She knew there were forty-six people in and around the library, and she'd learned all their names. She only tripped over two people's mental barrier and alerted them to the invasion of their mind, but she quickly got out and they were none the wiser. She was only going far enough to learn their names, so she didn't think that warranted any sort of prior approval.

Rokesh let her explore deeper into his mind, but Ambrose didn't want to participate.

I'll tell you my thoughts later, but you probably don't want to read them right now or you'll get embarrassed around everyone. He smiled deviously.

Butterflies fluttered in her stomach at just that statement, so he was probably right. She used Clark instead. After that, she felt like she'd learned enough to be proficient at what she needed to do for Ava.

Perhaps it could come in handy for a demon as well. Could she read a demon's mind like an ordinary person, or would it be different?

That was only one of the dozens of questions swarming her mind when she entered the healer's quarters to visit Cassie. Her condition hadn't changed, but her physical wounds were greatly improved. Her face and arms were unbandaged now, but her hands and the lower portion of her body was still covered. A patch of gnarly scars wrapped around both arms.

Sibyl wished she was able to read a regular human so she could tell if Cassie still had brain function or not. She supposed she'd have to rely on time to know the answer to that, just like everyone else.

"I'm going back to my room before dinner. I want to rest for a bit," Sibyl told Ambrose and Rokesh.

"Rokesh, can you walk her back? I'll meet you guys there in a few minutes. I need to get something," Ambrose said.

"Yeah. No problem," Rokesh agreed.

"Where are you going?" Sibyl asked.

"I'll see you back in your room." He gave her a gentle kiss on the lips then turned and walked off. Sibyl's cheeks heated as people openly gawked at her. Heads turned and whispers rippled in her wake as she left the healer's wing. People stared ever since she returned from Silvermar, but it was getting worse with every passing day.

"Don't people know it's rude to stare?" Sibyl said to Rokesh as they made their way to her room.

Rokesh chuckled. "You should get used to it. You're *the Druid* and you're dating Ambrose. Rumors fly faster than the wind in this place. Whatever happened five minutes ago, people knew about it four minutes ago," he joked.

"That's awesome," Sibyl said, sarcastically.

"I've never seen him like this."

"Like what?"

"Like he is with you." Rokesh met her gaze. "People notice."

Sibyl crisscrossed her fingers in nervous excitement. She'd heard the rumors about him when she first arrived. He'd been with many women and had quite the entourage of admirers who ogled over him, but was never serious about any of them, including Leabella.

Sibyl had no idea why or how she caught his attention, but it made her feel special and insecure at the same time. She had feelings for him, but were they serious? Was he serious? Was this a good idea? She wasn't staying beyond winter solstice. What would they do when she left? Have a long-distance relationship? That seemed like a silly idea to entertain. Or maybe this was just a fling for him. Their lives were headed in completely different directions in different worlds. There was no way he was taking this seriously.

Shaking off the thoughts, Sibyl tried to follow the advice of her friends. Just live in the moment. She didn't have to know all the answers to enjoy what they had going on now. That's probably what he was doing as well. Yes. That's what she was going to do, because so far, the moment was good. Really good.

When they got to her room, she left Rokesh outside the door and changed into something more comfortable, then she hopped into bed for a late afternoon nap. She was nearly asleep when she heard a knock on her door.

Sibyl. It's me. Ambrose's voice entered her mind.

It's open. Come in.

He came in and closed the door behind him. She sat up and yawned.

"Is everything ok?"

"Yeah. Just sleepy." She made to get up.

"Don't get up." He knelt in front of her. "Put your foot up here." He patted his knee. She did as she was instructed. Her pajama shorts were very baggy and short. She wondered how much of herself was exposed. Her heart rate ticked up when he put a hand on her calf.

He pulled out a large, sheathed knife that was tucked behind his back and her pulse quickened for an entirely different reason now. He pulled the knife from the sheath.

"Ok. This is a little weird. Should I be running or screaming right now?" she laughed halfheartedly.

"No." He chuckled and flipped the shimmering silver blade around and handed it over to her.

She took it and inspected the blade. "It's beautiful."

"It's yours. I had it made for you, and I imbued it with as much silver magic that I could cram into it."

Her mouth dropped open. "I don't know what to say. This is really nice, but I don't know how to use a knife."

"It's not that hard. The pointy end goes into anyone who tries to hurt you." He took it from her and re-sheathed it. He laid the knife across her thigh. "If you were wearing pants this would clip to your belt or belt loop." He showed her a snap that was attached to the top part of the sheath. "For now, I'll just snap it to the hem of your shorts." He clipped it to the top of her drawstring shorts.

"This piece." He held up a strap of leather. "Ties around your leg here." He pushed a hand under her thigh dangerously close to the split of her leg. Grabbing the other end of the strap, he pulled it under and tied it to the other end. A surge of desire pulsed through her.

"There's a loop on your pants that this would tie through," he said, without removing his hands. Those red-brown eyes connected with hers. She was about five seconds from tackling him.

"I have something else." He reached into his pocket. She slumped in disappointment at the lack of his warm hands on her leg.

He opened his hand to reveal about two dozen gems.

"What's this?"

"I got several gold and silver gems in case you're attacked or hurt or something. There's a couple of diamonds in case you're ever in the dark. Some rubies if you're cold and need heat. I only got one citrine. Be very careful with that one. It can be wild and difficult to wield. You can accidentally hurt yourself really easily with those. Here's an amethyst. Do you know what that one's for?"

"This is too much. These had to cost a fortune."

He shrugged and started to attach them to her necklace next to the bubble he'd given her. "There's also carnelian to enhance speed." He clipped it on her necklace. "If you need to run away, that's a good one to use. Azurite for strength." He added it on. "Opal for invisibility and camouflage, fluorite for water." Those went on her necklace as well. There were so many now that she had to lift her hair for him to get access to the sides of the necklace.

After he snapped the last one to her necklace, he kissed her neck, and she melted.

"I didn't bother getting you a moonstone since you don't really need one with your Druid magic, although now that I think about it. You could still use it for the enhanced sight and sound. I'll get you one." He sat down next to her on the bed. "You look beautiful. You're Tearnan now." He smiled but it didn't meet his eyes.

"I don't have words. Ambrose, this is too much."

"I want you to be safe and since you won't listen to reason and go home, the next best thing I can do is ensure you've got the resources to protect yourself. I can teach you how to use them if you want."

"I'd love that." She rubbed a hand over the necklace. It was heavy now, but surprisingly it didn't jingle when she moved around. He put the gems far enough apart, so they didn't clank against each other.

"I have a favor to ask." He moved closer and faced her.

All she could think about was his lips on her. She needed to taste him, feel him.

"If things go sideways, I want you to leave."

And that flame was immediately doused. "What are you talking about?"

"If the werewolves breach the wall and get inside Tearnanelle, I want you to get out. Get to safety."

"I thought bubbles didn't work within Tearnanelle walls."

"They don't work within the castle grounds and about a two-mile radius. You know how to get to the market, right?"

Sibyl nodded.

"If they breach the walls, go to town, and follow Market Street north until you get to the end. The last building is a stable. Ask for Fenrius. Tell him that you're with me and ask him to get you a horse."

"That I'm *with* you?"

"Yes." He said it like it was a given. She was with him.

"Take Market Street north out of town until you get to a fork in the road. It's about three miles. To the left is Rakau Road and to the right is Sigra. Take Sigra and go a few more miles until you see a sign that says Reston Family Farm."

"I don't understand why you need me to know all this. If something happens you can just take me wherever we need to go."

"This is if I'm gone."

Her heart hammered in her chest for completely different reasons than it did a few minutes ago. "I'm not having this conversation." She shook her head.

He grabbed her face, stopping her from shaking her head.

"Yes, we are. Please listen to me. If something happens to me, Sibyl, don't trust anyone but Rokesh, Demetrius, Clark, Wilson, or Ava."

"What do you mean?"

"Don't trust anyone, not even the Aruka. People are going to want you dead before they'll let you be captured. Get as far away from here as possible, and if the werewolves breach the wall, can you please take my family with you?" His face was heavy with pleading and desperation.

"I'm confused. Who wants me dead? Why?"

"If you get taken by the werewolves, you know that Alyssium will use your abilities to do horrible things. There are a lot of people who'd rather see you dead than let you get taken. The Aruka is one of them."

Sibyl couldn't believe what he just said. The Aruka wanted her dead. That couldn't be true. She assigned guards to protect her.

"So, if things go bad, you'll leave here, right?" He forced her to look at him.

She nodded.

"Will you take my family with you?"

"They don't know me. They're not going to go with some stranger who shows up at their door during an invasion."

"They know who you are. I've told them about you."

He told his family about her? In what capacity? His job assignment, the failed Druid experiment, a friend, his girlfriend?

"Will you get my family to safety?"

"Yes. Of course I will, but this is just paranoia talking." She tried to shake her head, but he wouldn't allow it. She grabbed one of his hands.

"Thank you." He kissed her then let her face go. They sat in awkward silence for a moment.

He cleared his throat. "I have an idea." His voice was light and playful again. So much different than a moment ago.

Sibyl was shell shocked. In one conversation she'd gone from hopeful flirting, to picturing his death and plans of escape, to being suspicious that people were trying to kill her. Her mind reeled with so much confusion that her heart didn't know what to feel at the moment.

"You asked earlier about getting rid of your guards."

Hope sparked inside her. "Did you talk to the Aruka? Did she say yes?"

"I haven't talked to her, but I thought maybe we could sneak out." He grabbed her hand and laced his fingers in hers.

"Sneak out?"

"You seem to have a knack for that sort of thing." He smiled playfully.

"If you remember correctly. I got caught. By you. So obviously I don't have a knack for it." She was trying to make light of things, but it was difficult.

"That's because you were working against us. Now you've got us in your court."

"Us?"

"Me, Rokesh, Demetrius, and Wilson."

"What do they have to do with sneaking out?"

"They'll cover for us. I thought I'd take you somewhere you haven't been before. It's called the cave of whispers. It's at the southern gate right past the tree tunnel bridge. We could go tonight after dinner if you want."

"Do you think it's safe to be that close to the wall and the gate right now?"

"Of course it is. I'll be with you." He gave her that look that twisted her all up inside.

"You are so arrogant," she teased.

"It's called confidence. Something you could use a bit more of."

She scoffed.

"I'm serious. If you were more confident right now, what would you do?"

She licked her lips. His eyes tracked the movement. What would she do if she was more confident? She'd make the move to kiss him. She hesitantly leaned into him. They were so close that she breathed in his exhaled air. Her heart hammered wildly.

He closed the space between them and filled her mouth with his tongue. Strong hands wrapped around her neck and swept her away in a sea of lust that rivaled the Pacific Ocean. Wrapping her arms around his waist she pulled herself onto him. He grabbed her ass and dove deeper into her mouth.

One of his hands moved under her flimsy shorts, and his thumb rubbed her right where she needed it. Her breath left her.

"I like your pajamas. They're accessible." A finger tucked under her panties and found the most sensitive part of her, driving her completely wild. His tongue found her mouth again and she spiraled into a lustful frenzy. She was at the end of a delicate tether of propriety that was about to snap, and then someone knocked at the door.

He growled into her mouth. Their expressions were mirror images of each other. A level of annoyance that would frustrate even the Pope.

"Ignore it," she said. They resumed making out and the knock came again a few seconds later.

"What do you want?" Ambrose yelled.

"Heads up," Rokesh said, from the other side of the door.

"What does that mean?" Sibyl dismounted and headed for the door. Pounding exploded on the door and the knob jiggled.

"Oh, for fuck's sake, hold on a minute." She reached for the knob.

"Sibyl, wait."

But she didn't hear him in time. With an impatient laugh, she opened the door. "What's up, Rokesh?"

But it wasn't Rokesh. Her heart dropped as five Mage Guard men pushed her to the side and stormed in.

"What the?" Ambrose shot up.

Before Sibyl knew what was going on, one of the men punched Ambrose in the center of his chest right over his heart. Ambrose toppled backward.

"AMBROSE! NO!" Sibyl launched for him, but someone grabbed her arms and restrained her. She glanced over her shoulder and met the face of a stranger. The man's eyes weren't kind or forgiving. He glowered at her with unfettered disdain.

Another man stepped in front of her and put a necklace over her head. His eyes dropped to her leg where the knife was sheathed. Pulling the knife out, he inspected it.

"Nice blade. I'll hold on to that." His eyes fell to her neck. "And this." Reaching around her head, he undid the clasp of her necklace. The one that Ambrose just filled with gems. Taking both items, he walked off.

"What's going on?" she asked.

No one answered her.

Ambrose regained his wits and was resisting the two men trying to subdue him. "What's this about?" he demanded.

Someone slapped a weird cuff around one of his wrists then twisted his arm behind his back. Ambrose shoved the man off easily and put a hand up defensively. Another man grabbed him and slapped a matching cuff around that wrist. Ambrose pushed back more force-fully that time.

Sibyl could tell he didn't want to openly fight the people who were supposed to be his colleagues, but he wasn't going to just roll over either. Before he was able to do anything, a third guard put a hand out in front of him as if he was casting a spell or something, and Ambrose fell to the floor as if he was pulled by his own arms.

"What's going on?" Sibyl asked again. Confusion and fear snaked around her mind and heart, threatening to squeeze the sense right out of her. She struggled against the man holding her. His grip tightened. She thrashed and kicked, trying to yank herself free. The man shoved her onto the bed face down and used his weight to hold her down.

"GET OFF ME!"

Ambrose's words rang inside her head. *People will want you dead before they'll let you be captured. The Aruka is one of them.* Panic fully seized her.

"TAKE YOUR HANDS OFF HER!" Ambrose shouted. He tried to get up, but his arms were stuck to the floor. Pulling against the cuffs, he rose a few inches.

One of the men punched him between the shoulders at the base of the neck and he collapsed. Ambrose pushed himself to his hands and knees and growled. He glared with feral anger at the man who hit him.

The man holding his hand out closed his fist and Ambrose roared in pain.

"Stay," the guard said, clenching his fist tightly.

"When I get out of this, Riah, you and I are going to have a talk," Ambrose said, through gritted teeth.

"You won't be getting out of this, traitor."

Ambrose's head snapped up. "What are you talking about?"

The Aruka walked into the room and Sibyl's heart sank. She was dressed in full armor as if she was about to go to war. As usual, her left arm was hidden beneath a sleeve, and a gilded cuff overflowing with various gems encircled her right arm. Ziv and Jameson flanked her.

Sibyl tried to move but the man pushed an elbow between her shoulders. Pain seared through her back. Squeezing her eyes closed, she whimpered against the pain. He didn't let up. She opened her eyes and met Ambrose's gaze. He was pissed.

Another man that Sibyl didn't know came from the bathroom. "All clear, Aruka."

Serellina surveyed the room. She looked healthy again. She'd obviously gotten over whatever illness was affecting her. Sibyl watched the woman suspiciously. It couldn't be true. Could it? The Aruka had never been warm toward Sibyl, but she was hospitable, and Ava's aunt, and the ruler of a magical kingdom. She was chosen by the Gods. Surely, they wouldn't choose someone who was bad.

"Serellina please. What's going on?" Sibyl asked.

The Aruka's green eyes locked onto Sibyl, as if she'd only just noticed she was there.

"Let her go," Serellina ordered.

The man released her.

Sibyl got up and shoved him back. "Don't touch me!" She scolded him as if he was a child who'd misbehaved.

The man smirked at her.

Rolling her shoulders, she stood up tall. She wouldn't let her fear get the best of her.

She reached for Ambrose telepathically. *Ambrose?*

There was nothing there. It's as if he didn't exist. Nothing and no one existed in the telepathic plane. She looked at the necklace around her neck. Osmium. Pulling it off, she flung it at the man who'd restrained her.

Ambrose, she said again, but he didn't respond. There was still a void, but this time it only existed around him. She moved toward him.

"No." Serellina stepped between them.

"Someone please tell me what's going on," Sibyl demanded.

"I'd like to know that too," Ambrose said. His fists pressed into the floor so hard his knuckles were turning white.

"Let him up." The Aruka watched Ambrose with deep contempt brewing behind her features.

The man named Riah put his arm down and the tension evaporated from Ambrose immediately.

Standing up, he rolled his shoulders, and eyed Riah with a threatening expression. Then his glare shifted to the man who'd held Sibyl down. "You better run when I get these off." Ambrose pointed at him.

The man huffed a laugh and crossed his arms challengingly.

"Don't try anything, Ambrose. The osmium spike in your chest won't allow you to use your magic, and the citrine around your arms can be activated within a split second. Don't make us use it," the Aruka said.

When it was obvious Ambrose was going to cooperate, she nodded to one of the men standing next to Ambrose. He undid the belt around Ambrose's waist, pulled it through the loops, and handed it to the Aruka. Ambrose glared at the man, but didn't resist.

"Do you have any other gems on you?" the Aruka asked.

Ambrose didn't answer. He stood in silent defiance.

"Search him."

The two men patted him down. Ambrose stood perfectly still for the entire process. When they came up empty handed, they nodded to Serellina and stepped back. She waved Jameson forward.

"Ambrose Reston, you're being detained and taken to the cells until a time can be scheduled to question you about your crimes against the kingdom." Jameson recited the line like it was Miranda rights.

"What crimes?" Ambrose asked.

"Leaking secrets and sensitive information to the enemy," Jameson answered.

Sibyl couldn't believe what she was hearing.

"Have you all lost your minds?" Ambrose exclaimed. "I'm not a spy."

"Can you account for missing Mage training sessions for weeks now?" Jameson asked.

"Yeah. I was sleeping. I've been assigned a swing shift, you fucking moron. I work until midnight every night. By the time I go to bed, the Empyrean star is three quarters across the sky sometimes, so I sleep in. Is that what this is about? Last I checked, I'm not a recruit. Mage training isn't mandatory for graduated guards."

"But you haven't missed one in years, and suddenly you're missing them all the time?" Serellina crossed her arms.

"Doing a job you assigned me to. This is bull shit."

"It's been reported that you had a foul odor on the night of WanG-1 Libnys?"

The veins on Ambrose's neck were popping out, he was so angry.

"Wait. Is that the night I was drugged at the tavern?" Sibyl asked.

"You were drugged?" Serellina asked.

"Yes. It was an accident. It's a long story. But that's the night they're referring to. Right?" She looked at Ambrose for confirmation.

He nodded his head.

"He smelled because something or someone was following us."

"Did you see this someone or something?" Jameson asked.

"No. It happened when I was unconscious."

"So, you have no proof of what or who this other thing was?"

"No, but this doesn't make sense. You're accusing him of being the spy because he smelled bad one night and he missed a few non-mandatory practices? This all seems circumstantial at best, and he hasn't smelled like that one single time since then."

"She would know what he smells like, wouldn't she?" one of the men standing next to Ambrose said.

They all laughed.

Quick as lightning, Ambrose throat punched the guy. He buckled over in a choking fit. Riah's hand flung up and Ambrose hit the floor.

"Knock it off, EVERYONE!" the Aruka shouted. "Willum, out! Now."

The choking man held his throat and headed for the door, kicking Ambrose in the back of the head on his way by.

Ambrose growled.

The man who searched the room took Willum's place next to Ambrose.

"Stand up Ambrose and behave!" the Aruka scolded.

Riah put his hand down and Ambrose stood.

"Sibyl, I know this is difficult to comprehend, but the evidence is stacked against him. It's obvious he's the spy."

Sibyl's anger flared. "Don't treat me like I'm ignorant. My dad and brother are lawyers. I know how due process works, and on Earth you must have significant supportive evidence to arrest someone. You don't have anything solid on him. You really think he's a demon?"

"This isn't Earth. This is Tearnanelle and by our laws we have plenty of proof that he is the spy. And, no, I don't think he's the demon. I think he's working with the demon queen, which explains why he had the smell on him, but hasn't since. She's a succubus you know." Serellina eyed Sibyl knowingly.

"That's ridiculous. What other *proof* do you have?" Sibyl challenged.

"Not that you're entitled to the information but, he has also defied direct orders, found to be negligent of his duties, and he's keeping secrets from his superiors that directly affects this kingdom. Without substantial evidence to prove otherwise, he will be detained in the O-cells for everyone's safety, including your own. This is how it works in our world."

"No," Sibyl said, barely louder than a whisper. He'd be locked behind a prison of osmium, rendering him powerless, and her unable to communicate with him.

"Wait. What if I can prove he's innocent?"

"How?" Serellina asked.

"I can look into his mind. Go back to that night and see if I can figure out who attacked us."

"You can do that?" she asked.

"I think so."

"Fine. Have at it." Serellina motioned to him. "Riah, remove the osmium spike."

"No," Ambrose said.

"What?" Sibyl couldn't believe what she was hearing.

He closed his eyes. "No. I don't want you to do that."

"Why not?" Sibyl asked.

He didn't answer her.

"Ambrose. Why won't you let me prove you're innocent?" She asked again, more demanding this time.

He remained silent, staring at the floor, fixated on some invisible point in front of the bed they were just making out on. His jaw ticked.

"He doesn't want you to look in his mind, because it won't prove he's innocent," Serellina said, matter-of-factly.

"No. It's not like that." Ambrose glared at Serellina.

"Ambrose." Sibyl tried to go to him, but she was blocked by Ziv.

Ambrose met her eyes. They were sad and apologetic, but unyielding.

"Sibyl, tell me something," Serellina said. "When did Ambrose show an interest in you? Was it before or after he learned how powerful you are?"

"What does that have to do with anything?" Sibyl's fingers tingled with riotous magic.

"Has he ever acted weird around you? Displayed unexplainable behavior?" Serellina asked.

Sibyl recalled how he hated her at first, then followed her and helped her, then acted like he couldn't stand her again. One minute he looked at her like she was some lost wounded puppy he needed to rescue, then the next he looked at her with disgust, then the next with longing.

She met his eyes. Those beautiful cognac eyes that always pulled her in. There was concern behind them.

His gaze darted between her and the Aruka then back to her again. He shook his head. "I can explain all of that, Sibyl." His chest puffed quicker than usual. He was losing the battle of composure.

"Has he recently told you not to trust anyone, especially me?" the Aruka asked.

Sibyl's head spun. It couldn't be true.

"Has he asked you to run away with him, perchance?"

"The cave of whispers," Sibyl mumbled to herself. Her knees buckled. Ziv caught her.

"Sibyl, it's not like that." Ambrose tried to go to her, but Riah closed his fist, and Ambrose fell back to the floor, groaning against some unseen pain.

"I'm being set up. Remember what I told you." His expression was desperate and his eyes pleading. The same eyes that pleaded to save his family. Save them from what exactly? Was it the werewolves he was afraid of? Or was he afraid of them getting caught up in a treasonous web of lies that he'd spun?

His eyes widened. "Don't believe it, Sibyl. Don't trust her." His voice cracked.

"And there it is. The traitor hangs himself with his own words." Serellina scoffed. "Silence him."

Ambrose fought to get up, but Riah punched his fist down so hard that Ambrose fell flat against the floor, writhing in pain. Sibyl couldn't do anything but watch, completely horror stricken, as they held him to the ground.

"Sibyl, I swear to you. I'm not a traitor. I didn't...."

Jameson buckled a leather collar around Ambrose's neck that had weird symbols etched onto it.

"What is that thing?" Tears streamed down Sibyl's face. She didn't realize she'd started to cry.

"It's just an ordinary strap of leather with silencing runes sewn into it," Serellina said, casually. "He was going to take you to the enemy. When were you supposed to leave and where were you going?"

Sibyl stared at the man she was about to sleep with less than ten minutes ago. The man she was about to sneak out with. The man who was slowly stealing her heart. Was it true? He mouthed something to her, but she couldn't tell what he was saying. She was a telepath, not a lip reader.

"Sibyl?" Serellina snapped her fingers in front of Sibyl's face. "When were you planning to run off?"

"We were just going on a hike. We weren't running away. It was just going to be a few hours."

Several men huffed and rolled their eyes at her. Serellina gave her a patronizing look. It did sound suspicious now that she said it out loud. Her heart sank further and further the more she put all the puzzle pieces together. He'd been hot and cold the entire time she'd been here.

"Tonight. After dinner. We were going to the Cave of Whispers," she finally said.

Ambrose closed his eyes and put his head on the floor. His entire body went limp. Sibyl felt the same way right now.

"Search the cave and take him away," Serellina ordered.

Two of the men dipped their heads and left. The others pulled Ambrose to his feet and marched him out the door. When he got close, he reached for Sibyl, but one of the men grabbed his arm and pushed him away.

Ambrose's mouth moved, but she had no idea what he said. Even if he spoke out loud, she's not sure she'd have understood. Her head was so mottled and confused. Staring blankly at him, she watched like a paralyzed statue as he was escorted out of her room.

Ziv finally let her go and surprisingly her legs held her up. The man who'd taken her knife and gem necklace tossed them haphazardly on the bed and gave her a condescending scowl before following the others out of the room.

She rushed out the door to find about a dozen guards in the hallway, barricading her from following as Ambrose was escorted down the hall.

He looked over his shoulder and mouthed something, but it wasn't directed at her. Sibyl's head robotically swiveled to the right. Rokesh nodded at Ambrose. Apparently, he understood what Ambrose said.

Sibyl turned toward Ambrose again. He locked eyes with her. He didn't try to say anything anymore. He just stared at her with sad eyes that ripped her heart out. One of the guards pushed his head forward and led him down the hall until they turned a corner and disappeared.

"I really am sorry Sibyl," Serellina said. "He fooled us all." She grabbed Sibyl's shoulder and squeezed. The Aruka was trying to be comforting, but Sibyl was too numb to feel anything. All she could do was stare at the empty hallway.

Serellina walked away and all the guards followed, leaving Sibyl, Rokesh, and several bystanders who now stared at Sibyl. A mixture of fear, confusion, loathing, and disgust pelted her. Not one single positive emotion came from anyone.

Tingling crawled up the back of her neck and creeped into her mind. Whispers scraped along the edge of her mental shield. Taking a deep breath, she tried to fortify it, but the tingling spread through her like a wildfire. She was in no state to fight the magic right now.

Rushing to the nightstand, she retrieved the osmium gem and clipped it onto her necklace with all the other gems then replaced it around her neck. Instant relief enveloped her, followed by a cascade of pain pouring into her heart. Her chest tightened. The osmium wasn't enough. She went to her backpack and dug around.

"What's going on?" Rokesh asked.

They weren't there. Hands shaking, she went to the dresser and dug through the drawers, not there. She pulled the drawers out and emptied the contents onto the floor. The room started to close in on her.

"No. No. No." She fell to her hands and knees.

"What's wrong?" Rokesh asked more urgently.

"I need my pills. The Ativan." It was really hot all of a sudden.

"Panic attack." She crawled toward the bathroom.

Rokesh helped her up and guided her to the bathroom where she fell to the floor pressing against the cold tile.

"What do you need?" he asked.

"Shower." She pointed but she didn't have the strength to stand. She was only a few seconds from passing out. If she could just get cold water on her, she could fight it off.

"What?" He sounded confused.

"Help me to the shower," she said, breathlessly. She was drenched in sweat, but it wasn't shocking her system enough to stave off the panic. She needed something stronger.

He half dragged, half led her to the shower. Once she was inside, she pulled the lever and ice-cold water poured over her. She immediately woke her up, and the anxiety bolted out of her like a frightened horse. Sliding down the wall, she sat on the floor of the shower stall letting the frigid water rain down on her while Rokesh paced.

Running a hand through his hair, he glanced at her every few steps. Desperation laced his features. Sibyl closed her eyes. She couldn't handle his anxiety right now. She could barely handle her own. She had nothing useful to say anyway.

What was she supposed to do? Ambrose was arrested for suspicion of being the spy. An act of treason punishable by death. She didn't know what to think or say or do. So, she did nothing except cry. At least with the water pouring down on her Rokesh wouldn't be able to tell the difference between the water and the tears, so she let them all come out.

CHAPTER 28
AVA
SASGAR WAXG-5/NOVEMBER 23RD

Gloom weighed heavily on Ava. She hadn't heard anything from Redly since his patrol shifts were changed a month ago. The moonstone was full of messages that she'd left for him every day. He hadn't gotten any of them.

Ambrose was locked up for being the spy. She invited him onto the council based on absolutely nothing except he happened to be one of the first people she met when she got here. How stupid could she be? She'd be more selective for future council members.

Cassie was still in a coma, and although her physical injuries were all but healed, she showed no sign of brain function. What on Earth was she going to tell Melody?

In less than a month, the kingdom would be under attack by a legion of werewolves roughly ten times the size of Tearnanelle's standing military.

Maybe her aunt was right. She was inheriting a doomed kingdom.

Demetrius and Clark huddled on the couch while Wilson laid on the love seat with his legs over the armrest. His eyes were closed, but Ava doubted he was asleep. Sibyl and Rokesh sat at the dining room table with forlorn expressions.

"What are we going to do?" Sibyl finally asked, breaking the depressing silence.

"We keep preparing for the battle to come." Ava went to the kitchen.

"But what about Ambrose?" Sibyl asked.

Of course that's all she was worried about. Her boyfriend.

"What about him?" Ava got a glass and filled it with water.

"We have to get him out. Can you talk to your aunt or something?"

"Why would I do that?"

"What do you mean why would you do that? You're the Arukas. You have authority. You can get him out." Sibyl furrowed her eyebrows.

"First of all, I don't have any authority. Arukas doesn't mean much except that I'm in training to have authority one day. This is a monarchy and my aunt's still in charge. Secondly, I don't think it's a good idea to get him out." Ava casually sipped the water. She could practically see Sibyl's freckles connecting themselves with as red as her face became.

"Why not?"

"Because I think he's exactly where he needs to be."

Sibyl walked to the counter opposite Ava. "You can't be serious? You think he's the spy?"

"I don't think we can dismiss the possibility."

Rokesh sighed and put his head on the table.

"That's absurd," Sibyl protested.

"Sibyl come on. You can't be that naïve." Ava walked to the other side of the counter so that they stood face to face. "He's acted strange since the moment we got here. He smelled suspiciously like a demon, he's had open arguments with the Aruka, and he's defied direct orders. You told us yourself that he asked you to sneak away with him."

"We just wanted some privacy."

Ava scoffed.

"If he was going to kidnap me and take me to Tearnanoak, he would have done it. He had many opportunities over several months."

"He was waiting for you to get your magic under control. Don't you think it's odd that right when you finally know how to handle your magic, he wanted to sneak away with you?" Ava tapped her temple. "Think about it Sibyl."

"That's a coincidence." Sibyl folded her arms over her chest.

"Coincidence. Really? Come on guys. Do you really think all these things are coincidence?" Ava looked at everyone else in the room.

"Ambrose is innocent," Rokesh said vehemently.

Ava rolled her eyes. "Demetrius, Clark?"

They acted like deer in headlights.

"I think we may need to consider the possibility that he might be guilty." Wilson sat up.

"Thank you. A voice of reason."

"You think Wilson is the voice of reason?" Sibyl said, sarcastically.

"Hey. I take exception to that," Wilson said.

"This isn't worth fighting about," Clark said.

"You just don't want to face the facts. You were so desperate for any kind of affection that you jumped right into bed with the first man to show interest in you since your boyfriend dumped you. You don't want to admit that he was using you."

Sibyl shook her head. "You don't know what you're talking about, and like you're one to talk. You sneak around nearly every day, going outside the walls like we were expressly told not to, and hopped right into bed with a werewolf. The enemy. The same people who killed your family. How does it feel sleeping with your family's murderers?"

Ava's temper flared. Before she could stop herself, she slapped Sibyl. The look of shock on Sibyl's face was priceless. A red handprint flared to life on her freckled cheek.

Wilson stepped between them. "That's enough you two."

Sibyl rubbed her face. "What's wrong with you? You think you can treat people like shit and expect us to just accept it because you've been through so much. That's why no one wants to be around you!"

"Really? You think no one wants to be around me? You're one to talk." Ava took on a whiny baby voice. "Oh, poor me. I have anxiety, waaah. I want to go home, waaah. I'm so pathetic and weak." Ava slammed her hand on the counter.

"Grow up, Sibyl. You've been sheltered so much that you can't function in the real world. That's why you came here, because no one could stand to be around you on Earth. You have absolutely zero redeeming qualities. You're a book nerd, and you're of no use to us, so why don't you just go back home, and take your meds like a good little crazy person." Ava twirled a finger around her ear making the cuckoo sign.

Sibyl charged toward Ava. Wilson held her back as she flailed and yelled all sorts of obscenities. Ava crossed her arms and glared at Sibyl, shaking her head.

"Look at this. Sibyl's grown a backbone. You want a go at me? Fine. Let her go, Wilson. This will be fun."

"Guys, can we just calm down please?" Clark stood up from the couch. Demetrius and Rokesh exchanged a concerned look.

After a minute, Sibyl finally calmed down, but Ava saw the rage burning behind those eyes that were now as dark as storm clouds. Wilson pushed her back, refusing to let her get any closer to Ava.

"You act all high and mighty, and like nothing bothers you. But it's so obvious that you want nothing more than to be loved and told everything's ok, because you never got that from mommy because she dumped your ass. You don't have any friends because you're a raging bitch that everyone hates!"

Ava saw red.

"OK. Sibyl. That was a low blow," Wilson said.

"Oh shit." Demetrius ran to intercept Ava. So did Rokesh, but they weren't quick enough.

The fog of battle overtook all her senses. Deflecting Demetrius as if he was nothing more than an irritating gnat, she elbowed him in the face. His nose crunched on impact. He rocked backwards as blood poured down his shirt.

Rokesh came at her, but she swiped his feet out from under him with barely a thought. He hit the floor, toppling over a chair in the process. Wilson was smart enough to step out of the way, letting Sibyl go, and Ava tackled her.

Sibyl was the weakest opponent she'd ever encountered. Ava had her in a choke hold within a few seconds. Wilson and Rokesh tried to pull Ava off, but her grip was solidly locked.

"Ava let go," Rokesh yelled, as he tried to dislodge her arms.

"You want to see raging bitch? Here she is, book nerd." Ava yanked Sibyl's head back.

Sibyl clawed at Ava's arms, digging her nails in so deep that she left marks. It stung slightly, but they healed within seconds.

"Come on ladies. This is ridiculous!" Wilson shouted.

"Let her go!" Rokesh yelled, but Ava had no intention of letting Sibyl go...yet.

"Apologize," Ava demanded.

"Fuck...you," Sibyl gritted out between clenched teeth. She punched Ava's shoulder, desperately trying to dislodge her, but it was pathetic. She was a kitten under a lion. Ava almost felt sorry for her. Almost.

She squeezed a little bit harder, and Sibyl's face turned an unflattering shade of blue. Sibyl glared at Ava with pure unadulterated hatred. Ava smiled and blew a kiss at her. It was a petty thing to do, but she couldn't help herself.

Sibyl's eyes started to change. Ice-white ribbons swirled within the dark grey hue of her iris creating a hurricane-like scene. As more and more white overtook Sibyl's eyes, the room got quieter, like a vacuum sucked out all the sound and air. It became difficult to breathe.

Sibyl pulled Ava's arm away and stepped out of her grasp like she was getting out of a car.

What the hell? Commanding her arm to regain her opponent, Ava watched as it did nothing but sit rigidly still suspended in space. She tried to move any part of herself, but she couldn't. She was paralyzed. Protesting against some unforeseen force that played her body like a puppet, Ava screamed. All that came out was a tiny whimper.

Sibyl glared down at Ava. "Kneel."

Ava's body moved into a kneeling position. Her mind screamed for control, but nothing worked. Her body was hijacked. She wondered if this was how Redly felt when Alyssium seized control of his mind.

"Look at me," Sibyl said.

Ava's head tipped up and she met Sibyl's stormy eyes. There was a level of anger on the freckled face that Ava had never seen.

Rokesh, Wilson, and Demetrius backed up.

"What's going on?" Demetrius asked, apprehensively.

Ava's lungs spasmed and her head squeezing in on itself from some invisible force. Her vision blurred. She needed air, but she couldn't take a breath. Her heart raced as panic set it.

She fought against the invisible paralyzing bonds that held her, but it was useless. Tentacles of rage ensnared her so completely that she was suffocating under their grip. She was completely at the mercy of Sibyl's magic.

"Sibyl." Clark cautiously stepped toward her. "Let her go."

Ava narrowed her eyes at Sibyl. She may not be able to move or breathe, but she could send a threatening glare. If Sibyl was going to choose now to be a murderous traitor, Ava would die fighting, even if it was just with her eyes.

"Next time you even think about laying a hand on me, remember this feeling." Sibyl's words were laced with a lethal calm. "The inability to control your own body and mind. Complete helplessness. Is it scary, Ava?" She cocked her head to the side. "This is where I've lived my entire life. You'll survive a minute or two."

Ava's chest burned. The room tunneled so that all she saw was Sibyl. Her head screamed in pain. She wouldn't last much longer without oxygen.

"You disregard the thoughts and feelings of everyone around you and treat us like we're the enemy. You think every problem can be solved by fighting." Sibyl shook her head. "Here's some advice from a book nerd." Sibyl knelt until she was right in front of Ava's face. "Don't fuck with the crazy ones." Then she walked out.

The moment she closed the door behind her, Ava fell to her hands and knees, and her lungs sucked in air of their own volition. She coughed and sputtered, trying to catch her breath. Once she was finally recovered, she sat back and looked at everyone. They all held shocked expressions.

"Damn. I didn't think she had it in her," Wilson said.

Rokesh shook his head at Ava as he walked out the door. Of course he would side with her. He was so far up Ambrose's ass; they were probably in a threesome.

Demetrius's face and shirt was covered in blood, and a bruise was already taking over his eyes and nose. Behind the swelling she could tell he was pissed. He stormed out, not saying a word.

"Come on. Demetrius. I'm sorry! I didn't mean to. I was in the heat of the moment."

He was gone. Ava looked at Clark sheepishly. Her expression was solemn. She walked out without saying a word.

"Well, that could have gone better." Wilson picked up the fallen chair and sat in it.

Ava joined him at the table. "Yeah."

Wilson laughed. "Remind me never to get on your bad side, or hers, for that matter." He ran a hand through his hair.

"She was being totally ridiculous," Ava argued.

"But was she?"

"What do you mean? Of course she was."

"We don't know that he's guilty. What's the harm in letting her believe that he's innocent? You don't have to beat people into agreeing with you."

"But she asked me to get him out."

"You could have just said 'no' without antagonizing her."

Ava sighed.

"I think next time you should both wear white shirts, and we can open up some fluorite on you two." He smiled.

"You're ridiculous."

Wilson stood from the table. "I'm going to bed. You good?"

Ava nodded.

"Alright. See you later." Wilson left.

Now what? They were supposed to be coming up with ideas for battle plans, not fighting with each other. Damn it. What a mess. Her aunt wasn't going to be pleased about a giant rift in the junior council. What a shitty Arukas she was shaping up to be.

CHAPTER 29
SIBYL
CAPBAY LASQ-4/DECEMBER 14TH

"Don't hold the blade like that." Rokesh demonstrated a proper knife hold for defense. "You don't want to hold your arm with the underside up as that leaves you vulnerable. Keep your arm like this." He held his arm with the underside facing in.

Sibyl nodded then did the stabbing movement again.

"Good." He laughed in a manner that made her believe it wasn't good.

"I'm not a fighter. I don't know why he gave me a knife."

"To defend yourself with. I'm not teaching you to fight. I'm teaching you to defend. Your number one goal, if you're attacked, is to run. Create distance between you and your assailant, then run. Got it?"

Sibyl nodded.

"If you can't run then your primary goal is to stay on your feet. That's the most important objective if you have to defend yourself. Ok?"

Sibyl nodded again.

"If you do fall, try not to fall flat out and hit your head. Tuck your chin and crunch up to protect your head."

"Ok. Chin in, got it."

"Second thing you do is don't turn your back on your attacker. Most people's gut instinct is to roll over to try to get up. You want to get back on your feet, but not by turning your back on your opponent while you're on the ground."

"How am I supposed to remember all this if I'm being attacked?"

"Stay calm. Don't panic. Use your brain. Do whatever you have to do to not panic."

"That's great. I'm really good at not panicking," she said, sarcastically.

He laughed. "We'll practice."

"Practice not panicking? I've done that my whole life."

"No. We're going to practice going to the ground so you can see what it feels like. That's how you remain calm. You do it until it's familiar. Release the knife."

"Ok." She let go of the blade and it fell on the ground.

Rokesh laughed. "Sorry. I meant sheath the knife. I forgot you're not a Mage. We release our magical tether, and the weapon disappears. It's just a habit to say "release."

She picked it back up and slid it into the sheath.

"You ready?"

"I guess so." She took up a defensive pose, spreading her feet apart, like he'd taught her. In less than five seconds, he faked a punch then swiped her feet out from under her, and she fell.

He was at least kind enough to guide her fall down so she didn't slam down on her ass. It was really awkward being on the ground with Rokesh towering over her.

"That was a decent fall. Remember to tuck your chin so you don't hit your head."

"Ok."

"Now that you're down, what's the first thing you're going to do?"

"Not turn my back on you."

"That's what you're *not* going to do. But you *are* going to stay calm."

"Right, stay calm, don't panic."

"Your adrenaline will be ramped up, so it'll be easier to focus in the heat of the moment. Once you're down, if you can't safely get up because your opponent is too close, you're going to put your legs between you and them to keep them away. Try it. Push me away."

She put her legs up and kicked out at him.

"Don't flail kick. Wait for an opening. Keep your opponent away from you, but not at the expense of just randomly kicking otherwise, he could just knock your legs to the side and grab you." Rokesh did exactly that and got Sibyl in a temporary choke hold.

Flashbacks from Ava's hold on her played through her mind. The whole not panicking thing went out the window.

"See." He let her go. "Let's do it again. Come on." Offering her a hand, he helped her up and they spent the next thirty minutes practicing falling down then keeping him away with her legs.

It was uncomfortable and uncoordinated the first few tries, but he made it kind of like a game, dancing around her, trying to get close. After a while, it got easier and more natural. Granted he was probably taking it easy on her, but at least she was learning a little bit, and she had to admit it was a little fun.

"That's it. All you do is keep your legs up and keep your opponent away. No matter what you do, don't let them get past your legs. Whether you spin, kick, block, whatever, use your legs to keep them away."

"Last thing, if you do get to the ground, and you can't get back up and your attacker does get to you." He shook his head. "That's when you'll probably want your knife. Do you know where to stab someone for the most effect?"

"Kidneys," Sibyl said.

"Yes. Kidneys are here." He pointed to her lower ribs. Also, the throat, eyes, or thigh are good areas. Whatever you can get to that's least guarded. And if you can't stab them then bite, kick, scratch, or yell. Whatever you have to do to prevent them from getting the upper hand, do it, and get back to your feet as soon as you can."

Sibyl's heart sank. "I don't have a shot in hell if someone attacks me. Do I?"

Rokesh sighed. "Ok. I'll be honest here. You're quite possibly the worst fighter I've ever seen."

"Me too."

They both turned to the man sitting on a bench. The Aruka had assigned Rokesh a new partner. His name was Tabaio, and he was as arrogant and obnoxious as he was large. Tattoos covered nearly every inch of his body except his face. None of them were ritualistic or mating bonds. He just wanted to look cool. If anything, the tattoos made him look more intimidating than he already was, and they were a stark contrast to his bright blond hair and icy blue eyes.

The Aruka must have assigned her most loyal guard, because he absolutely despised both Sibyl and Rokesh, and he was very open about it.

Ignoring Tabaio, Rokesh continued. "This is a last resort. You've got other strengths and skills. Your mind and your magic. Those are your primary weapons. Don't forget about them. Outsmart your opponent." He pointed to her necklace. "Use the gems like I've shown you, and if you still find yourself in a situation, then use the knife and fight with everything you have.

"A fight isn't over until you give up or you or your opponent is dead. Don't ever give up or you automatically lose."

"You're as good as dead anyway, so you could just give up and save everyone the trouble," Tabaio said.

"Shut up before I knock you straight into Mokor," Rokesh said.

"I'd like to see you try." Tabaio crossed his arms over his massively muscled chest.

Grumbling, Rokesh turned back to Sibyl.

She tried really hard to keep her composure, but she was about ten seconds away from a panic attack. How was she supposed to stay calm in a fight when she was panicking just by thinking she may have to fight?

Magic snaked up her arms and her hands started to tingle. She rolled her neck, trying to dispel the magic, anger, and pain.

"Ignore him. Pay attention to me," Rokesh said.

She swallowed down the building anxiety and the tingling lessened.

"Why are you helping me? You know this is basically pointless right?"

Rokesh's shoulders slumped. "Ambrose isn't the spy. I know it and you know it. He's like a brother to me. I'd do anything for him, and in extension, you. He asked me to train you, so I am."

"Is that what he said to you in the hallway?"

Rokesh nodded.

"I'm sorry."

"What for?"

"For you having to help me when you know as well as I do that it's a waste of time." She shook her head.

"Stop it. You're my friend, Sibyl. I'm happy to help. You're not a lost cause. You just..." Rokesh put his hands on his hips. "Ok. I'm going to tell you something that you're not going to like. Ava had a point."

Sibyl's hackles raised. "What are you talking about?"

"You need to stop being so defeatist and self-deprecating."

"She didn't say any of that," Sibyl defended.

"She did, in a roundabout way. The poor pathetic me, I can't do this, I don't know what to do attitude." Rokesh winced. "Look, Sibyl, I think you're great. You're sweet, caring, powerful, and smart. But you are your own worst enemy, sometimes. You're just so down on yourself. But every now and again, there's this fire that ignites and you come out of your shell. Like what you did to Ava the other night. That was awesome." He smiled.

"I didn't know I could do that. I just kind of snapped, and it happened."

"Good. Let that happen more often. Practice it. Control it. Use it.

Believe in yourself and trust your instincts. If you do that then you won't need this knife."

"You sound like Ambrose."

"He's a smart man. Listen to him, listen to me, and I know you don't want to, but listen to Ava. She said you finally grew a backbone. She was right. That woman you were when you put Ava in her place. That's who you need to be. Stop trying to be so prim and proper and contained all the time. Embrace the crazy."

Sibyl's head snapped to him. She hated when people called her crazy.

He nodded his head. "Embrace it."

"I hear what you're saying."

"Do you?" He cocked his head.

She knew he was right. She knew how to control the magic now, but she was still afraid to see how deep the rabbit hole went. She didn't know what was she fully capable of and if she got in too deep, would she be able to control it? There wasn't but so much time to learn all the ins and outs of her magical abilities and limitations. Trying to stuff it all into a few days seemed irresponsible and potentially catastrophic.

That didn't mean she should hide from it or try to suppress it though. She'd allowed herself to be a victim to her anxiety and fears for most of her life. It was time to be brave. Be in control. Be the master of her own mind. That's what she wanted since she could remember, especially since coming here.

"I hear you," she said.

"Why don't we quit for the day. We'll practice some more tomorrow."

"Yeah. Ok. I want to go by the O-cells again, anyway."

Rokesh sighed.

"I have to try."

"Ok." Rokesh gestured for her to lead the way. Tabaio hopped up from the bench and followed them to the O-cells.

"Can I see Ambrose Reston please?" Sibyl asked.

The man sighed impatiently, then ran a finger down the list in front of him. She'd come down here every day since Ambrose was arrested and requested visitation, and every day she was denied.

"Still no visitors allowed," he said dismissively.

She looked at the large ornate doors into the O-cells. The perimeter was lined with containment runes so the effects of the osmium wouldn't spill beyond the threshold. She could will the guard into letting her by, but the moment she stepped through the doors she'd be immersed behind a barricade of osmium and lose all her magic, at which point he'd wake up, and she'd likely be arrested and join Ambrose in the cells. That's a thought.

He stared at her, waiting for her next move. She'd tried nearly everything over the last couple of weeks. Pleaded, cried, yelled, negotiated, offered to trade her necklace of gems. She'd even thrown a temper tantrum, which resulted in her being escorted out.

She was kind of embarrassed about that. She was out of ideas at this point. It was hopeless. Rokesh had tried as well, and rumor had it, that Ambrose's parents had been down here too, and were met with the same results. The Aruka wasn't going to let anyone see him.

She slammed her hands on the table and walked away. Rokesh and Tabaio flanked her.

"That actually really hurt." She shook her hands when they got around the corner.

"What do you expect when you slap a table with an open palm?" Tabaio asked.

"Is there an appropriate way to slap a table?"

"Yeah. You don't do it," he said, sarcastically.

She rolled her eyes. They headed to the dining hall in silence.

Standing in line, tingling crept up her arm. Whispers grazed her mental shield. Dozens of people stared openly. Others quickly averted their gazes, but most everyone held contemptuous expressions.

"Don't worry about them." Wilson came up behind her. "They're just scared about the announcement."

The Aruka made an emergency announcement earlier this morning. Anyone who was close enough, attended in person. Everyone else listened via moonstone transmission.

Serellina informed the entire kingdom of the impending attack and laid out the plans for all the children, elders, disabled, and anyone else who was unable to defend themselves to take refuge in the S-cells and caves below Tearnanelle. She also said that the traditional winter solstice ceremony would go on as if nothing was any different than any other year.

Fear swept through the kingdom like a wildfire. All the bubbles were depleted as hundreds, maybe even thousands, escaped to other worlds. There were only a few bubbles remaining in all of Tearnanelle, and people hid them as a last resort. The one around her neck was one of them.

She grabbed the stone and held it. Her ticket out, if things went badly. She'd have to make her way to Ambrose's family first then they'd all get out. She had five more days before she'd either be forced home, dead, kidnapped, or the threat was over. She really hoped they survived, but with two-hundred thousand werewolves expected to attack, the odds weren't in their favor.

She felt stupid for staying, but she couldn't leave Ambrose or his family. She was still desperately searching for whoever the spy was, so she could prove his innocence, but they hadn't gotten any closer to uncovering their identity. The spy had gone underground, which really made Ambrose look guilty.

She still refused to believe it, though. He was being set up, just like he claimed. Ambrose was taking the fall for crimes he didn't commit. She knew it in her heart, no matter how oddly he'd behaved.

Someone bumped into her, nearly knocking the tray of food from her hands. She looked up and met the dark black eyes of Leabella.

"Back off!" Rokesh said.

Leabella feigned innocence then sat down with her friends who all stared daggers at Sibyl.

Sibyl made the mistake of glancing around the dining hall. So many unfriendly stares made her heart sink and tingling spiraled down her spine.

"Don't let them get to you," Rokesh said.

Easier said than done. They walked to their table, and she set the tray down. The people who were sitting next to them got up even though they weren't finished eating. What was this, high school?

It's all her fault. I bet she's the spy and she set him up.

She should just leave. She's the reason they're coming here.

Someone should just execute her, then all our problems will be over.

"SHUT UP!" someone yelled.

The entire room of people all stared at her now.

"Sibyl?" Wilson's brow knitted with concern.

Her hands shook, and magic engulfed her. She was the one who yelled.

Who is she to tell us to shut up?

"Just leave!" someone shouted.

"Knock it off!" Demetrius yelled.

She put her hands over her ears.

"Sibyl, just calm down and control the magic." Rokesh's voice was distant.

She's out of control.

What does he see in her?

She's crazy.

"I said SHUT UP!" The room became deathly quiet under Sibyl's glare. No one even dared to blink.

"I'm not crazy!" she yelled. "Please stop. Everyone, just stop." She squeezed her eyes closed and laid her hands on the table, willing them to stop shaking.

Rubbing along the wood grains, she concentrated on the rough texture. *Real.*

Magic poured from her like a waterfall, but no one spoke. The quiet soothed her. She repaired the mental wall and silence engulfed her. She relaxed.

She opened her eyes and met Rokesh's gaze. He was stone still, not moving or blinking.

"Rokesh?"

He didn't respond. She scanned the room. Everyone was in the exact same position as a few seconds ago, like they were frozen in time. Spinning in a circle, she frantically looked at everyone.

Shit. She'd subdued them all without realizing it. Remembering what Rokesh said about magical tethers, she decided to try the release tactic.

"Release!" she shouted, pushing magic out circumferentially from her heart. The entire room collectively inhaled. Trays fell to the floor, some people collapsed, Rokesh, Demetrius, Wilson and Clark all slumped in relief, inhaling large gulps of air.

Sibyl's heart raced. She backed up. "I'm sorry. I didn't mean to." Fear permeated every fiber of her being. Some was her own, but most of it wasn't. If they weren't afraid of her before, they definitely were now.

People stood up to get a better look at her. Some people pointed. She swallowed down the lump forming in her throat. Loud whispers took over the room, but they weren't in her mind. They were real.

"Sibyl. You got this. You're in control. Just relax and breathe." Rokesh made his way around the table to her. Wilson and Demetrius did as well. Tabaio rolled his eyes and sat down to eat like it was an ordinary day.

Rokesh, Demetrius, and Wilson escorted her out. After they got halfway out of the dining hall, Tabaio got up and begrudgingly followed them. Unlike them, he grabbed his tray of food and brought it with him. Nothing would stand between that man and his food. Sibyl had learned that about him over the last couple of weeks.

"Nothing to see. Nothing to fear. It was an accident. Sometimes that happens when we're learning to use our magic. Right?" Clark shouted. "Remember when you were learning? How many of you accidentally injured yourself or someone else? Raise your hand."

Sibyl glanced back over her shoulder. A few hands went up.

"Exactly. Shit happens. Don't freak out. It's a good thing she's on our side, am I right?" Clark laughed.

Sibyl heard some laughter coming from the dining hall. Damn. Clark was good at diffusing a situation.

They turned a corner, and Sibyl couldn't see or hear them anymore.

-—— Capbay WanC-5/December 19th ——-

Solstice? Sibyl called.

No one answered. It was nearly pitch-black outside. The moon was hidden by clouds, and it was so cold, Sibyl saw her breath.

Hello Sibyl, the familiar voice came to her.

Where are you? I don't see you.

I'm hidden and I'm going to stay that way. I have moved my herd to a safer location with the impending attack. I can talk to you, but I won't get any closer.

Oh. She stared into the darkness. Chills creeped up her spine, but not because of magic or anxiety. Just because she was creeped out being in an unfamiliar forest in the middle of the night surrounded by complete darkness. She backed up to a tree. It felt more secure having something against her back.

Do you think I should leave Tearnanelle? she asked.

Only you can answer that.

I'm asking for your opinion.

My opinion is no.

She sighed. Weirdly enough, that's the answer she wanted. She just needed to hear it for reassurance.

You don't need the opinion of some old unicorn. Why did you really come here?

Do you think I can break the curse on the werewolves?

It was silent for a few minutes, so long that she was about to repeat the question, thinking he may not have heard her.

Sometimes what we are destined to become is not obvious when we begin our journey.

Stop being cryptic and just tell me!

I don't know your purpose, Sibyl. The Gods have given you this gift, not me. My job in life is to protect my herd. I'm not usually involved in these matters.

Then why have you been coming to me all these years?

The Gods asked me to help, and I agreed I would.

In what capacity?

As a mentor to you and there are other things I'm helping them with that I'm not at liberty to discuss. I don't know their intentions or all that they have planned for you. I'm just here for guidance, until you are strong enough to commune with the Gods yourself. They don't tell me everything. Much information is withheld for the safety of us all. No one ever puts all their eggs in one basket.

So, you're completely useless to me then! she yelled telepathically.

I'm sorry I have disappointed you. I'm trying to help, but I can only offer so much. I know you are meant to stay in Tearnanelle, but I don't know all the reasons why.

You're no help! With a blink, she was back in her room.

Insufferable pretentious unicorn. She got out of bed and went to the bathroom. Staring at herself in the mirror, she tried to stay calm, but she could only think of one thing.

Two days. That's all there was between now and winter solstice. Ambrose was still in O-cells, Ava hated her and hadn't spoken to her in weeks, and everyone else feared her. What was she doing? This was insane.

Clutching the bubble, she thought about going home right now. That was the smart thing to do. Fuck all of them. Just save herself. But she couldn't bring herself to leave. She wasn't a coward. No matter how ineffectual she may be, she wasn't a coward. But she didn't know what to do. Why couldn't someone just tell her what she was supposed to do?

Anger consumed her and she screamed. She had to....do something. She spotted a bottle of soap, grabbed it, and threw it at the mirror, shattering it into a spider web of fractures.

Demetrius and Wilson busted into the room with silver swords drawn and frantic expressions. Once they ascertained there was no threat, they released the swords.

Demetrius's face was nearly all healed now, only shadows of bruises surrounded his nose and eyes. They weren't allowing people to use much gold right now to save as much as possible for the battle. He was given only enough to heal the fracture. The rest of the injury was left to heal naturally.

Running her fingers along the countertop, she recited the word. *Real.* She knew it was real, she just wanted to be one thousand percent positive for posterity's sake. If she was going to stay and potentially die for something, she might as well make damn sure it was real.

Ambrose was real. She could still smell, taste, and feel him. He was worth staying for, fighting for....dying for.

She looked in the mirror at all the versions of herself in the cracks. Tearnanelle was worth defending. All these people, even the enslaved werewolves of Tearnanoak, were all real, and all worth it.

"Sorry." She bowed her head. "I didn't mean to alarm you."

"No big deal. That mirror had it coming," Wilson joked.

She laughed. He always had a way of making a heavy situation lighter. She smiled at the six Wilsons in the shattered ruins of the mirror. That's just what the world needed, six of him. The thought made her smile.

She turned around and they both averted their eyes. Wrapping her arms around her chest, she remembered she was in nothing but her underwear and a camisole. No bra either, only a thin layer of silk between her and complete nudity.

"We'll be in the hall if you need anything," Demetrius said. They both walked out, leaving her to her thoughts. Her endless thoughts that prevented her from sleeping.

WINTER SOLSTICE
BATTLE OF THE TWIN KINGDOMS

CHAPTER 30

AVA

Ava rubbed her fingers over the moonstone on her cuff. Redly finally managed to sneak away and leave a message for her. At least she knew he was alive. She listened to his voice in her head.

> Ava
>
> I'm sorry I haven't been able to get here until now. Things are tense in Tearnanoak as the attack draws close. Alyssium plans to have her primary force attack the western wall. Her goal is to breach the wall using citrine and once inside, our primary objective is to find you and the Druid and kill anyone else who stands in the way. She, herself, will be staying safely in Tearnanoak. It'll be us coming for you.
>
> Another thing: she knows that Tearnanelle knows about the plan to attack. Hopefully you found the spy and plugged that leak, so she doesn't catch wind of any of

your specific defense plans.

Please do not engage in the fight. I don't know where I'll be, but even if you did find me, you wouldn't recognize the man beneath the monster. I'll be the enemy.

I'm so glad I met you. You're the only good thing that ever happened in my life. Even in the darkest depths of the beast, there's a remnant of you keeping me grounded. Hopefully that'll be enough to keep me alive and bring me back to your arms. Until then please don't worry about me, stay safe, and don't do anything stupid.

Love Redly

Tears pooled in her eyes. Damn it. Every time she listened to it, she had that reaction. She'd never been very sentimental, but the last couple of weeks she was an emotional wreck. She was becoming more like Sibyl than she cared to admit. Maybe that wasn't such a bad thing.

Ever since her fight with Sibyl none of their friends made an effort to speak to her. They were technically assigned to guard Sibyl, so she wasn't mad at them over it, but it still stung a little. They'd come to the council meeting, and were respectful, but things were strained between them, except Wilson. He was Switzerland in all this.

For the first time in a long time, Ava felt lonely.

Sighing, she clipped the moonstone back to her cuff. She told her aunt about the information Redly left, so they were busy planning defensive and offensive strategies accordingly. The Dragons agreed to send a battalion to help defend Tearnanelle. They arrived earlier this morning and were also busy with planning and strategies.

Ava tried to keep track of it all, but it was overwhelming, so she volunteered to help with the evacuation and protection of the citizens as a means to narrow her focus and keep herself busy. That's what she was doing now, waiting for the kids to arrive.

As if on cue, hundreds of kids came around the corner of the hallway heading toward the S-cells. Ava stood up along with a dozen other Mages.

"This way." A woman ushered them forward. When the kids got to them, scared eyes scanned Ava and the others. The children ranged from infant to seventeen, and more filed into the hallway with every passing second.

"OK, everyone, remember we talked about having a fun slumber party." The woman smiled huge and shook her body as if she was dancing. Some children smiled while others clung to each other, obviously seeing through the charade.

"Through these doors we have some amazing adventures planned for the fun winter solstice party. Are you guys ready to party?" she yelled.

Some cheered and clapped, but most just looked around apprehensively.

"OK. Let's go. This way."

They led the children through the archway that was lined with giant silver roots, and down the stairs into the S-cells below the main level of the castle. The cells were converted into bedrooms fully equipped with four sets of bunk beds in each cell. They tried really hard to make them not look like prison cells, but in the end, it just looked like bars with hanging decorations strewn about haphazardly.

A small cabinet full of food, drinks, and various gems were in each cell, along with various games, puzzles, coloring books, and crayons. A corner of each cell was curtained off for a makeshift bathroom, if needed. At least one adult was assigned to each cell to help take care of the children.

Hopefully, if things went well, they'd only have to spend the night in here, and the kids would never know the real reason they were down here until the threat was passed.

One of the guards, who helped escort the children, knelt in front of one of the cells. Two small children clung to his neck. He whispered something to them.

"I love you, Daddy." The little girl nestled her head into the crook of his neck.

Ava turned away. She didn't want to think of the possibility of him not returning to that little girl tonight. A few other guards bid their goodbyes to various children, spouses, and parents who'd been assigned to care for the kids for the night. It was too much emotion for Ava, so she made her way back upstairs.

After a few minutes, the closing of prison doors echoed up the caves, and Mage Guards started up the stairs. Once the last person exited, large doors were closed over the archway, locked, and barricaded with silver bars. She helped imbue even more silver into the doors, and they conjured silver spikes, similar to the thorns on the exterior walls of Tearnanelle.

"Assuming we survive the battle, our future is safe," someone said.

No one replied. What was there to say? This was either their safe place for the night or their tomb. Ava tried to swallow down the lump in her throat, but it wouldn't budge. The man who spoke wiped away a tear then walked away.

The two kids clinging to their father's neck burned in Ava's mind. She didn't know anything about her father. Was he as brave as that man, forced to leave his family to try and protect them? Was he a coward who left them to die? She made a mental note to inquire about her father, should they survive tonight.

Her friends' faces popped into her mind. She missed them. Her only friends. Who was she kidding? Her only family. Oh Gods. What if they died tonight? That thought scared her more than anything. "Hey, I have to do something really quick. I'll meet you guys down there, ok."

They all nodded then headed to their next assignment; escorting elderly and disabled into the caves beneath the castle. Chewing on her lip, she mustered the courage she needed for what she had to do.

Pushing through the doors of the healer's wing, she walked into complete chaos. People darted around, filling jars with weird healing herbs, stuffing extra bedding supplies under beds and on shelves, filling up bottles with water and other liquids.

She didn't see Sibyl anywhere. Going to Cassie's bed, she checked on her friend whose condition hadn't changed at all over the last month. It was looking grimmer every day for Cassie, but that was a problem she'd address tomorrow, assuming there would be a tomorrow.

"She moved a finger earlier."

Ava met the wrinkled face of Melinda. "Really? Is that a good thing or does that happen sometimes with coma patients?"

"It's a very good thing. She's still in there, I can feel it. She just needs a little more rest. Hopefully she'll wake up very soon." Melinda smiled.

Maybe it was best if she stayed unconscious for one more night.

"Where's Sibyl?" Ava asked.

"She's not here in the afternoons. She practices in the Mage training yard," Melinda said.

"Practices what?"

"Self-defense training."

That was a good idea. Sibyl was pathetic at defending herself as proven in Ava's room last month. Although, she probably didn't need it with her magical skill set. Either way, at least she was taking some initiative to help herself.

"Thanks." Ava turned to leave. When she got to the Mage training yard, she saw Sibyl in a choke hold by Demetrius. Rokesh talked her through techniques to get out of it. That probably would have been useful to her when Ava had her pinned.

Wilson sparred with a man covered in tattoos. Ava had seen him around. He was one of the best fighters on the Mage Guard, and he knew it too. He took Wilson to the ground with impressive proficiency. Ava wondered what his spirit animal was, rhinoceros maybe.

Sibyl feebly managed to weasel her way out of the choke hold with completely unrealistic chances of success in an actual fight. Rokesh praised her anyway. Ava rolled her eyes.

"That's not going to be good enough." She stepped onto the field. Everyone paused what they were doing and the atmosphere immediately tensed. She received no warm looks from anybody, including the tattooed guard, which surprised her. What did she ever do to him?

"Hi," she said once she was close. "Do you want some help?"

"No. We were just finishing up actually," Sibyl said curtly.

Ava nodded, trying to act natural. Shit, how did one grovel? "Where are you guys going?"

Wilson cleared his throat. "Dinner."

"Oh. I haven't seen you guys in the dining hall lately. I must keep missing you," Ava said casually.

"We've been eating in the piano room," Wilson said.

Sibyl glared at him. Wilson ducked submissively.

"Why?" Ava asked.

"Just because. See you later." Sibyl made to leave.

"Sibyl, wait. Can I talk to you for a second?" Ava jogged to catch up. Sibyl could walk insanely fast when she was mad, and right now, she was practically steaming.

"What do you want?" Sibyl spat.

Ava glanced back at the others. They all stood back, watching intently. Probably waiting for another fight to break out. This time Ava wasn't so sure of herself if they did come to blows. Sibyl could probably kick her ass without ever touching her.

"I just wanted to check on you, see how you're doing."

"I'm fine." She crossed her arms.

"Look, I wanted to say that maybe I was a little overzealous with my tone and I could have been a bit nicer. Things kind of got out of control." Ava met Sibyl's stormy hazel eyes. There was no warmth behind them.

"Kind of?" Sibyl said, sarcastically.

"Ok. Fine. A lot out of control. But I wasn't the only one being unreasonable."

Sibyl narrowed her eyes. "If that's all you wanted to say, I have things to do. I'll see you later." She turned to walk away.

Ava rushed to follow. "Come on, Sibyl. Look, I don't know if Ambrose is the spy. I just think that it doesn't hurt to keep him detained until we figure out for sure if he is or isn't. For everyone's safety including his own. If he is being set up, then he's a target. Someone may come after him."

Sibyl stopped and her eyes darted to the side. She was considering the sense of that statement. To be honest, Ava just made it up on the spot to sound more sincere. But it was something to consider.

"Let's just get through this night and tomorrow we'll both search for answers for Ambrose. How about that?"

They stood staring at each for a minute.

"Damn it, Sibyl. What do you want me to say? I'm trying here."

"Ugh. The only thing you're trying to do is NOT have faith in our friend and NOT admit you were wrong."

"I'm not going to admit I was wrong. But I will say...I'm sorry."

Sibyl furrowed her eyebrows.

"I am sorry. Ok. Even if we disagree, we can still be civilized and discuss it respectfully, as adults. I know I react quickly sometimes."

"Overreact," Sibyl corrected.

Ava's patience was waning. "My point is; we don't have to always see eye to eye on everything, but we can work together to find out the truth. Right? If we find the truth, then it will sort itself out." Ava kicked a rock. "I'm sorry I called you useless. It's not true. You're a big help and....a friend."

Sibyl's posture softened. "I'm sorry too. I didn't mean what I said about your mom. I just said it to piss you off."

"I know. It's fine, and I'm sorry I called you crazy."

Sibyl laughed. A for real laugh. "Well, I might be a tad bit crazy."

Ava smiled. "That kind of seems to be your superpower, doesn't it?"

They both giggled.

"Thank the Gods. Have you two finally made up?" Wilson threw his arms around their necks.

Ava weaseled out of the embrace. "That's enough sentiment for one day. Did you guys say you were heading to dinner?"

"Yeah. It's about an hour before dark so we'll eat then report to the fields with everyone else. After that I'm going to the healer's wing with Rokesh and Tabaio. Demetrius and Wilson have been assigned a post on the wall," Sibyl said.

"Why do you eat in the piano room?" Ava asked.

"I had a mishap a few days ago. People are scared of me, and I don't want to see them or hear them," Sibyl said.

"I heard about that. Intense."

"Yeah. Plus, Sibyl's an amazing piano player. She plays for us while we eat," Wilson said.

"Really? That's cool. I may have an idea that could make people less afraid of you." Ava smiled slyly.

"I don't think that's possible." Sibyl shook her head.

"Trust me. People will love you. It'll be great."

"Nothing good ever came from that statement," Sibyl said.

Ava looped her arm through Sibyl's, and they made their way to the dining hall. It felt good to have her friends back. Hopefully they'd all still be standing tomorrow.

It took some serious negotiation and pleading on her part, but Ava convinced her aunt to let Sibyl stand next to them on top of the platform for the winter solstice commencement. Ava stood between her aunt and Sibyl, hand in hand, above thousands of people. They were at least thirty feet in the air.

A silver crown of ornate twisted branches and oak leaves sat on her aunt's head, and much to Ava's dismay, her own as well. She detested the idea of being a princess, but if that's what was needed to be to bring hope to everyone, she'd grit her teeth and bear it.

"Ten. Nine. Eight," the crowd counted down. The moment they yelled out "One." Ava conjured a beautiful silver recurve bow. Her aunt conjured a matching one. They knocked a flaming arrow and shot it into the pyre that the people of Tearnanelle spent the last several weeks building.

Women, men, children, every single person in the kingdom added something to the masterpiece pyre. Flowers, hay, branches, paintings, wreaths, clothing, and countless other artifacts decorated the burning pyre in the center of the charred remains of their field crops. It was a symbolism of renewal.

Normally they would burn the fields every winter after harvest to infuse the land with essential vitamins and nutrients for next year's crops. This year it wasn't necessary since it had already burned, but it was still a tradition, and it held deeper meaning. Right now, that was needed more than ever.

Flames engulfed the structure within minutes, lighting up the dark sky almost as bright as the sun. The three women waved to everyone below before coming down from the platform. The blaze was so intense that Ava felt the heat from their distance. It drove away the bitter cold of the night, making it temporarily feel like summer.

Music started and people headed toward the castle grounds.

"That was cool," Sibyl said, once she set foot on solid ground.

"It's a tradition we've held for hundreds of years," Serellina said tersely. Tension between the two women was painfully palpable. Sibyl was still mad that the Aruka locked up Ambrose and Serellina still distrusted Sibyl. For now, they chose to put their differences aside in an effort to bring the kingdom together and present a united front. A common goal and life-threatening stakes can help resolve most disagreements, at least temporarily.

"That went well." Fulcinia joined them on their way to the festivities. It was decided to continue the party as if it was an ordinary winter solstice to help keep the citizens calm.

"The turnout is a tenth of what it usually is," Yilfin said.

"Between those hidden in the caves and S-cells, and the rest who have fled the kingdom, Runar reported an estimated twenty thousand residents remaining, not including the guards," Serellina said. It was a blessing to know that if things went bad, their people would survive, even if their home didn't.

Ava's heart beat wildly. Her home. Her people. It was a heavy weight that she hadn't held very long, but she was already possessive over it. She didn't want to lose it when she'd only just gotten used to having it.

Horns blasted from atop the wall.

"They're already here," Yilfin said, as if they needed an explanation.

Sibyl, Rokesh, Tabaio, Fulcinia, Yilfin, Serellina and Ava all stared toward the western wall. She wasn't expecting them so soon. The sun was barely set. Commotion behind them drew Ava's attention. Turning around, they came face to face with hundreds of people from the solstice celebration. Men and women of various ages held mixed expressions of anger, fear, and resolve.

A man stepped forward. "This is our home. We won't hide or run away. We'll help defend."

Yilfin, Serellina, and Fulcinia exchanged a look then nodded.

"We'll take all the help we can get," Serellina said.

Another horn rang out, followed by several others down the wall. Then howls. The hairs on the back of Ava's neck stood up. The music stopped and all heads turned toward the sound. The world went still. The only sound was the crackling embers of the fire that was already burned to ground level, and howls.

Ava swallowed down her fear. She hated to admit how afraid she was, but there was no denying it, at least not to herself. She was petrified. She tried to hide her shaking hands by her sides.

Sibyl grabbed one and squeezed. Ava met Sibyl's eyes. The hazel was nearly completely taken over with green almost as bright as her own.

Sibyl smiled but it didn't meet her eyes. "I'm going to the healer's wing."

"Change of plans," the Aruka said. "You're going with Ava. You two as well." Serellina pointed at Rokesh and Tabaio.

"What? Why?" Sibyl asked.

Serellina ignored Sibyl. "Ok. Everyone, get to your stations. Yilfin, will you take our volunteers to the wall?"

Yilfin nodded and signaled the new recruits to follow.

"Can we talk about my role?" Ava removed the crown from her head and handed it to Fulcinia.

"No. It's not up for discussion. Fulcinia, take my niece and Sibyl to the caves." Serellina also handed her crown to the raven warrior who blended in almost perfectly with the night, as if she was born from it. Fulcinia nodded and waved an arm to usher Sibyl and Ava toward the castle.

All the men and women who volunteered walked past them. Those people said they wouldn't hide and yet, that's exactly what Ava was about to do. Her aunt insisted she go into the caves with the others for the duration of the battle, to protect the future Aruka of Tearnanelle. It was a complete load of crap.

"Where are we going?" Sibyl asked, confused.

"We're hiding, like cowards," Ava spat.

"We're not hiding. We're protecting our future," Fulcinia countered.

When they got to the entrance there was a group of about twenty guards waiting for them. Fulcinia led them all down the stairs. They turned opposite from the cells and past the caves that were already full of people barricaded closed.

After a short walk through diamond lit tunnels, they came to another set of giant doors. When they passed the threshold, Fulcinia closed the doors behind them and pressed her thumb into a spot in the center. A rune glowed silver for a moment then vanished.

This tunnel was much narrower than the others. Only about four people could walk side by side. Molten silver flowed through giant tubes within the walls, like an underground network of rivers.

"It's the main roots of the God Tree. Pure raw silver magic," Fulcinia said. "The nervous

system of the Goddess Tearnanelle."

"I can feel her." Sibyl's eyes were wide with curiosity as she scanned the tunnel.

Ava ran a hand over one of the roots. It was warm and shimmered under her touch.

Once they got to the end of the tunnel there was another set of doors and beyond them was a large room with couches, tables, books. Basically, all the furnishings of a regular living room.

Everyone filed in, Fulcinia closed the doors, and repeated the process of the rune. Ava watched more closely this time. It was a blood lock. No one was getting in or out without Fulcinia's DNA, or they blew the doors off.

"This is where we stay until I am told it's safe to leave," Fulcinia said.

Ava flopped down on the couch. How pathetic. Hiding like a scared child while people fought and probably died to defend her. Sibyl took a seat next to her and Rokesh across from them both. Tabaio chatted with some of the other guards in a corner.

"This sucks." Ava crossed her arms and pouted.

CHAPTER 31
SIBYL

Pulling at the collar of her tunic, Sibyl attempted to relieve the suffocating restraint of the stiff leather. She wondered how the guards moved so quickly in these outfits. Rokesh managed to snag the armor for her. It didn't fit perfectly, but it was enough to keep her safe from most direct assaults to her person, should that situation arise. She didn't want to wear it, but he insisted.

The knife Ambrose gave her was sheathed at her hip, and the gemstone necklace was around her neck. Grasping the bubble, she held it for comfort. How would she get to Ambrose's family if she was stuck down here? How would she even know if she needed to? Could her magic work this deep below the surface? She was afraid to try. Part of her didn't want to hear, see, or feel what was going on above the surface.

No one spoke, except for Tabaio and a few other guards in the corner. The silence allowed in the faint distant sounds of battle. That started about fifteen minutes after they closed the doors. Muffled shouting and Dragons roaring made Sibyl's anxiety spike. Checking that her mental shield was firmly in place, she took a few meditative breaths to help keep calm.

An explosion vibrated the walls and floor, but the cave held solid, fortified by the roots of the tree. Mixed feelings of gratefulness and shame coursed through her. here. People were dying above their heads while she hid.

Ava jigged her leg. As the minutes ticked by her leg kicked more fervently until the whole couch shook. It wasn't in Ava's nature to hide from a fight. All the guards were restless. Fulcinia leaned against the wall with her arms crossed, her was expression unreadable, but Sibyl felt the frustration exuding from her. On a basic level, no one wanted to be here.

"This is stupid. We should be up there helping." Ava stood up.

"Sit down and relax. The night is young. We have many hours to go."

"No. I'm not a child or fragile elderly person that should be hiding. Everyone here is strong and capable. We should be up there defending Tearnanelle with everybody else." Ava stomped her foot. All the guards in the room nodded their heads.

"I agree," Tabaio said.

"No one asked for your opinion." Fulcinia shot him a look that promised death if he spoke again.

Sibyl's heart pounded. Ava wasn't going to give up. If there was one thing she'd learned about Ava, it's that she was as stubborn as an ox when she dug her heels in.

Sibyl's magic was restless. Dark magic scraped the edge of her mental shield, trying to find any weaknesses. Opening and closing her fists, she pumped blood to her fingertips, attempting to pacify the magic. Her hands weren't tingling. They were completely numb. She had just enough anxiety to keep her alert, but not so much that it was crippling.

"I'm going." Ava marched toward the door. Fulcinia stepped in her way.

"I'm the Arukas and I say move." Ava stuck her chin out.

Sibyl stood up, so did Rokesh. The tension in the room was so thick, Sibyl could probably slice through it with her knife.

"My orders come from the Aruka, who outranks you, so sit down," Fulcinia challenged.

"No." Ava stepped closer. "Let me by."

Ava wouldn't pick a fight with Fulcinia would she? Surely, she wasn't that stupid.

Another explosion shook the cave. Bits of pebbles fell from the ceiling. Sibyl swallowed down a ball of anxiety. Would the cave collapse on itself? Sibyl's fingers found themselves and started twisting on top of each other. Maybe being down here wasn't the best idea, but being out there wasn't much better. What would happen if they did get out? What would they do? Where would they go? What if there were werewolves right outside the door?

Panic slowly crept in. She shouldn't be here. She should be home, studying for boards. If she didn't show up for Christmas, her parents would think she was dead. If she didn't show up, it would mean she was dead or taken hostage. She didn't know what was worse.

"Ava, I understand your frustration. I want to be up there too, but our orders are to stay here." Fulcinia said.

"What's the point of hiding down here? If everyone dies up there then what's left for us to defend and protect? The people in this room? The people in the tunnels?" Ava looked around at everyone, trying to rally them to her cause. "We're supposed to defend our people and our home. I don't want to lose my home when I haven't had it very long. Come on guys. We have to help."

Another explosion shook the room with such intensity that they nearly fell down. Large rocks dislodged from the ceiling and walls. Diamonds fell and shattered into thousands of pieces, sending bits of light shards out like fireworks. Sibyl covered her head to protect herself from the ricochet.

"That doesn't sound good." Rokesh looked around apprehensively.

Sibyl pushed against the anxiety and magic that begged to be let free. The magic protested being locked down here just as much as Ava did. Fear and terror permeated her soul. Screams and voices echoed through her mind. It wasn't her own.

"They're inside the walls," Sibyl said. "The werewolves are in Tearnanelle. I can feel it." This wasn't a safe location. It's a corral. Suddenly feeling claustrophobic, Sibyl rushed to Ava's side. "We need to get out."

"No, you don't. You just said they're in the castle. The last place you need to be is out there," Fulcinia said.

"They got through the wall in less than three hours. The wall is ten times as thick as these doors. How long do you think it will take them to figure out we're down here and get in? We're trapped here. We've got a better shot out there." Sibyl pointed up.

"She can help. I've seen first-hand what she's capable of," Ava said.

Sibyl didn't want to fight. She just wanted to get out of this cave and go to Ambrose's family's house, so she could escape to safety.

"I think it's time for us to join the fight," Tabaio said. All the guards flanked him and crossed their arms.

Rokesh came up beside Sibyl. *Are you sure about this?*

No.

He took a deep breath.

"No," Fulcinia ground out.

"Let Me Out!" Sibyl said, with so much conviction that she surprised herself.

Fulcinia robotically moved toward the door, placed her finger on the blood lock and the door clicked open.

Ava rushed through and the guards followed.

Fulcinia turned on Sibyl. "What did you do?"

Sibyl stood dumbfounded. Had she done that? "I'm sorry. I didn't mean to. I just want out of here."

"Guys, come on!" Ava yelled from down the hallway.

"Come on." Rokesh escorted Sibyl around the fuming Fulcinia, who followed on their heels. Now they all stood in front of the door that led to the main level corridor.

Fulcinia glared at Sibyl on her way by. "If you get killed or taken, Ava, I'll be beheaded." Fulcinia pointed a finger at her.

"Then I guess you should keep me alive." Ava smiled arrogantly.

"And you." Fulcinia rounded on Sibyl. "Go to the healer's wing and stay there. We don't need you running around announcing to the werewolves where you are. You may have intangible abilities, but I've seen you fight. You're as helpless as a kitten."

Sibyl's mouth dropped open. She was offended, despite the truth of the statement.

"Tabaio, Rokesh, and you five." She pointed to the men behind Tabaio. "Escort her to the healer's wing. Do not let her out of your sight. Do you understand?"

They nodded.

Taking a deep breath, Fulcinia pressed a finger onto the door. The rune lit up and the door clicked open. She peeked through the crack then signaled to everyone it was clear. They filed through, one by one. The sounds of the battle were louder once they were back in the main tunnels of the castle.

"Come on," Fulcinia whispered.

They silently made their way past the cells and up the stairs toward the main level. With every step, the fighting came closer, and Sibyl's heart rate increased. When they reached the top, Fulcinia checked that it was clear, and they stepped into the hallway of the north wing.

Once everyone was up, they quickly made their way toward the healer's wing, but they came to a sudden halt when they turned the next corner. Sibyl's heart plummeted. A giant werewolf stood at the end of the hallway between the healer's wing and the permanent residence halls. The door to the healer's wing was right next to it, but it didn't see the door.

Melinda put concealing runes around the healer's wing that made it so anyone affected with dark magic wouldn't be able to perceive there was anything other than a wall.

The beast sniffed the ground and looked around. Its menacing eyes studied the door that only they could see. It knew something was there, but try as it might, it couldn't figure out where or what it was.

Fulcinia pushed them all back around the corner from which they came, and they all pressed against the walls trying to hide in the shadows.

"Let's go through the throne room, and dining hall, then out the side of the west wing. From there, we can go around back to the healer's wing," Fulcinia whispered.

Everyone nodded and headed the other direction. They made their way quickly and silently past the entrance to the caves from which they'd come, and down the hall to the giant doors to the backside of the throne room. One of the guards peeked through and nodded his head, signaling that it was clear. They made their way through then throne room, then the empty dining hall, and out the side door onto the terrace.

The sounds of battle were as brutal as the cold. Sibyl tried to block it out, but it was real. Her magic couldn't block out reality.

They crossed the terrace and were nearly to the back steps when voices slithered into Sibyl's mind.

Do you have anything?

No. The hallways are clear.

Sibyl slid to a stop and grabbed Ava's arm.

Ava's eyebrows creased with confusion.

I can hear them. Sibyl pointed to her temple.

Ava's eyes widened in understanding.

"What are you doing? Let's go," Rokesh said.

Everyone stopped and turned around, waiting for them to catch up.

Sibyl put a finger over her mouth. Peering across the gardens, she saw the werewolf who she accidentally heard in her mind. He was larger than the one on the beach, but not as large as some she'd seen in her dreams. She pointed to it.

Everyone scattered, taking up random hiding places behind trees, pillars, tables, whatever they could find to conceal themselves. Sibyl pressed her back against a vine covered post, between Ava and Rokesh. She closed her eyes and let her magic explore.

When she met the barrier of the werewolf's mind, she stepped inside just as easily as one would step into a pool. The putrid smell of dark magic engulfed her senses as she pushed silently by his mental shield, gaining access to his mind.

When she opened her eyes, she stood outside of a rickety old wooden fence. She pushed open the gate and stepped into a mental wasteland enveloped with a thick red fog. There was no individualized thought or feeling. Whoever this was, they were hijacked by the ominous red fog. She stepped into the wasteland. The red fog scattered like cockroaches.

Zini where are you?

The ground shifted. It felt like she was moving, despite everything staying the same.

We're in the gardens.

Sibyl looked toward the source of the outside voice. A path in the fog parted. She followed it, coming to a stake in the ground with a large rope tied to it. The golden rope was as thick around as her arm and contained a red snake-like tendril twisting its way around it. The rope went straight into the sky, disappearing into the mental abyss of Zini's mind.

Sibyl's magic pulled taut as Zini got further away from her physical body. She had to hurry before the connection snapped. She picked up a light jog, heading toward the source of the voice. The ground beneath her feet became soggy. She slogged through the mud as fast as she could go, feeling the tether of magic weakening with every step.

Finally, she stepped into a clearing and five werewolves stood around her.

The west corridors are clear, a large wolf named Henry said.

So are the north corridors, another wolf named Sarah followed up.

I checked the east. No one. I think they've all evacuated. No sign of either of the targets. That was Benjamin.

Sibyl turned a full three hundred-sixty degrees. Five werewolves surrounded her, but they couldn't see her. She was safely tucked inside Zini's subconscious.

The Queen is going to be pissed if we don't find them. They're here some-

where. Our last update from a few hours ago said the Arukas and the Druid were hiding in the castle. We need to find them.

Sibyl's breath caught. That was Benelli. She didn't have time to consider what he said as the mental connection finally snapped and she plummeted back into her own mind.

Ava stood over her with a concerned expression. "Are you ok?" she whisper yelled.

"Yeah."

"You've been unconscious for like five minutes, what happened?" Ava helped pull Sibyl to her feet.

"Sorry. I was in the werewolf's head."

"You were what?" Rokesh sounded outraged.

Sibyl ignored him. Turning to Ava, she said, "Benelli's out there."

Ava's green eyes became as wide as saucers. Before they could stop her, she bolted away.

"Ava NO!" Fulcinia yelled. It was too late. The Arukas was halfway down the terrace steps, headed to the gardens.

Shit. What had she done? She met Rokesh's concerned face. This was her fault. If she hadn't of said anything then Ava would still be here with them. Sibyl couldn't let her friend face five werewolves alone. She could help. She could immobilize them, hopefully. She still wasn't exactly sure how she did that. It just happened when she got overwhelmed.

Looking into Rokesh's eyes, she chewed on her lip.

He shook his head.

"Sorry." Sibyl dashed after Ava.

"Damn it, Sibyl," Rokesh yelled behind her.

CHAPTER 32

AVA

Ava ran as fast as her legs would carry her. Anger, pain, fear, all of it coalesced into an amorphous beast inside her. It was time to release that beast and take her revenge for the family that was stolen from her.

When she finally got close enough that the werewolf saw her, she came to a screeching halt. There were five werewolves. Annoyance blossomed. Sibyl didn't say there were five of them.

They whipped their heads in her direction. Ears erect, they stared. One of them was the Hanson's murderer. Squashing down the fear that threatened to break her, she walked toward them slowly, with purposeful effort. Conjuring her dagger sword, she made a large arc above her head in an exaggerated slow swipe and stared at them with a confidence she'd never felt before.

With every step closer to the creatures, her loathing and hatred grew until a dark storm brewed inside her so intense that her body barely contained it. The surprised looks on their faces was satisfying. They were probably expecting her to run or cower, but she was done with that. It was time to stand and fight.

A stream of fire lit up the sky as Dragons rained down a blazing inferno on nearby enemy. A pegasus with a rider darted through the cloudy moonless sky, but they disappeared when the flames burned out, once again leaving Ava under the dark wintry blanket of the night.

The Dragons were so far above they probably didn't notice the pack of werewolves surrounding the Arukas. That was fine by her. She could handle this on her own.

Ava stopped in the center of the circle of werewolves. She was far enough from each of them that it would only take a few steps in any direction to be within striking distance. They glanced at each other, then to her, uncertain how to react to their target walking right up to them.

Their orders were to take her alive. She was counting on that fact. She, on the other hand, had no such orders. Her plan was to kill every last one of them, starting with Benelli. There'd be no mercy for the monster who killed her family.

A werewolf stepped forward and stalked around her challengingly. The judgmental sneer on its hideous animalistic face made her cringe. This one was the smallest of them and looked vaguely familiar.

"Which one of you is Benelli?"

They stilled. The one in front of her cocked its head then looked over its shoulder to the second largest of them. That one glared at Ava with a look of contempt so intense, she knew it was him.

She pointed the sword at him. "You killed my family sixteen years ago."

An ear twitched and his eyes narrowed. Growls rumbled from the werewolves surrounding her. The one in front of her snapped its teeth in warning.

"I know you understand me. If you're the one who killed my family, face me in a fair fight. Or do you need them to fight your battles for you?" Ava fanned her arms in a circle and smiled antagonistically.

Footsteps stomped behind her. She, along with all the werewolves, looked toward the source. Fulcinia, the guards, Sibyl, and Rokesh came running into the clearing. Their faces morphed into surprise and terror. The werewolves snarled at her friends.

Sibyl's eyes widened. Taking a step back, she bumped into Rokesh, who grabbed her and pushed her behind the group of guards.

Ava. The one in front of you knows you. Sibyl's voice sounded in Ava's mind.

Turning to the small werewolf in front of her, Ava looked closer at the beast. It wasn't Redly. She'd seen him in his cursed form. The only other werewolves she'd ever seen was the one on the beach a few months ago and three from throughout her life. It came to her like a tidal wave.

"Sarah."

The small werewolf's lips curled into a malevolent smile.

"It is you, isn't it?"

The wolf didn't so much as blink as she held Ava's glare.

"You know, I've had this burning question for you since I came to Orlon." Ava took a step sideways so that she was just out of line with Sarah's body. "You told me all those years ago that I couldn't kill you because you're immortal."

Without any warning, Ava twirled and swung her sword in an overexaggerated strike pattern, sending the end of her blade ripping through the air. It flew within a few hairs of Sarah's face, sailed past her and lodged in a nearby tree.

Sarah shook her head.

She says, you missed, Sibyl said.

"Did I?" Ava smiled then yanked her sword backward, summoning the dagger with every ounce of magic she could muster. The blade exploded from the tree, sending splinters of bark into the air like shrapnel. In a streak of silver, the blade returned to Ava's sword. When it reconnected, Ava was nearly knocked off her feet from the force of the impact. Blood dripped from the tip.

The effect was delayed. Ava watched with satisfaction as Sarah blinked a few times before her head slid off her neck, landed on the ground, and rolled to one of the other werewolf's feet. A few seconds later her body toppled over too.

"I guess that was a lie, wasn't it?" she asked no one in particular.

The remaining werewolves paced around her, snarling and barking at one another.

"So, are you ready to face me, Benelli? Or are you afraid?" Ava wiped the blade on her pants. She didn't have to do that. It was just for show.

A few barks and yips were exchanged. One by one, the other three werewolves backed away. Ava smiled when Benelli stepped around Sarah's corpse and closed the distance between them.

Ava backed up equidistant. She didn't want to get in range of his claws. She rolled her shoulders a few times and popped her neck, then spread her feet hip width apart, pulled her arms in close, gripped the sword tightly with both hands and aimed it straight at his face. Benelli dropped his head low.

Perhaps she and Redly should have practiced with him in werewolf form. She'd only ever fought human opponents. No matter, it was the same basic structure. Two arms, two legs, a body, and a head to cleave off. She could handle it.

The other three werewolves stalked to her friends. Rokesh, Fulcinia, and several of the guards took ready stances. They had it handled. She couldn't worry about them right now. She had her own battle to fight.

As if he read her mind, Benelli attacked at the same moment the other three werewolves sprinted toward her friends. His legs were so long that he closed the distance between them in three strides. She underestimated how quickly he'd be able to get to her, so she was late with her strike.

She swung her sword, but he deflected the blow and plowed into her like a freight train. The force of the impact sent her flying. Rolling to a stop, she laid for a moment, dazed from the impact.

The ground vibrated as the giant beast charged toward her like an out-of-control semi-truck. She rolled out of Benelli's path at the last moment, barely missing his deadly claws. The wind from his swipe grazed the back of her neck. That was close.

Despite his size, he was agile and quick. Pivoting on his haunches, he launched at her again. She reconjured her weapon that she'd accidentally released and raised her sword just in time to slice open his chest as she spun out of his way again.

She rounded on him for a second strike, but he was quicker. His humanoid paw knocked her down with a teeth rattling right hook. Before she could regain her bearings, he was on her. Stepping on her sword arm with one of his front legs, he effectively immobilized her weapon, and with the other leg he stepped on her neck. His claws dug into her delicate flesh, but they didn't penetrate.

Damn. That went faster than she thought it would. Redly would be so disappointed.

Benelli snarled in her face. The putrid smell of dark magic made her gag. Blood from the wound across his chest dripped onto her. They stared at each other for a moment. Their expressions mirror images of pure unfettered hatred.

She spit in his face. Benelli grumbled low and pressed his weight into her throat. Slowly more and more of his weight pushed onto her neck until she felt it crack. Pain ripped down her spine, and she struggled to breathe through her crushed trachea.

He pressed down even harder. He was going to snap her neck. Maybe she'd underestimated his self-control, and he would actually kill her. Falling back to her training, she pushed the pain from her mind and forced herself to stay calm and think. Her body fought desperately to suck in air, but it was useless. Her trachea was completely occluded.

Conjuring a small dagger in her free hand, she slammed it into Benelli's elbow and twisted with all her strength. The joint dislocated and his leg collapsed, releasing her. He rocked back, roaring in pain. Before she let the weapon go, she sent more magic into it, creating large spikes jutting into his tissue to ensure he couldn't easily remove it. He backed up as quickly as he'd advanced on her.

Scrambling away as far as she could get, she backed up to a tree. Clawing at her neck, she felt the damaged tissue. Her neck was a smashed corrugated pipe. Nothing could pass through the structure in its current condition. The world swayed. Using the tree to hold herself upright, she waited. Her body would heal, she just needed time. Forcing herself to concentrate on the blade lodged in his elbow, she fought to hold the magical tether.

Her lungs spasmed painfully in a demand for air. A faint path in her throat opened and she sucked in with all her strength. She sounded like a poltergeist breathing through the crushed neck. Her vision tunneled. It wasn't enough. She needed more oxygen.

Come on. Heal faster! she screamed at herself.

Losing strength, she fell to the side but reinforced the tether of magic to the blade. She couldn't lose that blade.

Don't pass out, don't pass out. She watched Benelli pull at the blade in his elbow, then let it go in a roar of pain. His frustration and rage fueled her will to stay conscious.

Finally, the pain in her neck and the pressure in her chest lessened. Oxygen trickled in more quickly now. One heartbeat she could breathe through a straw. Another heartbeat after that and the obstruction in her neck dislodged completely.

The damn broke and precious air dove into her lungs. Taking a deep breath, she savored the feeling. Another few seconds and the pain ebbed away until finally she was whole again. Ava palpated her neck. It was fully healed, even though it still hurt like hell.

That was close. Too close. Taking deep calming breaths, she pushed herself up and regained her composure. She'd severely underestimated Benelli or overestimated herself. She wouldn't make that mistake again.

Glaring at the beast, she watched him take a few deep breaths, grab the blade with his pawish-hand and yank it free. Part of his arm ripped away with it. He swallowed down a roar behind gritted teeth.

Ava released the weapon, and the chunk of his arm fell to the ground. He narrowed his eyes at her and cradled his wounded arm. The Therian magic worked quickly to heal the injury. That went much faster than she remembered from the injured werewolf on the beach. It must be because dark magic was at its fullest potential right now.

Within no time, Benelli was whole again. Conjuring her sword, she took a ready stance and they both faced each other as if it was the first time.

She threw a quick sideways glance to check on her friends. They fought two of the three werewolves. Where was the other one? She didn't have time to consider it because Benelli came for her again. This time though, she was better prepared.

CHAPTER 33
SIBYL

Sibyl watched, in awe, as Ava fought with an ethereal elegance and speed that was unparalleled by any woman she'd ever seen, or man for that matter. Granted Sibyl hadn't seen many fights in her life. Ok, none, but it was still impressive, nonetheless.

Try as he might, but Benelli was unable to strike Ava even one single time outside of the first couple of blows where he'd used his body in a surprise attack. Ava was impressive to watch, but Sibyl didn't have time for the performance.

Fulcinia and half the guards chased after Henry, who ran off while Tabaio, Rokesh, and three remaining guards fought Benjamin and Zini, who were trying to get to her. Sibyl backed up against a lamp post on the terrace. Rokesh wasn't the largest man on the guard, but he was fast, resilient, and lethal. Taking a blow to the leg, he went down on one knee for a moment but was quickly up and fighting again.

Sibyl spun her magic out like a spider's web, reaching toward Benjamin. Creeping through his mind, she found his motor control and closed a fist around it. He froze mid strike, nearly landing a blow on one of the guard's heads. They looked at each other with confused expressions, then looked at her.

"I can't hold him forever," she said through gritted teeth.

Tabaio didn't hesitate. Swinging a large silver broadsword, he separated the beast's head from its body. Both parts fell to the ground. Blood sprayed from the neck just like she'd seen in movies. Sibyl slid down the post breathing heavily. The sight of blood didn't bother her, and she'd seen surgical decapitations, but she'd never witnessed something that gruesome.

Rokesh ran to her. "Are you ok?"

"Yeah." She wasn't faint or queasy, she was just overwhelmed.

Two of the guards still fought Zini. Flashes of silver from the Mage weapons winked in and out like strobe lights. Tabaio and one other guard stood behind Rokesh, protecting his back while he helped Sibyl up.

"We need to get you somewhere safe. They're probably sending half their army this way by now," Rokesh said.

"You're bleeding." She pointed to his leg where the werewolf scratched him. Remembering that their claws were infused with anti-gold, she knew the wound wouldn't heal normally especially considering he didn't have healing magic like Ava did.

"It's fine. Come on."

Out of the corner of her eye, she saw the other guard raise a silver bat.

"NO!" Sibyl shouted.

Rokesh spun just in time for the guard to knock him on the side of the head. Rokesh crumpled to the ground at her feet.

"What's wrong with you?" she yelled at the man who'd struck Rokesh.

Tabaio stepped in front of her and punched her in the middle of her chest right over her heart.

She remembered what Rokesh said about tucking her chin if she fell backward, but she didn't act quickly enough. The world tilted sideways as she fell flat out, knocking her head on the lamp post.

Her lungs struggled to breathe against a weight so heavy she may as well have been holding the world on her chest. There were voices but she couldn't comprehend them. The pain in her chest drowned out everything.

Pressure doubled, then tripled, then compounded on itself tenfold. It was unbearable. A tidal wave of knives slammed into her heart over and over and over again. Her heart pounded arrhythmically, fighting desperately against the pressure and pain, but the knives wouldn't cease their attack. When her chest was near implosion, the pressure finally fell away, and her heart steadied.

Coughing and gagging, she gulped down air and sat up. Her head felt like a hammer was taken to it. She gently touched the back of her head. It was wet. Looking at her hand, she saw eight swaying fingers. In a blink there were four blurry ones. One more blink and her vision cleared, revealing blood covered fingers.

A shadow blocked the light of the lamppost. Tabaio towered over her with a look of malice. Shuffling sideways, she tried to put distance between them like Rokesh taught her, but he followed her step by step, never letting the distance between them grow. A predator toying with his prey.

Throwing a hand up, she willed him to stop moving. Nothing happened.

He slapped her hand away. "I implanted an osmium spike in your heart. You can't use your magic on me."

Sibyl looked at her chest. Blood seeped from a wound under the leather armor. That explained the pain. He'd not only pierced the leather, but he managed to jam a shard of osmium so deep into her, she couldn't see it. She stuck a finger in the hole. Pain sliced through her chest when she brushed the edge of the spike. Screaming against the agonizing pain, she tried to dig it out, but it was no use. She couldn't grasp it.

He conjured a sword and pointed it at her neck. Shuffling away, she forgot there were steps off the terrace. She toppled down them. Luckily there were only three, but it was enough to hurt like a bitch. It did afford her a small distance from her attacker.

Bolting to her feet, she made to run, but a large arm wrapped around her waist, spun her around, and slammed her against a tree. Tabaio grabbed her neck and aimed the sword at her heart. She stilled.

Ambrose was right. Tabaio was the Aruka's man. He was told to stay with her at all times, probably for this reason. Sibyl was so stupid to trust the Aruka and Tabaio. Grabbing his arm, she clawed at it, and punched it, trying to get him to let go. He wasn't fazed by her feeble attacks.

"It's nothing personal. We just can't risk you getting taken by them."

"Please," she croaked out. Tears blurred her vision.

He shook his head, but his eyes were sad. Pulling his arm back, he prepared to shove the blade into her heart. Sibyl thought of her friends and her family back home. She would never return to them. She'd finally graduated from vet school, and she would never get to practice medicine.

Ambrose's face popped into her mind. She would never get to explore what they could have been. Her heart broke. The pain from the osmium shard was nothing compared to what she felt now. Squeezing her eyes closed, she accepted her fate, but her mind had a better idea.

She suddenly remembered the knife that Ambrose gave her. Snatching it from the sheath, she stabbed at Tabaio's torso, aiming for his kidney like Rokesh taught her.

Cat-like reflexes blocked her attack, but he had to release his weapon in order to grab her wrist. Bending her hand back painfully, he forced her to drop the blade. It hit the ground, and he kicked it away. Damn.

"Look at that. You learn quickly. Rokesh didn't completely waste his time after all."

She growled at him, kicking her legs desperately, aiming between his legs, but he was prepared for that too. Pivoting sideways, he blocked her kicks with his knee and thigh.

Now that his sword was gone, she could use both hands to punch. Frantically throwing jab after jab, she wailed on his arm, neck, and face. After a few punches to his elbow, he finally removed his hand from her neck, but he didn't back off.

Conjuring his sword, he put both hands on the hilt and pressed the cold silver blade against her neck. A new determination took over his features. Panting, Sibyl backed up solidly wedged between his blade and the tree at her back. She put her hands up in surrender.

"You're scrappier than I thought you'd be." His expression was almost impressed.

"I can help. Please," she begged.

For a brief moment, his conviction wavered, and a hint of sympathy flashed over his face. Just as quickly as it swept over him, it disappeared. Squaring his shoulders, he advanced an inch. The sharp edge of the sword dug into the skin over her carotid artery. His shoulders were so tense she could feel his muscles vibrating through the weapon. She squeezed her eyes closed, preparing for the pain.

When nothing happened, she opened her eyes. He stood over her, but his expression was as strained as his knuckles were white. Sibyl glanced to Ava. She still fought Benelli, and the two other Mages were so engrossed in their fight that they didn't notice Sibyl. Rokesh lay, unmoving, on the ground. The other guard stood over him with his arms crossed, staring at her with not a shred of compassion. She was on her own, weaponless, no magic, and not an ounce of fight training that could help her against Tabaio.

"Fine," she said.

Tabaio's steely countenance faltered.

Taking a deep calming breath, Sibyl willed her voice to stay steady. Taking a play from Ava's book, she decided that she wouldn't go down as a whimpering victim.

"I understand why you're doing this." A tear trickled down her cheek before freezing painfully to her face. "I forgive you. Make it quick and painless please." Her voice cracked.

It started to snow. They both looked up. At least she would die on a pretty night. Taking one last deep breath of the cold fresh air, she filled herself with a feigned bravery that she'd never felt in her life. Sticking her chin up, she leaned her head against the tree, fully exposing her neck to him, but she wouldn't close her eyes. She met his icy blue stare and waited, trying not to let her hands shake.

"Gods damn it." Tabaio lowered his sword and shook his head. His shoulders slumped and his weapon disappeared. His expression was mixed with regret and approval.

An ocean of relief flooded through her. Lowering her hands, she smiled, but before she could say anything a giant grizzly bear tackled Tabaio, sweeping him away in a tide of brown fur.

Within a split-second white fur joined the frenzy of fighting. A polar bear emerged from Tabaio's skin and punched the grizzly over the head, sending the brown bear sprawling across the snow-touched garden.

"Ambrose?" Sibyl yelled. The grizzly turned to her. Cognac eyes connected with hers. It was him. How? Where did he come from? How'd he get out of the O-cells?

The polar bear stood up on his hind legs. White fur blended in with the snowfall, making him nearly invisible. He was at least ten feet tall. The grizzly pulled himself up. While he was an impressive eight or more feet tall, Tabaio's spirit animal was larger in size and stature.

The bears collided with each other. Sibyl couldn't see much except white and brown tangling in a rage.

Ava still fought Benelli, another guard lay dead in a bloody heap. The man who'd struck Rokesh had joined the fight against Zini who was proving to be a formidable foe. Everyone was exhausted, carrying a few wounds each, and there was nothing she could do without magic.

A deafening roar pulled her attention back to the fighting bears. Ambrose knocked the polar bear down and stood over him. Tabaio stared at Ambrose, unmoving.

Rokesh stirred. Sibyl ran to him. Pushing himself to all fours, he shook his head. Sibyl checked the wound on the back of his head. Other than a concussion, he should be just fine. She helped him to his feet.

"What happened?" he asked.

"Tabaio turned on us, but then he had a change of heart and didn't kill me." She laughed weakly. "Then Ambrose showed up."

That got Rokesh's attention. She pointed to the grizzly who stood to his full menacing height over the polar bear. Ambrose raised a giant paw. Long deadly claws poised to strike. He was going to kill Tabaio.

"Ambrose no!" Sibyl forgot Rokesh and ran to them. The grizzly paused mid swing as she dove between them.

As far as crazy things go, this was probably one of the most insane things she'd ever done. Tabaio probably weighed around a thousand pounds of mostly muscle. Ambrose was at least six hundred and she stupidly sandwiched herself between them. A ton of predatory muscle, teeth, and claws surrounded her.

"Ambrose no." She put her hand up. Leaning protectively against the polar bear, she nestled into Tabaio's soft white fur and pondered her sanity. The man who tried to kill her only ten minutes ago was at her back, his chest rising and falling underneath her. He had a change of heart. He didn't go through with his order to kill her, and for that he deserved a second chance.

"No," she said sternly at the grizzly standing above her.

His massive paw was still suspended in the air as if held there by an invisible puppeteer. He was contemplating her request. After a few seconds he finally dropped his paw, and his face softened.

A ripple flowed through the brown fur like wind blowing through a wheat field and within a heartbeat Ambrose the man stood in front of her. Sibyl's wounded heart nearly gave out. She tackled him. He wrapped his arms around her.

"You're supposed to be with my family. What are you still doing here?" he scolded.

She couldn't help but laugh. Of course he would fuss at her when she nearly died ten minutes ago. She looked into his face. His beard was twice as long as when she saw him last.

Rubbing a hand over his jaw, she asked, "are you real?"

He kissed her. Their tongues collided in a desperate craze that both excited and calmed her. Earthy spices and cedarwood scent enveloped her.

When he pulled away, he asked, "what do you think?"

Fiery snow fell all around them. Sibyl reached out a hand. Ice mixed with burning embers landed in her palm. The burn was tempered by the snow that melted the moment it touched her skin. A beautiful liquid fire flowed from a Dragon hundreds of feet above them. Ambrose stared in awe at the sky.

"Real." She nestled into his arms as close as she could get while the ice fire rained down around them.

CHAPTER 34

CASSIE

SCORPLEM/OCTOBER: 2 MONTHS AGO

Cassie inhaled the fumes off the strip of aluminum foil, letting the rush of the meth whisk her away. Sibyl went to Silvermar. Tacey was busy with harvest and other family obligations that kept her busy nearly every evening. Ava was sneaking off every day, probably to see some secret lover. Cassie didn't have anyone to hang out with the past few weeks.

The library was boring. She couldn't go with Ava or participate in Mage training, and Tacey acted like Cassie was in the way most of the time. She felt like a burden. She thought about going home, but it wasn't much different there either. She'd just work as a cook in her sister's restaurant and be constantly reminded of how inadequate she was. At least here no one looked down on her. They just overlooked her completely.

Hiding in one of the green houses, she sucked in another cloud of smoke. Orgasmic tingles rippled inside her head, through her neck, and down her spine. She could feel every beautiful beat of her heart, and the blood pumping through her body. The life force of her soul. Everything was enhanced to its purest form of energy and life. The smell of vegetables, herbs, and fruits, the perfect temperature of the greenhouse, the leaves of various plants tickling her skin. Every sensation and perception morphed into a euphoric state of pleasure and vitality.

Heart pounding with so much power that her body struggled to contain it, Cassie stood up. Her mind reeled with thoughts and ideas. She could do something to show everyone how useful and helpful she could be. There were plants in the greenhouse that were ready for harvesting. Some needed trimming, others repotting. She could get a ton of work done in one night so tomorrow, maybe Tacey would have more time to hang out with her.

The door opened. Cassie dropped to the ground. No one was supposed to be in the greenhouses at night. That's why she chose this place to enjoy her high without interruption or disturbance. If she got caught in here, she might get in trouble, especially considering her current intoxicated state.

Ducking behind a large plant, she tried to blend in within the greenhouse jungle. The person rifled around a bit but didn't come to the far end of the greenhouse where Cassie hid. After a few minutes, Cassie's curiosity got the best of her. Crawling on her hands and knees as quietly as possible, she snuck a peek.

Poking her head above a row of plants, she watched the back of a person as they removed a box from a cabinet behind a bunch of nutrient bags in the corner. Cassie didn't know there was a cabinet back there. She wondered if Tacey knew about it.

The person mixed various substances in a bowl like they were about to cook a meal. Craning her neck, Cassie tried to get a better look. The person paused and glanced over their shoulder. Cassie ducked quickly, accidentally knocking over a pot. It fell to the floor and busted in a loud clash.

"Who's there?"

That voice. Tacey? What was she doing here and what was she doing? Great. Now Cassie would have to explain what *she* was doing here. Stepping up sheepishly, Cassie faced her friend.

"What are you doing here?" Tacey demanded.

"Nothing. Just getting away for a bit. I wanted s-some time to mys-s-self."

"Why are you talking like that?"

"L-l-like what?" Sometimes meth made her mind work faster than words could form. She knew what she wanted to say, but her mouth couldn't keep up with the speed of her thoughts.

Tacey furrowed her eyebrow. A horrid smell overpowered the herbs and flowers.

"Oh Gods. W-w-w-what's that smell?" Cassie plugged her nose and fanned her hand. "Dude. Did y-y-you fart?"

"No. Get out, Cassie. No one's supposed to be here at night."

"What-t-t are you doing h-h-here?" Cassie asked.

"That's not your concern. I'm the head gardener. I'm allowed to be here. I'm preparing for the harvest."

Cassie lit up with excitement. "I c-c-can help." She bumbled toward Tacey. Tripping over her own feet, she crashed into Tacey, spilling the concoction that she was preparing.

"Ahhh. Cassie. What have you done?" Tacey bent over and desperately swept up the powders with her hands.

"Sorry dud-d-de. Here I can help pick it up."

"No. Don't touch it!" Tacey practically yelled at her.

Cassie slumped with embarrassment. No matter how much she tried to help, she ruined everything for everyone.

"Ugh. Now there's not going to be enough. I need at least four more doses," Tacey mumbled.

The smell in the room was vomit worthy. Cassie sniffed her friend's shirt. It was all over her. What had she gotten into? Cassie sniffed the air. Her senses were heightened when she was high. That's one of meth's superpowers. She was practically a bloodhound. Following the odor closer and closer to Tacey until she was right on her, Cassie scrunched up her nose in confusion. Tacey was the source.

"Jeeze d-d-dude. When was the last time you sh-sh-showered?" Cassie gagged.

"I said BACK OFF!" Tacey shoved her.

Cassie toppled backward into the wall. "What's your p-p-problem?"

"You're a menace. You ruined everything." Tacey's eye was full of rage.

Cassie leaned against the wall for support. Her mind and heart raced. She wasn't sure which one was going faster at the moment. She remembered a couple of months ago, Sibyl, Ava, and the guys were talking about demons having a foul odor, and they suspected a demon spy in Tearnanelle. Her drugged mind slowly puzzled it out.

"Tacey, what h-h-happened to you in Tearnanoak-k-k ten years ago?"

The blonde-haired woman laughed maniacally. Cassie swallowed hard. There was no way this was happening.

"I'll give you props. No one here ever figured it out. Not even the imbecile's parents could tell the difference. All I had to do was play a victim and they all passed off the differences in behavior as a trauma response." Tacey sauntered toward Cassie.

Cassie sidled toward the back where her bag and the back door was.

Stopping just inches from Cassie's face, Tacey said, "once her body was weak enough to possess, I took over. When Tacey finally died a few minutes later, I was able to keep her body alive by consuming blood. All these years I've been in this vessel." The non-Tacey person surveyed herself. "At first, I wasn't sure how I was going to get into the inner circle of the kingdom, but the Aruka herself came to *my* house and invited me to the palace."

The not-Tacey demon-person cackled. "It was so easy. The bleeding-heart bitch brought me right in and gave me the food source to the kingdom." She fanned her hands out. "Over the years I've been selectively killing off the biggest threats to Tearnanoak, and when the Arukas arrived, I started to poison the Aruka. By the time winter solstice rolls around, she'll be dead, we'll take the Druid and the Arukas, and Tearnanelle will be ours!"

Cassie's heart rate spiked even higher, if that was physiologically possible. If she didn't have meth in her system, she might have passed out, but meth was pure adrenaline that kept you strong and awake.

Thinking furiously, she tried to figure something out. She remembered her friends saying you can't kill a demon. That fucking sucked. She was in trouble. There must be a way out of this. She tried to buy some time.

"Wow. The villain divulging their entire plan to the good guys in the final scene. So, cliché." Cassie sidestepped.

Tacey followed her in a dominating stalking fashion that made Cassie swallow nervously.

"It's more satisfying to let your victim know how pathetic they are, and how hopeless it is right before you kill them. I am quite hungry. Fresh blood will be delicious, even blood tainted with Earth chemicals." Tacey lunged, teeth bared.

Cassie ran backward, tripped over her bag, and fell to the floor. Tacey pounced on her. The demon was incredibly strong, but with the power of meth, Cassie was able to hold her back.

Tacey snapped furiously at Cassie's neck and raked her razor blade nails over Cassie's arms tearing up her flesh in a painful tapestry of bloody art.

Mustering all her strength, Cassie head butted Tacey. Pain blossomed on her forehead as putrid blood poured from the demon's nose.

"Gross." Cassie spat out the cascade of blood falling onto her face and mouth. She turned her head away and saw her butane torch lighter that she used to get high laying on the floor a few feet away.

She lunged while Tacey was distracted. Grabbing the lighter, she clicked the button and tossed it into the spilled powders.

"NO!" Tacey screeched as the torch landed in the pile of powder and exploded on contact.

Meth's not bomb proof, and no matter how much you have in your system, it would not protect someone from blunt force trauma. Cassie and Tacey catapulted backward, and the world zapped out.

———-—-— Winter Solstice ———-—-

Cassie opened her eyes. Shouting, bright lights, and commotion swam around in a chorus of confusion. Was she under the water? She tried to get up, but her arms were too heavy to lift. Yes. She must be really deep under water to not be able to move her arms. But how was she breathing if that was the case?

It took concerted effort, but she finally managed to lift her arm to scratch an itch on her nose. Ok. Not under water then.

She took in her arm and gasped. A pink fleshy spider web of skin covered the entire hand and distal half of her arm. She flexed and extended her fingers. The skin pulled tightly, but it didn't hurt. What the hell happened?

She looked around, but didn't recognize anything. Dozens of people with various wounds scurried about. A guy lay on the bed next to her with a missing arm. The stump dripped blood in a large, congealed puddle on the floor.

Cassie sat up and took in the horror around her. Large lacerations to faces and torsos, a missing eye, missing limbs. People in weird blood covered cloaks darted about frantically. Was this some kind of trippy hospital? She remembered getting high recently. This was the weirdest meth dream she'd ever had. It was so vivid and real.

"What's going on?" Her voice came out as a barely audible scratchy whisper. Coughing, she tried it again. "Hello." That was better, but no one acknowledged her. They were all too busy with other wounded people to notice her.

She was so confused. What was the last thing she remembered? Nothing. Her mind was blank. Had she finally overdosed and stroked out or something? That's it. She was quitting meth for good this time.

"Get the gold and calendula poultice!" Someone shouted.

Gold? What the fuck do you need gold for?

"Breathe this in. It's a sleeping potion mixed with Em. It'll put you to sleep while we suture up your wound," a cloaked nurse said to a woman in a bed across the room.

Em? That sounded familiar. The fog in Cassie's mind cleared slightly. Em. Orlon. Ava. Sibyl. She was in a magical world called Tearnanelle. Cool. Magic was real. She remembered now, but how did she get here?

Looking at her scarred arms again, she tried hard to remember, but her mind was full of mud, and she was a sloth, knees deep trudging through it. The scars looked like burns. It must have been a serious burn to cause this much damage. Did she drop her torch lighter on herself?

Her friends always made fun of her for using that giant torch lighter for her meth. They kept telling her she'd burn her house down eventually. Shit. Did she burn the place down? She was in for a world of trouble.

She thought so hard her head hurt. Finally, a raging river of memories crashed into her mind.

"TACEY!" Cassie launched out of bed and fell face first on the floor right in the puddle of blood. "Are you kidding? Gross." She stood up, grabbed a cloth, and wiped it off.

"You're awake!" an old woman exclaimed.

"Yeah, I'm awake. Do you have some real clothes? What's going on? How long was I asleep?"

"Two months," Melinda said. Cassie remembered her name.

"Shit. Where's the Aruka?" She didn't have much time if two months had already passed. She needed to warn them.

"The council room," Melinda said.

"Where's the council room?"

"Same wing as us, next to the dining hall."

"Okay, thanks." Cassie bounded off as fast as her sluggish uncoordinated legs would go. Apparently being in a coma for two months makes you weak and slow, not that she was strong or fast to begin with.

When she got to the hallway, the freezing cold night air dove beneath her skimpy hospital robe making her entire body shiver uncontrollably within seconds.

"Holy shit, did someone turn off the heat?" Her breath fogged in front of her face. Her bare feet turned to ice cycles. She hopped around like she was playing a game of hot potato, only it was cold potato. Hopping ungracefully, she moved as fast as she could, heading for the council room. She only tripped about three times, which was impressive considering everything.

When she saw the door that said 'Council Room' she threw it open and ran inside, slamming the door closed behind her. Dozens of Mage Guards huddled around a large table. Everyone stopped what they were doing, and silence took over the room as they stared at her with confused expressions.

She bolted toward them. As if they were one, they conjured swords and took aim at her. Cassie slid to a stop, heart thundering in her chest. She was out of breath from fear and the run here. Damn, she probably should have taken Sibyl's advice and done more cardio exercise.

"I need to-" Breathe. "the Aruka-" Breathe. "Now. It's-" Breathe. "-an emergency." She buckled over, leaning her hands on her knees. The guards exchanged confused looks with each other.

"I'm Cassie."

"The Arukas's human friend who burned down the field crops?" one of the women asked.

"WHAT!? I didn't-" Breath "-burn down the crops!" Shit did she do that? The Aruka stepped from behind the guards. Nearly every inch of her body was covered in silver armor except her head.

"Cassie." Her expression hardened and she crossed her arms.

"I didn't burn down the crops. It was Tacey. Tacey's the spy!"

The Aruka's eyebrows shot up. "What are you talking about? Ambrose is the spy. We have him locked up," Serellina said.

Cassie shook her head. "No way, man. It's Tacey. I was getting high in the greenhouse, and she came in. She had all these powders and shit. I tripped and she saw me, then we got in an argument. Then I was like 'what are you doing?' and she was like 'none of your business' and I was like-"

"Ok. Ok. Get to the point," Serellina said.

"She was poisoning you, and she said after you were dead, they'd attack on winter solstice and take Ava and Sibyl. They're going to attack us on winter solstice!" Cassie yelled.

"We know that. It is winter solstice. They're here," Serellina said.

"Oh shit. No way. Tell me you at least captured Tacey," Cassie said.

"No. She's been missing since the fire. You know, the fire you caused," a man she didn't know said crossly.

"Yeah. Sorry about that. I only meant to torch the poison she was mixing in The Aruka's food, but then it kind of exploded. I don't remember anything after that."

"Our intel says that Alyssium was still receiving information as recently as a few days ago, so Tacey must still be alive and be out there. We never suspected Ambrose was the demon, just that he was working for the demon," Serellina said. "Jameson, go to Tacey's home. Take iron and a dozen guards. Be careful."

The man named Jameson nodded and stormed off with a host of guards trailing behind him.

"Dude, there's no way Ambrose is a spy. He's like the most strait-laced, uptight, rigid guard you have. He wouldn't betray this kingdom," Cassie said.

"You seem really confident about that," Serellina said.

Cassie shrugged.

"For the record, I never believed it was him either," Yilfin said.

Serellina shot him an exasperated look. "He stays in the O-cells until Tacey is apprehended and we get the truth out."

An explosion startled them.

Serellina buckled over as if she was punched in the gut. "They're at the wall," she said grimly. Yilfin wrapped his arms around the Aruka and helped steady her.

Cassie swallowed down her fear. "Where's Ava and Sibyl?"

"Safely hidden in the royal cave below the castle." Serellina stood back up again, seemingly recovered from whatever ailment had temporarily affected her. "You can stay here with us as long as you stay out of trouble."

Serellina looked at Cassie's feet then trailed her eyes up her entire body to her face again. "For Gods' sake, would someone get this girl some clothes?"

Cassie tried to sit still, but that was damn near impossible. Her nails had grown two inches long while she was asleep, and she spent the last two hours chewing them all off until a couple of her fingers bled.

Finally, Jameson returned. Cassie shot to her feet.

"You may want to come yourself," Jameson said.

Another explosion shook the diamond lights and rattled the furniture. Serellina gripped her stomach as if she was about to vomit. Everyone held their breath, waiting for something to happen. When nothing did, they all relaxed and Serellina took a deep breath, collected herself, then stormed out of the room.

Cassie ran behind her. Serellina opened her mouth to say something, but Cassie stuck her chin out. The Aruka sighed and snapped her mouth shut. Heading down the corridor, surrounded by a small legion of Mage Guards, they went down several hallways until they entered a giant doorway lined by iron and runes.

"These are the iron cells. We call them I-cells for short. They're used to house any dark magic wielders as iron helps suppress dark magic," Serellina told Cassie.

They descended some stairs and entered a dungeon-like room with several prison cells lining each wall. At the very end was Tacey. When they got close to her cell, the horrific odor overwhelmed Cassie. She put a hand over her nose as did everyone else.

Tacey's violet eye widened when she saw Cassie. The other eye socket was fully exposed, along with the scars across her face. Tacey didn't seem the least bit concerned that the wounds were on display. Was the insecurity of her injuries faked as well?

Even without the empty socket, Tacey looked terrible. She was deathly skinny, pale, and her hair was a knotted mess.

"You're awake. How fortunate for you. I tried to sneak into the healer's wing so many times to finish you off, but I never could get past all the guards. Pretending to be dead has its disadvantages," Tacey sneered.

"Are you working with anyone?" Serellina asked.

"You mean in your kingdom?" Tacey laughed. "You Mages are incredibly dim-witted. I would never align myself with any of you. Although it was entertaining watching you detain the wrong person. I nearly had the Druid during Wan-G Libnys when lover boy was making out with her, but then he looked up at the last moment." Tacey laughed again. Her voice wasn't the timid shy one that Cassie was used to. This Tacey's voice was like fingers down a chalkboard.

"I'll admit, I wasn't strong enough to fight that one. He's quite the large brute, so I had to run away that night." Tacey giggled. "But you all thought it was him after that." She laughed so deeply she coughed and choked.

After she finally regained herself, she said, "you think I would deign to align myself with the peasants of Orlon. Even one as strong as that one? I would rather be strung up by my toes and fileted in the open sun and eaten by crows."

"You already smell like you've done that," Cassie said.

A few guards chuckled. Serellina shushed them, but Cassie saw a slight tug of her lips.

"Keep me here as long as you want. I don't care. My queen will free me when she arrives. Our werewolves have already breached your gates by now. You'll all be enslaved to us soon."

Another large explosion stabbed through the night, shaking the castle so violently that pebbles and dust fell from the ceiling. Serellina fell to her knees. Jameson kneeled beside her as the Aruka panted from unseen pain that racked her body.

Tacey smiled wickedly. "They're here."

Chills climbed up Cassie's spine.

"Aruka, we need to release Ambrose," Yilfin said.

Serellina's eyes darted around like she was working out a puzzle that only she could see.

"Aruka?" Yilfin asked.

"Yes, release Ambrose immediately," Serellina whispered.

Jameson nodded and ran out.

CHAPTER 35
AVA

Ava dodged a blow from Benelli's dinner plate sized paw. She barely had time to recover her balance before he swiped again and then lunged with a snap of his jaw. Ava tripped and nearly fell on her ass, but she managed to maintain her balance.

Using the momentum to twirl, she brought her blade around in a powerful slash, missing Benelli's abdomen by inches. He jumped backward then side stepped and punched out. She swung the sword to the side releasing the end piece which flew past him wedging deep into the side of a lamp post. Ava growled in frustration.

Glancing toward Sibyl, she saw her friend laying on the ground with Tabaio standing over her with a sword.

What's going on, Sibyl?

No answer. Two other guards fought one of the other werewolves a dozen yards away. Rokesh laid on the ground unmoving. Ava couldn't tell from here if he was alive or dead. Another guard stood above him, protecting him from attack. She didn't have time to consider their predicament. Hopefully things were under control.

Benelli stormed at her, the ground jolted with each of his powerful steps. She sidestepped a few feet then rushed backward. He charged again. The gap between them shrank. She backed up more, the gap shrank more.

She needed a few more steps. There it was; the opening she was waiting for. She summoned the dagger back to her. It flew from the post and struck Benelli's shoulder as he raised an arm to punch her. Losing his footing, the beast fell to the ground in an earth-shaking thud. Ava smiled.

Reaching around, he tried to grab the blade, but it was at the perfect location that neither arm could reach. Flailing around, he twirled several times before finally abandoning his attempts to dislodge the blade and faced Ava once again. Malice burned hot behind his crazed eyes. They circled each other, taking the moment to catch their breath.

This time she made the first move. Dashing toward him, she raised her arm ready to strike. He ducked, as she knew he would. Dropping her hip, she put all of her strength into an uppercut. Her fist connected with the beast's jaw. Pain shot through her hand and arm. The beast stumbled slightly, but he didn't go down. She didn't expect him to.

While he was distracted, she twirled, releasing the next dagger of her sword which embedded into his torso about six inches away from the first one.

He split the air with a deafening roar and sprinted toward her. He was on her in two strides. She couldn't back up fast enough to get out of his range.

He swiped.

She dodged, but not fast enough. His paw grazed her cheek. Razor blade claws ripped through her flesh. Screaming, she rolled sideways, dropping her sword. Concentrating as hard as she could, she held the magical tether. She couldn't lose those daggers.

When she finally came to a stop, she got to her hands and knees just in time to see Benelli charging her again. She summoned the sword, and it sprang to life, flying into her hand at the last second. Doing a backbend, she avoided his punch and shoved the sword up, stabbing him in the armpit on the same side as the other two blades.

Releasing the tip of the blade, she pulled the sword out and rolled from under him.

She had a short sword now, as three of her daggers were securely lodged within the beast.

He stumbled, no doubt from the monstrous amount of silver that was leaching into his bloodstream. She dumped as much as she could spare into the sword.

The inky night lit up with specs of white snow. The cold flakes were refreshing against her sweaty skin, especially the wound on her cheek, but it made for shit visibility.

A giant grizzly bear charged through the wintry garden. For a second everyone paused their fighting and watched the bear tackle Tabaio. What the hell? Were there weregrizzlies?

Tabaio shifted almost immediately into a polar bear, and the two bears fought furiously, dancing between the snowfall which muffled the sounds of battle. Ava didn't have time to revel in the cold beauty or watch the bear fight play out, because Benelli turned his attention back to her.

She sidestepped. He matched it. And so, another round started. She was getting tired and the wound on her cheek stung. The anti-gold in his claws prevented it from healing. Hopefully it didn't scar. Another step, and they completed a half circle around each other. She was losing patience. It was time to end this.

"How does it feel to be losing to a human woman?" she asked mockingly.

The bait worked. He came at her, a rabid rage fueling his advance, but he was lame and slow. This would be easy now. She feigned a right hook then stabbed with her sword. He'd learned her technique though, and when she came through with the strike he reared up and knocked the blade from her hand. She used all of her focus to not release it.

Benelli stomped on the weapon and stared challengingly. She conjured another sword, but as a single unit. She didn't think she'd be able to manage twelve daggers. The magic strained against her. The tethers held together like stretched thread a breath away from unraveling. One wrong move and some or all of them would break.

Benelli's werewolf eyebrows shot up. Guess he didn't think she'd be able to maintain them all. If she ever saw Redly again, she'd be sure to thank him for the multiple weapon training.

His voice played in her mind. *Don't do anything stupid.*

Ava smiled. She had a really stupid idea. If it worked, though, it would be epic. Redly would be appalled and impressed. Hopefully she'd live to tell him about it.

Gathering up all her energy, she sprinted toward Benelli. He reared up just like she thought he would do. She watched his right hip drop as he prepared to swing. She just needed to get a little closer, within his arm span.

Right when his paw came down, she dropped to her knees and slid across the ground, which was now slick with ice and snow. His paw grazed over her head, barely missing her. She tipped sideways and stabbed her sword into his paw then released it at the same moment that she grabbed her dagger sword. Then she stabbed him in the rear leg on the same side as the other daggers and released the tip with a twist. He fell over in a whimpering rage. She slid to a stop and got quickly to her feet.

Remarkably, Benelli got to his feet. His fortitude was impressive, she'd give him that.

While he was distracted and weak, she positioned herself so that he was between her and the daggers embedded in his body.

Shaking his head, he took a few ataxic steps but managed to stay standing. Ava glanced at the others. The final werewolf lay on the ground in a bloody heap. Only one guard remained standing. Two bodies lay unmoving on the ground nearby. She wasn't sure if they were alive or dead, but she didn't have time to check.

She glanced at Sibyl, who knelt defensively on top of the polar bear, holding up her hand. Ava had no idea what was going on with her friends, but she'd have to wait just a little bit longer to find out. She only needed one more minute.

The sky lit up with an orange fiery cloud as another Dragon let loose atmospheric lava. Embers and snowflakes poured down around them like fireworks. Ava watched in awe for just a moment before reality set back in when Benelli stumbled around in front of her. He wasn't watching the sky or her. He was dazed and stumbling in disoriented fashion. She took up a defensive pose and waited.

Every step Benelli took, she matched it keeping him in line exactly where she wanted him. Finally, his eyes focused on her. That's what she was waiting for.

"This is for my family." As the fiery rain poured down all around her, she slammed her sword point to the ground behind her with as much force and magic that she could muster. Releasing a scream of rage, she summoned the blades back to her in reverse order that she'd let them go.

The blade she implanted into his hind leg tore through his abdomen and catapulted out the other side, flying to her sword. Next was the one lodged in his armpit. It pulled from his flesh easily. Too bad his other front leg was between it and her sword. It severed his leg cleanly in half before returning to her. Benelli fell to the ground.

Next was the one in his torso. It yanked through his body, likely breaking a few ribs and ripping up his lungs in the process. She wasn't quite sure what internal damage it ravaged, and she didn't care, as long as it was a lot.

The final blade was the one she was waiting for. She paused. The beast lay sternal, panting. Blood dripped from his mouth. His expression was full of defeat and resolve.

The guard who'd fought the other werewolf stared with his mouth agape. Ava found Sibyl's gaze. She stood in Ambrose's arms, and they both watched. Rokesh, Tabaio, Fulcinia, Jameson, Ziv, Wilson, Demetrius and finally, Ava's eyes met Cassie. Her heart leapt. Cassie was awake. Other than that, there were at least twenty other guards all watching her. She had an audience. She better make it good then.

Turning back to Benelli, she summoned the last dagger. Time slowed down as the blade disappeared into his chest, then emerged from the other side with something stuck to the end of the blade. Blood sprayed the ground from the exit point, leaving a bright red stain on the powdery snow.

The dagger zoomed through the air and snapped onto the end of her sword. Her eyes widened at Benelli's unbeating heart that was impaled on the end of her blade. Satisfaction bored through her when the monster, formerly known as Benelli, slumped to the ground. He wouldn't be able to heal from that.

Wilson ran to Ava and swooped her up into a big hug.

"Holy shit dude. Where'd you learn that?" Cassie exclaimed, running to her.

"I'd like to know that too. It's definitely not something we teach," Fulcinia said.

"My source. He's been teaching me to fight."

Demetrius checked the werewolf's pulse. It was a formality, but it was satisfying to watch him shake his head in confirmation.

"He killed my family. The people who adopted me, The Hansons. They were kind and innocent, and he slaughtered them like animals. He ripped their throats out." Ava kicked him one more time for good measure. No one chastised her.

Someone gripped her hand. The gesture startled her. When she met Sibyl's hazel eyes, a wave of emotions overwhelmed her, and her eyes started to burn. No. Not now. She didn't want to feel that right now.

Sibyl pulled her in for a hug. Ava positively despised hugs. Too touchy feely. Cassie crashed into her other side. She met Cassie's brown eyes and saw tears pooling. Ava leaned into her friends. Maybe hugs weren't so bad.

The pain she'd endured her entire life at the loss of the Hansons wasn't gone. It didn't even lessen, but there was something else there to help the pain not hurt so bad. Love. A lot of love from her friends and family. She was literally surrounded by love, and for the first time in her life, she was relieved and grateful for it. She hugged Sibyl and Cassie even harder for another minute.

Finally pulling out of the embrace, she surveyed everyone. Rokesh had a wounded leg that oozed with an unhealthy shade of black-red blood. The guard who was fighting the other werewolf looked pretty bad too, boasting several wounds along her arms and one across her abdomen. Fulcinia and Yilfin also had a few minor wounds, as well as several of the guards she didn't know, but all in all, they weren't in terrible shape.

Then her eyes fell on Ambrose. "How are you here?"

"Cassie." A faint smile tugged at his lips.

"It's Tacey. I caught her." Cassie squared her shoulders proudly.

Jameson coughed; his dark eyes alight with playful reprimand.

"OK. Jameson caught her, but I discovered her real identity. Tacey died in Tearnanoak ten years ago. A demon possessed her body and has been masquerading as her this entire time, waiting for her time to strike which was when you guys arrived." Cassie nodded to Sibyl and Ava. "She was also poisoning your aunt, but I figured it all out and I blew her up....sort of."

"What do you mean she was poisoning my aunt?"

"That's why your aunt's been so sick lately, but I stopped her." Cassie beamed.

"You didn't have to burn down half the kingdom to do it though," Jameson admonished.

"I've never been a secret agent before. I think I did pretty good for my first mission."

They all laughed.

Rokesh winced and leaned on Ambrose for support. "Anyone have any gold gems?"

"I have one." A guard handed it to him. They smashed it and a golden thick liquid pooled in a silver bowl that Demetrius conjured to catch the healing magic. Several of them grabbed a handful to rub on their wounds. Ava rubbed a dab on her cheek. The relief was immediate as the gold seeped in to help heal the wound her innate blood couldn't handle on its own.

"That's it for me. I'm out now," the woman who'd given them the gold gem said.

"I have three," Sibyl said.

"Keep them. We're all good for now," Wilson said. "We should probably get to the wall and see what's going on there. How much longer until sunrise? Anyone have any idea? I can't tell since the clouds are blocking the Empyrean star."

"Midnight." Sibyl held up her cell phone.

"Only halfway through the night. Great." Wilson wilted.

Howling tore through the atmosphere, interrupting their conversation. It was close. Too close. Chills ran up Ava's spine as something moved in the darkness behind the falling snow along the forest line. A few sets of eyes reflected in the diamond lamps along the garden pathway.

Ava siphoned magic from the moonstone on her cuff and stared into the dark forest. Creatures paced along the edge of the forest. Lots of them.

Another blast of fire lit up the sky and Ava's stomach dropped as hundreds of werewolves stepped out of the darkness. It was difficult to tell how many there were through the snow, which fell more heavily now, but it was a significant amount that outnumbered them at least ten to one. The werewolves came in from all sides. Everyone crowded into each other.

"Oh shit," Cassie said.

That was the understatement of the century. They were completely fucked.

CHAPTER 36
SIBYL

Sibyl swallowed nervously. Ambrose conjured a sword and pushed her behind him protectively. Cassie clambered up a nearby tree as skillfully as a moose would accomplish the task. Bits of bark and pine needles mixed with the falling snow cascaded down as Cassie made her way up.

"What are you doing?" someone asked.

"Dude, I can't fight, and I have no magic. I'm hiding." Cassie climbed further up into the evergreen until she disappeared completely.

"Sibyl, you know that trick you did in the dining hall a few nights ago. How about doing that again now?" Ava conjured her sword, as did all of the Mages. They pressed into each other more closely.

"I can't." Sibyl tried to keep her nerves from completely undoing her, but it was difficult as hundreds of werewolves slowly surrounded them.

"Damn it, Sibyl. Now's not the time to have self-doubt, just fucking DO IT!" Ava snapped.

"What did you do?" Ambrose asked, not taking his eyes off the approaching werewolves.

"I froze everyone."

Ambrose turned to her with raised eyebrows.

"I've learned a few more tricks since you've been gone, but I don't exactly know how I did it. It just happened when I was super stressed."

"I don't know about you, but I'm pretty stressed right now," Wilson said.

Ava glared at Sibyl, determination burning behind her emerald eyes. "Do it again." It wasn't a request.

"No. I mean I can't. I have an osmium chip in my chest."

"What is that?" Ava asked.

"It's how a Mage is subdued without hindering the ability of those around them. A tiny chip of osmium is implanted into your chest," Ambrose said. He shot a glance at Tabaio. "That moron put one in Sibyl."

Tabaio shrugged like it was no big deal.

"Well get it out!" Ava yelled.

"It's not that easy. There are spikes that anchor it in the heart. It's a sedated procedure," Jameson said.

"There are spikes of osmium in my heart?" Anxiety threatened to cripple Sibyl.

Jameson nodded; a strand of his dark hair fell into his face.

The werewolves sat down in a circle around them. Rows and rows of werewolves concentrically placed around their group that huddled helplessly in the center. They yipped and barked at each other as if they were talking.

"I really wish I knew what they were saying," Demetrius said.

"Sibyl can understand them, if she wasn't incapacitated." Ava shot a reprimanding look at Tabaio.

He wasn't paying attention. His gaze was fixed on the perimeter of werewolves. Holding a sword in each hand, he swung them around threateningly.

"Ok." Ambrose released his weapon and turned to Sibyl. Stepping into the center of the protective formation, he stared down at her, his brow furrowing in deep concentration. Someone immediately filled his spot so that there was no gap in the protective barrier around them.

Sibyl looked into Ambrose's cognac eyes. Something brewed in that head of his. She could sense it, even without her magic. Cupping her cheeks, he studied her face then kissed her like no one was watching. Sibyl lost herself. His hands held her tight, and she temporarily forgot the horrible situation. She loved the feel of his lips on hers.

"Oh, my Gods you two. This isn't the time for a make out session," Ava snorted.

And with that, Sibyl came back to reality. The very grim reality. Ambrose held Sibyl's gaze. A very stern, very serious expression took over his features. "We're going to have to get that chip out of you, if we have any hope of getting out of this." He rubbed a thumb over her cheek reassuringly, but it didn't work. Terror poisoned Sibyl's mind and heart. The heart that contained a shard of osmium.

"What does that entail?" She was afraid to know the answer.

"Keep the werewolves off of us," Ambrose said to no one in particular. "Jameson, you're helping. Sit down," Ambrose told her.

"What's going on?" Sibyl asked, but it was rhetorical. She knew what they were about to do. They were going to attempt to remove the shard from her heart, in the middle of the night, on the ground, while werewolves surrounded them. This was definitely not a sterile environment, and it was her heart. It's not just a simple wound. It's her freaking heart!

Sibyl started to shake, but not from the cold. The snow and cold was probably the only reason she hadn't passed out yet. She sat on the ground. Her butt was instantly soaked from the wet snow.

"Take your armor and shirt off." Ambrose and Jameson knelt in front of her.

She paused briefly, glancing around at everyone. Maybe it was silly to be bashful. There was nothing and no one here that was remotely interested in anything other than survival at the moment, but it was still a bit unnerving to undress in the middle of her friends, strangers, enemies who wanted her dead or hostage, and Ambrose.

She met his expressionless gaze. No more playful banter or warm affection. Ambrose the Mage Guard was on duty. She marveled at his ability to turn his emotions on and off like a light switch.

Taking a deep steadying breath, she pulled the leather armor off. She glanced at Rokesh, who'd given her the armor. He turned away and put his eyes back on the werewolves who sat and watched in silence. What were they doing? Why weren't they attacking?

Pulling her shirt over her head, she winced when she lifted her left arm. The only thing between her and complete nakedness was her bra, which did nothing to make her feel less exposed. The cold air bit at her skin, teasing goosebumps to the surface.

Ambrose's eyes flicked over her then he tore his gaze away. His jaw ticked, but he said nothing. This wasn't the way she'd pictured him seeing her for the first time.

Ambrose balled up her shirt and put it behind her for a makeshift pillow. He helped her lay on her back. The moment her head hit the fabric the wound on the back of her head screamed. She'd forgotten about it, until that moment.

"What was the song you played that night in the piano room?" Ambrose asked.

Her mind had split in a thousand directions, but that wasn't one of them.

Jameson inspected the hole that dove into her chest over her left breast. His hands were cold against her bare skin. Blood trickled from the wound in a slow congealed ooze that froze almost immediately. It was trying to clot, but with every beat of her heart, new blood pumped fresh liquid out. She began to shiver.

"I need a knife. A real one," Jameson said.

A knife!!! What the hell? Panic fully gripped her. She tried to get up, but Ambrose put a hand on her shoulder and pushed her back down. She felt faint. Her entire body shook uncontrollably.

"Hey." Ambrose rubbed her cheek soothingly. "We won't do this if you don't want to." His expression disagreed with what he said. He was fighting between being the warm affectionate man she'd come to know, and the hard lethal warrior he needed to be right now.

She grabbed his hand and held on as if her life depended on it. If she couldn't use her magic, they were all as good as dead. Sibyl shifted her gaze to Jameson. He watched her with a determined desperation, but he didn't move. He wouldn't do this if she said no.

Sibyl looked at Wilson, Demetrius, Rokesh, Ava, Fulcinia, and countless others who all took turns avoiding her gaze. None of them would force her, but they all knew if she didn't agree, they were doomed.

A tear streamed down her cheek and froze before it had a chance to drip off. She didn't even know if she could immobilize all the werewolves. They were putting their hope in her, and she may not be able to save them, but there was no other good option. Fighting their way out, twenty-five to two hundred, was certain death for everyone, except her and Ava. That thought scared her shitless. She'd rather die than get taken.

She bit down on her lip, looked at Ambrose, and nodded.

He reached over and fidgeted with the sheath at her hip.

"Where's the knife I gave you?" he asked.

Sibyl locked eyes with Tabaio. He had pretty bright blue eyes, as pure as ice.

Ambrose followed her gaze.

"She tried to stab me with it." Tabaio pulled the knife from his belt and handed it to Ambrose.

"Good. You deserved it." Ambrose grabbed the knife. "Next time don't miss," he said to her.

She laughed halfheartedly.

Ambrose handed the knife to Jameson. The two men exchanged a look, some unspoken conversation passing between them. Ambrose grabbed her hand and squeezed so tight, she thought he may accidentally crush it. "You never told me that song."

Panic took over every facet of her being. She knew a distraction technique when she heard one. She did the same thing to her patients, only with cheese and ear scratches. With humans you talk to them about something completely unrelated to what was going on. She wasn't a fool. Her eyes shifted to Jameson.

"No. Look at me," Ambrose said.

Her gaze returned to him.

"You ready?" he asked.

Sibyl shook her head a split second before a searing pain ripped through her chest. Screaming, she tried to pull her hand from Ambrose and get away.

"Hold her still!" Jameson shouted.

Someone grabbed her legs, and another person grabbed her shoulders and her arm that Ambrose wasn't holding. Looking at the source of the pain, she confirmed what she thought. She was being stabbed.

Jameson pried the end of the knife blade into the hole, trying to weasel the shard out. Her body fought against the assault of its own volition. She'd never experienced any pain so profound. Lava poured into her chest and the edges of her vision tunneled in. Her voice screamed itself out, her head rolled to the side, and what she saw made the pain seem like child's play.

The werewolves advanced. That's what they were waiting for; distraction.

Chaos broke out around her as the world faded into darkness.

———————— Earth Home ————————

Soaking in a hot bubble bath, Sibyl basked in the warm scent of lavender and chamomile soaps. A Knock on the door startled her.

"Sibyl, do you need anything?"

"No, Mom. I'm good." Sibyl's mom had always been a loving and caring mother, but this amount of doting was over the top. Even on her birthday, she never got this much attention. It must be because she'd missed her daughter. Sibyl had been gone for so long.

"We're going to wait for you to pick a movie for us to watch tonight, so hurry up darling," her dad called from outside the bathroom door.

"Ok, Dad. I'll be out in a minute." She just wanted to bask in the relaxing hot water for a few more minutes. She was so cold.

"Hey, Sibs, do you want to shoot some hoops after you're out?" her brother Jonathon asked, from the other side of the door. What was he doing home? She thought he was going to Monica's for Christmas. Weird.

"No. It's too cold outside," Sibyl answered.

"Oh, ok then." His words were laced with disappointment.

Footsteps walked off. Closing her eyes, she submerged herself deeper into the nice....*cold* water! What the hell? In the last thirty seconds the water had not only cooled down, but became like ice, as if her body chilled it.

She got out of the frigid water and grabbed a towel. Wrapping it around herself, she waited for the warmth to sink in, but it didn't happen. The towel felt like aluminum foil. An edge of the crisp metal cut her chest.

"Ouch." Sibyl looked at the small cut over her heart. Blood poured from the wound like a water hose, soaking her entire front side in red within seconds. It froze to her bare skin in an ominous tapestry of gore.

Throwing the aluminum foil towel down, she grabbed another towel from the cabinet and wrapped that one around her. It, too, felt like cold, stiff metal.

"Why doesn't this feel right?" She rubbed the fabric of the towel between her fingers. It was cold and brittle, nothing like a towel should feel.

More blood drained from her, and she became lightheaded. Losing her balance, she fell against the wall of the bathroom and slid to the floor. The towel she'd wrapped around her provided no warmth and it was becoming more soaked in blood as her life force drained out.

"This isn't real," Sibyl said as her consciousness waxed and waned. Her eyelids grew heavy.

"Wake up!" she yelled at herself.

In a flash, the scene changed. She stood in the middle of a field at night. Snow fell from the sky in silent misty flakes. A pain burned inside her chest. She pulled the collar of her shirt down and saw a hole over her heart. *What the hell?*

What are you doing here? How did you find me? A large bay unicorn appeared in front of her.

Sibyl backed up so fast, she tripped over her own feet and fell down.

"Who are you? What are you? How come I can hear you talk?" This felt familiar. Hadn't she seen him before? "Are you real?"

Yes, but the more important question is are you really here?

"What does that mean?"

Where are you, Sibyl?

Sibyl looked around the unfamiliar forest. Odd bulbous shaped trees with skimpy branches stuck straight into the sky which had two moons, one with rings around it.

Sibyl's jaw hit the ground. "Where are we?"

Where we are doesn't matter. Where you are is the question we need to answer.

"I'm right here. What do you mean?"

No, you're not. I can't feel your soul.

"Is that something you should feel?"

Yes. Whether we meet in physical form or metaphysical form, we should always have our soul. Yours isn't here, Sibyl. Where is it? You should never separate your soul from your consciousness. If your metaphysical self is here but your soul and physical self are somewhere else, you risk losing your soul.

"What happens if I lose my soul?"

You die.

A pain ripped through her chest like someone stabbed her. She fell flat out, hitting her head against the hard ground. She wasn't supposed to do that. She was supposed to tuck her chin when she fell. Someone had told her that once. Who was it?

The pain was unbearable. It was hard to breathe. Her lungs turned to stone. Electric needles stabbed and shocked her heart until it stopped beating. Her heart actually stopped, and her entire body froze in time, unable to move.

Cold enveloped her, but it was a peaceful type of cold.

Go back, Sibyl! The unicorn towered over her, Solstice. That was his name. She remembered him. He helped her find Orlon and Tearnanelle. Ava, Cassie, Ambrose. She needed to get back to them.

The pain evaporated as the cold consumed her completely. She became numb and sleepy.

Sibyl, GO BACK!

She would go back to them in just a minute. She needed to rest for only a minute. Closing her eyes, she let the beautiful pain free numbness take her away.

CHAPTER 37
AVA

Ava watched in horror as Sibyl's body went limp.

"No! No! Jameson do something!" Ambrose shouted desperately.

"The fucking thing's too deep. I can't get it," Jameson said. His hands and arms were covered in blood. Sibyl's blood. Ava's sword vanished. She forgot about it.

"Sibyl!" Ambrose shouted into the freckled face. Everyone except Ambrose, Jameson, and Ava fought the werewolves all around them. That's what Ava was supposed to be doing. Keeping the werewolves away while they performed a simple procedure to remove the osmium shard from Sibyl's chest. It wasn't supposed to be a big deal. What was happening?

"WAIT! I got it." Carefully, Jameson tipped the edge of the knife sideways and pulled out a tiny square gray stone with two-inch-long spears jutting off the four corners. He threw it into the snowy night.

Ava watched her blood covered friend for any signs of life. Flashbacks of the Hansons filled her mind. Sibyl looked like they did. Her lips were blue from the cold or lack of blood, Ava didn't know. Sibyl's face was so pale, even her freckles lacked their normal dark brown luster. Her body was covered in blood, along with the ground all around them. But, unlike the Hansons, she looked as if she was sleeping. Her eyes were closed peacefully.

Holding her breath, Ava watched her friend closely, waiting.

Ambrose grabbed a gem off Sibyl's necklace and shoved the golden sphere into the hole in Sibyl's chest. He lifted her head. "Come on, Sibyl. Come back to us," he pleaded. After a minute, nothing happened. He took another golden gem from her necklace and shoved that one in the hole as well. The bleeding finally stopped, but her color was still terrible.

"Come on." Jameson watched the wound, but still, nothing happened.

"Why isn't it working?" Ava asked.

"Sibyl." Ambrose's voice cracked. It was suddenly really hot outside despite the temperature. Ava's chest squeezed painfully. Her hands shook and her knees trembled. Closing her eyes, Ava willed herself to stay calm. Stay standing. Stay focused. Don't lose her shit now.

"It's working!" Jameson exclaimed.

Ava's eyes flew open, and her hope soared as she watched the hole in Sibyl's chest slowly close in on itself. Ava couldn't take her eyes off the wound. After half a minute, there was barely a tiny opening anymore. After a full minute, the hole was gone, and color seeped back into Sibyl. After another minute, her friend sucked in a breath, and her hazel eyes shot open.

Everyone collectively released a breath. Sibyl grabbed at her chest in a panic, looking around with a confused and scared expression.

Ambrose pulled her into his arms. "Thank Empyrean."

Jameson smiled and patted Ambrose on the shoulder. Ava slumped with relief. The moment was short lived as a blood curdling scream rang out.

Wilson thrashed frantically underneath a werewolf, trying to gain a foothold. A blue sword stabbed into the beast's abdomen on top of him, but the werewolf had him by the neck. A deep wound laid open Wilson's chest. Blood poured from four claw marks that spanned the entire width of his torso. Wilson's feet slipped on the slick ground making it impossible for him to gain any traction. He could get free if he used his hands, but he'd have to let his blade go.

Ava watched in horror as Wilson used all of his strength not to pull himself free, but to plunge the sword deeper into the animal until it burst out the backside of the werewolf.

Ava sprinted toward him, but she was too far away. The beast closed his jaws around Wilson's neck and ripped her friend nearly in half before it fell to the ground.

"NOO!" Ava shouted. Sliding to a stop next to Wilson, she shoved the monster off him. He held his neck, blood poured from around his hands.

"I NEED GOLD!" Ava shouted. Wilson tried to say something but only managed to cough up blood.

"Don't talk," Ava said. "SOMEBODY BRING US SOME gold!" She could barely get the last word out as she choked on a sob. Someone came up beside her. Ava stared at her friend. Wilson's dark green eyes were full of terror.

"Here." Sibyl yanked a gem from her necklace. Ambrose snatched it from her and pried open Wilson's mouth shoving it in. Wilson choked. Sibyl moved one of his hands from his neck to reveal nothing but macerated tissue and blood. The golden gem fell out from the wound.

"It can't go down. His esophagus is ruptured," Sibyl said.

"Then what the fuck are we supposed to do?" Ava shouted at her.

"Give it to me," Ambrose demanded.

Sibyl handed it over.

"Move his other hand," Ambrose said.

Ava took Wilson's hand in hers. It was slick with warm blood. Wilson gripped her tightly.

Holding the gem a few inches above the wound, Ambrose smashed it in his palm and liquid gold burst from the sphere. There had to be at least a gallon of gold inside it. An impossible amount for such a tiny object.

Gold covered the wound and lit up to a beautiful swirly mixture of red and glowing gold. Wilson choked and tried to take a breath, but he gurgled instead. Remembering that it took Sibyl's more than a minute to fully take effect, Ava waited impatiently.

Wilson flailed his other arm. Sibyl grabbed Wilson's hand and held on tight. All three of them sat beside him as the light left his eyes and his body spasmed a few times before going completely still.

His grip loosened in her hands. "No. Why isn't it working?"

Wilson's face looked just like her adopted parents' faces had. Vacant, unseeing eyes stared at the dark sky. Sibyl threw a hand over her mouth, and her eyes pooled with tears. Ambrose's shoulders slumped.

"More gold," Ava demanded.

"We're out," Sibyl said.

Ava shook her head.

"There isn't any more," Sibyl said, as if she needed to clarify.

Incisive pain bit at her heart like a savage animal. How come she kept living while those she cared about died? "If only I could give you my healing blood." Ava gripped his hand tightly.

Sibyl stared at her, mouth agape. Ava didn't know what was going on in Sibyl's mind and she didn't care. Her heart was about to give out. This was too much, all of it. Killing Sarah then Benelli, surviving to embrace her friends, nearly losing Sibyl, and now Wilson was dead. Ava choked on a sob. Wilson's face was forever frozen in pain and fear. Ava pulled his eyelids down, closing his eyes.

"I-" Sibyl started to say something, but a werewolf came out of nowhere and tackled her.

Ambrose shot to his feet, conjured a sword, and ran after her.

Ava set Wilson's hand down and stood on shaking legs. Four werewolves surrounded her. She shook her head clear and glanced over each of them. Just like that, the battle went on as if Wilson's death was just a speed bump.

Shoving the pain into a chest in the back of her soul to be dealt with later, she put up her shield of anger. Her heart hardened over, and the familiar calm of rage overtook her mind. Conjuring her weapon, Ava jumped into the fight with what remained of her friends and family.

CHAPTER 38
SIBYL

The world tripped over itself so many times, Sibyl's brain trampolined off her skull at least a dozen times. When she finally stopped rolling, she laid for a moment, trying to get her bearings. The snow spun sideways in a blast of wind that rivaled the violence of the battle. The flimsy shirt she'd put back on did nothing to keep the cold air out of her bones.

Once the world stabilized, she attempted to get up. Her legs were as uncoordinated as a newborn foal, but she stood strong, only to immediately be taken back to the ground by a large werewolf who came out of nowhere, knocking her sideways.

Putting a paw on her chest right over her heart, he held her there. The weight of the beast pushed down on her like a mountain. Flexing his claws in warning, he dared her to move. She didn't, lest one of the talons pierce her recently healed heart. Their orders were to take her alive, but that didn't mean uninjured.

He snarled in triumph. The putrid smell of his breath made her gag. He lowered his head until he was within inches of her face. Thinking quickly, she grabbed her knife and stabbed the beast in the throat like Rokesh taught her. Unlike the last time she used the weapon, this time it met her intended target, sinking deep into his leathery flesh.

It didn't surprise her how easily it penetrated his throat. She'd performed surgery on animals before. This was nothing like that, but the ease with which a blade cut through flesh was not a new feeling.

He tried to roar but his voice was sliced in half just like his throat. In one last gurgling attempt to dominate his prey he backhanded her. Sibyl saw stars, but the weight of the beast lifted from her.

Cold kisses tickled her face as a cyclone of white crystals spiraled down on her. Orange colors bloomed through the sky as bright as the sun. Hope swelled in her chest. Day had finally arrived, and their torment was at an end, but the color wicked out as quickly as it appeared, taking her hope with it.

Burning ice cascaded down from the Empyrean in a beautiful curtain of fire that looked like millions of bright orange fireflies danced chaotically around her. When the fire rain burned out, the blanket of darkness lay back over her.

Sounds trickled in from the valley outside of her perception. Her mind kicked and fought as fierce roars slowly pulled her back to reality. She didn't want to return to the battle, but she had no choice. Reality crashed back down, and she sat up.

A large grizzly bear fought one of the monsters from her nightmares. The werewolf roared at the bear who matched his battle cry with equal magnitude. The bear charged and smashed into the werewolf. The two creatures fought violently. One of them would die before it ended. She hoped it wasn't the grizzly.

Blood splattered the snow, creating a sharp contrast of brutal colors. Uncertain who it belonged to, Sibyl's heart pounded so hard she thought it may spring out of her chest. Getting to her feet, she looked around for someone who could help, but everyone was busy with battles of their own.

Rokesh valiantly fought against three large werewolves, firing every weapon he could think of as fast as possible. Silver streaks whirled around like the swords from space movies. Blood dripped from

Rokesh's side, and he still limped from the wound he'd partially healed earlier. He wouldn't last long if this kept up.

Two guards, she didn't know, fought back-to-back against six werewolves. She watched in dismay as one of the men was decapitated with one swipe from a werewolf. The beast sliced through the man's neck like a knife cutting through butter. Dread sank into her bones.

Ava's silver sword that broke into pieces cut through the night and anything in its path. A beacon of hope amidst the grim carnage of battle. She fought like a character out of a superhero movie, spinning around in violent choreographed patterns, moving so fast sometimes she was little more than a blur.

But when one werewolf fell or retreated, two more replaced it. Even Ava wouldn't last much longer at this rate. Sibyl had to help somehow. What was she supposed to do? She couldn't fight. Her power was her mind, and she couldn't think her way out of this. Another blast of fire tore through the sky, lighting up the land in an orange glow. Dozens of Dragons circled above. Dragons!

Aiden, are you there?

Yes.

We need help. We're outnumbered and dying. Please help us.

He didn't answer for a few minutes. She was about to ask again when his voice boomed in her head.

I heard you can paralyze their movement.

I did that by accident.

Do it on purpose then. Move your people out of the way and hold the enemy still. We'll do the rest. You have two minutes before we fire.

Sibyl shook her hands. There was no room for negotiation or doubt. She just had to do it. Closing her eyes, she took a deep breath and knelt on the ground, figuring it could help stabilize her in this world.

She sent a blast of magic out and searched for her people. One by one, she found them. Earthy spices and cedarwood; Ambrose. Prairie on a summer day; Ava. Wild garlic growing in a marsh; Fulcinia. She'd memorized all of them over the last few months.

She called them in, and those she didn't know, she had to hazard a guess based on the fact that there was no dark magic within them.

Everyone fall in to me now.

They all received the order, and most ran to her without question. A few hesitated though. They either doubted what they heard, or they didn't understand where the command came from. She screamed down the signature tethers.

Retreat to us, NOW! There was no time to argue.

Pulling magic from her heart in massive quantities, she siphoned it to the surface. Her skin hummed with power, and she continued to pull more. Tingling churned all over her body as an ocean of magic amplified a thousand times on itself until it felt like millions of bees stinging every inch of her. When her skin was about to melt off, she yelled down the signature path to the Silvermar Aruko.

NOW!

She released the magic with a scream of energy. A shimmering white chakram exploded from her, expanding its diameter exponentially until it swept over the entire garden and everything in its path. Whenever it met a werewolf, the creature was catapulted backward a hundred feet.

Everyone around her stared. Equal parts shock, fear, relief, and awe exuded from them. She could relate. She had no idea she could do that.

Ambrose helped her to her feet and pulled her into his arms.

"That wasn't exactly what I intended to do. I was trying to freeze them, but the magic had a different idea."

"This is better," he said, looking out at the dazed beasts.

"Just wait. It's not done yet." She smiled deviously.

The werewolves slowly got to their feet, stumbling around in disoriented confusion. Deep drumming pounded the sky above them. As if their heads were on a swivel, everyone looked up. A fissure split the snowfall, and a flicker of orange ignited in the dark atmosphere. A fiery red orb lit up, then another, and another, and another, until a dozen shades of red, yellow, and orange orbs dotted the sky like floating lanterns.

The wind shifted, blowing the snow sideways moments before a thunder of Dragons descended around them. Their throats glowing with tempered fire ready to expel. In the very center, a waterfall of blue flames tore from a Dragon's mouth. The Aruko of Silvermar with his blue fire led the aerial charge.

The beating of wings kept time for the symphony of fire that fell from the sky, burning every werewolf that surrounded them. The heat was overwhelming. The snow melted instantly, and it felt like the hottest day of summer in the center of a ring of fire.

Everyone cheered. Relief and happiness flooded into Sibyl, some her own, but most was from her comrades. Ambrose pulled her in close, his arms a shield against the world.

When the fires receded, hundreds of charred bodies scattered the destroyed gardens. Hopefully the Aruka wouldn't be mad. Between her and Cassie, they'd managed to set most of Tearnanelle on fire. At least this time, the wet snow and lack of flammable vegetation prevented the blaze from spreading.

Before the fire was completely burned out, the Dragons sailed back into the sky.

"That was fortuitous timing," Rokesh limped up. "I was about to lose my head, I think." He held his hand over a large bleeding wound.

"Let me see your wound." Sibyl moved to him instinctively.

He removed his hand, wincing. "I'm nearly out of silver."

"Me too," Ambrose said.

Several others voiced their agreement.

"Let's get out of here before they come back," Demetrius said.

"Too late." Tabaio pointed.

Sibyl's gaze followed the direction he pointed, and her heart dropped. Another legion of hundreds of werewolves walked out of the dark forest. They were calm, fresh, and well rested as if they'd been sitting around waiting for their turn.

"Fuck me," Demetrius said.

"We're going to die," someone Sibyl didn't know said.

The werewolves fanned out just like the previous legion did.

Everyone huddled close, again. The werewolves paused a healthy distance from their group and stared at them.

It was quiet, too quiet. The only sounds were the gentle hiss of snow falling on the remaining embers from the Dragon's fire.

Something tugged at Sibyl's consciousness. A mental booby trap she'd set for herself had been tripped.

"Call the Dragons back," someone said.

Sibyl shushed them, listening carefully, although it couldn't really be defined as listening as much as feeling. Pine needles in the autumn. An unfamiliar signature, but one she'd been waiting for.

Sibyl met Ava's tired green eyes. *Redly's here.*

Hope and fear battled themselves behind Ava's eyes as they widened to fist-sized spheres. Sibyl grabbed Ava's hand and pulled her away from the group. Everyone stared at them with confused expressions. Ambrose made to follow, but Sibyl signaled him to wait there. He stopped with a puzzled expression.

Once they were far enough away that they couldn't be overheard, Sibyl turned her back on the group and faced the werewolves who paced and yipped at the edge of the tree line. Staring into the darkness, she found a pair of mocha-colored eyes with a bright green tapetum reflecting in the lamp post lights. Sibyl pointed.

Ava stepped forward and squinted into the night, staring where Sibyl indicated. Ava's lips parted.

He, and about another dozen werewolves stalked out of the woods and surrounded the pair. Right as the formation of the circle closed around them the remaining legion of werewolves attacked their friends. They'd walked right into a trap.

The fight resumed as if there had never been a reprieve. Spinning around desperately, trying to see a way back to Ambrose, Sibyl started to panic.

Several werewolves snapped at her and Ava. They backed up to each other, and the circle closed in tighter.

"If I call the Dragons back, Redly will die."

Sibyl felt the turmoil inside her friend. They both knew what they *should* do, but neither of them wanted to do it.

"Look!" Ava pointed to a gap in the circle. "Ready?" she asked.

No.

"GO!" Ava shouted.

Sleet stung Sibyl's face as they ran for the gap between the circle of werewolves. The melted snow from the Dragon's fire had frozen into a sheet of ice so their sprint was akin to clumsy ice skating. They weren't nearly as quick as normal, but they managed to reach the gap of werewolves and run through.

Once they were outside the circle, they kept running until Ava slowed pace.

"What are you doing? Come on!" Sibyl turned and then stopped.

The werewolves trotted calmly behind the pair like they didn't have a care in the world. Casually, they reformed the circle around the two women, leaving the same gap in the same location. Backing up to her friend, Sibyl surveyed the perimeter of werewolves who weren't acting hostile.

"Wait here," Ava said. She walked to the gap. None of the werewolves moved a muscle. The two beasts closest to her watched with predatory stillness as Ava walked leisurely out of the circle. She walked a few yards in the direction of Tearnanoak, and the beasts did nothing. Ava stopped and looked back at Sibyl.

Odd, Sibyl said.

Ava walked in a different direction. Several of the werewolves lunged at her, snapping their jaws threateningly, but they weren't delivering any blows. Ava rejoined Sibyl in the center of the circle.

Sibyl grabbed Ava's hand and walked toward the gap. The werewolves matched them step for step. If they tried to go a different direction, the circle of werewolves became hostile, but as long as they moved in the general direction of Tearnanoak, the werewolves remained amiable.

"They're herding us," Sibyl said.

"Yep." Ava nodded her head. "I have an idea. Wait here." Ava stared at Redly, who watched her tentatively. She stepped toward the werewolf.

Sibyl sent a wave of magic toward the animal, dipping a toe into his mind. A cold red mist full of malice and violence greeted her. There was no hint of recognition or friendliness. He was a cursed beast with a single motivation. Capture them and kill anyone else.

"Ava don't," Sibyl whisper yelled, as if the werewolves wouldn't hear her only ten feet away.

Ava waved her off and took another step closer to Redly whose hatred grew stronger.

Sibyl's stomach flipped on itself.

CHAPTER 39
AVA

"Hey there Redly." Ava extended a hand toward him, cautiously, as if one might do when approaching a scared dog.

Redly's hackles raised. His eyes glared at her with malice. An expression she wasn't used to seeing on him. He must be in there somewhere, though. Replaying his message in her head that she'd listened to a hundred times, she recalled what he said.

Even in the darkest depths of the beast, there's a remnant of you keeping me grounded.

If that were true, then maybe she could reach him. The real him. Taking another step, so slow her movement was nearly imperceptible, she closed the distance between them. Redly dropped his head low and a low growl rumbled from his chest. Swallowing hard, she took another step. She was close enough now that in one stride he could be on her.

"Redly," Ava said.

The werewolf's ears perked and his expression transformed into one of confusion.

"You know me. We're friends." She bobbed her head. "Sort of. We're more than friends, you and I."

He arched his neck and narrowed his eyes to lethal slits.

"Please remember." Ava took another step. She was so close now that she had to look up to meet his eyes. They were his beautiful mocha eyes, but all the joy and playfulness was gone from them. They were hard and uncaring.

Don't do anything stupid, his moonstone message also said. Did this count? Ava's heart thundered nearly as loud as the Dragons' wing beats had.

He says you must have hit your head because he doesn't know you, Sibyl said in her mind.

Redly's gaze shifted to Sibyl.

"Do you remember a pretty little hawk?"

His eyes flashed and his face softened. A hiccup in the curse. A spilled memory, but with one blink it was gone. The monster resurfaced again.

He says the only thing he knows is that you destroyed his home and killed his family, and he wants to take you in to get justice.

Ava stood up straight and confident. Willing her hands, legs, and voice to stay steady, she said, "the demon usurper lied to you. *She* killed your family and mine too." Ava took a half step. She could touch him if she wanted.

He was massive. She'd forgotten how large he was in his cursed form. Holding out her hand, which shook despite her best effort, she wiggled her fingers, inviting him to hold her hand like he'd done for her the last time they saw each other.

"I love you."

The beast looked at her hand then back to her face, confusion written across his features. "I didn't kill Selaney or your parents."

His mocha eyes widened. Before Ava could react, his face transformed into violent hate and his hand came across her face so hard she rolled across the wet snow coming to a halt in a half-frozen mud puddle. The freezing water on her face soothed the pain from his punch.

"AVA! Look Out!" Sibyl shouted.

A mountain landed on top of her, submerging her head in the shallow frozen mud. Four knives stabbed into the sides of her neck and a thousand lightning bolts shot down her spine. Then she became weightless.

The dark sky, swirling snow, and ground zipped around in a chaotic jumble. She couldn't tell what was up and what was down. Her entire body hurt. She'd never experienced a pain so severe. It consumed every inch of her, making it impossible to move or fight back. She was tossed around like a rag doll from the back of her neck.

Trying desperately to keep her senses through the myriad of pain, she conjured a war hammer and threw her arm backward blindly. The spike met a target and the pressure from her neck vanished at the same instant a crack in her spine released all the pain.

Falling to the ground, she didn't move. She couldn't move. Desperately pulling herself across the muddy frozen ground by her hands, she attempted to get away from the beast. Her entire body, from the waist down, was numb.

Oh, Gods, Sibyl. I think I'm paralyzed!

Hang on! I'm coming! AH! Sibyl was blocked by the other werewolves. Ava was on her own. Rolling to her back, she faced Redly. He yanked the weapon out of his shoulder and threw it away. His glare was lethal.

"Redly please," she pleaded for the man she loved to return.

The beast fell on all fours and roared so loud that her ears rang.

Digging her hands into the soil, she dragged her broken body across the ground further away from him, but she was too slow. He sauntered toward her with determined intent.

Prickles of sensation blossomed in her spine and down her legs. She was healing, but would it be quick enough? Her toes regained sensation. She wiggled them inside her boots.

Redly overtook her. She flattened herself to the ground. The putrid scent of dark magic washed over her, not the pine needles in the autumn that she loved so much.

The death lust ran deep within his eyes. His orders were to take her alive, but she'd struck a nerve by mentioning his sister. Sometimes it's difficult to control yourself when lost in the fog of battle and revenge. Redly opened his mouth and prepared to strike.

"Redly," Ava pleaded.

But there was no hint of recognition. Redly was gone, consumed by the curse.

Ava sobbed. She knew it was him or her. She was all he had, but she had an entire kingdom depending on her. He wouldn't be able to live with himself with the death of another loved one on his hands. She would survive the pain. She had to, for everyone else she loved and cared about.

"I'm sorry Redly." With tears streaming down her face, she shoved the large silver spear she'd conjured into his chest.

His eyes widened. He'd forgotten to secure her arms. The first lesson he ever taught her. Gasping for air, his knees buckled. Her legs regained enough function to sluggishly pull herself out from under him a split second before he fell.

Ava released the weapon and looked into his eyes. The death lust was gone, replaced by agony. His breathing was strained, but he didn't take his gaze from hers. His expression was empty. No hate, no fear, no anger, but also, no recognition or love. He was simply empty. A shell of someone she knew and loved.

"I'm sorry," she choked out. "I do love you."

His eyes closed and his head slumped.

Ava's broken body was nothing compared to her broken heart.

CHAPTER 40
SIBYL

Sibyl tried to get around the werewolves who blocked her from Ava, but they were perfectly placed, obstructing her from seeing what was going on or getting to her friend.

MOVE! she demanded.

The wolves stepped back in surprise.

You heard me. I said move!

No, one of them said.

A roar sounded from behind her. Spinning on her heel, she searched desperately for him. There he was, across the gardens, entangled with two large werewolves. The grizzly bear was pinned to the ground.

"NOOO! Ambrose!"

His head pivoted toward her. Reddish-brown eyes locked onto hers right before the werewolf stabbed his claws into the bear's abdomen. Sibyl tried to run for him, but another set of werewolves stepped in front of her.

MOVE! she commanded again. This time the beasts' eyes glazed over with a film of white, and they stepped to the side obediently.

Sibyl ran to the bear. A second werewolf raised his hand, dagger-like talons poised for the killing blow.

NO! Sibyl shouted. The monster froze in place. Sibyl rushed to Ambrose, diving between him and the frozen werewolves, whose eyes were consumed with white.

Leave, she said, calmly.

They both fell to all fours and walked away mechanically.

Sibyl dropped to Ambrose's side. A river of red flowed from the wound in his abdomen. The contents that should remain inside hung out in a massacred mess. Sibyl surveyed the damaged entrails. This was not repairable without significant amounts of magic that they didn't have.

She scooped up the bear's giant head. Ripples fluttered across the brown fur, and within a few seconds Ambrose the man lay his head on her lap. His face was pale. He winced. Waves of agony poured out of him as quickly as his blood did.

"Oh Gods. Somebody help him!" She searched desperately for anyone to help, but everyone was fighting as more and more werewolves poured into the gardens from every direction.

Sibyl, his voice sounded in her head.

Clenching her eyes closed, she stepped into the metaphysical realm. An uninjured Ambrose stood above his body. She ran to him and threw her arms around his neck. He kissed the top of her head and pulled her into a strong embrace.

You have the power to end this. He flickered. *The Gods chose you for this amazing gift because you're as strong as you are compassionate, and you're so damned smart. It's infuriating sometimes.* He cupped her face.

Sibyl leaned into his touch that faded with every passing second.

That's why I've completely fallen in love with you.

The words crashed into her heart like a stone tossed in a river. His figure flickered a few times and faded until he was barely perceptible. This couldn't be happening. He healed her heart and now it was going to break again.

Don't go, she pleaded. Tears streamed down her cheeks. *Just hang on a little longer and someone will help.*

Moving his head toward hers, their lips touched, barely a whisper of a kiss. Ambrose faded to a thin outline of a man.

Please. She grabbed his shirt, but her fingers sifted through the material.

You will survive this. Use your strengths. You can save everyone, I know it. Then Ambrose disappeared. The stone in her heart morphed into a beast scarier than the werewolves. The stoney teeth gnawed at her heart until there was nothing left. She didn't just have a broken heart. There was nothing inside her but agony.

She didn't know what to do. Between the crippling sorrow and the imminent defeat, there was nothing she could do. She stared at Ambrose who looked as if he was sleeping peacefully. She moved a stray lock of hair out of his face. He was still warm.

Gently removing his head from her lap, Sibyl backed away.

Rokesh ran to his friend. "Ambrose!"

Another guard joined him, and they started to evaluate the wounds and his status, but the scene blurred behind a film of tears.

Shuffling backward, Sibyl put as much distance between herself and Ambrose as possible. Ringing in her ears drowned everything out. The world tilted and she collapsed onto the frozen ground. Curling into a ball, she held her throbbing head between her arms. It hurt so much that she couldn't breathe.

Someone grabbed her and tried to pull her up. They spoke to her, yelled her name, but she couldn't hear them over the ringing. She choked on a ball in the back of her throat. Even when Ava had her in a choke hold, it hurt less than this.

She'd failed. Wilson was dead. Ambrose was dead.

Someone shook her but she barely felt it. The only thing that existed was pain. They were going to die, well not her or Ava. They'd be taken hostage and used, probably raped and tortured, and it was all her fault. She should have let Tabaio kill her. Sybil's heart shattered into a thousand pieces and with it, all hope left her. She failed everyone.

Rolling over, Sibyl stared into the sky. The dark black of night gave way to a deep blue, promising a beautiful sunrise. Sounds of muffled fighting echoed around her. A voice called her name in the distant pit of her mind. It was so far away. A tear tickled her cheek. Ambrose's face popped into her mind. He would haunt her for the rest of her days, however many she may have left.

Voices of thousands pushed into her head. All in pain, consumed with terror. A woman held her baby, hiding beneath the floorboards of their home. A young boy, no older than twelve, conjured a blue sword and ran alongside his father toward the castle. Screams of dying innocent people as the beasts invaded every corner of Tearnanelle, echoed through her mind.

The men and women who cooked their food every day were barricaded in the cellar, but it was no match for the werewolves as they busted the doors down and attacked the basically defenseless people. Sibyl rolled into a fetal position and covered her head, willing it to stop.

Demetrius fought a beast right next to her. Tabaio knelt in front of her.

"Sibyl, get up!" the large, tattooed man yelled.

Why did they still defend her? They should just leave her to die. She didn't deserve any of them. She'd failed them.

Sibyl.

His voice took her breath away.

Sibyl, I can be with you here. Ambrose knelt next to her. He rubbed his hand over her cheek. *Come on. Get up. Come with me.*

Taking his hand, she stood up. *I thought I lost you.*

No. I've been waiting for you here.

Falling into his arms, she nestled herself so close that no force in the universe would be able to pry them apart. Leaning her head into the crook of his neck, she breathed in his scent. Nothing. There was no cedarwood and earthy spices. Weird. Maybe he'd bathed in a different soap. She laid her head against his chest. No heartbeat. Pulling back from him, she searched his eyes. They were the right color, but there was no spark of life behind them.

This isn't real. She stepped away from him.

Of course it is. What are you talking about? It's me. He pulled her to him again and kissed her. It wasn't warm or cold. It was nothing. Drinking tepid distilled water. Rubbing a hand over his bearded jaw, she let the hairs tickle her fingers. It felt like straw. Not the normal coarse yet soft texture of his whiskers.

Not real, she said.

Stay. He gripped her tightly.

The real Ambrose wouldn't want me to stay.

Of course I do.

What about our friends? What about Tearnanelle?

They're fine. They don't need us, but I need you. He cupped her face. Her heart skipped a beat, but it petered out just as quickly. His hands were void of all texture. She put a hand over one of his, wishing it was real, but she had to face the truth. She would never again feel his touch.

You would never say that. This is my mind playing tricks on me, she whispered.

He smiled at her, but it was different. It wasn't his smile.

Goodbye Ambrose.

Sibyl opened her eyes, this time truly seeing, hearing, and feeling.

Werewolves descended on them by the hundreds. What guards remained fought with everything they had left, which wasn't much. Demetrius, Tabaio, Rokesh, and countless others still defended their home, and they would continue until their last breath.

Rokesh wouldn't last much longer in his state. Kneeling on one good leg, completely out of silver, barely keeping them back, he swung a sword in wild desperation against his attackers. The unmoving Ambrose lay behind him.

Sibyl squeezed her eyes closed. Deep inside her soul a small ember ignited. She would not let anyone else die while she laid down and gave up. Ambrose would be so pissed at her if she did that.

Taking a deep calming breath, she shielded her mind from the suffering and dying. She couldn't hear them right now. For good measure, she created a second wall made from her own pain. Swallowing the lump in her throat, she called the magic from her broken heart.

It flowed easily, a fierce determination built by anger and pain fueled her. If Ava had learned to use it, then so could she. Entering the minds of the beasts around her. she yelled at them. *STOP!*

At once, they all stilled. Their eyes turned completely white, and a silence fell over the gardens. The forest became eerily quiet as the entire kingdom was swept into a storm of stillness. Everyone around her slowly stood up and stared around apprehensively. Uncertainty laced through the atmosphere that transitioned from deep blue to violet. No one moved in fear that the beasts would reanimate.

"Retreat," Sibyl said, calmly.

The werewolves backed up slowly. Too slow.

"LEAVE!" she screamed.

They turned tail and ran.

Finding an icy countenance inside her heart, she stood up and surveyed the gruesome scene. Tired men and women fell to their knees, breathing heavily, taking the moment, uncertain how long it would last, to rest.

A slow boil simmered under her skin. She was done being a victim to her own inadequacies and failures. It was time she embraced her crazy mind. She formulated a plan, a really crazy plan.

Alyssium couldn't control all the werewolves on her own, that's why she wanted Sibyl so bad, because Sibyl could. Breathing in and out rhythmically, she summoned the magic again, sending it out in snaking tendrils. When she found the first werewolf, she dove into its mind.

Walking through the smokey red mist, she searched for the one thing that could turn this battle around. The rope she saw in Zini's mind earlier must represent the cursed connection.

When the mist parted, she followed it. After a while, she came to the rope rising into the atmosphere. It was nearly identical to Zini's, a thick golden rope with a red twisted pattern. Sibyl craned her neck. At the end of that rope must be the connection that Alyssium had over them.

Sibyl lifted from the ground. The weightlessness was weird. She knew it wasn't real on a physical level, but it felt as if she was flying.

Following the rope, she ascended further and further until she pushed through an invisible barrier and floated into the open sky. A deep orange-red line spanned the horizon, pushing back the darkness. Thousands of ropes, similar to the one she followed, traveled to a centralized location, converging at some unseen point. Stepping into hyperdrive, she sped through the sky until she came to a large structure that all the ropes attached to. An anchor holding thousands of ships in a harbor, only the ships were enslaved souls.

Most of the ropes were red, some were yellow, others contained streams of silver and yellow undulating back and forth. Some ropes were frayed so thinly that they were barely holding by a thread. One rope snapped, startling her. It uncoiled and vanished into a red mist. The closest rope to her was completely red. Sibyl grabbed it, and a searing pain burned her palm.

"Ah." She let go of the rope, some of her skin peeled off. Her palm looked like melted plastic. The pain was almost unbearable, but it was nothing compared to what resided in her heart. The pain kept her grounded in this mental maze of insanity. Ripping a piece of fabric from her shirt, she wrapped it around her wounded hand and pulled it tight.

Inspecting the structure that held the ropes, she tried to find a way to manipulate it or break it. There was no way to sever the connection. Intangible magic was one thing, but this was dark magic which worked on a completely different set of rules, but she could use the curse even if she couldn't break it. Leaning in close, Sibyl whispered down the ropes, "Retreat."

A horrible screeching noise, like nails scratching on a chalkboard, vibrated through the ropes. Sibyl covered her ears against the auditory assault. The werewolves fought the request. Maybe she needed to be more forceful.

"RETREAT!" she yelled down the ropes.

This time the ropes pulled taut and went silent. One by one, they changed color to a pure white. Cheering erupted in the distance.

Sibyl's wounded heart beat a little stronger. She smiled at her triumph. Tearnanelle was safe now. Ambrose would be proud of her. A pang of sorrow pulsed through her.

Swallowing it down, she walked alongside the base of the anchor. A few ropes remained a dull yellow color. Why were these ones different? She jumped to the other end, skipping the flight this time.

Once she touched the forest floor, she found a dying werewolf, too weak to comply with the order to retreat, but still clinging to life, just barely. The yellow rope grew fainter by the moment. They weren't just cursed tethers. It was their tether to life itself. No wonder they couldn't disobey Alyssium. If they did, the rope would fray and snap, and they would die.

Sibyl's heart broke for whoever this person was. They were nothing more than a pawn. Once they were no longer useful to the demon usurper, she abandoned them to die.

Sibyl knelt next to the beast and placed a hand on her head.

Whimpering beneath the touch, the beast pleaded, *help me.*

Sibyl's breath hitched. Back home on Earth, people always said to a veterinarian *I couldn't be a vet because I could never euthanize an animal,* but that wasn't a problem for most vets. It's an act of kindness in the last moments when nothing else would save them. A gift that only a few people were strong enough to provide. No one deserved to suffer in the end. Part of Sibyl's oath as a veterinarian was to relieve suffering, and that's exactly what she was going to do.

Sibyl willed peace into the animal's soul, and the werewolf's body relaxed. Sibyl watched the pain drift away with the snow fall. *Rest now.*

The animal closed her eyes, and the rope broke, releasing the curse and her spirit. Sibyl bowed her head and breathed in a heavy sigh. Dozens of remaining yellow ropes flickered around her. She couldn't let them suffer. They were souls, after all.

One by one, she went to each fading yellow rope and brought eternal peace to the dying. The pain in her heart, the Twin Kingdoms, and Orlon became lighter with each passing, until she finally came to the last tether.

A large puncture wound in the center of his chest oozed blood. Under him was a pool of blood nearly the span of his entire body. He was in excruciating pain. Placing her hand on his paw, she prepared to send him to his final resting place, but the connection startled her. Pine needles in the autumn, and a piece of Ava's essence was inside this one's heart. Sibyl had come full circle back to the garden.

Redly.

His eyes opened and his pupils constricted on her. He whimpered. His pulse was weak. He barely clung to life. Silver circulated throughout his entire body. Cautiously, she flipped up one of his lips; white as a ghost. He'd lost so much blood. The most humane thing she could do was end his suffering. There was no way to recover from this without blood transfusions, surgery, and medicine. Even then, the prognosis was grave.

"Damn it," she said to herself.

The werewolf whined. Sibyl placed her hand on him again, preparing to send him away, but her heart dipped painfully. Pulling her hands back, she wilted. She lost people she cared about tonight. Wilson and Ambrose's faces popped into her mind. The pain in her heart threatened to take over again.

Shaking it off, she looked at Redly. She couldn't lose anyone else. She couldn't let Ava lose someone else she loved. There must be something she could do.

Placing a hand back on the scary looking paw, she sent more

calming energy into him. His breathing became shallow and the rope that tethered him to the demon faded to an almost imperceptible hue. The pain in her hand momentarily intensified. Turning it over, she saw a sheen of silver coating her palm.

"What the hell?"

She recalled something Solstice said to her months ago; *you can sense someone's magic and even transfer magic between beings, like a current of energy.*

Ava made a comment earlier when Wilson was dying. She wished she could share her healing magic. Sibyl's mind raced faster than a cheetah.

"I can transfer magic," she whispered to herself.

Putting her hands on his shoulders, she summoned the silver magic into herself. She didn't have to wield the magic to will it to move. That's all she was doing. Slowly the silver flowed from Redly and into her hands. It stung her injured hand, but she ignored the pain and kept going.

The rope that tethered Redly to Alyssium became brighter, his breathing deepened, his pulse became stronger, and his heart beat rhythmically in his chest. His chest started to glow a bright golden hue, and the wound laced itself together. When the last bit of silver flowed into her hands, Sibyl raised them above her head and released it into the atmosphere. The wound that nearly killed him was completely healed now.

"Get up."

The large beast stood up and looked down at her. The milky white tendrils in his eyes matched his tether of life.

"Go home, Redly."

The mangy wolf bowed to her then turned and walked away.

Sibyl stared at her hands in awe, a smile spread over her face. She had an idea.

CHAPTER 41
AVA

The darkness of the night released its grasp on the world. They say it's always darkest before dawn. It would seem that were true figuratively and literally.

The sun was rising, and the werewolves were retreating. If the battle lasted even thirty minutes longer, they may all be dead. Ava was nearly drained of silver, and she was exhausted. She couldn't imagine how others felt who didn't have nearly as much magic as she did.

Cassie skittered down from the tree she'd hidden in all night. Other than being nearly frozen to the bones and a bit shaken, she was unharmed. Demetrius, Fulcinia, Rokesh, and everyone else who was still alive hobbled over to them.

The sun crested the horizon, shining through the tree canopy of the giant God Tree. Ava nearly cried at the sight. Relief flooded through her with such force that she thought for a moment she may faint. The relief was diluted with pain and devastation as she surveyed the scene.

Hundreds of bodies scattered the once immaculate gardens. What should be a beautiful wintry scene was a gruesome reminder of everything they'd lost. Ava's eyes scanned to where Wilson's body lay under a blanket of snow that wasn't as white as it should be. Her heart dipped. Then her gaze slipped to Redly, and her jaw dropped. He was gone. Before she could ponder his whereabouts, a blinding light that wasn't the sun grabbed her attention.

A luminous white blanket engulfed Sibyl. Even as bright as the light was, Ava couldn't take her eyes away.

After the werewolves retreated, Sibyl remained in a meditative state, just sitting on the ground in the middle of the garden, unmoving, eyes as white as the snow. That's how she remained, until now.

"Look at that." Demetrius pointed toward Tearnanoak. Even from this far away, through the trees and snow, Ava could see a shimmering white wave climbing smoothly into the sky. As if someone pulled up a curtain from the ground the white blanket rose. The dome-shaped forcefield wrapped around Tearnanoak, rising higher and higher into the atmosphere, until it disappeared into the clouds.

The sun rose adjacent to the forming structure. The bright orange ball of hope pushed the clouds away and ceased the falling snow. The forcefield refracted the sun's rays creating tiny barely perceptible rainbows all throughout the sky. Wave after wave, the forcefield fortified itself, becoming more opaque with every undulation, until, with one last ripple, it snapped into place, glowed bright white for a few seconds, then disappeared.

Cheering echoed along the wall surrounding Tearnanelle. Sibyl created a prison and trapped the demon queen behind it. Cassie jumped up and down, nearly pulling Ava down. Ava wrapped her arms around her friend. Everyone smiled and embraced each other in happy crying hugs. It was truly over.

"What in Empyrean's name?" someone said. A spike of anxiety shot through Ava. What could be going on now?

Ava turned and her anxiety morphed into curiosity. Sibyl stood with unblinking eyes completely consumed with white, staring vacantly into the forest. Serpents, so white they were nearly blue, shimmered and slithered through the air around her, hissing at anyone who got too close. Sibyl walked mechanically to a pile of werewolf corpses.

Raising her arms, she pushed a white mist into the air from the palms of her hands. It fell over the dead werewolves, forming a thick blanket before being absorbed into them.

Shimmering golden streams surfaced all over their bodies. The gold glitter spilled from the corpses in amorphous beads that floated into the morning air coalescing in a pool of sparkling gold above their heads. The pool grew larger and larger until an entire ocean swam above them. Sibyl lowered her arms, and the floating pool of gold hovered in a churning storm.

She walked to Ambrose, the golden lake following her and the aerial serpents who still guarded the freckle-faced, white-eyed version of Sibyl.

Everyone parted to let her by. A guard who'd been futilely trying to patch up the eviscerated Ambrose, backed up apprehensively. Kneeling beside Ambrose, Sibyl placed one hand on his chest and the other on his head.

The pool of gold swirled above their heads in a large whirlpool. At first it was gentle, like a lazy river, but it quickly escalated to hurricane force currents, flowing in turbulent rotations above the pair. The white serpents swam calmly through the magical storm as if they were immune to it. The wind was so strong the trees bent sideways, and people scrambled back to a safer distance.

Cassie grabbed Ava's hand; wide brown eyes full of trepidation stared at the hurricane of magic. The liquid gold moved faster and faster until it spiralized into a narrow tornado and dove into Ambrose.

His entire body glowed gold, and the horrific wound on his abdomen laced itself together within seconds. The magic flowed into him faster and faster until it zapped out as if someone turned a switch. The white serpents were gone, Sibyl's white glow was gone, the wind died down to a gentle cold breeze, and Sibyl collapsed next to Ambrose.

The pinks, golds, and purples of dawn settled over the land, bringing hope and anticipation with it. No one moved. They all watched and waited. With every passing second, Ava's heart beat harder.

Finally, a finger moved on Ambrose's hand, and laughing exploded all around them.

Cassie squealed and yanked Ava over to Ambrose who opened his eyes right as everyone came upon them. Ava rolled Sibyl over. She was unconscious, but alive.

Hot tears streamed freely down Ava's face.

Rokesh pulled a confused Ambrose into a hug. Ambrose's color wasn't good, and he couldn't stand up, but he was alive. Sibyl saved him. Ambrose held Rokesh and glanced around at everyone with wide confused eyes.

Ava looked at the snow-covered body of Wilson, and her heart twisted into a painful knot. Sibyl was going to hate herself for not being able to save them both. Ava knew she would, because Ava hated herself for not being able to save him.

Then Ava's gaze fell to the vacant spot where Redly had been. An ember of hope ignited in her heart. If he wasn't here, then he must still be alive. He had to be. She wouldn't accept any other possibility.

CHAPTER 42
SIBYL
CAPBAY WAXC-1/DECEMBER 24TH

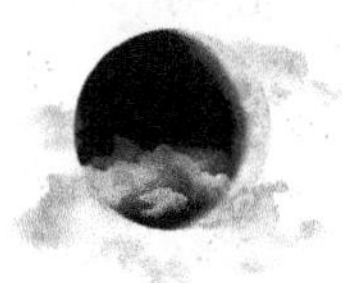

Sitting on the bed, Sibyl leafed through the book *Legends and Myths of Silvermar.*

Six months ago, she opened this book in the middle of the night and read about Dragons. Thinking it was just a stretch of fiction, she lost herself in the stories, avoiding thoughts of the tasks ahead that she found so daunting.

Laughing at herself, she set the book on the nightstand. A knock on the door sounded a split second before Ava entered.

Sibyl rolled her eyes. "What's the point of knocking? You just come right in anyway."

Rokesh, Demetrius, Clark, and Tabaio entered behind her.

"I knew this time it was just you and Cassie, so no worry of interrupting anything." Ava smiled deviously. "Unless there's something I should know about you and Cassie."

"She's not my type." Cassie laughed.

"Ha ha," Sibyl said.

Ava plopped down on the bed next to Sibyl. "You guys all packed?"

"Yeah," Sibyl and Cassie answered in unison.

"Don't you want to come?" Sibyl asked. "You could spend Christmas with me and my family."

Ava scrunched up her nose. "No. This is my home now. My family is here, and the rest of my family will be coming back after the holidays. Right?"

Cassie nodded and Ava looked at Sibyl expectantly.

"In a few months, after boards," Sibyl said.

"That's good. There's a certain someone who I'm sure you don't want to be away from for too long." Ava bumped Sibyl's shoulder teasingly.

Sibyl winced. Her entire arm ached from the burn in her hand, but she pushed down the pain and giggled at Ava.

"I'll take your bag," Rokesh limped over and grabbed Sibyl's backpack.

"Slow down, gimpy. You're still healing. I'll take the bag." Demetrius took it from Rokesh and slung it over his shoulder. "We'll be outside when you guys are ready."

"I'm ready now." Cassie hopped off the bed and headed out the door with everyone, leaving Ava and Sibyl alone.

Sibyl knew Ava was waiting for her to move but her legs were frozen. She'd been pining for home for so long, and now that it was finally time to go, she didn't want to. It was a strange feeling to not want to leave, but the real world beckoned.

That's what was confusing though. This was real too. This world called to her for years, begging her to come. She just hadn't recognized it. Now, her heart was split between two worlds.

"You know there's time to visit him one last time before you leave. It'll take them forever to get to the gates with all the adoring fans," Ava said, mockingly.

The entire kingdom was buzzing about Sibyl's miraculous save and imprisoning the demon so that she and her cursed werewolves couldn't bother anyone anymore. People who were scared of Sibyl days ago were now adoring fans. Everywhere she went, people would stop and shake her hand, bow, hug her, give her gifts. Some people even left things at her door.

She had more gems and stones than she knew what to do with, along with letters and pictures drawn by kids. It was overwhelming, but if she was being completely honest with herself, she loved it. It was nice to be revered, instead of feared.

"Why don't you meet us at the bridge? If you have an opal, I'd recommend using it." Ava winked.

Sibyl nodded then Ava left the room. Grabbing a few remaining small trinkets, she shoved them into her pockets and headed to the door. Pausing, she surveyed the room she called her home for the last six months. With great effort, she willed the lights out and closed the door.

The walk to the healer's wing took longer than she'd anticipated for the exact reason Ava warned about. She should have taken Ava's advice and used her opal to be invisible. By the time she made it to the doors to the healer's quarters, she'd been hugged at least a dozen times, thanked profusely, and an entourage of small children followed her.

She turned and she smiled at them. They dispersed like pappus seeds on the wind in a giggling frenzy. Sibyl laughed and pushed open the doors to the healer's wing, nearly running into Serellina. She looked exhausted, like everyone else. She wore her usual silver armor around her torso and her left arm was covered.

"Oh. Sorry. I didn't see you there." Sibyl swallowed nervously. Things were still awkward between them.

Serellina inhaled a long, strained breath and squared her shoulders. "Sibyl, I owe you an apology." Serellina looked her straight in the eye. "I'm sorry."

The apology took Sibyl by surprise. It was so direct and sincere. Sibyl felt the sincerity behind the words. The Aruka felt contrition for her actions.

Sibyl nodded her head but couldn't figure out what to say. *I under-*

stand why you tried to have me killed. You were doing what you thought was best for your people. The words sounded bitter, because they were.

"You have an entire kingdom of people to think about. I can't imagine what a burden that must be, what choices you have to make sometimes to ensure their safety."

The Aruka fidgeted. "I hope that you can find it in your heart to forgive me because, as you stated, I was thinking of my people and, if I'm being honest, I was scared. I made a mistake, and I misjudged you." The Aruka folded her hands in front of herself and stood proudly. She would admit to her mistake, but she wouldn't grovel.

The bitterness toward the woman lessened. Sibyl nodded and smiled, although it didn't meet her eyes. The Aruka nodded back and walked off. That was the best Sibyl would get, and she supposed, it was enough.

Sibyl made her way to the back of the healer's wing and through another door. Ambrose was in one of the private rooms. She found him lying in bed, staring out the window with a pensive expression. He smiled when he saw her, and Sibyl's heart somersaulted. She sat on the bed next to him.

He took her hand in his and laced his fingers through his. "You're leaving now?"

Sibyl stiffened. Damn. She didn't want to. She really really didn't want to. This was a lot harder than she thought it would be.

"I'm coming back in a few months."

"By the time you get back, I should be all healed up and back to my regular self again." He smiled, but there was sadness behind his eyes.

"That's unfortunate," she teased.

He laughed and winced a little.

"Easy there. Don't laugh."

"Yes ma'am." His thumb brushed the top of her hand lightly. "Come here."

He didn't have to ask her twice. She laid down next to him. He scooted over tenderly, making room for her on the bed. Cradling his arm tightly to her chest, she scootched into his spoon as close as she could get without hurting him. His warm lips kissed the back of her neck, working their way down to her shoulder, then he gave her a quick teasing lick.

"What are you doing?" She giggled.

"I told you I'd get you over this licking phobia."

Another lick grazed over her ear. It was slimy and tickled, but she loved it.

"Stop it." She feigned disgust.

He did it again and she squirmed. He pulled her in closer.

"Don't make me kick an injured man," she threatened.

"Ok. Ok." He nestled back down, and they laid there silently. The pain in her hand and arm was completely gone. As time passed, her legs fell asleep, her shoulder went numb, and her eyelids became heavy. The slow rhythm of his breathing and heartbeat lulled her to sleep. Wrapped in his arms, his smell, his body, she felt warm and secure. He felt like home.

Remembering what he said moments before he nearly died, she wondered if he actually said that or was it an apparition of her imagination?

She opened her mouth to ask him if it was real when a healer walked in.

The woman skittered to a halt; eyes wide. "I'm sorry. I didn't realize anyone was here."

Sibyl pulled herself away with difficulty, like trying to separate two pieces of adhered duct tape.

Ambrose grabbed her arm.

She turned to him.

His eyes were.... everything.

"I'll come back in a little while." The healer curtsied and walked out.

"Did she just curtsy?" Sibyl asked.

They both laughed. He pulled her down to him and their lips collided. Sibyl's heart frolicked and butterflies danced in her stomach in timing with their tongues. After a few moments, she finally pulled herself away.

He groaned.

"I have to go," she whispered.

He laid back down on the bed and sighed. "Stay safe and don't forget to listen to your heart, Sibyl Murphy."

A lump formed in her throat, preventing speech so she smiled at him one last time then walked out before she lost the courage. With every step away from him her legs became heavier and the pain in her hand got stronger. Her body protested leaving just as much as her heart did.

This time, she used the opal to render herself invisible otherwise it may take a century to get to the gate. Carefully navigating her way through the crowds of people, she made her way through the gardens and to the bridge that led to the southern gate. Dozens of people cleaned up the aftermath of the battle.

Sibyl glanced to the western side of the gardens where the wall peaked above the trees. A large gap interrupted the structure where the werewolves had gotten through just two nights ago.

She thought of Wilson. The hole in the wall was as big as the hole in her heart.

A gentle snow started to fall. Swallowing down the pain, she trudged on, leaving the broken wall, the gardens, and Tearnanelle behind.

Her friends were exactly where Ava said they would be, standing in front of the gates. Letting go of the opal's magic, she materialized.

"There you are," Cassie said.

"Yep. Here I am. Let's go." Sibyl didn't pause. She walked past them and into the forest. If she didn't keep her legs moving, she may turn around and run back to him.

Once they got to a small clearing, she finally stopped. At this distance outside the gates bubble travel would work. It was a highly trafficked area where most people came for bubble portaling. This was the southern bubble hub in Tearnanelle. There were a couple of others on the outskirts to the north and east. The western one was destroyed in the war at some point.

Demetrius handed her the backpack.

"Thanks." She shouldered it.

He pulled her into a hug. "Take care of yourself and come back to us soon."

Sibyl nodded and pulled away, but she couldn't look him in the eyes. Demetrius and Wilson were a pair. It didn't feel right without Wilson here. A pea in their pod was missing because she wasn't quick enough. Pushing the thoughts down before the weight of the pain crushed her, she reached for Clark and pulled her into a hug.

Next was Rokesh, then Ava, and Tabaio was last.

Sibyl sighed at the giant man who nearly killed her forty-eight hours ago. He wasn't apologetic at all. She shook her head and smiled. He shrugged and smiled back. They gave each other a quick curt hug.

"Don't try to kill anybody while I'm gone," she said in his ear.

"No promises. If your boyfriend mouths off too much I may need to remind him, I let him win."

"Yeah right," Sibyl snorted.

"Ok, it's time to go." Sibyl held her hand out and Cassie gripped her tightly.

Smiling to her friends one last time, she crushed the bubble. The familiar pressure of the portal magic consumed her. The lights winked out, the air pulled from her lungs, and the cold enveloped her. Unlike the first time though, she didn't panic, she didn't try to breath against the odd feeling, and she didn't pass out, she just waited patiently.

Within a few seconds, she stood in a forest not much different than the one she'd just left. Sibyl placed her uninjured hand against the bark of a nearby tree. The spirit within danced in jubilant recognition.

Putting one foot in front of the other, she and Cassie headed to the cabin nestled in the Appalachian Forest of North Carolina. The trees greeted her as old friends when she passed by.

Home. Such a funny bitter-sweet word.

CHAPTER 43
AVA
ALDAQ WANC-3/JANUARY 25TH

Sitting beneath the apple tree in the forest between The Twin Kingdoms, Ava waited impatiently. She'd come here every day since winter solstice, but Redly had yet to show up. Three weeks had passed, and she was beginning to think the worst.

Sibyl said he survived, and she left a pathway through the force-field for him, so he should be able to get here. If that was the case, then where was he?

The wall wouldn't allow anyone else from either side to pass through, so Ava couldn't go find him, which thoroughly pissed her off. She tried, repeatedly. She'd slammed herself against it, banged on it, threw conjured bombs at it, but all it did was flicker slightly against her assaults.

She called Sibyl and demanded that she fix it so that she could pass through, but Sibyl said it was impossible to modify and told her to just be patient. Patience was not one of Ava's virtues.

Checking the moonstone for the hundredth time, she sulked. It was full of her voice letters, but nothing from him. She tucked it back under the tree root and leaned her head against the tree. Pulling the cuff of her coat up tighter around her neck, she sighed. Her exhaled air clouded in front of her face.

The new year brought the coldest part of winter with it. Ava was a summer girl at heart, so this sucked on all levels. The sun would set soon, and it would get even colder. She had no intention of being here at dusk.

She stared toward Tearnanoak longingly. She couldn't keep making excuses for her absence every day either. Her aunt and Fulcinia were already hounding her, trying to figure out who the mystery man was. They assumed it was someone from Tearnanelle and Ava didn't make any effort to correct them. They wouldn't understand the truth, and the deception wouldn't last forever. Someone would eventually discover where she was going and who she was meeting with. Hopefully by that time, the curse would be broken, and it wouldn't matter.

Blowing warm air into the palms of her hands, she headed home, shoulders slumped as low as her heart felt.

"Leaving already, pretty little hawk?"

She stilled. His voice immediately warmed her heart like a marshmallow over a campfire. She turned back around to find him standing at the edge of the meadow. Leaning against a tree with his arms crossed over his chest, he smiled wide.

She ran to him, tackling him so hard he nearly fell down. Breathing in his beautiful scent of pine needles in the autumn, Ava melted into his arms.

"I was so worried about you," she said into the crook of his neck, trying desperately to contain the sobs that threatened to spill out.

"Me? Nah. I'm ok. It just took me a while to heal completely. Someone stabbed me through the chest with a silver spear."

Ava's stomach dropped. Did he know it was her? She searched his eyes. That ridiculous eyebrow ticked up and his lips curled into a mischievous smile. Ava bit her lip.

His eyes flicked to her lips a split second before he leaned down and kissed her so deeply that her knees weakened. As if spring had arrived and melted the winter away, the cold vanished. She was engulfed in hot passion. Nothing and no one existed beyond him and this moment.

Every time she tasted him; it was like the first time. Their tongues danced to a song only they could hear. They explored each other for several minutes until Ava was lightheaded.

When he came up for air, he asked, "I want to know about this Mage woman who stabbed me. Do you have any idea who that might be?"

Ava shook her head. "No idea. I'll ask around."

"You do that. She's pretty hot. Maybe I can hook up with her sometime."

Ava punched his shoulder.

"I mean, I know it couldn't be you since I directly told you not to do anything stupid, and an Arukas fighting in the trenches with the rest of the infantry is incredibly stupid, so I know that it couldn't have been you."

Ava punched his shoulder again.

"Ouch. That's mean. Somebody stabbed me with a silver spear, you know." He hunched over and moaned as if in significant pain.

"Oh, I'm sorry. Did that hurt?" She punched him again. "Don't call me stupid."

"Did I say that?" He stood straight up, miraculously uninjured.

"You know I can kick your ass."

"If I remember correctly, I kicked your ass."

"I thought you didn't remember newm nights?"

"I usually don't, but a Druid allowed me to keep my memories from the last one."

"Well, if that's the case then you should remember that I kicked your ass."

"So, it was you!" He wrapped his arms around her and lifted her from the ground.

She wrapped her legs around him.

"Naughty little hawk," he growled, then kissed her. Making his way clumsily to the apple tree, he laid her down on a patch of ground that didn't have any snow. Pressing his body onto hers, he met her lips again.

Ava could scarcely breathe under the weight of him. Every inch so close it was tantalizing. Her body responded to him instinctively as she drove her hips into his.

"You forgot to secure my arms," she said, breathlessly.

He pulled her hands from around his neck, secured them over her head. "Is that better?"

"Yeah. Don't ever forget to do that again."

He looked into her eyes with a questioning expression.

"I could have gotten your heart," she said seriously.

"You already have."

What little composure she had left completely unraveled. The sun dipped behind the trees, cloaking their bodies in shadow, but the cold air didn't bother her. His hands kept her warm as they explored every inch of her body. Ava shed all of her worries at the same rate she shed her clothes. Passion was the only form of heat they needed.

EPILOGUE: REDLY
ALDAQ WANC-3/JANUARY 25TH

Redly stepped through the forcefield and back into Tearnanoak just as the last bit of sunlight disappeared. The warm tide of magic spilled over him with one step then disappeared with the next step. Pulling through the barrier was like walking against a gentle river current, but unlike a river, it pulled against him no matter which direction he traversed.

There was no indication of a wall separating the Twin Kingdoms. Someone could accidentally walk right into it, which would result in getting knocked backward as if they'd been sucker punched. The force-field matched whatever force was applied to it. If someone gently laid a hand on it and pushed, it pushed back evenly. But if a person were to run at it full force, they'd be catapulted backward violently. Redly watched this happen several times, which he found endlessly entertaining. The moron twins actually did it at least six times each. *Idiots.*

Luckily, he didn't have the same problems as everyone else. Thanks to Sibyl, the magical imprisonment didn't apply to him. He could traverse freely through it from either direction.

Now that he was back on Tearnanoak's side of the fortress, he made his way through the desolate forest and emerged into the bustling market street. Slogging into the ankle-deep mud and filth, he headed to the patrol guard office to make his report for his shift.

The putrid smell of dark magic mixed with mud and smoked meat clogged his senses, effectively pushing out Ava's beautiful lingering scent of the prairie on a summer day. Bitterness pooled in his stomach. At least he could still feel the phantom touch of her hands and taste her sweet soft lips in his memory. No matter how much filth covered him, the memories were always sharp and vivid. That kept him going every day.

Before he reached the office, a claw scraped his subconscious. He hissed in detest. Alyssium summoned. His heart thrummed nervously. Others around him gasped and bemoaned. She was summoning everyone, not just him. Some of his nerves dissipated.

He knew this day was coming eventually. She hadn't made a peep since the battle. Everyone was nervous about what she was going to do about their loss. She certainly wouldn't accept the loss as her fault. She was probably about to doll out a ridiculous number of unjust punishments. He just hoped she didn't single him out.

It was fully dark outside when he got to the castle ruins. The temperature had dropped to the negatives. Everyone around him was tense from anxiety and cold. He blew into his hands, trying to warm them.

The mud pit amphitheater was once a grand throne room completely housed by the Goddess Tree. Redly was told that before the war, this throne room was nearly identical to the throne room in Tearnanelle. He wouldn't know, since he'd seen neither. Now that the tree was gone, all that remained was this giant mud pit and the throne stump that had a faint yellow glow.

The magical glow pissed Alyssium off. She loved to cake mud over it, claw at it, piss on it, or degrade it any possible way she could think of. Her pathetic way of desecrating the fallen Goddess even more. Despite it all though, the beautiful golden glow always returned, which frustrated the demon endlessly.

Cursed Therians crowded in as far as the eye could see, disappearing into the cold dark night beyond the torch lights' reach. It was impossible to fit everyone close enough so that they could see or hear the queen, but attendance was mandatory, regardless if you could actually hear her speech. The message would be relayed later.

Redly stood, expressionless, waiting for the demon who called herself a queen to arrive.

He didn't have to wait long. A tall angular woman walked through an old archway behind Tearnanoak's stump throne. Raising her cadaverous arms, she smiled widely. Cheers and roars erupted from the crowd. No boos. If you didn't approve, you remained silent or faked approval. Any negative display would be dealt with swiftly and lethally by the soldiers who made rounds in the crowd.

Most of the soldiers were chosen strictly for their unwavering loyalty to the demon queen, their short temper, and love for violence. It only took the perception of a wrong look to earn a punishment. Redly had mastered feigned support of the demon usurper long ago.

Alyssium waved her arms and fanned out her black-taloned fingers as if she conducted an orchestra. She loved to make an entrance. A red-lipped serpentine smile swallowed her pale features. Large wings folded neatly over her back, blood red on the underside with a black outer shell like a hardened lava. Long, thick, black hair curled down the sides of her body and blended in with the wings, making it difficult to know exactly how long her hair was, especially in the dark torch light.

The two small horns on her head extended another three feet above her, and the tips of her wings came to dark lethal poisoned points. A thick red tail swiped under the edge of her blood red dress to hold it out of the muck as she strode across the dais.

"My beautiful subjects, I have a few announcements." Her voice was an elegant evil hiss that sent chills down Redly's spine.

The crowd became silent.

"I have promoted a new werewolf captain to stand beside general Abigor in the next phase of our war against the traitorous Mages." Alyssium gestured to her side where a large murderous looking man stood with his arms crossed over his chest. "This is Jameck."

Everyone cheered and clapped. Redly joined in robotically.

"I know it's concerning that we have been temporarily blockaded, but do not fret. This was all part of the plan." She smiled sweetly.

Redly temporarily faltered in hiding his confusion. A soldier took a second glance at him. He immediately schooled his features and plastered a large smile to his face and added a shout of 'hooray' for good measure. The soldier walked on.

"I assure you; our plans are moving along quite nicely. In fact, things went better than I ever imagined possible. We didn't lose the battle, and we most certainly are still winning this war! All we have to do now is wait. The Druid will come to us soon enough." The demon queen laughed maniacally. "I think she'll find that she won't be able to stay away." Her laughs echoed in the cold night.

A cacophonous riot of cheers drowned the atmosphere. Redly did his best to join in with the cheering, but uncertainty and fear made his skin crawl.

THE END

Look out for book 2 in
The Twin Kingdoms Trilogy
The Lost Ones

PLAY LIST

Girls Just Want to Have Fun | Cyndi Lauper
Interlude | Stormzy
Smells Like Teen Spirit | Nirvana
Crazy | Daniela Andrade
Reflection | Christina Aguilera
Darkside | Sam Tinnesz
All of Me | The Piano Guys
Being Good Isn't Good Enough | Glee Cast
Hogwild | Twisted Pine
Do or Die | Natalie Jane

Acknowledgments

First, I want to express my deepest gratitude to my husband, who read the first, second, third and twentieth drafts of this book. Without him, this book would not exist. Thank you for being my constant cheerleader, for believing in me even when I doubted myself, and for always encouraging me to keep going, no matter the obstacles.

Second, I'd like to thank my dad who also read the first few drafts and has been a constant supportive voice from day one.

To my incredible editor, Cynthia Merrill, your expertise and keen eye have shaped this book into something far better than I could have imagined. Your feedback was invaluable, and your commitment to excellence pushed me to be a better writer. I am deeply grateful for your dedication to this project.

Finally, I want to thank my amazing critique partners. Your honest feedback, thoughtful suggestions, and moral support were crucial throughout the writing process. You all offered perspectives that challenged me to dig deeper and think differently, and I couldn't have completed this book without you.

To all of you, thank you for being part of this book's journey. Your contributions, encouragement, and belief in me mean the world.

About the Author

When Aurelia isn't pretending to be an author, she is working hard at her "real" job as a veterinarian. She was one of those obnoxious children who wanted to be a veterinarian from the day she could talk. She's always been drawn to animals. From a young age, she wondered what it would be like to either shape shift into various animals, or at the least, talk to them.

Being a veterinarian is full of ups and downs. Aurelia cuddles with cute puppies one minute then helps people say goodbye to their furry family member the next, and solves complex medical cases to improve the life of her patients. There's also a lot of fingers up butts, various colors of fluids from many different orifices, and a lot of dick pics....of dogs. One of the only professions where it's perfectly normal to crawl around on the floor trying to get a better look at a dog's rear end. Just kidding....sort of.

When Aurelia isn't at the clinic, she's spending time with the love of her life and amazing husband, and her beautiful daughter. They love to travel, go hiking, camping, floating, and go on many other adventurous activities.